The Lyfe of
Sir Thomas Moore, knighte

Early English Text Society.

Original Series, No. 197.

1935 (for 1934).

Sir Thomas More
by Holbein

The Lyfe
of Sir Thomas Moore, knighte,

written by

William Roper, Esquire,

whiche maried Margreat,
daughter of the sayed Thomas Moore

AND NOW EDITED FROM THIRTEEN MANUSCRIPTS,
WITH COLLATIONS, ETC.,

BY ELSIE VAUGHAN HITCHCOCK, PH.D., D.LIT.,
FELLOW OF UNIVERSITY COLLEGE, LONDON.

LONDON:
PUBLISHED FOR THE EARLY ENGLISH TEXT SOCIETY
BY HUMPHREY MILFORD, OXFORD UNIVERSITY PRESS
AMEN HOUSE, E.C. 4.
1935.

OXFORD
UNIVERSITY PRESS

Great Clarendon Street, Oxford OX2 6DP
United Kingdom

Oxford University Press is a department of the University of Oxford.
It furthers the University's objective of excellence in research, scholarship,
and education by publishing worldwide. Oxford is a registered trade mark of
Oxford University Press in the UK and in certain other countries

© The Early English Text Society 1935

The moral rights of the authors have been asserted

Database right Oxford University Press (maker)

First Edition published in 1935

All rights reserved. No part of this publication may be reproduced,
stored in a retrieval system, or transmitted, in any form or by any means,
without the prior permission in writing of Oxford University Press,
or as expressly permitted by law, or under terms agreed with the appropriate
reprographics rights organization. Enquiries concerning reproduction
outside the scope of the above should be sent to the Rights Department,
Oxford University Press, at the address above

You must not circulate this book in any other form
and you must impose this same condition on any acquirer

Published in the United States of America by Oxford University Press
198 Madison Avenue, New York, NY 10016, United States of America

British Library Cataloguing in Publication Data
Data available

Library of Congress Cataloging in Publication Data
Data available

Original Series, 197

ISBN 978-0-85-991931-9

TO
THE FRIENDS OF MORE,
R. W. Chambers
AND
A. W. Reed,
THIS BOOK IS DEDICATED

PREFACE

An edition of Roper's *Life of More* in 1935 can claim recognition only as an old friend in a new dress; for over three hundred years, through the various earlier editions, students of More and of English literature have been acquainted with Roper's work. On account of the innocuous nature of the variants, the result of the labour of collating the manuscripts is rather disappointing; but as long as these variants remained untested and unrecorded, the text of the older editors could not be blindly accepted as authentic. I plead this justification.

My sincere thanks are due to the Cambridge University Library, the Bollandist Library, Brussels, and the Rt. Hon. John Burns for the loan of their manuscripts to the British Museum for my collation. The Delegates of the Clarendon Press generously gave me permission to use the Emery Walker plate of the Holbein portrait of More which was formerly in the Huth Collection. (In 1912 this portrait was purchased by Mr. H. C. Frick, and is now in the Frick Museum, New York.) The notes kindly supplied to me by Professor C. J. Sisson and the Rev. S. L. Greenslade are quoted below in the section on William Roper (pp. xxxi, xxxix, xli–xlii) and those by Mrs. Probert and Mr. Reginald Hine were used for the Note to 82/8–9.

Professor R. W. Chambers' Historical Notes to Harpsfield have made it easy to annotate in summary form the Roper text; and for those Notes which were left over for the Roper volume, he has put his material at my disposal. Though the limits of Roper's *Life* have precluded more than a few references to Professor A. W. Reed's *Tudor Drama* and his other contributions to the study of the More Circle, I owe to these and to him a general debt which it is not always easy to specify. He and Professor Chambers have read the proofs, and made most helpful corrections and suggestions. I acknowledge with pleasure the assistance and encouragement of these two eminent More scholars, and dedicate this book to them as a token of gratitude and affection.

Mr. Thomas More Eyston has supplemented from his archives the table (pp. 112–113) relating to his branch of More's descendants, and I look back with delight on his hospitality and my introduction to him and Lady Agnes, Thomas More, Mary and John. Four centuries after More's execution they carry on his name, and a Lord Chancellor's simple drinking-mug and a Bishop's wooden walking-staff are their priceless possessions. By 1603 the stock of the royal murderer was no more, and no relic of kingly pomp compares with little Thomas More's inheritance.

" A man may lose his head and have no harm."

E. V. H.

University College, London,
 6 February, 1935.

CONTENTS

	PAGE
PREFACE	vii
INTRODUCTION	xi
DESCRIPTION OF THE ROPER MANUSCRIPTS	xi
RELATIONSHIP OF THE ROPER MANUSCRIPTS	xxi
EARLIER EDITIONS	xxv
WILLIAM ROPER	xxix
EDITOR'S SUMMARY OF CONTENTS OF ROPER'S *Life of More*	xlix
TEXT	1
HISTORICAL NOTES	105
GLOSSARY	129
GENERAL INDEX	133

INTRODUCTION

DESCRIPTION OF THE ROPER MANU-SCRIPTS

Thirteen Roper manuscripts have been collated for this edition.[1]

I, II, III. MSS. HARLEIAN 6254, 6362, 6166.

There are three Roper manuscripts in the Harley collection, British Museum—MSS. 6254, 6362 and 6166.

MS. H² — MS. 6254 is used as the basis of the critical text. Throughout this edition it is referred to as H^2.

It is a paper folio, in a modern binding. The leaves measure $11 \times 6\frac{3}{4}$ inches. A line of writing measures about 6 inches. Each page contains about 40 lines, and has a catchword.

The *Life* is paginated in ink, and occupies pages 2–47. Before the text are three leaves, the first press-marked, the second blank, the third (paginated as 1) having pasted on its verso an engraved portrait of More as Chancellor. Following the text are three blank pages.

The handwriting is uniform throughout, and is a good firm cursive of the late sixteenth century. The text runs on continuously, without paragraph breaks, but the commencement of a new section or topic is generally indicated by enlarging and thickening of the first word or words of the sentence.

The punctuation of the manuscript is good for the period, but has been modernised in this edition, for the sake of the general reader.

The *Life* has no title. At the end is written "Finis. Deo gratias."

MS. H³. — MS. 6362 is denoted in this edition by H^3. It is a paper quarto, in a modern leather binding. The

---
[1] See list, p. 2, below.

leaves measure 8 × 6 inches. A line of writing measures about 4 inches, the text being enclosed by doubly-ruled guide-lines. The number of lines per page varies, being usually between 25 and 30.

The text occupies the leaves marked in modern pencil 3–47, and in a contemporary hand in ink 1–45. On the recto of the leaf preceding the text, in the same hand, runs the title : " The lyfe of Sir Thomas Moore sometyme Chancellor of Englande written by his sonne in lawe Williame Roper of Eltham in the Countye of Kente Esquier." Before the text there is a variation of this: " The lyfe of Sir Thomas Moore knighte written by William Roper Esquire whiche maried Margreat daughter of the sayed Thomas Moore."

On the verso of the leaf preceding that containing the title is a note by Joseph Planta : [1] " Sir W^m. Strickland, Bar^t, a descendant from Sir Th: More, has another copy of the following Life very similar to this."

The transcript is necessarily before January 4, 1602, that being the date of a note (not however connected with the transcript) following the text on p. 48.

The hand is of the late sixteenth century, a good clear cursive. The manuscript is executed with care. The first few words of the title, of the heading before the text, of the Preface and text, and the initial letters of the first words of new sections are in red. The text is written continuously, but these red initial letters indicate important new paragraphs and fresh topics. A marginal summary, contemporary with the text, but not by the same hand, runs throughout.

MS. H¹.   MS. 6166 is denoted in this edition by H^1.

It is a large-paper folio, in a modern binding. The leaves measure $15\frac{1}{2} \times 9\frac{1}{2}$ inches. There are 44 tracts in the volume. Nos. 1–31 are in the same hand, and are copies of some of the Collections of Francis Thynne, which now form MS. Additional 11388 (see below). The Roper *Life* is the first. It is foliated in pencil 3–20, and

---

[1] Appointed Keeper of the Manuscripts, British Museum, 1776.

paginated in ink 1–35. A line of writing measures between 5 and 6 inches. The number of lines per page varies. Each page has a catchword.

Before the text is the title : " The lyfe of Sr Thomas Moore K^{nt} written by William Rooper Esqr who marryed Margarett Daughter of þ^e sayd Sr Thomas, this William liued at Eltham, & dyed about, &c."

The *Life* carries the date of Thynne's transcript: "Finis. 26° Maij 1598."

The hand is of the seventeenth century, clear and neat, but the varying slope gives it a displeasing effect. The text is divided into numerous short paragraphs. The first few words of the Preface and text are larger and bolder. The pronoun " I " is usually much thickened, as is often the initial letter of a paragraph.

IV, V. MSS. ADDITIONAL 11388, 4242.

Among the Additional MSS. in the British Museum are two of Roper's *Life*—11388 and 4242.

MS. 11388 is denoted in this edition by A.   MS .A

It is a folio on paper, in a shabby modern binding. The pages measure 13 × 8½ inches. The volume contains the Collections of Francis Thynne, Lancaster Herald from 1564–1606—chiefly treatises on alchemy, heraldry and topography. Roper's *Life* occupies folios 46^b–63^b (modern pencil foliation). A line of writing measures about 6 inches. The number of lines per page varies.

The *Life* has the title : " The lyfe of Sir Thomas Moore knight written by Willm Roper esquier, whiche maryed margaret daughter of the sayed Thomas Moore. This Willm dwelt at Elthame in kent and dyed aboute." At the end is written " Finis. 26 maij 1598," the exact date of the transcript. Other transcripts by Thynne in the volume are dated, and some signed.

The hand is a good firm cursive. The text is written continuously, without paragraph breaks. There are frequent corrections and interlineations. The first few words of the Preface and *Life* are larger and bolder.

MS. A².   MS. Additional 4242 is denoted in this edition by A².
It is a small-paper quarto, in a leather binding. The leaves measure $7\frac{1}{4} \times 5\frac{1}{2}$ inches. A line of writing measures about 4 inches. The number of lines per page varies. Each page has a catchword.

There are i + 43 leaves. The text occupies folios 3ᵃ—43ᵃ. The manuscript is imperfect at the end; folios 39–43 have been supplied from MS. Additional 4474 (see below, p. 89); but a leaf is still missing between the folios marked 38 and 39. It is much injured by damp, particularly towards the end (fols. 34ᵃ—43ᵃ), so that many words are lost round the edges. There are pasted on the fly-leaf the initials " H.M.," and on folio 2ᵇ an engraved portrait of More.

At least three hands appear in the transcript, all apparently of the early seventeenth century. The text is split up by paragraph spaces. Before the Preface, and again (with slight variations) before the *Life* itself, is written : " The Life of Sʳ Thomas Moore knight somtimes Lᵈ Chancellor of England."

VI. MS. SLOANE 1705.

MS. S.   There is also a Roper *Life* in the British Museum Sloane collection—MS. 1705. It is denoted in this edition by S.

S is a paper manuscript in small folio, in a modern binding. The pages measure 12×7 inches : these are not the originals, but those on which the originals have been imposed. The edges of these originals are frequently worn away.

The manuscript now consists of 94 leaves. Roper's *Life* is the first tract, occupying fols. 1ᵃ—32ᵃ ; the *Life* of Fisher[1] occupies fols. 33ᵃ—94ᵇ. The foliation is modern, and in red ink. The Roper is imperfect : the first complete page, 2ᵃ, deals with the Speech of More when made Speaker, commencing " manner appointed " (see below, p. 14, l. 9). On 1ᵃ and 1ᵇ are imposed fragments of the

---

[1] This is the *Life* wrongly attributed to Richard Hall. It was printed by Van Ortroy from the Stonyhurst MS. in *Analecta Bollandiana*, X and XII, and by Ronald Bayne from MS. Harleian 6382 for the E.E.T.S., Extra Series, 117.

earlier part of the same speech, and of the words in Roper immediately preceding. The Fisher *Life* is imperfect at the end; following it is a blank leaf.

Nothing seems to be known of the earlier history of the manuscript. The notes scribbled here and there are trivial, referring to hands of cards, etc., and give no indication of the possessors.

The handwriting is probably of the late sixteenth century, and the same throughout, a clear, firm cursive, with few scribal corrections or slips. The text is written continuously, the only paragraph break I have noted being that after More's Speech, fol. 3ª. A marginal summary, in a finer hand, accompanies the text, and was evidently allowed for, as the line of writing is carefully restricted to about 5 inches. The number of lines per page varies, being usually 28 or 29. Each page apparently had a catchword.

VII, VIII. MSS. BURNS.

There are two Roper manuscripts in the Library of the Rt. Hon. John Burns. These are denoted in this edition by J and B.

MS. J is a paper folio, in a modern binding. The leaves measure $11\frac{9}{10} \times 7\frac{1}{2}$ inches. A line of writing measures about 6 inches. The number of lines to a page varies, many having 39 lines, others 34, others only 28 or 29. Catchwords are the rule, but are sometimes wanting, in some cases owing to cropping.

There are 63 pages of text, paginated. Preceding the text is a leaf, originally blank, on the recto of which are now written two notes in later hands:

> This is written by William Roper son in law to Sʳ Thomas Moore.
> I lent this MS to Mr Hearne who published it at Oxon in 8°.

On the verso of the first fly-leaf are some modern pencil notes:

> Written circa 1600–1620.
> £35.

xvi *Introduction*

This Manuscript was the one used by Thos. Hearne for his Latin Edition of Mores Life 1716.

Sir T. Phillips Library?

On the verso of the following fly-leaf we have:

John Burns. August 26, 1921.

The handwriting is the same throughout, a clear cursive of the late sixteenth or early seventeenth century. Latin words and quotations are in italic.

The manuscript has no title, but the text is headed " In hoc ✠ signo vinces."

MS. B.   MS. B is also of paper, in a modern leather binding. It is a quarto, 7 (nearly) × 5 inches. There are no guide-lines. A line of text measures about 4½ inches. There are commonly 22 to 24 lines to a page. There are now no catchwords, but there may have been originally, as even the last line of the text is frequently cropped, so that the wording can only be ascertained by checking with other manuscripts. Paragraph breaks are indicated.

The manuscript consists of 64 leaves, not paginated or foliated. The text begins on the second leaf. On the recto of the first is the title " The Life and Death of Sr Thomas More knight sometymes Lord Chauncellor of England. Written by William Roper his Sonne in Lawe Anno Domini 1535." This title also occurs before the text as heading: apart from this there are no headings or headlines.

The hand is the same throughout—a clear cursive, probably of the late sixteenth century.

IX. MS. Mm. IV. 21.

MS. M.   MS. Mm. IV. 21, in the Cambridge University Library, is denoted in this edition by M.

It is a folio, on paper, the leaves measuring 12 × 7½ inches. The number of lines per page varies, the average being 35.

The text occupies folios 2^a—28^b. On fol. 1^a is written: " Sr T. Mores Life by his son in law William Roper." Fol. 1^b is blank. Preceding fol. 1 are nine blank leaves, of which six are cut short. A blank leaf also follows the text.

The hand is a neat, clear cursive of the early seventeenth century. Latin words are written in a larger italic. The text is written continuously, without paragraph breaks.

The top of the pages is injured by damp, but the words can always be made out.

A transcript of the manuscript (now MS. Harleian 7030) was made by the antiquarian Thomas Baker (1656–1740) because of its damaged condition even at that date, being " much eaten, and in some places consumed with moisture."

X. MS. DYCE 46.

MS. Dyce 46, in the Dyce and Forster Collection in the Library of the Victoria and Albert Museum, S. Kensington, is denoted in this edition by D.

It is a paper quarto, in a modern binding. The leaves measure $7\frac{1}{2} \times 5\frac{1}{2}$ inches. A line of writing measures about $3\frac{3}{4}$ inches. The number of lines on a page varies, there being frequently as many as 28. Each page has a catchword.

There are 51 folios written—102 pages. The foliation is in ink and contemporary; the pagination is in modern pencil. In the foliation 49 is omitted: hence the discrepancy between foliation and pagination. The text begins on the recto of folio 1, and ends on the verso of the folio marked 52 (actually 51). Before the text are three leaves: the first blank; the second a factitious title-page, with engraved ornamental border, embracing the portraits of King James and Queen Anne; the third occupied by a portrait of More. At the end there is one leaf blank.

The factitious title-page runs: " The Life and Death of Sir Tho: More K^t: somtyme Lo: Chaunccellor of Eng: written by Wm Roper his Sonne in lawe: An: Do: 1535."

On the fly-leaf is pasted an engraving of the More Family Group, from the picture (presumably in part by

Holbein) once at Well Hall, Eltham, the seat of the Roper Family. This picture later passed, by marriage, to Sir Rowland Winn, of Nostell Priory, near Wakefield. Pasted on the fly-leaf is a cutting, describing the picture, from the Catalogue of the Exhibition of National Portraits at Kensington, 1866.

The writing is the same throughout, a neat cursive of the late sixteenth or early seventeenth century. There are a number of paragraph breaks. The first recto is headed " The life of Sir Thomas More." After that each verso is headed " The life of Sir," and each recto " Thomas More."

XI, XII. MS. BODLEY 966, AND MS. WILLIS 58.

In the Bodleian there are two Roper manuscripts.

MS. T.   MS. Bodley 966 is denoted in this edition by T.

The manuscript is on paper, and contains xxiv + 684 pages. It comprises copies of about fifty papers dealing chiefly with English history of the sixteenth century, and was written probably about 1610. It was presented to the Bodleian by Sir Peter Manwood in 1620.

The Roper *Life* occupies pp. 193–220. The leaves measure about $16\frac{1}{2} \times 10\frac{1}{2}$ inches. A line of writing measures about $7\frac{1}{2}$ inches.

The *Life* is written in a neat, cursive hand of regular slope, with no paragraph divisions. Each page has a catchword. Quotation marks are used. At the beginning is the heading : " Jesus Amen."

MS. W.   MS. Willis 58 is denoted in this edition by W.

The MS. is on paper, and contains i + 488 leaves. It comprises a collection of copies of treatises, in English and Latin, on English history, and was written probably between 1580 and 1640. Each article is practically a separate manuscript.

Roper's *Life of More* occupies fols. 2ᵃ—75ᵃ : the title being on 2ᵃ, 2ᵇ blank, and the text beginning on 3ᵃ. The leaves measure about 12×7 inches. A line of writing occupies about 5 inches.

Introduction

The hand is a much-flourished cursive.

The matter is divided into paragraphs, with indented first line and large flourished capital. Each page has a catchword.

XIII. MS. 544, BOLLANDIST LIBRARY, BRUSSELS.

This manuscript is denoted in this edition by X. MS. X.

It is a small-paper quarto, in a modern leather binding. The leaves measure $7\frac{1}{2} \times 5\frac{7}{10}$ inches. Up to folio 47^b, lines are ruled to enclose the text, giving a text-space of about 4 inches. These bounds are observed by the first scribe, whose work ends l. 5, fol. 24^a; but the writing of the second scribe frequently overflows the margins. The number of lines on a page varies, the average of the first scribe being 24. Each page has a catchword (occasionally cropped towards the end). The pages are not headed.

The two hands seem to be both of the late sixteenth or early seventeenth century. The first hand is a good, firm cursive; the second is loose and careless, particularly towards the end, where the scribe seems to be writing very fast; this second hand varies so much, according to the degree of care used, that it gives at first sight the impression of different writers. Both scribes use paragraph breaks.

The manuscript is foliated throughout in pencil, and the pencil foliation is the one used for this description. An ink foliation, numbered 3–15 (end of first hand), corresponds to the folios marked in pencil 12^a–24^a. There are 87 leaves. The Roper text occupies fols. 11^a to the bottom of 79^a. The leaves following the text are blank.

Preceding the text are various notes on the leaves noted below :

Blank leaf inserted by binder.	Edm. Waterton, 1866.
fol. 1^a.	RR. PP. Bollandianis 1871.
fols. 2^b—3^a.	Genealogical tree showing descent of the owner of the MS., Edmund Waterton, from Sir Thomas More.

xx Introduction

fol. 8ª. 1535 (in hand of first scribe). Sr Tho Moore (in hand of second scribe).

fol. 9ª. A note in a seventeenth-century hand by a " Tho Bushell," possibly Sir Francis Bacon's protégé, the speculator and farmer of the royal mines, who lived from 1594–1674 :

> When the fraile bark of man is frawted with a see of sorowes and sailes by noe other gale but the billowes of sithes, woe be to that passengre, for as death is the tribute due to nature soe itt is the hauen of his happines. Tho Bushell.

fol. 10ª. The life of Sr Thomas More knight sometime Lord Chauncellor of England. Written by Willm Roper his sonne in Lawe Anno Domini 1535.

On the left-hand inner cover are the arms of Edmund Waterton (1830–1887), F.S.A., of Walton, Yorkshire. As stated on the blank leaf preceding fol. 1ª, the MS. was in his possession in 1866.

RELATIONSHIP OF THE ROPER MANUSCRIPTS

The critical text of Roper's *Life of More*, which follows, is derived from a collation of the thirteen manuscripts H^2 J H^3 H^1 A M S A^2 D T W X B described above (pp. xi–xx). H^1 is a copy of A. MS. H^2 has been chosen as basis.

From a consideration of common errors,[1] these manuscripts may be tentatively grouped in some such form as below; but the relationships of S and M are too uncertain for the diagram to satisfy all the data.

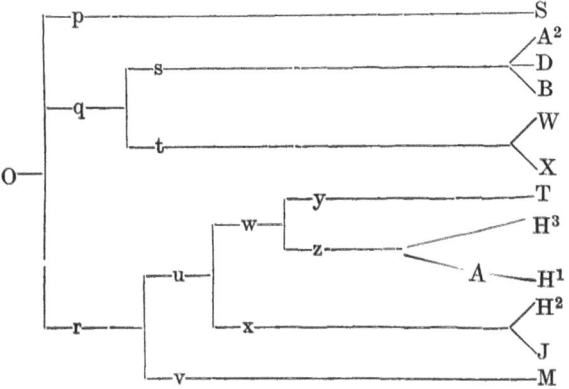

Genealogical tree of the Roper manuscripts.

O represents the author's original; the small letters, p, q, r, etc., denote parent manuscripts now lost, and the capitals S, A^2, etc., the extant manuscripts.

Lists of corrupt readings in the various manuscripts may be easily constructed from the collations. The manuscript groups A^2 D B, W X, A^2 D B W X, H^3 H^1 A, H^2 J, are obviously justified by the inheritance of many errors in common. An interesting peculiarity of the

MS. groups.

---

[1] For the principles of text-editing from multiple manuscripts, see Harpsfield, Introduction, pp. xxi–xxxi.

W X sub-group is the use of direct speech in the passage, p. 41, below.

S, T, and M are more difficult to class.

Independent tradition of S.   S is a good manuscript, and if complete would have had considerable claim to be taken as basis for the critical text. There are no striking errors justifying the connection of it with any other extant manuscript or manuscript group.

Evidence for grouping T with H³ H¹ A.   T shows conflicting affinities, but errs most often with H³ H¹ A. The following common errors seem to warrant the grouping of T with those manuscripts:

10/7, *woulde none in our lawe be founde* for *could be none of our Lawe founde.*
12/2, *misliked* for *mysliking.*
14/3, *my* for *most.*
24/4, omit *familiar.*
29/6, omit *very.*
48/16, *noble* for *notable.*
62/11, *his* for *this.*
63/1, omit *vnto her.*
68/16, *receyve* for *receaued.*
89/12, omit *as.*
90/1, omit *materiall . . . statute* (*Eyeslip.*)
90/11, *honorable* for *noble.*
90/14, *worthy* for *waighty.*
96/16, omit *our.*
101/20, *with* for *of.*

Independent tradition of M.   M is a very good manuscript, with few individual errors and few in common with other manuscripts. The trifling ones that do occur are not in common with any manuscript or manuscript group at all consistently. Cf. collations, 11/9, 12/4, 15/21, 17/18, 20/25, 31/5, 56/10, 71/18, 89/11. All that can be safely said is that M seems more remote from the manuscripts derived from p and q than from those derived from u: hence its position in the preceding diagram.

After the merits of MS. M had been made clear by the collations, it was with much hesitation that H² was retained as basis for the critical text. It is obvious that

Introduction

M was made by a more careful scribe, and if used as basis, less emendation would have been necessary. But the spellings of H^2 point to an earlier date. Its *tradition* seems as good as that of M, and its individual errors are easily recognised and corrected by checking with the other manuscripts of its group. The isolation of M makes for difficulty, and though its value in settling textual problems must be clearly recognised, it seems preferable to print *in extenso* MS. H^2.

Where the evidence of Roper manuscript authority is so balanced, or so at variance, as to make decision difficult, the text of Harpsfield is taken into account. Harpsfield himself must have had access to a good and authentic manuscript of Roper, and the Harpsfield manuscripts may be fairly used to control and aid the editor of Roper, just as the Roper manuscripts may help to settle a dubious reading in Harpsfield. Where, however, the evidence of Roper manuscript authority is clear, Harpsfield is not allowed to weight a variant, even if the Harpsfield text seems preferable, *e.g.*:

The value of the Harpsfield MSS. in settling Roper readings.

(1) Roper, 7/8, as compared with Harpsfield, 19/21 : *and play but for their sauce* H^2 J M A^2 D B, little stronger than H^3 H^1 A T W X, which omit *but*. As all Harpsfield manuscripts omit *but*, and the balance of Roper manuscript authority is so nearly even, *but* is omitted in the Roper critical text.

(2) Roper, 9/16, as compared with Harpsfield, 22/24 : *his seruice* H^2 J H^3 H^1 A M T, a stronger combination than A^2 D W X B, which read *his Graces seruice*. All Harpsfield manuscripts read *his Graces seruice*, but the reading of H^2 J H^3 H^1 A M T is followed.

(3) Roper, 9/26, as compared with Harpsfield, 23/7 : here the Roper readings vary erratically, and *that then was* of J M D B, as supported by all the Harpsfield manuscripts except C, is read in the Roper text.

(4) Roper, 15/6–7, as compared with Harpsfield

29/20 : *best spoken* H^2 J H^3 H^1 A A^2, little weightier than *the best spoken* M S D T W X B. Hence *the best spoken* of the best Harpsfield manuscripts has settled the Roper reading.

(5) Roper, 32/14, as compared with Harpsfield, 45/7 : *thexpositions* H^2 S, *exposicione*, J H^3 H^1 A A^2 D X B, *exposicions* M T, omitted in W. Here all the Harpsfield manuscripts read *the expositions*. The plural is read by four good Roper manuscripts; for the singular we have the solidly united evidence of one group H^3 H^1 A, but the contradictory evidence of A^2 D X B as against T and of J as against H^2. The plural therefore, so strongly supported by Harpsfield, the best Roper tradition, and sense, is read in the Roper text.

In cases where the readings of Harpsfield are of importance or special interest, they are noted in the Roper collations, even if not adopted in the Roper critical text.

The Harpsfield manuscripts are referred to by the following symbols :

E = MS. Emmanuel 76.
L = MS. Lambeth 827.
R^2 = MS. Rawlinson D. 107.
Y = MS. Yelverton 72.
C = MS. (Colchester) Harsnett H. b. 35.
H = MS. Harley 6253.
R = MS. Rawlinson D. 86.
B = MS. Burns.

EARLIER EDITIONS

The *Life* had circulated in manuscript for many years before it was printed first by a certain " T.P." [1] in 1626. The editions of " T.P." (1626), Thomas Hearne (1716) and the Rev. John Lewis (1729, 1731, 1765) cannot be considered to represent faithfully even such an approximation to the original text as can be arrived at from detailed collations.

The manuscript used by " T.P.," which he " had come upon in a Friend's house," was one of the class in which the dialogues are in the third person. MS. Eton 167 and Mr. Fagg's manuscript are similar (see below, p. 2). This version differs considerably from the regular Roper tradition, as may be seen from the following comparisons :

"T.P."

(1) " T.P." begins : " Syr Thomas More was borne in London of worshipfull Parents. His father was a Student of Lincolnes Inne, and brought him vp in the Latin tongue at S. Antonyes Schoole in London, who was very shortly after, by his Fathers procurement, receiued into the house of that Worthy and Learned Prelate, Cardinall Morton." Cf. text below, p. 5.

(2) " T.P." ends : " Which speach of the Emperour was afterward related by Syr Thomas Eliot vnto M. William Roper & his wife, being with him at supper in the presence of one M. Clement, M. Heywood, and their wiues." Cf. text below, p. 104.

(3) " T.P." transposes the earlier Nun of Canterbury passage so as to follow the Gresham case, and

[1] " T.P." still remains unidentified—Thomas Plowden has been suggested.

thus brings together the whole of the matter concerning the Nun. Cf. " T.P.," pp. 103–119, and text below, pp. 59–61, 64–71.

(4) The various dialogues between More and Roper refer to Roper in the third person; e.g. " T.P.," p. 31 : " As soone as his Maiesty was gone, M. William Roper, a Gentleman of Grayes Inne, who had married Syr Thomas Mores eldest daughter, said vnto him, ' Father, how happy a man are you '," etc. Cf. text below, p. 21.

Cf. also " T.P.," pp. 36–8, 54–7, 115–16, and text below, pp. 24–5, 35–6, 69–70. " M. Roper " is used throughout for " I," " me," etc., and " his daughter Roper," etc., for " my wife."

Hearne. Hearne based his text on " Mr. Burton's copy," one of the two Roper manuscripts now belonging to the Rt. Hon. John Burns (= MS. J in this edition). Collation soon shows that this is not the best manuscript. Hearne notes at the end " various readings " from other MSS. One of these was " Mr. Murray's copy." The Roper now belonging to Mr. Fagg (see below, p. 2) belonged to Alexander Murray. It carries the signature " Alexander Murray " on an illuminated title, 1679, and has an early eighteenth-century bookplate of Alexander Murray of Broughton.

Lewis. Lewis's text does not tally exactly with any of the thirteen MSS. collated for this edition. It was taken from a manuscript lent to Lewis by Mr. Thomas Beake of Stourmouth,[1] and Lewis's transcript of it exists in the Bodleian, MS. Rawl. D 787.

Singer. S. W. Singer, in his 1817 edition (in the original spelling) took " Lewis's text as groundwork, and ingrafted upon it the readings which appeared preferable " in Hearne and "T.P." (p. vii). This "ingrafting" is done silently, so that the student can only discover the source of any read-

[1] The manor of Stourmouth or Northcourt was left to Christopher Roper, William's younger brother, by their father.

Introduction

ing by laborious comparison. Singer's book is, however, most useful in that it incorporates Lewis's Preface and Appendix of the More Letters, the portion of Hearne's Preface relating to the Roper *Life*, and " T.P." 's Dedication to the Lady Elizabeth, Countess of Banbury. Singer also includes the Letter from More to Cromwell concerning the Nun of Kent.

In the 1822 edition, Singer unfortunately chose to " reform the unsettled and wretched orthography." He used a manuscript lent him by Sir William Strickland,[1] Baronet, of Boynton in Yorkshire, and " another manuscript " for the revision of his 1817 text. Sir William Strickland's manuscript belonged to Roper's family. The last male descendant of Margaret and William Roper in the direct line was Edward Roper, who died in 1708, unmarried. His sister Elizabeth married Charles Henshaw. One of their daughters, Susanna, married Sir Rowland Winn of Nostell, and another, Catherine, married Sir William Strickland. Singer notes that some complimentary lines under the Leigh and Egerton arms opposite the first page of the Strickland MS. are signed " Fra. Wynne."

There are several modern reprints of Singer's 1822 text, *e.g.* Gollancz's for the *King's Classics* (1903).

George Sampson in 1910 brought out a very readable text[2] based on four of the manuscripts in the British Museum (Harley 6362, 6254, 6166, and 7030). Sampson writes : " The first and second, both written in a sixteenth-century hand, have been taken as the main authorities, and compared with 6166 and 7030, the latter of which is a copy of an old manuscript at Cambridge "[3] (see p. 2, below). Also : " The text thus obtained differs from Singer's only in matters of detail."[4] But the editor gives no collations or notes by which his work may be

Sampson.

---

[1] This Strickland MS. is referred to on a fly-leaf of MS. Harl. 6362 : " Sir Wm Strickland Bart, a descendant from Sir Th. More, has another Copy of the following Life very similar to this."
[2] The *Utopia* of Sir Thomas More . . . with Roper's *Life of More*, etc. Edited by George Sampson. Bell, 1910.
[3] *Ibid.*, p. vi.   [4] *Ibid.*, p. vi.

controlled, and a composite text, so edited, can hardly be said to give us Roper's *Life* in its " final form." [1]

Though the variants of the Roper MSS. are not of much significance, students like evidence, and there seems room for a critical text with collations, which are the only check on the editor's wisdom of choice in any particular reading. Such a work as Roper's *Life*, handed about for many years only in manuscript, and frequently and probably hurriedly transcribed, is particularly liable to trifling errors. As long as the copy made good sense, there would be little attempt to keep punctiliously to the exemplar in the case of common synonyms, or the arrangement of words in simple phrases. But we want a text as near Roper's as possible, and it is hoped, therefore, that this edition will have its appeal.

[1] Sampson, *op. cit.*, p. vi.

WILLIAM ROPER

WILLIAM ROPER came of a wealthy Kentish family, landowners for many generations, and with records [1] going back to the time of Henry III. Harpsfield gives the following account of his lineage:

Family.

> Ye come of a woorthye pedegree, both by the Father and mothers side: by the fathers side of auncient gentlemen of longe continuance; and by the mothers side of the Apuldrefeles, one of the chiefest and auncient families in Kent, and one of the three chiefe gentlemen that compelled William Conquerour to agree and to confirme the auncient customes of Kent; daughter to the great, wise and right woorshipfull Sir John Fineux, chiefe Justice of the Kinges benche ... whose steppes in vertue, wisedome and learning, as also your woorshipfull fathers (who was Attorney to King Henry the eight,[2] and whom ye in the office of the Pregnatorie in the kinges benche [3] haue immediately succeeded ...) ye haue ... well and gratiously troade after.[4]

Roper's family tree [5] may be mapped out as on p. xxx.

Genealogical tree.

John Roper, William's father, was an active member of Lincoln's Inn, and closely associated there with Sir Thomas More and his father, Judge John More.[6] He was autumn reader, 1503–5, and a governor, 1507–8. He held various public offices other than those noted by Harpsfield: [7] he

John Roper William's father.

---

[1] See Collins' *Peerage*, Vol. VI, p. 621.
[2] See *L. & P.* III, no. 1389: *1521. 3 July.* "For John Rooper. To be Attorney General, during pleasure, with fees, and the appointment of officers."
[3] See below, p. xxxv.   [4] E.E.T.S. ed., p. 5.
[5] See *e.g.* Collins' *Peerage*, Vol. VI, pp. 621–6. For further information, see Harpsfield, Hist. Notes, 5/4, 5/8, 5/13–14; Hasted's *History of Kent*, 1778–99, *passim*: particularly Vol. I, pp. 55–7 (Well Hall); Vol. III, pp. 589, etc. (St. Dunstan's, Canterbury); Vol. III, pp. 640–1 (Manor of Stourmouth, *alias* Northcourt); also new ed., *Hundred of Blackheath*, ed. H. H. Drake (1886), p. 189.
[6] See *Pub. Mod. Lang. Assoc. America* (*PMLA*), Vol. XLVII, June, 1932, *Sir Thomas More's connection with the Roper Family*, by Pearl Hogrefe.
[7] See quotation above.

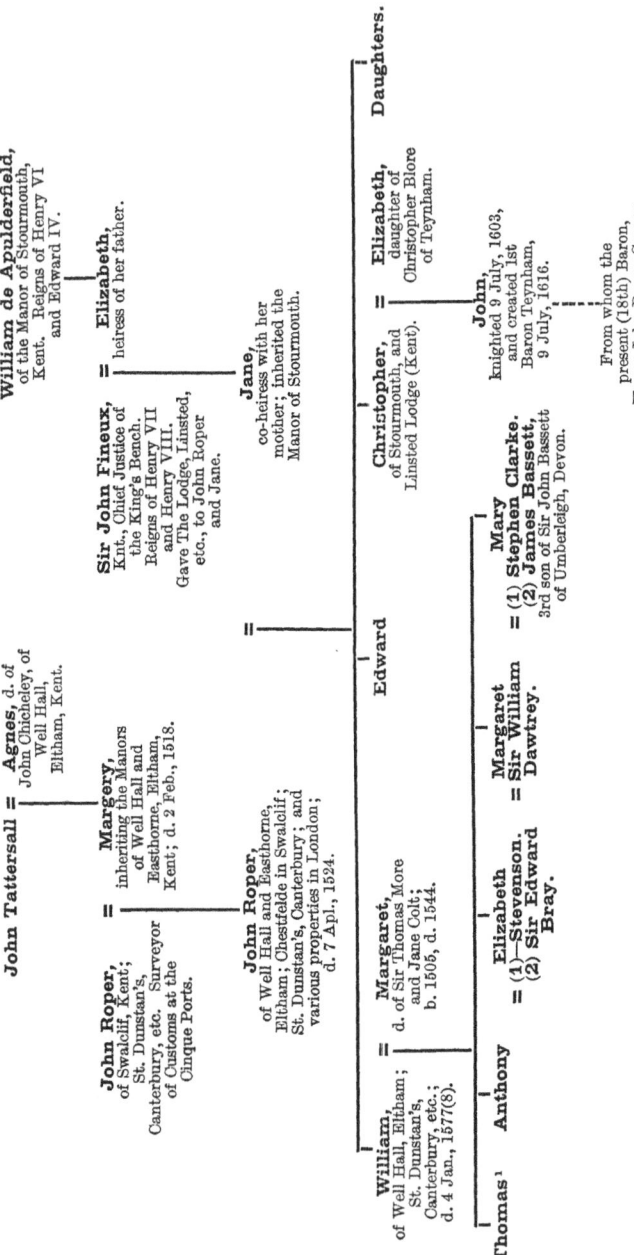

Professor Sisson notes that Thomas Roper describes himself as being thirty years of age on 11 June, 1564. The order of the children is not clear: the sons are therefore given first in the Table.

Introduction

was Sheriff of Kent, 1521, and sat many times on commissions of the peace (often with Sir John More) for that county.[1] With Sir John Fineux, his father-in-law, he was in charge of the Records at Bridewell Palace.[2] As noted in his Will,[3] he secured for William his office of Clerk of the Pleas, or Prothonotary in the Court of King's Bench. He died 7 April, 1524.

William Roper's birth-date has been commonly estimated[4] as 1496. The old epitaph at St. Dunstan's (recorded by Somner, and given in Lewis's edition of Roper's *Life*) stated that he was 82 years of age when he died on 4 January, 1577(8). Professor Sisson's researches throw doubt on this statement. He communicates to me the following note:

Birth of William Roper.

Roper as Steward of the Manor of Stepney, and the date of his birth.

Roper appears in Chancery depositions in suits arising out of disputes in connection with Lord Wentworth's Manor of Stepney, and gives evidence in his capacity as Steward of the Manor. I am unable to say at present in what year he began, and in what year he ceased to hold this office. On 14 May, 1562, when he appeared before the examiners, he is described as William Roper of Lincoln's Inn, Steward of the Manor of Stepney, aged sixty-four; and again on 24 February, 1563 (N.S.), when he gives the same estimate of his age. This would appear to fix the date of his birth between 25 February, 1498 and 15 May, 1498.

Incidentally, the dates of the births of some of Roper's children may be similarly fixed. I find, for example, a note of evidence given, in connection with a suit of the Heron family, by Thomas Roper, aged thirty on 11 June, 1564.

Wood,[5] on what authority I do not know, states that *Education.*

---

[1] See Hogrefe, *op. cit.*, with references to the *Patent Rolls* and *L. & P.*

[2] See *L. & P.* III, 2, no. 3678 (p. 1522); and E. G. O'Donoghue, *Bridewell Hospital* (1923).

[3] Made 27 January, 1523(4). For text, see *Archæologia Cantiana*, Vol. ii, pp. 153–74; *Statutes of the Realm*, III, 309 ff. See below, p. xxxv.

[4] See Wood, *Athen. Oxon.*, Vol. I, col. 41; Collins' *Peerage*, Vol. VI, p. 623; Epitaph below, p. xliii.

[5] *Athen. Oxon.*, Vol. I, col. 36.

Roper was educated "at one of the Universities"; but of his youth and studies we as yet know nothing.

Marriage with Margaret More.

The year in which Roper entered Sir Thomas More's household is not certain, but it must have been some time before he married Margaret. Their marriage took place [1] on 2 July, 1521, and More went to the Tower on 17 April, 1534. As Roper had been "xvj yeares and more in house conversant with him," [2] 1518 seems indicated. In this year Roper was admitted to the Society of Lincoln's Inn, [3] and the arrangement was probably made for the young law-student's convenience.

Birth of the first child.

By 1523 a child had been born to William and Margaret. Writing to Margaret in 1523, Erasmus says:

> William Roper, who is gifted with such nobility and gentleness of character that, were he not your husband, he might seem to be your brother, has given you (or if you prefer it, you have given to him) the most fortunate first-fruits of your union, or, to put it better, each has given to the other a child—to whom a kiss is to be sent. I send you another child. . . .

Erasmus then goes on to speak of the Christ-child, and how he is sending husband and wife his commentary upon the Christmas hymn of Prudentius. The Christ-child, he says:

> will not disdain to be celebrated by such a pair as you, whose purity of life, peace, concord and simplicity are such, that few, even from among the number of professed monks or nuns, would dare to compare with you.
> (*Commentary on the Christmas Hymn of Prudentius.*)
> See Harpsfield, Note to 80/23-5.

---

[1] See *Harleian Soc. Pub.* Vol. XXV, *Allegations for Marriage Licences issued by the Bishop of London*, 1520–1610. Extracted by ... J. L. Chester, ed. by G. J. Armitage:

2 July 1521: William Roper of St. Andrew, Holborn, & Margaret More of St. Stephen's, Walbrook.

In the autumn (? Sep.) of 1521, Erasmus writes to Budæus:

Habet [Morus] filias tres, quarum maxima natu, Margareta, iam nupta est iuueni, primum beato, deinde moribus integerrimis ac modestissimis postremo non alieno a nostris studiis (*Opus Epist. Des. Erasmi*, IV, p. 577).

[2] See below, p. 36.   [3] See below, p. xxxiv.

Introduction

The most famous of the five Roper children [1] was Mary,[2] later Mistress Bassett, who inherited the literary gifts of her grandfather and parents, and translated into English More's *Passionis Expositio* and several learned works. She died 20 March, 1572; William Roper was an executor to her Will,[3] which was proved on 19 April following.

Roper's daughter, Mary Bassett.

Sir Thomas More did not always find Roper a docile son-in-law. In early life he was attracted to the Lutheran doctrine of justification by faith. Harpsfield zestfully describes how Sir Thomas rescued him " by his good counsaile and aduise, or rather by his instant and deuout prayers to God," recovering his "lost soule, ouerwhelmed and full deepe drowned in the deadly, dreadfull depth of horrible heresies." [4] Roper, " at what time he maried with mistris Margarete More, was a meruailous zealous Protestant, and so feruent and withall so well and properly lyked of himselfe and his diuine learning, that he tooke the brydle into the teeth, and ranne forth like a headstronge horse, harde to be plucked backe againe. Neyther was he content to whisper it in hugger mugger . . . he longed so sore to be pulpited . . . thinking . . . that he should be better able to edifie and profite the people then the best preacher that came to Paules crosse." [5] He was charged with open heresy before Wolsey, but " for loue borne by the Cardinall to Sir Thomas More . . . was with a frendly warning discharged." [6] More reasoned and argued with him to no avail, and at length, perceiving " none of all this able to call him home," decided to "cleane geue him ouer and gett . . . to God and praye for him." [7] Roper remained ever after a steadfast Catholic, " the singuler helper and patrone of all Catholikes, to relieue and ayde them in their distresse, especiallye such as eyther were imprisoned [8] or otherwise troubled for the

Roper's temporary lapse into heresy.

Charity to distressed Catholics.

---

[1] See pedigree, p. xxx, above.
[2] See Harpsfield, p. 83, and Notes thereon.
[3] For Will, see *Notes and Queries*, 11th Ser., Vol. VI, 3 Aug. 1912, pp. 87–8. [4] *Op. cit.*, p. 5.
[5] *Op. cit.*, pp. 84–6.   [6] *Op. cit.*, p. 86.   [7] *Op. cit.*, p. 87.
[8] In 1569 Roper bequeathed to the Worshipful Company of Parish Clerks a freehold estate in Candlewick Street, and some tenements in Bermondsey Street, on condition that they should distribute £4 among the poor prisoners in Newgate and other gaols—"to four prisons on All Saints' Day for ever." See below, pp. xxxix–xl.

xxxiv *Introduction*

Consequent imprisonment and fine, 1542.

Catholike fayth. For which cause in the latter time of king Henry the eight, for relieuing by his almes a notable learned man, Master Beckenshawe, he suffred great trouble and imprisonment in the towre." [1]

Roper's legal training at Lincoln's Inn.

Roper's legal training at Lincoln's Inn is recorded in the *Black Books*, Vol. I. The most important entries are :

1518, Christmas Day. William Roper, son of Mr. John Roper, was admitted to the Society by George Treheyron, then the Marshal, and on Feb. 26, 1520, he was pardoned all vacations, past and future; he may be at repasts at his pleasure.

1525, Ascension Day [May 25]. Roper . . . to be called to the Bar at the next moot.

1534, June 24. . . . Roper is discharged of his amercements for refusing office, and shall henceforth be exonerated; he shall be an Assistant of the Bench,[2] and may have a clerk at the yeomen's commons for 14*d.* a week, and a " bower " to his chamber when in commons as Outer Barristers have. He paid £5.

1535, Hilary Term. Mr. William Roper was called to the Bench. He paid £5.

From 1535 to 1565 there are numerous entries marking the interest and activity of William Roper as a Governor, Dean of the Chapel, etc. Further entries of importance are :

1565, July 1. William Rooper, a Bencher, . . . obtained admission to his own Chamber for his sons, Thomas and Anthony, Fellows of this House, and afterwards for William Dawtrey, his daughter's son, who was thus the junior, and not able to claim benefit thereof against the other two. Order for his quiet enjoyment.

1568, June 24. The House having borrowed £60 from William Roper, he is to be repaid at All Saints' next.

[1] *Op. cit.*, p. 89. For Roper's imprisonment in the Tower and fine of £100, see *L. & P.* 1542, no. 267 :

29 Feb., brought in to the King by Sir Richard Southwell, one of the General Surveyors, for the fine of William Roper, being in the Tower of London, 100 l.

For Bekynsaw's story, see *D.N.B.* (IV, p. 141, *Bekinsau*) and Hist. Notes to Harpsfield, 79/1–3 ; also *L. & P.* 1544, Pt. i, no. 610 (62), for his pardon for " all treasonable colloquies at Paris with the detestable traitors, Reginald Poole," etc.

[2] An " Assistant " or " Associate " of the Bench seems to have been a kind of honorary Bencher.

1573–4. It is noted in the printed edition of the *Black Books*, Vol. I, that William Roper ceased to reside in the Inn in this year, there being a list of the Fellows of Lincoln's Inn in the Burghley Papers, MS. Lansdowne 106, fo. 90, where his name is marked with the " d " = " discontinuing."

Roper held the office of Prothonotary for 54 years. When his father made his Will, on 27 January, 1523(4), he and William were holding the office jointly. In his turn, William, in 1577, at the end of his life, procured the post for his elder son, Thomas. It is interesting to note that at one time William Roper held the office conjointly with Richard Heywood [1] (brother of John, the dramatist) and shared quarters with him at Lincoln's Inn.[2] Richard Heywood was present in a legal capacity at More's trial—Roper himself being absent—and was one of Roper's authorities for the account of it.[3]

{Office of Prothonotary.}

This office of Prothonotary was of such value that John Roper evidently thought that his securing of it for William should be taken into account when William's share of his estate was under consideration. That the father knew his division of the property would not be considered just by William is obvious from the Will : [4]

{John Roper's will.}

> Fyrst, forasmoche as I have provydyd and caused myn eldest soone Willyam to be prefferred, and to be Joynt offycer with me in the office of the chief clerke of our Sovereigne lorde the King, for plees before the same King to be holden, and perceyve the proffyttes thereof after my decesse, the Atteyning of which office was to me no litle charge, And also where the grete parte of my saide manours, landes, and tenementes, to the yerelye value of one hundreth poundes and above, ben of the tenure and nature of Gavylkynde, and that londes and tenementes of the same tenure and nature of Gavilkynde within the saide Countie of Kent ben, and the tyme that no manne's mynde ys to the contrary

[1] See A. W. Reed, *Tudor Drama*, p. 82.
[2] See *Black Books*, Vol. I : 1567, Aug. 19. Mr. William Rooper and Richard Heywode, Esqs. . . . admitted to the two east chambers beneath in the middle rooms of the new building.
[3] See below, p. 96.
[4] For full text, see *Archæologia Cantiana*, Vol. ii, pp. 153–74.

hathe ben, parted and parteable emonge heyres males, and to thintente my soones after my decesse shall have no cause to varye amongst them selffes, or to stryve for the partycyon and devyding of the same, I therefore openly declare this my saide last will, etc.

So much did John Roper's sons and widow vary and strive among themselves after his decease that his estate was not settled till 1529, when Parliament finally disposed of it. It was a source of trouble between Warham and Wolsey (see *Letters and Papers*, IV, nos. 1118, 1157). The examinations of witnesses before the Will was proved, point to the main questions having been the validity of the document, and the probability of the widow having influenced her husband in favour of the youngest son Christopher, and to the prejudice of William. One witness "had heard Jane Roper often say, when she was merry, and her husband in good health, 'Would God you would let Christopher your son have your manor in St. Dunstan's without Canterbury, and your eldest son some other thing;' but never heard her counsel him to do so at the time of making the will." (*L. & P.* IV, no. 1518). Under the same entry: John Abery (who had been servant to John Roper for 30 years) examined before the commissary of the Archbishop of Canterbury, 23 March, 1526, deposed "that John Roper was of sound mind, and that after the reading of his will on one occasion, he said to his son William, 'All trust and familiarity is set apart between thee and me.'"

The final disposition of Parliament was considerably more favourable to William than was the document alleged to be John Roper's last will and testament. Estimating the estate at over 300 marks a year, the widow was to receive 100 marks, the two younger sons (Edward and Christopher) 40 each, and William the remainder. He was also allotted Well Hall, Eltham, and the St. Dunstan's property.[1]

Roper's public career.

William, like his father, occupied prominent public positions, mostly connected with Kent, where he held his

---

[1] See Hasted, *History of Kent*, new edition, ed. Drake, p. 189; *Statutes of the Realm*, III, 309 ff. For an interesting discussion of the Roper Will and the action of Parliament in personal cases, where domestic bickering seemed likely to affect the public peace, see Hogrefe, *op. cit.*, pp. 529 ff.

most important property. As far as one can gather from the scattered and superficial notices that exist, he does not seem to have suffered seriously from Henry's displeasure against More and his family. He took the oath, and his conduct was watched: there are Cromwell's *Remembrances*, "to send for Wm. Roper, to send for Lady More" (*L. & P.* 1535, no. 218); in Cromwell's hand there is a List of Names of "nearly forty gentlemen, including . . . Robert Fyssher, the Bishop of Rochester's brother, and Will. Roper of Chelchyth" (*L. & P.* 1535, no. 1077). But Roper's public career continued: *L. & P.* have frequent notices of his sitting on Commissions of the Peace for Kent, and receiving grants (*e.g.* 1537, Dec., Grants, 28; 1542, Nov., Grants, 22); also on Commissions for Middlesex (1543, Pt. I, 100 (21)). He draws an annuity from monasteries (*L. & P.* 1543, Pt. I, 436 (55)). For the Army for Flanders he can contribute "10 foot" (*L. & P.* 1543, Pt. I, 832). There was no forfeiture of his ancestral estates. For his imprisonment in the Tower and fine, see above, p. xxxiv.

Roper sat several times as Member for Parliament. In 1529, in the very Parliament in which his father's Will was at last settled, he was Member for Bramber in Sussex.[1] In the reign of Mary he sat for Rochester (1554) and twice for Canterbury (Oct. 1555 and Jan. 1557(8)). Under Mary, his staunch Catholic principles stood him in good stead.

Member for Parliament.

[1] See *L. & P.* Vol. IV, Pt. iii, no. 6043. The list contains many interesting names connected with the More family and their history:

Nomina Militum
Cambridge—Sir Giles Alyngton
Oxon.—Sir John Dauntsey

Nomina Civium
Colchester—Rich. Riche
Rochester—Rob. Fyssher
Midherst—John Basset
Brambre—Wm. Roper
Wilton—Geoffrey Pole
Downeshed—John Rastell
Thetford—Giles Heron, William Dauntsey

Cf. A. F. Pollard: Thomas Cromwell's Parliamentary Lists, *Bulletin of the Institute of Historical Research*, ix, 25 June, 1931.
Cf. also A. F. Pollard in *T.L.S.*, 27 March, 1930, quoted below in Note to 40/19.

In trouble under Elizabeth.

But they equally got him into trouble in the reign of Elizabeth. On 8 July, 1568, he was summoned before the Privy Council on the charge of having financed religious exiles, who had printed books against Elizabeth's government. On 25 Nov., 1569, he entered into a bond to be of good behaviour, and to appear before the council when summoned : [1]

> 1568, July 8. No. 7. Submission of William Roper before the Lords of the Privy Council, for having relieved with money certain persons who have departed out of the realm, and who, with others, have printed books against the Queen's supremacy and government.
> 1569, [Nov. 26]. No. 37. Justices of Peace for the Lathe of Sutton-at-Hone, Kent, to the Council. Certify their proceedings relative to the Act for Uniformity of Common Prayer. *Inclosing* . . . 37. II. Bond of William Roper, of Eltham, Kent, to be of good behaviour, and to appear before the Council when summoned, 25 Nov. 1569.

He seems to have kept the bond literally, and was no further molested.

Roper nominated Visitor for life of St. John's College, Oxford.

Roper was nominated with the Master of the Rolls, Sir William Cordell, as Visitor for life of Sir Thomas White's new foundation of St. John's College, Oxford, a nomination contested by Robert Horne, the anti-Catholic Bishop of Winchester.[2] "The first three heads of this College, appointed by Sir Thomas himself, were either deprived, or resigned their appointment, owing to dissatisfaction with the settlement of the Church under Elizabeth."[3] Roper and Sir Thomas were evidently close friends. "In March, 1558, at the funeral of Sir Thomas's first wife at S. Mary, Aldermary, their daughter, Lady Laxton, chief mourner, was led by Mr. Roper. The sympathies of both White and Roper with the old forms probably drew them together in more ways than one."[4]

---

[1] *Cal. State Papers, Dom.* 1547–80, pp. 311, 347.
[2] See *Cal. State Papers, Dom.* 1547–80, p. 417.
[3] *Some Account of Parish Clerks, more especially of the Ancient Fraternity . . . of S. Nicholas, now known as the Worshipful Company of Parish Clerks* . . . by James Christie (1893), p. 99.
[4] *Ibid.*, p. 99.

Introduction xxxix

I am indebted to the Librarian of St. John's College (Mr. S. L. Greenslade) for the following note :

> White received letters patent to found St. John's on 1 May, 1555. The deed of foundation is of 29 May, 1555. The position seems to be that the founder, in the original statutes, laid down that the Bishop of Winchester should be visitor, and closed that clause with a proviso that Roper and Cordell should have authority such as his own as long as they lived. Whether that took effect at once, or at his death on 12 Feb. 1567, I cannot say.

White and White's College were connected with the Merchant Taylors, and to this Company Roper offered property which he later bequeathed to the Parish Clerks : *Roper's bequest to the Parish Clerks, 1569.*

> It may have been this friendship [with Sir Thomas White] which led Roper to offer in 1569, to the Merchant Taylors' Company, with which White and White's new college were closely connected, the property at Bermondsey which, on their refusal to accept, he afterwards made over to the Parish Clerks. In the minutes of that Company, as given in " Clode's History of the Merchant Taylors Co.," it is recorded, 10th November, 1569, " whereas Mr William Roper hath made an offer to give certain tenements of his lying in the parish of S. Olave, in Southwark, in the County of Surrey, unto this mystere for ever, upon condition that this mystere shall yearly for ever give and distribute four pounds to, and amongst the poor prisoners at the four prison houses of Newgate, Ludgate, the King's Bench and the Marshalsea, viz., to every of the same four prison houses 20/- in bread or coles; and to keep the same in due reparation, which said tenements were sometime in the tenure and holding of Mr John Jenkyns, while he lived, citizen and Merchant Taylor of London; it is agreed by the aforesaid masters, and wardens, and assistants, that the said tenements shall be first viewed, and if it shall happen upon the view thereof had that it will be profitable for this house to take the same lands, then this house to accept the same offer, and if it shall appear otherwise, then this house to make refusal of the accepting the said offer, and yet, nevertheless, to render their hearty thanks to the said Mr Roper for his good will to them; whereupon, after view made of the said tenements, they, the said masters, wardens, and others,

the viewers, agreed to refuse the said land according to the aforesaid offer to this house, for that same land be now in great ruine and decay, and like to fall down."

This is probably the property which the Parish Clerks held by deed from Roper under the same conditions. To this property was added part of another in Candlewick Street, by the same deed. What the richer Company declined the poorer, despoiled as it had been over twenty years before, accepted.[1]

Portrait described as "William Roper" in the Parish Clerks' Hall.

In the Parish Clerks' Hall there is a picture [2] of a man of early middle age, described on the portrait as "William Roper Esqre A Worthey Benefactor to this Company of Parish Clerkes," and in the Inventory of 1674, as the "effigies" of William Roper. Now Roper's bequest to the Company was in 1569, when he was over seventy years of age. The picture is probably much later than Roper's day, and can hardly be a portrait of him.

Governor of a Grammar School.

To the end of his life Roper was taking interest in all sorts of affairs. He was one of "the twenty discreet governors" who appointed the pedagogue and sub-pedagogue of the "Free Grammer Schoole of Queene Elizabeth in Lewsham," [3] which was not founded till 1574.

"Old Mr Roper," 1576.

An interesting reference occurs in connection with the correspondence carried on for the collection of information concerning the Life of Bishop Fisher, preserved in MS. Arundel 152. "Old Mr Roper" and Mr. [Allan] Langdale are noted there as the only two surviving people likely to be of assistance in the search: "I know no moo that can say any thing." [4] This would be about 1576.

More's conveyance of land to Roper and Margaret.

Sir Thomas More, foreseeing probable confiscation of his lands by the King, had tried to make provision for his

[1] *Some Account of Parish Clerks, more especially of the Ancient Fraternity ... of S. Nicholas now known as the Worshipful Company of Parish Clerks ...* by James Christie (1893), p. 100.
The Company of Parish Clerks must be considered in connection with the survival of Church Music from pre-Reformation to post-Reformation times. See P. H. Ditchfield's *The Parish Clerk*, 1907.
[2] The thanks of the Editor are due to the Worshipful Company of Parish Clerks for permission to inspect the portrait, and to reproduce it for this edition, if it had been suitable.
[3] *Hundred of Blackheath*, p. 268.
[4] See *Analecta Bollandiana*, X, 159, 160.

family. His conveyance for the disposition of his lands after his death had been set aside, and the lands seized after his attainder; Roper and Margaret alone had been fortunate enough to have their portion earlier assured to them in immediate possession.[1]

We should like to think that this good fortune had made Roper particularly careful as to any claim on More's possessions by his other children and widow. But researches of Professor C. J. Sisson in the Record Office have revealed family strife between Roper and Dame Alice. Professor Sisson communicates to me the following note: *Roper at law with Dame Alice.*

Roper and More's Battersea property.

In 1561 William Roper defended a suit in Chancery against Henry Royden who sought to establish a claim to lands in Battersea formerly held by Sir Thomas More and subsequently by Roper. Roper obtained a lease from the Court of Augmentations some years after More's attainder. Royden set up a lease obtained under Edward VI in conflict with Roper's lease from Henry VIII and a later lease from Mary, the latter being clearly a confirmatory renewal. The lands were originally granted to More by the Abbot of Westminster in February 1529. After More's execution, it appears from the evidence, Henry allowed Dame Alice More to continue in possession for some eight years. When the lands were leased to Roper, Dame Alice took it very ill, "was greatly displeased therewith," as one witness put it. Another witness, a servant of Dame Alice, reports that she

"hard . . . Dame Alice many tymes talke thereof & was very angry when so euer she chaunced to speke of the same vntill such tyme as she and . . . Mr Roper were agreed agayne."

It is further stated that Dame Alice and Roper went to law about the property, that Sir Giles Alington finally arbitrated an agreement, and that Roper made some payment to Dame Alice under the agreement.

The rival lease was made under Edward VI to John Philpot, who conveyed it to Henry Royden. The new lease made to Roper under Mary, on 23 December, 1553,

---

[1] See below, pp. 79-80.

protected his rights until Elizabeth came to the throne, when Royden evidently took fresh heart, made entry upon the lands and was able to dispossess Roper. Two years later, on 8 May, 1561, Roper retorted in kind, drove out Royden's cattle at midnight, and forced an issue in Common Law, in the Court of Common Pleas. He did not, he points out, take recourse to the Court of Queen's Bench,of which he was an officer, as he might well have done, for he seeks pure justice,

"to the end that the plaintiff should not vniustly slaunder the Justices and Mynysters of the same Courte."

Royden found the Common Law suit likely to go against him, and therefore entered suit in Chancery.

Most of the witnesses claim personal acquaintance with both Sir Thomas and Dame Alice More, as well as William and Margaret Roper. One witness is of peculiar interest, Margery Hillary, widow of Sebastian Hillary. She was seventy years of age on 3 June, 1561, when she gave evidence. She informed the Court that her husband died at Shrovetide in 1545, and that Margaret Roper "died at Christmas then next before," *i.e.* at Christmas 1544.

Roper first took effective possession of the Battersea lands, she said, in 1543, farming part of them himself, and letting the rest to tenants. The vicissitudes of Roper's battle for Battersea seem to indicate clearly that he continued to hold to his Catholic faith at any rate until 1561, if we may judge by the relative strength and weakness of his position under the three sovereigns who succeeded to Henry.

I hope to give subsequently a fuller account of this hitherto unknown property of Sir Thomas More and of its history.

This lawsuit and the friction over his father's Will prove that where property was concerned, Roper was of a doggedly litigious disposition.

Death of Roper.

Roper died on 4 January, 1577(8), and was buried in the Roper vault at St. Dunstan's, Canterbury.[1] His wife had

[1] The Ropers had for generations been benefactors of St. Dunstan's. See *Archæologia Cantiana*, Vols. xvi and xvii. In 1402-3 John Roper, William's great-grandfather, had founded a chantry on the south side of the chancel, in which the chaplains were to sing

Introduction xliii

died at Christmas, 1544, and been buried in the More Tomb at Chelsea Old Church (not at St. Dunstan's, as stated in the Epitaph and often elsewhere).

Lewis, in his edition of Roper's *Life*, p. 6, gives the epitaph of William Roper, recorded by Somner, once to be seen in the chapel of the Ropers on the south side of the chancel of St. Dunstan's, Canterbury : this, even in Lewis's time, had totally disappeared : {Epitaph.}

> Hic jacet venerabilis Vir Gulielmus Roper armiger, filius et heres quondam Johannis Roperi armigeri, et Margareta uxor ejusdem Gulielmi, filia quondam Thomæ Mori militis summi olim Angliæ Cancellarij, Grecis, Latinisque literis doctissim[a],[1] qui quidem Gulielmus patri suo in officio prothonotariatus supreme Curie Banci Regij successit, in quo cum annis 54 fideliter ministrasset idem Officium filio suo primogenito Thomæ reliquit. Fuit is Gulielmus domi forisque munificens, mitis, misericors, incarceratorum, oppressorum, et pauperum baculus. Genuit ex Margareta uxore (quam unicam habuit) filios duos et filias tres, ex ijs vidit in vita sua nepotes et pronepotes, uxorem in virili ætate amisit, viduatus uxore castissime vixit annis 33. Tandem, completis in pace diebus, decessit in senectute bona ab omnibus desideratus die quarto mensis Jan. Anno Christi salvatoris 1577, ætatis [2] vero sue 82.

Cresacre More, in his *Life of More*, discussing Roper's recovery from heresy, pays tribute to his charity, and records the following marvel : {Cresacre More's tribute.}

> euer after he was not only a perfect Catholike, but liued and dyed a stoute and valiant Champion thereof, whose almes in charitable vses was so great, that it is sayd that he bestowed euerie yeare to the value of

---

mass at the altar of St. Nicholas, and where he was buried. The Accounts of the Churchwardens from 1484 to 1580 show several entries relating to payments by the Ropers—sometimes in arrear : *e.g.*

[Aug. 8, 1557–Aug. 7, 1558.] First of William Roper Esquyer for therrerages of certayne pece of ground called the Lome pyttis for xxx[ti] yeres past, viz. euery yere a peny . . . ijs. vjd. (Vol. xvii, p. 113.)

[1] Lewis: *doctissime*.
[2] See Wood, *Athen. Oxon.* Vol. I, col. 41, and discussion above, p. xxxi.

fiue hundred pounds,¹ especially in his latter daies in which he enioyed an office of great gayne and commoditie; and after his death I haue heard it reported by them that were seruants in his house, that whilst his bodie lay vnburied for three or foure daies there was heard once a day for the space of a quarter of an hower the sweetest musike that could be imagined, not of anie voices of men, but angelicall harmonie, as a token how gratious that soule was to Almightie God and to the quires of Angells.²

Cresacre's supernatural embroidery is well-known, but the story makes a pleasing ending.

Roper's *Life of More*: literary value, and relation to Harpsfield's *Life*.

As far as we know, the *Life of More* is Roper's only contribution to literature. It is not a biography in the modern sense, where the author aims at chronological sequence, careful arrangement of matter, and completeness. Nicholas Harpsfield had been selected by Roper himself as More's official biographer,³ and Roper, "at the desire of divers worshyppfull freinds" of his,⁴ is merely setting forth " such matters towching his life " as he " could at this present call to remembraunce." ⁵ To Harpsfield the memoir served as Notes, and though he incorporated them word for word, and fully appreciated the literary value of these " good instructions, diligently and truely by . . . industrie gathered," "the moste orient of pretious pearles and stones," ⁶ he treated them as Notes, arranging them more logically, weaving them into his other material, and constructing from Roper and his other sources a true biography. We have only to look at what is *not* Roper in Harpsfield, to realise the labour and skill with which Harpsfield " gleaned good grapes and leased good corn." ⁷

---

¹ "Ro. Ba.," writing in 1599, described a much greater amount: "His ordinarie almes, as yet to be seene in his booke of accountes, amounted yearelie to 1000ˡⁱ; hys extraordinaries were as much, and sometymes more; sometymes 2, 3, 4 thousand poundes a yeare" (MS. Lambeth 179, p. 46). These figures seem incredible, even though Roper was a wealthy man and held the Prothonotary's office.
² *Life*, 1726 ed., pp. 121–22.
³ Harpsfield, p. 4: "If I haue erred, you also haue erred in your choyse, in that you appointed no meeter person. And I comfort my selfe . . . that I haue satisfied your request."
⁴ See below, p. 4.   ⁵ See below, p. 3.
⁶ Harpsfield, p. 6.   ⁷ *Ibid.*, p. 6.

Introduction xlv

The literary value of Roper is, as it were, accidental, unpremeditated. His aim is merely to "*sett forth* . . . so much as in his poore iudgment seemed worthy to be remembered."[1] There is no verbosity, padding, or preaching, no literary vanity. All is clearly narrated, dignified, effective. "Roper can tell his tale, and leave it to work its effect, without any attempt to enforce it."[2]

Roper regrets that "very many notable things, not meete to haue bine forgotten, throughe neckligens and long contynuans of tyme are slipped out of my mynde."[3] He is writing some twenty years after More's death, certainly not before Mary's reign—it was dangerous to circulate, or even to write, such memoirs earlier—and probably not long before 1557, the date of publication of More's *English Works*.[4] *Date of Roper's Life of More.*

Some of the omissions interest us. The only reference to More's books is to his writings "in defens of the true *Omissions.*

[1] See below, pp. 3–4.
[2] R. W. Chambers in *The Continuity of English Prose*, Introd. to Harpsfield, p. clxi. See also pp. xlv–vi, clxi, clxxi.
[3] See below, p. 4.
[4] Rastell's dedication of More's *English Works* to Queen Mary is dated 30 April, 1557. Harpsfield dedicated his *Life of More* to Roper as a New Year's gift, and in the course of his work (p. 100, ll. 15–19) remarks, "we trust shortlye to haue all his englishe workes . . . in print." The New Year of 1557 is probable, though an earlier is, of course, not excluded. Roper's *Life*, therefore, must have been used by Harpsfield before 1557. It is true that Roper speaks as if writing when the *English Works* were already in people's hands—"may be found in certaine letters of his . . . remayning in a greate booke of his workes" (p. 73, ll. 16–20), "as appeareth by his examinations in the said great book" (p. 84, ll. 10–11), "a letter . . . contayned in the foresaid booke of his workes" (p. 99, ll. 13–14). Roper may well have had an advance copy of pp. 1–1458. Prof. A. W. Reed has pointed out (*Mod. Lang. Review*, Vol. XXIX, No. 2, April 1934, p. 190) that there was probably an interval between the completion of these sheets, and the printing off of the Index, etc., and Rastell's dated preface.
Prof. Chambers suggests that Roper may be referring to a *manuscript* collection of More's writings, and that MS. Royal 17 D. XIV may well be indicated. This manuscript contains material which was printed, with a very few exceptions, in the 1557 volume, and the *Catalogue of the Royal Manuscripts* concludes that it was for this edition that the transcripts were probably made. The letters to Margaret (two of which describe the examinations in the Tower) are included, fols. 393ᵇ ff.
Roper's own copy of the 1557 edition of More's *English Works* is in the Library of St. John's College, Oxford; but only came there in the 18th century.

xlvi   *Introduction*

Christian religion, against hereseies "—work on which More was actually engaged during Roper's personal contact with him.¹ Roper does not even mention *Utopia*; his attachment to More's household almost certainly dated from the period after 1516. We do not learn from him that More married twice: "the eldest daughter of Master Colte"² is not differentiated from "my Lady, his wife," who visits More in the Tower, and tries to scold him into submission to the King's wishes.³

Errors.   Roper's errors are somewhat surprising—of the sort attributable to "neckligens" rather than to "long continuans of tyme":

(1) (*a*) Roper makes More Treasurer instead of Under-Treasurer, 12/8; Harpsfield corrects, 24/10.
(*b*) And More followed in this office Sir John Cutte, not Weston; Weston followed More. Harpsfield⁴ here reproduces Roper's error.
(2) The speech in which More excused himself from the office of Speaker is reported by Roper as "not now extant," 12/14; Harpsfield relates the Hannibal-Phormio portion, 26/19-27/7.
(3) Roper errs as to the dates of More's position as Chancellor of the Duchy of Lancaster—actually 1525-9:
(*a*) 23/3-4. The embassy of More and Wolsey to Charles into Flanders was in August, 1521. Harpsfield incorporates statement from Roper, but omits reference to date, 39/14-17.
(*b*) 29/19-20. Adrian was elected Pope in 1522. Harpsfield (p. 42) does not state that this was during More's Chancellorship of the Duchy, but follows Roper in attributing Wolsey's resentment to the election of Adrian.⁵
(4) 31/8. "The Frenche kings Sister" is an error for Renée, daughter of Louis XII. Harpsfield⁶ follows Roper, adding "the Dutchesse of Alanson," 43/8-9.
(5) 34/16-17. (*a*) The brief was not found in the Treasury of Spain, but among the papers of the English ambassador of 1494-1509; and (*b*) only a copy was

---

¹ See below, p. 46.   ² P. 6.   ³ Pp. 82-4.
⁴ See Harpsfield, Hist. Note, 24/9-10.
⁵ Dr. A. F. Pollard suggests that "Roper is vaguely remembering the rumour of Clement VII's death in 1529" (*Sir Thomas More's Richard III*, p. 225).
⁶ See Harpsfield, Hist. Note, 43/8-9.

sent to England. Harpsfield, 46/20-3, adopts Roper's errors.[1]

(6) 57/9, 13. (a) The Court determining the marriage void was held at Dunstable Priory, not at St. Alban's; and (b) the marriage to Anne had preceded. Harpsfield,[2] it is surprising, follows Roper, 148/5-6, 9-10.

(7) 99/9-10. Five days, not seven, elapsed between More's judgment (1 July) and his execution (6 July). Harpsfield,[3] 200/18-19, follows Roper.

(8) 103/18-104/10. Elyot's embassy to Charles was in 1531-2. Harpsfield [4] follows Roper, 205/16-206/8.

But these are minor blemishes. For all the More *Lives*, Roper's ranks as the *biographia princeps*, and has always been recognised as one of the masterpieces of English literature.

[1] See Harpsfield, Hist. Note, 46/20-3.
[2] *Ibid.*, Hist. Note, 148/5-6.   [3] *Ibid.*, Hist. Note, 200/18-19.
[4] *Ibid.*, Hist. Note, 205/16-206/8.

EDITOR'S SUMMARY OF CONTENTS OF ROPER'S LIFE OF MORE [1]

	PAGE
Roper's Preface	3–4
More's education: St. Anthony's School—Morton's household—Oxford . .	5
Legal studies and practice	5, 6–7
Lectures on the *De Civitate Dei* . . .	6
In the Charterhouse	6
Marriage; his children	6–7
Early public career: Member of Parliament, opposes King's subsidy—an Under-sheriff of London—embassies in interests of English merchants	7–9
Case of the Pope's ship	9–10
Enters the Royal service: Master of Requests—Privy Councillor—Knight—wins the King's affection—Under-Treasurer. .	10–12
Speaker: plea for freedom of speech for the Commons	12–16
Wolsey's visit to the Commons, More incurs his displeasure	16–20
Chancellor of the Duchy of Lancaster . .	20
The King visits More at Chelsea: "If my head could win him a castle in France," etc.	20–21
Modesty in argument; *ex tempore* orations .	21–22
Embassies with Wolsey	23
The Water-bailiff jealous for More's reputation	23–24
Foresight: three things needed in Christendom	24–25
,, the growth of heresy . . .	34–36

[1] Roper's arrangement of matter often lacks sequence. In this Index references to the same topic are grouped together.

Summary of Contents

	PAGE
Foresight: his family prepared for future trouble	55–56
,, the administering of oaths	57
,, "*Quod differtur non aufertur*"	71
,, "I shall die to-day and you to-morrow"	71–72
,, the fall of Anne Boleyn	77
Virtues, virtuous practices and counsels	25–28, 43, 72
Margaret's recovery from the sweating sickness	28–29
Divorce, events preceding the	29–31, 33–34, 57
Divorce, More consulted on the	31–33, 37–38, 49–50
Embassy with Tunstall to Cambrai	36–37
Stokesley's quarrel with Wolsey	38–39
Fall of Wolsey—More made Chancellor—his speech	39–40
A just Chancellor: accessibility to all suitors—decree against Heron—care concerning subpœnas—righteous injunctions	40–45
Refuses reward from the clergy	45–48
Shirt of hair and other austerities	48–49
Announces judgement of the Universities concerning the marriage	50–51
"A parish clerk"	51
Resigns the Great Seal—the King's promise	51–52
Poverty—discusses economies with his family	52–55
"Madam, my Lord is gone"	55
Advice to Cromwell: "If a Lion knew his own strength," etc.	56–57
Refuses to be present at Anne's coronation—warns the Lords by the parable of the offending virgin	57–59
The matter of the Nun of Canterbury	59–61
Incorruptibility: the Vaughan, Crocker and Gresham cases	61–64
Attainted of misprision of treason in the case of the Nun—accused of inciting the King to write the *Assertio septem sacramentorum*—his name struck out of the Bill	64–71

Summary of Contents

	PAGE
Summoned to Lambeth—refuses the Oath—committed to the Tower	72–75
Conversations in prison	75–78, 80–84
Illegality of the Oath administered to More	77–78
Arranges conveyance of his lands	79–80
Envies martyrs going gladly to execution	80–81
Verses on flattering Fortune	82
Examinations in the Tower	84
The Rich episode	84–86
Trial and condemnation	86–97
Farewells and preparations for death	97–102
Martyrdom	102–103
The Emperor's tribute to More's wisdom	103–104

Roper's Life of More

The Roper manuscripts collated for this edition are referred to by the following symbols :

H² = MS. Harleian 6254, British Museum : the basis of the critical text.
J = A MS. in the possession of the Rt. Hon. John Burns : the one used by Hearne.
H³ = MS. Harleian 6362 ⎫
H¹ = MS. Harleian 6166 ⎬ British Museum.
A = MS. Additional 11388 ⎭
M = MS. Mm. IV. 21, Cambridge University Library.*
S = MS. Sloane 1705 ⎫ British Museum.
A² = MS. Additional 4242 ⎭
D = MS. Dyce 46, Dyce and Forster Collection, S. Kensington.
T = MS. Bodley 966 ⎫ Bodleian.
W = MS. Willis 58 ⎭
X = MS. 544, Bollandist Library, Brussels.
B = A second MS. belonging to the Rt. Hon. John Burns.

The Eton Roper (MS. 167) and a manuscript now in the possession of Mr. W. Fagg of 275, Church Rd., Crystal Palace, S.E. 19, the dialogues of which are in the third person, and which differ somewhat from the regular Roper tradition, have not been collated, as they would have needlessly cumbered the footnotes.

For the Harpsfield manuscripts and the symbols denoting them, see above, p. xxiv.

The reading of the critical text (based on H²) is to be assumed to be that of all manuscripts not noted in the collations as differing. Readings adopted from other manuscripts as emendations of H² are placed in the text within square brackets. Where an emendation cannot be thus signified, an asterisk in the text calls attention to the collations below.

The spelling of variant readings is that of the first manuscript cited. That of other manuscripts is not differentiated unless of special interest. The same applies to varieties of inflectional form.

Such common varieties as the following, which the scribes seem to have considered interchangeable at their own fancy, are not included in the collations, unless for some reason of importance :
afore, before ; farther, further ; on, vpon ; till, vntil ; to, vnto.

No note is usually taken of scribal corrections in the text of manuscripts other than H². If, however, the correction throws light on the text of the manuscript or of other manuscripts, the correction is recorded. This is also the editor's practice with regard to obvious spelling blunders such as *concering* for *concerning*, or careless repetitions like *of of, yet take yet take*, etc.

The collations provide few interesting or important variants. There are many careless scribal errors and the usual random transpositions and substitutions of synonyms. As even innocuous variants may throw light on manuscript relationship, it has been thought useful to include them in the collations.

The paragraphing, punctuation and marginal summary are the Editor's.

---

* MS. Harleian 7030 is a copy by Thomas Baker of this Cambridge University Library MS.

MS. Harleian 6254.

[The Lyfe of Sir Thomas Moore, knighte, written by William Roper, Esquire, whiche maried Margreat, daughter of the sayed Thomas Moore.]

[p. 1] FORASMUCHE as *Sir* Thomas Moore, knighte, some- More is worthy perpetual famous memory.
tyme lorde Chauncelor of England, a man of singular
vertue *and* of a cleere vnspotted consciens, as witnessethe
Erasmus, more pure *and* white then the whitest snowe,
5 *and* of such an angelicall witt, as England, he saith,
neuer had the like before, nor neuer shall againe,
vnyvarsaly, as well in the Lawes of our owne realme (a
study in effecte able to occupy the whole life of a man)
as in all other sciences, right well studied, was in his
10 dayes accompted a man worthy *per*petuall famous
memory: I, William Roper, thoughe most vnworthy, Roper qualified to write More's life.
his sonne in lawe by mariage of his eldest daughter,
knowing [at this daye] no one man [livinge] that of him
and of his doings vnderstood so much as my self, for
15 that I was contynually resident in his house by the space
of xvj yeares and more, thought it therefore my *pa*rte
to sett forth such matters towching his life as I could
at this present call to remembraunce. Amonge wh*i*ch Although

MSS. H² J H³ H¹ A M A² D T W X B *only*.

The title above is that of H³. MS. H² *has none.* *For titles of the other* MSS., *see descriptions, pp.* xi–xx. 2. *of singular*] of a singuler M. 3. *a*] *Omitted in* H¹; a most D. 3. *cleere vnspotted*] cleare and vnspotted A² D X B. 6. *neuer had*] had neuer W. 6. *nor neuer*] nor euer W; nor D. 7. *owne*] *Omitted in* J D T; *interlineated in* A. 8. *effecte*] affection T. 8. *of a man*] of man W. 10. *perpetuall*] *Omitted in* J; of perpetuall X B. 13. *at this daye*] *Omitted in* H² J. 13. *livinge*] *Omitted in* H² J. 14. *of*] *Omitted in* H³ M A² W. 18–p. 4, l. 2. *Amonge . . . bine*] Among which the verie manie noble thinges not meete to hau bin W.

he has for-
gotten many
memorable
things.

things, very many notable things (not meete to haue bine forgotten) throughe neckligens *and* long contynuans of tyme are slipped out of my mynde. Yeat, to thentent the same should not * all vtterley perishe, I haue at the desire of divers worshyppfull freinds of mine (thoughe 5 very farre from the grace *and* worthines of them, Neuertheles as farr forthe as my meane wit, memory, *and* [knowledge] wold serue me) declared so much thereof as in my poore iudgment seemed worthy to be remembred. 10

MSS. H² J H³ H¹ A M A² D T W X B *only*.

1. *things* (1)] *Omitted in* J.   2. *bine*] *Omitted in* M.   3. *are slipped*] being slipped W.   3. *my*] *Omitted in* W.   3. *mynde*] memory D.   4. *should*] shall J M A² D.   4. *not all*] not at all H²; not H³.   4. *vtterley perishe*] perish vtterly W. 4. *I haue at*] I haue here at W.   4–5. *the desire*] the earnest desire A² D B.   6. *and*] or T.   6. *them*] him T. 7. *Neuertheles*] yett W.   7. *my*] by M.   8. *knowledge*] learning H² J.   8. *wold*] will D W; should A².   8. *serue*] suffer H³ H¹; fuffer A.   9. *poore*] simple W.   9. *seemed*] seemeth W.

This Sir Thomas Moore, after he had bine brought vpp More at St. Anthony's School.
in the Latyne tongue at St. Anthonies in London, * was
by his fathers procurement receaved into the house of And in Morton's household.
the right reuerend, wise, and learned prelate Cardinall
5 Mourton; where, thoughe he was younge of yeares, [1490.]
yeat wold he at Christmas tyde sodenly sometimes Impromptu acting.
steppe in among the players, and neuer studyeng for the
matter, make a parte of his owne there presently among
them, which made the lookers on more sporte then all
10 the plaiers beside. In whose witt and towardnes the Morton predicts More's greatness.
Cardinall muche delightynge, wold often say of him
vnto the nobles that divers tymes dined with him:
"This child here wayting at the table, whosoeuer shall
liue to see it, will proue a mervailous man."
15 Wherupon for his [better] furtheraunce in learninge, Sent to Oxford. [1492.]
he placed him at Oxford; where when he was both in
[p. 2] the greake and latine tongue | sufficiently instructed, He Enters New Inn. [1494.]
was then for the study of the lawe* of the Realme put
to an Inne of Chauncery called Newe Inne, where for his
20 tyme he very well prospered; And from thence was
admitted to Lincolnes Inne, with very small allowans, Admitted to Lincoln's Inn. [1496.]
contynewinge there his study vntill he was made and
accompted a worthy vtter barrister. Made an utter barrister. [? 1501.]

MSS. H² J H³ H¹ A M A² D T W X B only.

1. *Before the* Life *proper,* D *has heading :* The Entrance into the matter.   1. *brought vpp*] brought vp and instructed D.
2. *in London was*] in London he was H² J; in the Cittye of London hauing an extreordinary witt and Capacite for his tyme was D.   3. *procurement*] greate laboure and industrie D.
5. *younge of yeares*] yong and very tender of yeares D.   6. *sometimes*] Interlineated in H²; *omitted in* W; *transposed so as to follow* stepp *in* X.   7. *studyeng*] standinge T.   8. *presently*] presente H³ H¹ A T.   10. *towardnes*] towards A².
11. *delightynge*] delighted T.   12. *nobles that*] Nobles which W.
15. *better*] Omitted in H² J.   15. *furtheraunce in*] Omitted in J.   16. *where*] Omitted in H¹.   17. *greake*] Greek tongue T.   17. *latine*] the latynne H³.   17. *tongue*] tongues A² D W X B.   18. *lawe*] lawes H²; Common Lawes W X.
18. *the* (3)] this X.   19. *of Chauncery*] of the Chauncerie J.
20. *prospered*] profited W.   21. *admitted*] committed J.
21. *with*] where with X.   22. *contynewinge there*] he continued X.

Lectures on St. Augustine's *De Civitate Dei*. [1501.] Grocyn one of his audience.

After this, to his greate commendacion, he redde for a good space a publike lecture of St. Augustine, *de ciuitate dei*, in the Churche of St. Lawrens in the old Jury; whereunto there resorted Doctor Grosin, an excellent [cunninge] man, *and* all the cheif learned of the City of London.

More Reader at Furnival's Inn. [1501.]

Then was he made reader of Fvrnivals Inne, so remaynynge by the space of three yeares and more.

Four years without vow in the Charterhouse. [1499–1503.]

After wh*i*ch tyme he gaue himselfe to devotion *and* prayer in the Charter house of London, religiously lyvinge there, without vowe, about iiij*er* yeares; Vntill he resorted to the house of one m*ast*er Colte, a gentleman of Essex, that had ofte invited him thither, having three daughters, whose honest conue*r*sation *and* vertuous educacion provoked him there specially to sett his affection. And albeit his mynde moste served him to the second daughter, for that he thought her [the] fairest *and* best favoured, yeat when he considered that it wold be both greate greif *and* some shame also to the eldest to see her yonger sister in mariage preferred before her, he then of a certayne pity framed his fancy towardes her, *and* soone after [maryed] her; Neuer the more discontynewinge his study of the lawe at Lyncolnes Inne, but applieng still the same, vntil he was called to the bench, *and* had read [there] twice, w*h*ich is as

Marries [Jane] Colt. [? 1505.]

Bencher of Lincoln's Inn, reading there twice. [Autumn, 1511; Lent, 1515.]

MSS. H² J H³ H¹ A M A² D T W X B *only*.

1. *greate*] very great T.   1. *commendacion*] Comendacions X.   2. *space a*] space in a A² B.   2. *St.*] *Omitted in* A².   4. *there*] *Omitted in* H³.   5. *cunninge*] learned H².   5. *and*] *Omitted in* A² B.   8. *by*] *Omitted in* H³; there by X.   10. *of London*] *Omitted in* A²; in London W X.   10. *religiously*] religious T.   11. *without*] whithout H².   11. *vowe*] vewe H³ A.   12–13. *a gentleman of Essex*] a gentleman in Essex H³; gentleman in Essex H¹; of Essex (*omitting* a gentleman) A²; of Essex a gentleman D B.   13. *having*] who hauing W X.   15. *provoked him*] *Omitted in* T; A² damaged.   15. *sett*] settle H¹.   16. *his mynde*] A² damaged.   17. *the* (2)] *Omitted in* H².   18. *best*] *Interlineated over* most *crossed through* H³.   19. *greate greif*] a greife H³; a greate greife A² D B.   20. *in mariage preferred*] preferred in marriage X.   22. *maryed*] did marry H².   22. *her* (2)] *Omitted in* W.   22–23. *Neuer the more discontynewinge*] neverthelesse not discontinuing J.   23. *at*] of B.   24. *applieng still the same*] applieing himselfe to the same W X.   25. *there*] *Omitted in* H² J; the (*end of line*) B.

Enters Parliament; opposes King's subsidy

often as [ordinarillye] any Judge of the Lawe doth reade.

Before w*h*ich tyme he had placed himself *and* his wife at Bucklersbury in London, where he had by her three
5 daughters [and one Sonne], in vertue and learning brought vpp from their youthe, whom he wold often exhorte to take vertue *and* learninge for their meate, *and* play * for their sawce.

Residence at Bucklersbury. His children.

Who, ere euer he had bine reader in Courte, was in
10 the latter tyme of king Henry the seaventh made a burgesse of the p*ar*liame*nt*, wherein there were by the king demaunded (as I haue hearde reported) about three Fifteenes for the mariage of his eldest daughter, that then should be the Scottishe Queene. Att the last
15 debating whereof he made such arguments *and* reasons there against, that the kings demaundes thereby were cleane oue*r*throwne. So that one of the kings privy Chamber, named m*aster* Tyler, being present thereatt, brought word to the kinge out of the p*ar*liament house
20 that a beardles boy had disapointed all his purpose*. |

Burgess of the Parliament. [1504.]

Opposes subsidy demanded by Henry VII consequent upon Margaret's marriage to James IV of Scotland. [1504.]

[p. 3] Wherevppon the kinge, conceaving greate indignacion toward*es* him, could not be satisfied vntil he had some way revenged it. And, forasmuch as he nothinge having, nothing could loose, his grace devised a cawseles
25 quarrell against [his] father, keeping him in the tower

Resulting hostility of Henry VII towards More and his father. [1504.]

MSS. H² J H³ H¹ A M A² D T W X B *only*.

1. *ordinarillye*] Omitted in H² J; A² D B *omit here, but insert after* doth. 5. *and one Sonne*] Omitted in H² J. 6. *often*] after A² B. 8. *play for*] play but for H² J M A² D B. (*All* Harpsfield MSS. *omit* but.) 9. *ere euer he*] before he X. 10. *of king*] of the Raigne of king X. 10. *Henry the seaventh*] Henry the vij^th raigne D. 10. *made*] kayng made A². 11. *of the*] in the J. 11. *there*] they M D. 12. *reported*] it reported J. 12. *about*] Omitted in W. 16. *against*] against the same W X. 16. *thereby were*] were thereby J T X. 17. *cleane*] Omitted in J; vtterli W X. 17. *So . . . kings*] And therevpone one of the Kinges W X. 18. *present*] there present W X. 19. *word*] word with speed W X. 20. *that a*] that the M. 20. *purpose*] purposes H² J. 23–24. *forasmuch . . . loose*] forasmuch as he had nothing he could loose W. 23–24. *having*] Omitted in A²; had X. 25. *his*] Sir Thomas Moores H²; interlineated in J. 25. *the tower*] the tower of London A² D B.

vntill he had made him pay to him an hundrethe pounds
fyne.

Dr. Fox, Bishop of Winchester, strives to entrap More.

Shortly herevppon it fortuned that this Sir Thomas
Moore, cominge in a suite to Doctor Fox, Bishoppe of
Winchester (one of the kings privy Counsaile) the Bis- 5
hoppe called him aside, and pretendinge greate favour
towardes him, promised him that, if he wold be ruled
by him, he wold not faile into the kings favour againe
to restore him; meaning (as it was after coniectured) to
cause him thereby to confesse his offence against the 10
kinge, whereby his highnes might with the better coler
haue occasion to revenge his displeasure against him.

More is advised by Whitford to return no more to the Bishop.

But when he came frome the Byshoppe, he fell in communicacion with one master Whitford, his familiar friend,
then Chapleine to that bishoppe, and after a Father of 15
Syon, and shewed him what the bishop had saide vnto
him, desiringe to haue his advise therein; who, for the
passion of god, prayed him in no wise to followe his
Councel: "For my lord, my master," quoth he, "to
serve the kings torne, will not sticke to agree to his owne 20
fathers death." So Sir Thomas Moore retorned to the
Bishoppe no more. And had not the king soone after

Death of Henry VII. [1509.]

died, he was determined to haue gone ouer [the] sea,
thincking that being in the kings indignacion, he could
not liue in England without great daunger. 25

More made an Under-sheriff of London. [1510.]

After [this] he was made one of the vndershirifs of
London, by which office and his learninge together (as

MSS. H² J H³ H¹ A M A² D T W X B only.

1. *he had made*] he made H³ H¹ A T.   1. *he . . . pay*] he
had payed J.   1. *to him*] him J; *omitted in* A² D B.   2.
fyne] *Omitted in* A² D B.   5–6. *the Bishoppe*] They J.   6.
called] calling M.   6. *pretendinge*] pretended T.   7. *that, if
he wold*] yf that he woulde H³ H¹ A.   8–9. *faile . . . restore
him*] faile to restore him againe into the kings fauour D; faile to
restore him into the kinges fauour againe W X.   9. *coniectured*] *Omitted in* T.   11–12. *his highnes . . . revenge*] *Omitted
in* W.   14. *Whitford*] Whitfeild W.   17. *desiringe*] desiring
him D.   17. *to haue*] to heare T.   20–21. *owne fathers*]
fathers owne M.   21. *So*] And soe W X.   21–22. *retorned
. . . more*] returned no more to the Bishopp W X.   22.
king] kinges maiestie A² D B.   23. *to haue gone*] to goe A².
23. *the*] *Omitted in* H².   23. *sea*] Seas X.   25. *great*]
greater A² D B.   26. *this*] *Omitted in* H² J.   27. *by*] *Omitted
in* B.

I haue herd him say) he gayned without greif not so   Makes about £400 yearly.
litle as foure hundreth pound*es* [by the] yeare; Sithe
there was at that tyme in none of the princes courte*s* of
the lawes of this realme, any matter of importans in
5 controuersie wherein he was not with the one p*a*rte of
Councell. Of whom, for his learninge, wisdome, know-   Embassies in interests of the English merchants. [1515, 1517.]
ledge, *and* experiens, men had such estimacion that,
before he [came] to the seruice of king Henrye the eight,
at the suite *and* instaunce of the Englishe merchaunt*es*,
10 he was by the kings consent made twise Embassador in
certaine greate causes betweene them *and* [the] mer-
chaunt*es* of the Stilliarde: Whose wise *and* discreete   Success in embassy. The King desires to get him into the royal service. Manages for a time to keep out of State affairs.
dealinge therin, to his highe comendac*i*on, coming to
the kings vnderstanding, provoked his highnes to cause
15 Cardinall Wolsey (then Lord Chauncelor) to procure
him to his seruice. And albeit the Cardinall, according
to the kinges request, earnestly travailed with him
therefore, amonge many other his p*er*swasions alleaging
[p. 4] vnto him howe deare his service | must needes be vnto
20 his ma*i*estie, w*h*ich could not, [with] his honor, with les
then he should yearly leese thereby, seeme to recompence him; yeat he, loth to chainge his estate, made
such meanes to the kinge, by the Cardinall, to the contrary, that his grace, for that tyme, was well satisfied.
25   Nowe happened there after this, A greate Shippe of   Ability he shows in the case of the Pope's ship causes the King to engage him in his service.
his that * then * was Pope to arive at Southampton,

MSS. H² J H³ H¹ A M A² D T W X B *only*.

1. *herd*] often heard A² D B.   2. *by the yeare*] *Corrected to*
that yeare H²; a yeare A² D B.   3. *princes*] kynges H³ D.
4. *in*] or T.   5–6. *with . . . Councell*] with one parte in
Councell W X.   6. *Of whom, for his*] who for his W X.
6. *wisdome*] wisdome and J.   7. *had such*] had him in such
J W X.   8. *came*] was come H² J.   8. *the* (1)] *Omitted in* A².
9. *the* (2)] our X.   10. *twise Embassador*] Ambassadour twice M.
11. *the*] *Omitted in* H².   13. *dealinge*] dealings T.   13. *highe*]
highnes W.   13. *comendacion*] comendacions T X.   14.
provoked] provokinge J.   16. *his seruice*] his Graces
seruice A² D W X B. (*All* Harpsfield MSS. his graces seruice.)
16. *And albeit*] wherevppon albeit W X.   18. *amonge*] And
among W.   18. *alleaging*] alleadged W X.   20. *with* (1)] of
H² J W X.   20. *les*] *Omitted in* A².   21. *yearly*] *Omitted
in* D T.   21. *seeme to*] *Omitted in* D.   25. *Nowe . . .
this*] Afterward it happened that A² D W X B; Now happened
that T.   25. *this*] *Omitted in* M.   25–26. *A greate . . .
arive*] a greate Shippe of his that then was Pope to arive J M;

which the king clayminge for a forfeyture, the Popes
Embassadour, by suite vnto his grace, obteyned that he
might for his master the Pope haue Councell learned in
the lawes of this realme, and the matter in his owne
presens (being himself a singuler Civillian) in some 5
publique place to be openly heard and discussed. Att
which tyme there could * none of our lawe be found
so meete to be of councell with this embassador as Sir
Thomas Moore, who could reporte to the Embassador in
Latyne all the resons and argumentes by the learned 10
Councell on * both sides alleaged*. Vppon this the
counsaylors [of] either parte, in presens of the lord
Chauncelour and other the Judges, in the starre Chamber
had audience accordingly. Where Sir Thomas Moore
not onlye declared to thembassador the whole effecte of 15
all their opinions, But also, in defens [of] the Popes side,
argued so learnedly himself, that both was the foresaid
forfeyture to the Pope restored, and himself amonge all
the hearers, for his vpright and comendable demeanor
therein, so greatly renowmed, that for no intreaty wold 20
the king from thenceforth be induced any longer
to forbeare * his service. Att whose first entry

MSS. H² J H³ H¹ A M A² D T W X B only.

a greate Shippe of his then that was Pope to arive H²; a great
shippe of his that was then Pope to Arive H³ H¹ A; T as
H³ H¹ A, but good for greate and the Pope for then Pope; a
greate Shipp belonging to the Pope that there was did arive
A² X; D B as A² X, but then was for there was; a great shipp of
the Pope did arriue W. (All Harpsfield MSS. except C, that then
was; C that was then.)
 1. for a] as X B.   3. learned] learned and wise H³.   5.
himself] Omitted in M.   7. could . . . found] could be none
of our Lawe be found H²; woulde none in our lawe be founde
H³ A T; H¹ as H³ A T, but were woulde.   8. this] the M.
10. and] of A².   11. on] in A²; of W X.   11. on both
sides alleaged] alleaged on both sides H².   12. of (1)] vppon
H²; on J.   12–13. of the lord Chauncelour] of the learned
Chauncellor M.   13. in] of H³ A² W X B.   15. not]
Omitted in B.   16. in defens] in the defense A² D W X B.
16. of] on H² (after of crossed through); on J.   17–18. that
both . . . amonge] that thereby not onely the foresaid forfeiture
was to the Pope restored, but allso he himselfe among A² D W X B.
18. to the Pope restored] restored to the Pope T.   19. hearers]
peares M.   21. thenceforth] henceforth J M T.   21. any
longer] Omitted in A² D B.   21–22. any longer to forbeare his
service] any longer to forbeare him to be in his service H² (him to
be in being interlineated); to forbeare his seruice any longer W.

Enters the Royal service; the King's favour 11

thereunto, he made him * mayster* of the requests (hauing then no better roome void) and within a moneth after knighte, and one of [his] privy Councell. And so from tyme to tyme was he by the [Prince]
5 aduaunced, contynewing in his singuler favour and trustie seruice twenty yeares *and* aboue; A good *parte* whereof vsed the kinge vppon holidaies, when he had done his owne devotions, to send for him into his travers, *and* there sometyme in * matter[s] of Astronomy,
10 Geometry, Devinity, *and* such other Facultyes, and sometimes of his worldly affaires, to sitt *and* confferre w*i*th him. And other whiles wold he, in the night, haue him vppe into his Leades, there for to consider w*i*th him the diu*er*sities, courses, motions, *and* op*er*acions of the
15 starres *and* planet*es*. And because he was of a pleasaunte disposition, it pleased the kinge *and* Queene, after the Councell had supte; * at the time of their sup*per*, for their pleasure, comonly to call for him to be merry w*i*th them. Whom when he p*er*ceaved so much
[p. 5] in | his talke to delight, that he could not once in a
21 moneth gett leave to goe home to his wife *and* * children (whos company he moste desired) *and* to be absent from

Made Master of Requests and Privy Councillor. [1517]; Knight [1521.]

His company sought by Henry VIII.

Also by Queen Katherine.

His liberty thereby much restricted.

MSS. H² J H³ H¹ A M A² D T W X B *only.*

1. *thereunto*] there into X.   1. *he*] his maiestie A² D B; *omitted in* W X.   1. *mayster of the requests*] one of the maysters of the requests H² (one of the *being interlineated*) A² D B; master of requestes H³.   2. *a*] one A² D B.   3. *his*] the H².   4. *he*] Omitted in J H³.   4–5. *by the Prince aduaunced*] by the kinge aduaunced H²; advanced by the kinge A² D B.   5. *in his*] still in his A² X B.   7. *whereof*] thereof T.   7. *vsed the kinge*] the King vsed A² D W X B.   8. *owne*] Omitted in H³.   8. *devotions*] devotion A² D T W X B.   8. *for him . . . travers*] for Sir Thomas More into his owne Traverse A² D W X; *so* B *but* vnto *for* into.   9. *in matters*] in a matter H²; in matter M.   10. *Devinity*] & Diuinity H¹.   11. *of his*] in his J.   13. *into*] in A².   13. *his*] the J.   13. *for*] Omitted in A X B.   14. *and*] and other H³.   14. *diuersities, courses*] diuerse scituations courses W X.   16. *Queene*] the Queene A² D B.   17. *after*] manie times after W X.   17. *at*] and at H².   18. *comonly*] Omitted in W.   18. *him*] Sir Thomas More W X.   19–20. *with them . . . delight*] with them but when he perceaued the king in his talke to take soe much delight W X.   19. *Whom*] Omitted in J; Who T.   20. *in*] Omitted in A² D B.   21. *to his*] to se his A² D B.   21. *and children*] and his children H².   22. *and to be absent*] nor be suffered to be absent A² B; nor be satisfied to be absent D; And that he could not be absent X.

the courte two dayes together, but that he should be thither sent for againe, He, much mysliking this restraint of his libertie, began therevppon somewhat to dissemble his nature, and so by litle *and* litle from his former [accustomed] myrthe to [disvse] himself, that he was of them frome thenceforthe at suche seasons no more so ordinarily sent for.

<small>Made [Under]-Treasurer of the Exchequer. [1521.]</small>

Then died one m*aster* Weston, thresurer of thexchequer, whose office, after his deathe, the kinge of his owne offer, without any askinge, freely gaue vnto S*ir* Thomas Moore.

<small>Chosen Speaker. [18 April, 1523.]</small>

In the xiiijth yeare of his graces raigne was there a p*ar*liame*nt* holden, whereof S*ir* Thomas Moore was chosen speaker; who, beinge very lothe to take that roome vppon him, made an oration (not nowe extant) to the kings highnes for his discharge thereof; wherunto when the kinge wold not consent, he spake vnto his grace in forme folowinge :

<small>Speech before the King, pleading for toleration for himself and freedom of speech for the Commons.</small>

" Sythe I p*er*ceiue, most redoubted soue*r*aigne, that it standethe not w*i*th y*o*ur high[e]* pleasure to reforme this election *and* cause it to be changed, but haue by the mouth of the most reue*r*end father in god, the legate, y*o*ur high[nes] Chauncellor, therunto geuen y*o*ur most royal assent, *and* haue of y*o*ur benignity determyned, farre aboue that I may beare, to enhable me *and* for this office to repute me meete, rather then ye should seeme

MSS. H² J H³ H¹ A M A² D T W X B *only*.

1-3. *but that . . . restraint*] without sending for againe, he somewhat disliking this restraint W; without sending for againe he somewhat misliking he much dislikinge this restraint X. 2. *mysliking*] misliked H³ H¹ A T; disliking W. 2-3. *restraint*] distraynte H³ H¹ A. 3. *his*] *Omitted in* H³ H¹ A. 4. *and so by litle and litle*] and soe a little H³; and soe litle and litle H¹ A M T. 5. *accustomed*] *Omitted in* H² J. 5. *disvse*] refrayne H²; dispose A² B. 5. *he*] *Omitted in* W. 6. *of them*] *Interlineated in* H². 6. *at suche seasons*] *Omitted in* J. 9. *whose*] who X. 10. *without . . . freely*] *Omitted in* A². 10. *gaue vnto*] gave it to T. 11. *graces*] maiesties A² D B. 13. *that roome*] this roome T. 19. *standethe*] standes M. 19. *highe*] highnes H² J M. (*All* Harpsfield MSS. high.) 21 *most*] *Omitted in* A². 21. *father*] *Omitted in* B. 22. *highnes*] highe H² A² D B. (*All* Harpsfield MSS. highe.) 22. *therunto*] there into D; *omitted in* W. 23. *assent*] consent J. 25. *to*] *Omitted in* H¹. 25. *me*] *Omitted in* W. 25. *ye*] you A² D T W B.

to impute vnto your comons that they had vnmeetely
chosen, I am therefore, and alway shalbe, ready obediently to conforme my self to thaccomplishment of your
highe commandement, In my most hvmble wise be-
5 seeching your most noble maiestie that I may with your
graces favour, before I farther enter therunto, make
mine humble intercession vnto your highnes for two
lowly petitions : The tone privately concerning my self,
the other * the whole assembly of your comon house.
10 " For my self, gratious Soueraigne, that if it misshapp
me in anye thinge hereafter that is on the behalf of your
comons in your highe presence to be declared, to mistake
my message, and in [the] lack of good vtteraunce, by
my misrehersall, to perverte or impaire their prudent
15 instructions, It may then like your most noble maiestie,
of your aboundant grace, with the eye of your accostomed pitye, to pardon my simplenes, geuing me leave
to repaire againe to the comen house, and there to conferre with them, and to take their substancial aduise
20 what thing and in what wise I shall on their behalf vtter
and speak before your noble grace, To thentente their
prudent [de]vises and affaires be not by my simplenes
[and] Folly hindered or impaired : which thing, if it
should so [mis]happe, as it were well likely to mishappe
25 in me, if your gra[tious] benignity releaved not my
ouersight, It could not faile to be during my life a per-

MSS. H² J H³ H¹ A M A² D T W X B only.

1. to impute] Omitted in T.   3. conforme] confirme H³;
confirme corrected to conforme A.   4. highe] highnes A² D B.
4. my] Omitted in H³ H¹ A T W.   6. farther] father M.
9. the other the] the other for the H² (for being interlineated); the
other concerninge the W.   9. comon] Commons H¹ W X.
10. For] and for J.   11. on] in J A² D B.   12. highe] highnes H³ A² D W X B. (All Harpsfield MSS. except B, high.)
13. in the lack] in lack H²; for lacke J.   14. my] me J.
14. their] the J.   15. It may then] that it may then J; it may
D B.   15. most] Omitted in H³ H¹ A.   17. simplenes]
simplicite J.   18. to repaire againe] againe to repaire J.
18. comen] Commons H¹ W X.   20. wise] case A² D B.
20. on] in H¹ W X.   21. their] that their W.   22. devises]
advises H² J.   23. and] or H².   23. or] and A² B.
23. it] Omitted in M.   23-24. it should so] it so should A² D X B.
24. mishappe] happen H² T W; happ J.   24. likely] like T.
25. gratious] graces H² J M.   25. releaved] relieue A² D B.
26. could] woulde T.

petuall grudge *and* hevines to my harte, | The helpe *and* [p. 6] remedy whereof, in manner aforesaid remembred, is, most gracious soue*r*aigne, my first lowly suit *and* humble petition vnto yo*ur* most noble grace.

" Mine other humble request, moste excellent Prince, is 5 this : Forasmuch as there be of yo*ur* comons, heare by yo*ur* highe com*m*andm*en*t assembled for yo*ur* p*a*rliament, a greate number w*h*ich are, after thacustomed manner, appointed in the comen house to treate *and* advise of the comon affaires among themselfes aparte; 10 And albeit, most deere leige Lord, that according to yo*ur* prudent advise, by yo*ur* honorable write*s* euery wheare declared, there hath bine as due diligens vsed in sending vpp to yo*ur* highnes courte of p*a*rliam*en*t the most discreete p*e*rsons out of euery quarter that me*n* 15 could esteeme [meete] thereunto, Wherby it is not to be doubted but that there is a very substanciall assembly of right wise *and* polliticke p*e*rsons; yeat, most victorious Prince, sith among so many wise men neyther is eue*r*y man wise alike, nor among so many men, like well 20 witted, euery man like well spoken, And it often happeneth that, likewise as much folly is vttered wit*h*

To l. 9, manner appointed, MSS. H² J H³ H¹ A M A² D T W X B *only; then the first complete folio* (2ᵃ) *of* MS. S *commences, but this is damaged at the right-hand edge.*

2. *aforesaid*] afore H¹ A X B. (*All* Harpsfield MSS. afore.)
2. *remembred*] menconed A² D B.   3. *most*] my H³ H¹ A T.
3. *and*] *Omitted in* A².   4. *most*] *Omitted in* W X.   6. *Forasmuch*] That forasmuch W X.   7. *highe*] highnes A² D B.
8. *thacustomed*] your accustomed T.   9. *in the comen*] to the Common T; in the Commons H¹ W X.   9. *treate*] intreate T; treaty B.   10. *advise*] dev[ise] S (*imperfect at end of line*).   10. *the*] your H³; *omitted in* S.   11. *most deere leige Lord*] my leige lorde J; H¹ *has* leige *interlineated.*
12. *prudent advise*] most prudent devise S.   13. *as*] *Omitted in* W.   16. *could*] woulde T.   16. *meete*] *Omitted in* H².
17. *that*] *Omitted in* X.   18. *wise*] wise men T.   18–19. *victorious*] vertuous D W X B.   19. *among*] *Omitted in* A².   19–21. *neyther . . . spoken*] neither is any man alike nor amongst soe many like well witted euery man like well spoken H³ H¹ A; M *omits* men like (l. 20); neither is any man wise alike nor amonge so many like well wittie euery man like well spoken T; neither is euerie man like nor among so manie men like well witted nor euerie man like well spoken W; neither is euery man wise alike nor among so many men all like well witted nor euery man like well spoken X.   21. *often*] oftneth J.   22. *likewise*] like D X B.

painted polished speache, so many, boystyous *and* rude
in language, see deepe indeed, *and* giue right substanciall
councell; And sithe also in matter[s] of * great importaunce, the mynd is * often so * occupied in the
5 matter that a man rather studieth what to say then
howe, By reson whereof the wisest man *and* [the] best
spoken in a whole country fortvneth among, while his
mynd is fervent in the matter, somewhat to speake in
such wise as he wold afterward wishe to haue bine
10 vttered otherwise, *and* yeat no wors will had when he
spake it, then he hath when he wold so gladly chaunge
it; Therefore, most gracious soueraigne, considering
that in * your highe court of parliament is nothing
intreated but matter of weight *and* importance concern-
15 ing your realme *and* your owne roiall estate, It could not
faile to let *and* put to silence from the geving of their
advice *and* councell many of your discreete comons, to
the greate hinderaunce of the comon affaires, excepte
that euery of your comons were vtterly discharged of all
20 doubte *and* feare howe any thing that it should happen
them to speake, should happen of your highnes to
be taken. And in [this] point, [though your] well
knowen *and* *proved benignity puttethe euery man in

MSS. H² J H³ H¹ A M S A² D T W X B.

1. *speache*] speeches J.   1. *many, boystyous*] many men boysterous S; manie which are boysterous W X.   2. *see*] so M.   2. *see deepe indeed*] are deepely read W X.   3. *matters of*] matter of so H².   4. *is often so occupied*] is so often occupied H² T; is so occupied often S.   6. *By reson*] by what reason J.   6–7. *the best spoken*] best spoken H² J H³ H¹ A A². (*Best* Harpsfield MSS. the best spoken.)   7. *whole*] Omitted in J.   7. *fortvneth among, while*] among them while S, fortvneth *having been omitted, and* them *interlineated*; fortuneth sometime while W X.   8. *in*] on J.   10. *vttered*] Omitted in T.   10. *will*] witt S.   10. *had*] had he S; he had A² D W X B.   11. *it*] Omitted in T.   11. *chaunge*] clayme M.   13. *in your*] in all your H² J.   13. *court*] courtes J.   14. *matter of*] of matters of J; matters of W X.   15. *could*] would A².   17–19. *to the . . . comons*] Omitted in J.   18. *of the*] of your S A² D W X.   19. *euery of*] euerye one of H³ H¹ A.   20. *doubte*] doubtes H³ H¹ A T W.   20. *it*] Interlineated in H²; omitted in J.   21. *them*] then H³; omitted in M A².   21. *them . . . happen*] Omitted in M.   22. *this*] that H².   22. *though your*] Omitted in H²; your J.   23. *and proved*] and approved H² S D W X B; omitted in J. (*All* Harpsfield MSS. proued.)   23. *puttethe euery man*] putteth away euery man T.   23. *in*] to A²; to a B.

ryght good hope, yeat such is the waight of the matter, such is the reuerend dread that the tymorous hartes of your naturall subiectes conceave toward your highe ma*i*estie, our most redoubted king *and* vndoubted soue*r*aigne, that they cannot in this point finde themselfes satisfied, except your gracious bounty therin declared put away the scruple of their timorous myndes |, *and* animate *and* incourage them, *and* put them out of doubte. It may therefore like your most aboundant grace, our most benigne *and* godly kinge, to giue to all your comons heare assembled your most gracious licens *and* pardon, freely, w*ithout* doubte of your dreadfull displeasure, euery man to discharge his consciens, *and* boldlye in euery thinge incident among [vs] to declare his advise; *and* whatsoeue*r* happen any man to say, [that] it may like your noble maiestye, of your inestimable goodnes, to take all in good p*ar*te, interpreting euery mans wordes, howe vnconingly soeue*r* they be couched, to p*r*oceed yeat of good zeale towardes the p*r*ofit of your realme *and* honor of your royall p*er*son, the prosperous estate *and* preservation whereof, most excellent soue*r*aigne, is the thinge w*hi*ch we all, your most humble loving subiectes, according to the most bounden duty of our naturall alleageans, moste highlye desire *and* pray for."

Wolsey's visit to the Commons. [1523.]

At this p*ar*liament Cardinall Wolsey found himself much greaved w*ith* the Burgesses thereof, for that nothing was so soone done or spoken therein but that it was ymmediately blowen abrode in euery Alehouse.

MSS. H² J H³ H¹ A M S A² D T W X B.

1. *ryght*] *Omitted in* H³ H¹ A; a right A².   2. *that*] of B.
3. *conceave*] conceaued A² W B.   3. *highe*] highnes A².
8. *incourage them*] encourage T.   8. *and put them*] *Omitted in* J.   9. *most*] *Omitted in* S D.   9. *our*] *Omitted in* A²; or B.   9–10. *our . . . kinge*] our most gratious kinge J. 10. *to all*] all H³ H¹ A T W.   14. *vs*] *Omitted in* H² J.   14. *to*] *Omitted in* J.   15. *happen*] happneth J.   15. *that*] *Omitted in* H² J.   16. *noble*] *Omitted in* H³ H¹ A; most noble S. 16. *inestimable*] most inestimable W.   18. *vnconingly*] cunningly T.   19. *of good zeale*] of a good zeale J.   19. *towardes*] to H³ H¹ A.   21. *is*] in A².   22. *loving*] *Omitted in* H³ H¹; *crossed through in* A.   23. *duty*] *Interlineated in* H². 25. *this*] which S.   26. *much greaved*] verie much agreeued W X.   27. *soone*] *Omitted in* H³ H¹ A W X.

It fortuned at [that] parliament A very greate subsedy to be demaunded, which the Cardinall fearing wold not passe the comon house, determined for the furtherauns thereof to be there [personallye] present himself. Before
5 whos coming, after Longe debating there, whether it were better but with a fewe of his lordes (as the most opinion of the house was) or with his whole trayne roially to receave him there amongest them : "Maisters," quoth Sir Thomas Moore, "forasmuch as my lord
10 Cardinall lately, ye wote well, laid to our charge the lightnes of our tongues for thinges vttered out of this house, It shall not in my minde be amisse with all his pompe to receave him, with his maces, his pillars, his pollaxes, his crosses, his hat, and greate seale too; [to]
15 thentent, if he find the like faulte with vs hereafter, we may be the boulder from our selues to lay the blame on those [that] his grace bringeth hither with him; " wherunto the house wholy agreainge, he was receaved accordingly.
20 Where, after [that] he had in a solemne oration by manye reasons proved howe necessary it was the demaund there moved to be graunted, and further shewed that les wold not serve to mainetayne the princes purpose, he, seing the company sittinge still silent, and therunto

Wolsey gets no answer from the Commons or the Speaker.

MSS. H² J H³ H¹ A M S A² D T W X B.

1. *at*] that at A² D B; also at X.   1. *that*] this H².   2. *to be*] was A² D B.   2. *demaunded*] granted S.   2. *wold*] it would J D; that it would A² B.   3. *comon*] Commons H¹ T X.
4. *there personallye present*] there present H² J; *in* H³ there *is interlineated, in* A² D B *omitted*; personallie present there W X.
5. *whether*] whither D X.   6–7. *as . . . was*] as the opinion of most of the house was W X.   7. *the house*] his house T.   7. *his*] a J.   7. *roially*] Royall H³ H¹ T.
8. *him*] them M.   10. *ye wote*] yet not A².   12–13. *in my minde . . . him*] be amisse in my mynd to receaue him with all his pompe J.   12. *his*] this A².   13–14. *maces . . . too*] Maces his hatt his pillors his pollaxe his Crosses & his great Seale too S ; the greate seale A² D T W X B. (*All* Harpsfield MSS. the great Seale.)   14. *to*] Omitted in H² W.   15. *if*] that if J.   16. *be*] Omitted in T.   16. *to lay*] lay T.   17. *that*] Omitted in H².   17. *hither*] Omitted in J S; thither T.
18. *the house*] the whole house M S.   20. *after that he*] after he H² J S.   20. *had in a*] had made a W X.   21. *demaund*] demandes J.   22. *moved*] vsed A².   22. *shewed*] sayed J.
23. *to mainetayne*] Omitted in J.   23. *princes*] Kinges J.   24. *company*] People W X.   24. *sittinge still*] still J; still sittinge T.

nothing awnesweringe, *and* contrary to his expectacion shewing in them selfes toward*es* his request[es] no towardnes of inclynacion, said vnto them :
"Maisters, you haue many wise *and* learned men amonge you, *and* sithe I am from the kings owne p*er*son sent hither vnto you for the preservacion of y*ou*r selfes *and* all the Realme, I thincke it meete you giue me [some] resonable awneswer." Whereatt eu*er*y man holding his peace, Then began he to speake to one m*aster* Marney (after lord Marney) : "Howe say you," quoth he, "m*aster* Marney?" Who making [him] no awneswer neyther, he seuerally asked the same question of divers others accompted the wisest of the Companye.

| To whom, when none of them all wold geeue so much [p. 8] as one word, being before agread, as the costome was, by their speaker to make awneswer : "Maisters," quoth the Cardinall, "vnles it be the maner of y*ou*r house, as of likelihood it is, by the mouth of y*ou*r speaker, whom you haue chosen for trusty *and* wise, as indeed he is, in such cases to vtter y*ou*r mindes, here is w*i*thout doubte a me*r*vailous obstinate silens."

And thervppon he required awneswer of master speaker ; who first reuerently vppon his knees excusinge the silence of the house, abashed at the presence of so noble a p*er*sonage, able to amase the wisest *and*

MSS. H² J H³ H¹ A M S A² D T W X B.

1. *awnesweringe*] answered S.   2. *shewing in them selfes*] in shewinge themselues S, *with* in *interlineated before* shewinge. 2. *requestes*] request H².   6. *your selfes*] our selues W X. 7. *some*] a H² J.   9. *his*] *Omitted in* M.   9. *Marney*] Varney X.   10–11. *after . . . Marney*] *Omitted in* J (*Eyeslip*). 10. *Marney*] *Omitted in* X.   10. *Marney . . . he*] Marney you Sir quoth he W.   10. *say*] saith T.   11. *Marney*] *Omitted in* X.   11. *him*] *Omitted in* H².   12. *he seuerally asked*] he asked seuerally S.   12. *divers*] *Omitted in* S. 15. *agread*] decided A².   15. *was*] is H¹.   16. *their*] the A² D W X B.   17. *maner*] order H³.   17. *your*] the S. 18–19. *by . . . is*] *Omitted here in* J, *but inserted after* mindes *below, l.* 20.   18. *speaker, whom*] Speaker to make answere whom H¹.   19. *you haue chosen*] haue you chosen T.   20. *cases*] causes J.   20. *mindes*] mind W.   20. *is*] *Omitted in* J.   21. *a*] *Omitted in* B.   22. *thervppon*] therefore T. 22. *he required*] required the J ; required he S.   22. *master*] *Interlineated in* H² *before the* crossed through.   23. *first*] *Omitted in* J.

More incurs Wolsey's anger

best learned in a realme, and after by manye probable
argumentes proving that for them to make awneswer
was it neyther expedient nor agreable with the auncient
libertie of the house, In conclusion for himselfe shewed
5 that thoughe they had all with their voices trusted him,
yeat excepte euery one of them could put into his one
head all ther seuerall wittes, he alone in so waightye a
matter was vnmete to make his grace awneswer.

Whervppon the Cardinall, displeased with Sir Thomas
10 Moore, that had not in this parliament in all things
satisfied his desire, sodainelye arose and departed.

Wolsey's consequent anger against More.

And after the parliament ended, in his gallery att
whitehall [in] westminster, vttered vnto him * his
greifes, saienge : " Wold to god you had bine at Rome,
15 master Moore, when I made you speaker." " Your
grace not offended, so wold I too, [my lorde]," quoth he.
And to wind such quarells out of the Cardinalls head, he
began to talke of that gallery, and said : " I like this
gallery of yours, my lord, much better then your gallery
20 at hampton courte." Wherewith so wisely brake he
of the Cardinalls displesaunt talke that the cardinall at
that present (as it seemed) wist not what more to say to
him. But for revengement of his displeasure, councelled the king to send him Embassodor into Spayne,
25 comending to his highnes his wisdome, learning, and

Wolsey's unsuccessful plot to send More to Spain.

MSS. H² J H³ H¹ A M S A² D T W X B.

1. *best learned*] most learned S.   1. *in a*] of a X.   1.
probable] *Omitted in* J; profitable A².   2. *argumentes*]
reasons J.   3. *was it*] it was T; was yet S; was W X.
3. *nor*] and T.   6. *euery*] *Omitted in* T.   6. *could put*]
could not put A².   6. *one* (1)] *Omitted in* J.   6–7. *his
. . . seuerall*] his head of their seuerall T.   6. *one* (2)] *Omitted
in* T W; *interlineated in* X.   7. *head*] *Omitted in* H³ H¹ A.
8. *vnmete*] vnfitt T.   8. *awneswer*] answeared W.   10. *this*]
his T.   12–13. *in his gallery . . . westminster*] *Omitted in* J.
12–13. *att whitehall*] in whitehall M; S *has at interlineated over
in crossed through*.   13. *in westminster*] at westminster H²;
omitted in J; neere Westminster A² D B. (*All* Harpsfield MSS.
at.)   13. *vttered*] he vttered S.   13. *him his*] him all his
H² J.   16. *I*] *Omitted in* W.   16. *my lorde*] *Omitted in* H².
17. *the Cardinalls*] his W X.   19–20. *gallery* (1) . . . *hampton
courte*] Gallerie at Hampton Court J. (*Eyeslip.*)   20. *courte*]
Omitted in S.   21. *that*] *Omitted in* J.   22. *more*]
Omitted in W.   23. *revengement*] revenge A² D B.   23.
displeasure] *Omitted in* H³ H¹ A.   24. *into*] to S.

meetenes for that voyadge; *and* the difficulty of the cause considered, none was there, he said, so well able to serve his grace therein. Whiche, when the king had broken to S*ir* Thomas Moore, And that he had declared vnto his grace how vnfitt a iourney it was for him, the nature of the countrye and disposition of his complexion so disagreing together, that he should never be [likelye] to do his grace acceptable service there*, knowing right well that if his grace sent him thither, he should send him to his graue; But shewinge him self neue*r*theles redy, according to his duty, [al] were [it] w*i*th the losse of his life, to fullfill his graces pleasure in that behalf; The kinge, | allowing well his awneswer, said vnto him : [p. 9] " It is not o*ur* meaninge, m*aster* Moore, to doe you hurt, but to doe you good wold * we * be glad; we [will] therefore for this purpose devise vppon some other, *and* imploy yo*ur* service other wise."

More made Chancellor of the Duchy of Lancaster. [1525.]

And suche entire favor did the kinge beare him that he made him Chauncelor of the duchy of Lancaster vppon the death of S*ir* Ric*hard* Wingfeild, who had that office before.

The King visits More at Chelsea.

And for the pleasure he took in his company, would his grace sodenly sometimes come home to his house att Chelsey, to be merry with him; whither on a tyme, vnloked for, he came to dinner [to him]; *and* after dinner, in a faire garden of his, walked w*i*th him by the

MSS. H² J H³ H¹ A M S A² D T W X B.

1. *meetenes*] meekenes S.   2. *none was there*] there was none X.   2. *he said*] sayd he S.   2. *he said, so well able*] so well able, he sayd J.   2. *well*] Omitted *in* M.   4. *had*] Omitted *in* W.   7. *should*] coulde T.   7. *likelye*] able H² S; able nor likelie W X.   8. *there*] therein H² D B.   8. *right*] Omitted *in* H³ H¹ A.   10. *to*] into W X.   11. *redy*] Interlineated *in* H².   11. *al were it*] although were *as correction of* al were it H²; although it were W X.   11. *with the*] to the A² B.   12. *his* (1)] Omitted *in* T.   12. *pleasure in that behalf*] pleasure therein J.   14. *meaninge*] pleasure M.   15. *wold we*] we wold H² J A² D B.   (Harpsfield MSS. *vary*.)   15. *will*] Omitted *in* H²; omitted here in J, *but inserted before* devise *below*, l. 16.   18. *beare him*] at that time beare him W X.   20. *Wingfeild*] Winfeild J; Winkfeild W.   24. *att Chelsey*] Corrected *from* to Chelsey H².   25. *vnloked for . . . to him*] vnloked for he came to dinner H² J M; vnlooked for he came to dinner to him vnlooked for W.   26. *walked*] walking W X.

space of an houre, holdinge his arme aboute his necke. As soone as his grace was gone, I, reioycing thereat, told Sir Thomas Moore howe happy he was, whom the king had so familiarly entertayned, as I * neuer had * seene 5 him to doe to any [other] excepte Cardinall Wolsey, whom I * sawe [his grace] once * walke with, arme in arme. "I thancke our lord, sonne," quoth he, "I find his grace my very good lord indeed, and I beleeave he dothe as singulerly favour me as any subiecte within 10 [this] realme. Howbeit, sonne Roper, I may tell thee I haue no cawse to be prowd thereof, for if my head [could] winne him a castle in Fraunce (for than was there warre betweene vs) it should not faile to goe."

This Sir Thomas Moore, amonge all other his vertues, 15 was of suche meekenes that if it had fortuned him with any learned men resortinge to him from Oxford, Cambridge, or els where, as there did divers, some for desire of his acquaintaunce, some for the famous reporte of his wisdome and learning, and some for suites of the vni-20 uersityes, to haue entered into argvment, wherein fewe were comparable vnto him, and so farre to have

Marginalia: More realises the insecurity of kingly favour.

"If my head could win him a castle in France, it should not fail to go."

Meekness and courtesy in disputation.

MSS. H² J H³ H¹ A M S A² D T W X B.

2. *thereat*] *Omitted in* J; much thereat S. 4. *neuer had*] had neuer H² J S A² D B. (*Order supported by* Harpsfield MSS.) 5. *to doe*] doe H³ H¹ A M S T X. (*All* Harpsfield MSS. *except* H, to doe.) 5. *to any other*] to any before H² J; any other M D T. (Harpsfield MSS. *vary*.) 5. *excepte*] before excepte H² J. 6–7. *whom . . . arme*] whom I once sawe him walke with arme in arme H². 6. *sawe*] see A² D T B. 6. *once walke with*] walke with once A². 6. *with*] *Omitted in* W. 8. *beleeave*] doo beleeve H³ H¹ A T. 9. *as* (2)] *Omitted in* H¹. 9. *within*] in H³ H¹ A. 10. *this*] the H²; his H³ J T. 10. *thee*] you A² D B. 11. *cawse*] greate cause A² D B. 11. *for if*] but if W. 11. *could*] wold H² J. 12. *a castle*] but one Castle A² D B. 12. *for than was there warre*] for then there was warre J X; for then was the warre H³ H¹ A; for then was there warrs T. 12–13. *for . . . betweene vs*] for at that tyme there was mortall warr betwixt vs and France A²; D B *as* A², *but* betweene *for* betwixt. 13. *goe*] goe off D B. 15. *had*] *Omitted in* A² X. 16. *men*] man J X; man or young student A² D B. 17. *some*] *Omitted in* M. 17. *for desire*] for the desire J H³ H¹ A A² D B. (*All* Harpsfield MSS. for desire.) 18. *some*] *Interlineated in* H². 19. *wisdome and learning*] learninge and wisdome J. 19. *suites*] followeinge of suits A² D B. 19. *of the*] as the W. 20. *to haue entered*] to enter in H³; to haue entred in H¹ A T. 20. *fewe*] very few A² D B. 21. *were comparable*] was comparable T.

discoursed with them therein that he might perceiue they coulde not, without some inconveniens, hold out much further disputacion against him; Then, least he should discomforte them, as he that sought not his owne glory, but rather wold seeme conquered then to discourage studentes in their studies, euer shewinge himself more desirous to learne then to teache, wold he by some witty devise courteouslye breake of into some other matter, *and* geeve over.

<small>Employment by the King for *ex tempore* answers to orations.</small>

Of whom, for his wisdome *and* learninge, had the kinge suche an opinion, that at suche tyme as he attended vppon his highnes, takinge his progresse either to oxford or Cambridge, where he was receaved with very eloquent orations, his grace wold alwaies assigne him, as one that was * prompte *and* ready therein, ex tempore to make awneswer therevnto. Whose manner was, whensoeuer he had occasion, either here or beyond the sea*, to be in any vniuersity, not onely to be present at the readinge *and* disp[uta]tions there comonly vsed, but also learnedly to dispute amonge them himself.

MSS. H² J H³ H¹ A M S A² D T W X B.

1. *discoursed*] discoursed and disputed A² D B.   2. *inconveniens*] inconvenience or disgrace A² D B.   3. *against*] with A².   4. *discomforte*] discourage and discomforte A² D B.   4. *glory*] prayse and glory A² D B.   5. *seeme*] be A².   5. *then to discourage*] then discourage W X.   5-6. *then . . . studies*] Omitted *in* S *here, but between* teache *and* wold (*l.* 7) S *inserts* or to discourage Students in their studies.   6. *studies*] endeavours and studies A² D B.   7. *to learne*] to learne and be taught A² D B.   7. *teache*] teach others A² D B.   7. *by some*] by his W X.   8. *devise*] device or other A²; D B *as* A², *but omitting* over.   10. *wisdome and learninge*] singuler wisdome and profound learning A² D B.   10. *had the kinge*] the King had X.   11. *tyme*] tymes S X.   11. *attended*] intended T.   13. *Cambridge*] Chambridge or any other place A² D B.   13. *very*] Omitted in A² D B.   14. *orations*] Orations as the Custome is in many places A² B; D *as* A² B, *but* Such places *for* many places.   15. *was prompte*] was most prompte H².   17. *he had occasion*] he had any occasion J; he heard that there was an Oration to be made A² D; B *as* A² D *but* any *for* an.   17. *here*] here at home A² D B.   17. *the sea*] the seas H² S X; Sea T.   17-18. *to be in any vniuersity*] in any of their vniuersities never to fayle to be at the delivery thereof A² D B.   18. *not onely*] And not only A² D B.   18. *at the readinge*] at Readings A² D B; at the Readinges X.   19. *disputations*] dispitions H².   20. *to dispute*] to argue and dispute A² D B.   20. *himself*] Omitted in A².

Who, beinge Chauncelour of the duchie, was made Embassador twice, ioyned in Comission with Cardinall Wolsey, once to [the] Emperour Charels into Flaunders, the other tyme to the French kinge into Fraunce.

[p. 10] | Not longe after this, the water-baily of London, 6 sometyme his servant, hearing, where he had bine at dynner, certeine marchantes liberally to raile against his old maister, waxed so discontented therewith that he hastely came to him, *and* told him what he had herd.

10 " And were I, S*ir*," quoth he, " in such favour *and* aucthoryty w*ith* my prince as you are, such men [surelye] should not be Suffred so villainously *and* falsly to misreporte * *and* slaunder me. Wherefore I wold wishe you to call them before you, and to their shame for 15 their lewd malice to punishe them."

Who, smilinge vppon him, said : " Why, master Waterbayly, wold you haue me pvnyshe those by whom I receiue more benefitt then by you all that [be] mye freindes ? Let them a gods name speake as lewdly as 20 they list of me, *and* shoote neuer so many arrowes at me, [as] long as they do not hitt me, what am I the worse ? But if they should once hitt me, then wold it indeed not a litle trowble me. Howbeit I trust, by gods helpe,

More and Wolsey twice joint Ambassadors. [Aug. 1521; July–Sept. 1527.] The Waterbailiff jealous for More's reputation.

But More is tolerant of slander.

MSS. H² J H³ H¹ A M S A² D T W X B.

1. *Chauncelour of the*] *Omitted in* A² B.   1–2. *was* . . . *twice*] was twice made Ambassadour A² D B.   2. *ioyned*] and ioyned A² D B; *omitted in* T.   3. *once*] one A².   3. *the Emperour*] Emperour H² M S T; A *has the interlineated.*   3. *Charels*] Charles the fift A² B; Charles the first D.   3. *into*] in W.   5. *Not longe after*] Not long tyme after M.   6–7. *at dynner*] at a dinner H³ H¹ A T.   7. *liberally*] *Omitted in* D.   7. *to raile*] rayle S X.   8. *therewith*] therewithall B.   8–9. *he hastely*] he H¹; hastilie he A²; hastily B.   10. *Sir, quoth he*] quoth he Sir S; quoth he D; Sir, saith he W X.   10. *quoth . . . favour*] in such favour quoth he A².   11–12. *surelye should not*] assuredlye should not H²; should nott suerly W X.   12. *be Suffred*] *Omitted in* X.   12–13. *misreporte and*] misreporte of me and H².   13–14. *wishe you*] wishe and advise you A² D B.   16. *Why*] *Omitted in* J; what S.   17. *those*] them J T W X.   18. *you all*] all you M S W X.   18. *be*] are H².   19. *a gods name*] on godes name W X.   20. *of me*] by me H³.   21. *as long*] so long H² J.   21. *as* (1) . . . *me*] *Omitted in* M. (*Eyeslip.*)   21–22. *what . . . hitt me*] *Omitted in* A² B. (*Eyeslip.*)   22–23. *indeed not*] *Omitted in* J.

there shall none of them all once be able to touche me. I haue more cause, I assure thee, master waterbaily, to pyty them then to be angry with them." Such fruitefull communicacion had he oftetimes with his familiar Freindes. 5

The three things in Christendom that More wished to see.

So on a tyme, walking with me alonge the teames side at Chelsey, in talking of other things he said vnto me : " Nowe wold to our Lord, sonne Rooper, vppon condicion that three things were well established in Christendome, I were put in a Sack, *and* here presently 10 caste into the Thames."

" What greate things be those, Sir," quoth I, " that should moue you so to wishe ? "

" Wouldest thow knowe what they be, sonne Roper ? " quoth he. 15

" Yea, marry, with good will, sir, if it please you," quoth I.

" In faith, sonne, they be these," said he. " The first is, that where the [moste] parte of Christen princes be at mortall warre, they were [all] at an vniuersall peace. 20 The second, that wheare the Church of Christe is

MSS. H² J H³ H¹ A M S A² D T W X B.

1. *them . . . able*] them all be able once J; them once be able H³ H¹ A T; them all be once able M S D B; them all be one able A²; them be able W; them be once able X.   2. *I assure . . . waterbaily*] Master water bayly, I assure thee J S.   2. *waterbaily*] Baylie T.   4. *communicacion*] communicacions H³ H¹ A.   4. *oftetimes*] often H³ H¹ A; many times M.   4. *familiar*] Omitted in H³ H¹ A T.   7. *at Chelsey*] with me at Chelsey J.   8. *to our Lord*] to god J.   9. *that*] Omitted in J.   9. *well*] Interlineated in H²; omitted in A² D B.   10. *were put*] were heere put D.   10. *in*] into H¹ S A² D X B.   10. *presently*] Omitted in D.   11. *the*] Interlineated in H².   12. *those*] theise D.   12. *Sir, quoth I*] quoth I, Sir S.   14. *what they be*] Omitted in A² W.   16–17. *marry . . . I*] marry sir with a good will if it please you quoth I, J; marrye withe good will, Sir, quothe I, yf yt please you H³ H¹; *order of words in* W X *same as in* H³ H¹, *but* a good will *and* said I.   16. *with good will*] with a very good will A² D B; with a good will T W X.   18. *In faith . . . he*] I faith they be these sonne quoth he J; in faith sonne they bee said hee theis M; In faith they be these sonne said he S.   19. *is*] Omitted in A² D B.   19. *that*] Omitted in H³.   19. *where*] wheras J H³ M.   19. *moste*] more H².   20. *mortall*] interlineated in H².   20. *warre*] warrs B.   20. *all*] Omitted in H² J.   20. *an vniuersall*] vniuersall J H³ H¹ A W X; *in* T an *is interlineated*.   21. *second, that*] seconde is that H³ H¹ A S W X.   21. *of Christe*] Omitted in S.

Holiness of life

[at this presente] sore afflicted with many errors *and* heresees, it were setled in a perfecte vniformity [of] religion. The third, that where the kings matter of his mariage is nowe come in question, it were to the glory of
5 god *and* quietnes of all partes brought to a good conclusion." Whereby, as I could gather, he iudged that otherwise it wold be a disturbance to a greate parte of * Christendome.

Thus did it by his doings throughe out the whole *Not ambitious*
10 course of his life appere that all his travaile* *and* paynes, *of worldly honour or* without respecte of erthly comodities, either to himself, *reward.*
[p. 11] or any of his, were | onely vppon the seruice of god, the prince, *and* the realme, wholy bestowed *and* imploied; whom I herd in his later tyme to say that he neuer asked
15 the kinge for himself * the valewe of one penye.

As Sir Thomas Moores cvstome was daily, if he were *Family* att home, besides his private prayers, with his children to *prayer.* say the seuen Psalmes, * letany *and* suffrages Folowinge; So was his guise nightly, before he went to bed, with
20 his wife, children, *and* houshold to goe to his chappel, *and* there vppon his knees ordinarily to say certeine psalmes *and* collectes with them. And because he was *His New* desirous for godlye purposes sometyme to be solitary, *Building: devotes his* *and* sequester himself from worldly company, A good *Fridays there to spiritual* MSS. H² J H³ H¹ A M S A² D T W X B. *exercises.*

1. *at this presente*] Omitted in H². 1–2. *errors and heresees*] heresies and Errors J. 2. *setled*] well setled J. 2. *a perfecte vniformity*] an vniformity J. 2–3. *of religion*] in religion H². 3. *The third*] the last S; the third is W X. 4. *nowe*] Omitted in S. 4. *come*] brought H³. 4. *in*] into J. 5. *god*] god Allmightie A² D B. 5. *and quietnes*] and quiet H³ H¹ A; and to the quietnes A² D B. 7. *disturbance to*] disturbance and trouble of A² D B. 7. *of*] of all H². 9. *his doings*] this doeings T. 10. *travaile*] travailes H² J S W. 11. *comodities*] commoditie S A² D X B. 11. *either*] Omitted in H¹. 14. *whom I herd*] when I heard him A² B; whom I haue heard W X. 14. *whom . . . say*] whom in his latter tyme I hard to say J. 14. *to say*] say S. 14–15. *asked . . . himself*] asked of þe king himself J; asked of the king for himself S A² D T W X B. 15. *the valewe*] to the valewe H². 17. *prayers*] prayer H¹. 18. *Psalmes*] penitenciall psalmes A² D B. 18. *letany*] and letany H²; the letany H³ H¹ A A² D T B; lettanies S. (*All* Harpsfield MSS. letanie.) 19. *So*] Omitted in J. 19. *his*] yt his H³ H¹ A. 19. *guise*] guise and vse A² D B. 20. *wife, children*] wife and children H³ H¹ A. 23. *sometyme*] Omitted in T.

distaunce from his mansion house builded he a place called the newe buildinge, wherein there was a Chappell, a library, *and* a gallery; In w*h*ich, as his vse was vppon other dayes to occupy himself in prayer *and* study together, So on the Fridaie* there vsually contynewed he from morning till evening, spending his time only in devoute praiers *and* spirituall exercises.

And to provoke his wife *and* Children to the desire of hevenly things, he wold sometymes vse thes word*es* vnto them:

Counsel to his family: no merit in "being carried up to heaven by the chins."

"It is nowe no maistry for you children to goe to heaven, for euery body geueth you good councell, * eu*er*y body geeueth you good example; you see vertue rewarded *and* vice pvnished, So that you are caried vppe to heven euen by the chynnes. But if you live the tyme that no man will geeue you good councell, nor no man will geeue you good example, when you shall see vertue punished *and* vice rewarded, If you will then stand fast *and* firmely stick to god, vppon paine of my life, [thoughe] you be but half good, god will allowe you for whole good."

Sickness and sorrow must be met patiently: people cannot "go to heaven on featherbeds."

If his wife or any of his children had bine diseased or troubled, he wold say vnto them: "We may not looke at our pleasure to goe to heaven in fetherbeds: it is not the way, for o*u*r lord himself went thither

MSS. H² J H³ H¹ A M S A² D T W X B.

1. *builded he*] build he M; he builded A² D B.   1. *place*] howse A².   2. *called*] calle J.   2. *buildinge*] buildings X.
2. *there*] Omitted in H³ H¹ A T.   5. *Fridaie*] Fridaies H² J.
5. *there*] he there X, *with omission of* he *after* contynewed.
6. *till*] to H³ H¹ A.   6. *only*] Omitted in S.   7. *praiers*] prayer T.   8. *the*] Omitted in H³ H¹ A M.   8. *desire of*] Omitted in M.   9. *sometymes vse*] vse sometymes W X.   11. *you*] Omitted in T.   12–13. *euery body*] and euery body H².
13. *example*] examples T.   15. *to heven euen*] euen to Heauen W X.   15–16. *live the tyme that*] live in the tyme that J; liue the tyme will come that S; live at that tyme when A²; liue at that time that B (at that *interlineated*).   16. *will geeue*] giveth A² B.   16. *nor*] Omitted in S A².   16–17. *no man*] anie man W X.   17. *will geeue*] give H³ H¹ A; woulde giue T.
17. *you* (1)] Omitted in H³ H¹.   17. *good*] a good X.   17. *see*] Omitted in W.   19. *firmely*] Omitted in M.   19–20. *vppon . . . good*] Omitted in M. (*Eyeslip.*)   19. *my*] Omitted in J.
20. *thoughe*] if H² J A² D B.   20–21. *god . . . good*] Omitted *in* T. (*Eyeslip.*)   24. *pleasure*] pleasures S T.

Pious counsels to his family 27

with greate payne *and* by many tribulacions, w*h*ich was
the path wherein he walked thither; [for] the servaunt
may not looke to be in better case then his m*a*ster."
And as he wold in this sort p*er*swade them to take
5 their trowbles paciently, So wold he in like sorte teach
them to w*i*thstand the divell *and* his temptacio*n*es
valiantly, sayeng :
"Whosoeuer will marke the divell *and* his temptacio*n*s, shall find him therein much like to an Ape. For,
10 like as an Ape, not well loked vnto, wilbe busy *and* bold
to do shrewd turnes, *and* contrarywise, being spied, will
sodeinely leape back *and* adventure no farther; So the
divell, finding a man idle, slouthfull, *and* without resist-
aunce redy to receiue his temptacio*n*s, waxeth so hardy
15 that he will not faile still to contynue w*i*th him, vntill to
his purpose he [haue] throughly brought him. But on
thother side, if he se a man w*i*th dilegens p*er*seue*r* to
preuent and w*i*thstand his temptacio*n*s, he waxeth so
[p. 12] wery that in conclusion | he vtterly forsaketh him. For
20 as the divell of disposition is a spirite of so highe a pride
that he cannot abide to be mocked, so is he of nature
so envious that he feareth any more to assaulte him,
least he should therby not only catche a fowle fall himself, but also minister to the man more matter of merite."
25 Thus delighte[d] he euermore not only in vertuous
exercises to be occupied himself, but also to exhorte his

They must withstand valiantly the temptations of the devil, who is likened to an ape.

MSS. H² J H³ H¹ A M S A² D T W X B.

1. *with greate*] in greate T.   1. *payne*] paines X.   1. *was*] is J.   2. *wherein*] where H³ H¹ A.   2. *walked*] walke J.   2. *thither*] *Omitted in* X.   2. *for the*] and the H² J S.   3. *may*] must D.   5. *sorte*] case J.   7–9. *valiantly . . . temptacions*] *Omitted in* D. (*Eyeslip*.)   8. *Whosoeuer will marke*] that whosoever will observe will observe and marke A²; B *as* A² *but* will obserue *once only*.   9–10. *For, like as an Ape*] for as an ape J; for like as the ape H³ H¹ A A².   11. *contrarywise*] otherwise T.   12. *leape*] looke M.   13. *finding*] seeinge J.   15. *faile still*] sticke still W X.   16. *haue*] hath H² J M X. (*All* Harpsfield MSS. hath.)   16. *throughly*] *Omitted in* J.   16. *him*] *Omitted in* A².   17. *perseuer*] present J; to perseuer T.   18. *temptacions*] temptacion T.   19. *vtterly*] *Omitted in* J.   19. *him*] *Omitted in* H³.   20. *of* (1)] by J X; in S.   20–21. *spirite of . . . of nature*] spirit of nature J. (*Eyeslip*.)   21. *mocked*] wicked D.   23. *least*] least þat J.   23. *not only*] *Omitted in* H¹.   24. *matter*] cause A².   25. *delighted*] delighteth H².

Margaret's
miraculous
recovery
from the
sweating
sickness
at the
prayer of
More.

wife, children, *and* houshold to embrace and followe the same. To whom, for his notable vertue *and* godlines, god shewed, as it seemed, a manifest miraculous token of his speciall favo*ur* towarde*s* him, at such tyme as my 5 wife, as many other that yeare were, was sick of the sweating sicknes; who, lieing in [so] great extremity of that disease as by no invention or devises that phisitions in such case[s] comonly vse (of whom she had diuers both exp*er*te, wise *and* wel learned, then continually 10 attendant aboute her) she could be kepte from sleape, So that bothe phisitions *and* all other there dispaired of her recou*er*ye, *and* gave her ouer; her father, as he that most intirely tendred her, being in no small hevines for her, by praier at gods hand sought to get her remedy. 15

Whervppon goinge vppe, after his vsuall maner, into his foresaid newe buildinge, there in his Chappell, vppon his knees, w*ith* teares most devoutly besought all-mighty god that it wold like his goodnes, vnto whom nothinge was impossible, if it were his blessed will, at 20

MSS. H² J H³ H¹ A M S A² D T W X B.

1. *wife, children*] wife and children H³.   4. *it*] he J.   6–7. *wife . . . sicknes*] wife his dearly beloved daughter was very extreame and dangerously sicke (as many others were that yeare) of the sleepinge sicknes A²; D B *as* A², *but* in that yeare *for* that yeare.   7. *in so great*] in that great H²; in so greate and dangerous A²; in so great & greiuious D B.   7–8. *of that*] of the S.   8. *invention*] inuentions H¹ S A² D B. (*All* Harpsfield MSS. inventions.)   8. *devises*] devise H³.   8. *that*] the H¹; tha A; of M.   9. *such cases*] such case H² J M; such or the like cases A² D B. (*All* Harpsfield MSS. except L, case.)   9. *comonly vse*] vse commonly D; doe commonly vse B.   10. *experte, wise*] experte and wise H³ H¹ A W. 10. *wel*] Omitted in A² D B.   10. *then*] Omitted in H³ H¹ A. 11. *attendant*] attendant and conversant A² D B.   11. *aboute*] vpon J.   11. *sleape*] sleeping W X.   12. *bothe phisitions*] the phisitions H³ H¹ A; both the phisitions A² D T B; phisitions W X.   12. *all*] Omitted in A².   12. *there*] Omitted in S; present A²; there present B.   12–13. *of her recouerye*] her health and recovery J; *omitted in* M.   13. *ouer*] ouer for dead A² D B.   13. *her father*] heere after T.   13. *as he*] and hee M.   14. *hevines*] greife and heavines A² D B.   15. *hand*] handes J M W.   15. *her*] Omitted in J.   16–17. *Whervppon . . . buildinge*] Where vpon after his vsuall manner going vp into his new lodginge J.   16. *vsuall*] vsuall and accustomed A² D B.   17. *buildinge*] buildinges X.   18. *most devoutly*] devoutly H³ H¹ A; most instantly and devoutly A² D B. 18–19. *allmighty god*] god Almightie S.   20. *will*] his will X.

his mediation to voutchsafe gratiously to heare his
[humble] petition. Where incontynent came into his
mynd that a glister shold be thonly way to helpe her.
W*h*ich, when he * told the phisitions, they by *and* by
5 confessed that, if there were any hope of health, that * was
the very best helpe indead, much marvailinge of themselfes that they had not before remembred it.

Then was it ymmediately ministred vnto her sleapinge,
w*h*ich she could by no meanes haue bine brought vnto
10 wakinge. And albeit after [that] she was therby
throughly awaked, gods markes, an evident vndoubted
token of death, plainely appeared vppon her, yeat she,
contrary to all their expectacion[s], was, as it was
thought, by her fathers fervent prayer myraculously
15 recoue*r*id, *and* at length againe to p*e*rfect health restored.
Whom, if it had pleased god at that tyme to haue taken
to his mercye, her father said he wold neuer haue medled
w*i*th worldly [matters] after.

Nowe while S*i*r Thomas Moore was Chauncello*u*r of
20 the Duchy, the sea of Roome chaunced to be void,

MSS. H² J H³ H¹ A M S A² D T W X B.

Cardinal Adrian elected Pope. [1522.]

1. *mediation*] meditation *corrected to* mediation J; meditacion H³ A.   2. *humble*] *Omitted in* H² J.   2. *petition*] petition for her recouery A² D B.   2. *incontynent*] incontinently T B.   2. *came*] came yt H³ H¹ A S X; it came A² D B.   2. *into*] to S W X.   3. *glister*] clyster D.   4. *told*] had told H² J H³ H¹ A X. (*All* Harpsfield MSS. tolde.)   4. *phisitions*] phisition T.   4. *by and by*] presently A² D B.   5. *health*] her health D B; helpe W X.   5–6. *health . . . helpe indead*] health indeede that that was the verie best helpe M.   5. *that was*] that that was H² H¹ M A T; that yt was J H³. (*All* Harpsfield MSS. that was.)   6. *very*] *Omitted in* H³ H¹ A T.   6–7. *of themselfes*] of it them-selues S; that of themselues B.   7. *that*] *Omitted in* D B.   8. *was it*] it was J.   9. *she*] *Omitted in* H³ A.   9. *by*] *Omitted in* X.   9. *meanes*] waies X.   10. *wakinge*] meltinge T.   10. *after*] *Interlineated in* H².   10. *that*] *Omitted in* H² J.   11. *throughly*] cleerelie W.   11. *an*] *Omitted in* J.   11. *vndoubted*] and vndoubted A² B; *omitted in* D.   13. *expectacions*] expectacion H² J H¹ A; expectacions and the ordinary Course of the disease A² D B.   14. *fervent*] fervent and devout A² D B.   14. *prayer*] prayers W.   14. *myraculously*] miraculous D.   15. *againe*] *Omitted in* T.   15. *to perfect*] to her perfect H³ H¹ A.   15. *to perfect health restored*] restored to perfect health W.   16. *had*] *Omitted in* M.   16. *at that tyme*] *Omitted after* god *in* S, *but interlineated after* taken.   16–17. *taken to*] tooke to A²; to D B; taken her to T.   18. *matters*] affaires H².

Wolsey's consequent anger with Charles the Emperor.

which was cause of much trouble. For Cardinall Wolsey, a man very ambitious, *and* desirous (as good hope and likelyhod he had) to aspire vnto that dignity, p*er*ceaving himself of his expectacion disapointed, by meanes of the Emperour Chare[l]es so highely comendinge one Cardinall Adrian, sometyme his scholemaster, to the Cardinalls of Roome, in the tyme of their election, for his vertue and | worthines, that therevppon was he chosen Pope; who from Spayne, where he was then resident, cominge on foote to Roome, before his entry into the Citye, did put of his hosen *and* showes, barefoote *and* barlegged passing throwe the streates towards his pallaice, with such humblenes that all the people had him in greate reuerence; Cardinall Wolsey, I say, waxed so wood therw*i*th, that he studied to invent all waies of reuengm*en*t of his grief against the Emp*er*our; wh*i*ch, as it was the begininge of a lamentable tragedye, so some p*ar*te [of it] as not imp*er*tinent to my present purpose, I recknid requisite here to put in remembraunce.

Wolsey's revenge against Queen Katherine.

This Cardinall therefore, not ignorant of the kings inconstante *and* mutable disposicion, soone inclined to withdrawe his devotion from his owne most noble, vertuous, *and* lawfull wif, Queene Katherine, awnt to

MSS. H² J H³ H¹ A M S A² D T W X B.

1. *was cause*] was after the cause A² D B.   1. *trouble*] trobles T.   5. *Chareles*] Charees H²; Charles that then was A² D B.   5. *comendinge*] commended T.   5. *one*] our J.   7. *their*] our J.   7–8. *for his vertue and worthines*] for his singuler vertues and much worthines A² D B.   8. *that*] and S.   8. *was he*] he was H³ B.   8. *chosen*] chosen and elected A² D B.   9. *where*] when A² B; omitted in D.   9. *then*] there T; omitted in W.   9. *he . . . resident*] Omitted in D.   10. *the*] that J.   11. *hosen*] hose J.   11. *barefoote*] barefooted J D T W X B. (Harpsfield MSS. vary.)   12. *streates*] streete S; Citty streets T.   12. *towards*] vnto H³.   14. *I say*] Omitted in J S.   14. *wood*] chafed S.   15. *invent*] Interlineated in H² over revenge *crossed through*.   15. *all . . . reuengment*] of revengement allwayes T.   16. *grief*] greifes H³ H¹ A; greife and discontentment A²; greefe and discontent D B.   17. *a lamentable*] the lamentable T.   17. *some parte*] in some part W.   17–18. *of it . . . impertinent*] thereof as not impertinent H²; thereof not impertinent J; of yt not impertinent H³ H¹ A T W; of it not pertinent X.   18–19. *recknid requisite*] thought fitt and requisite A² D B.   19. *here to put*] to putt here W X.   20. *This*] The H³.   20. *therefore*] Omitted in M.   22–23. *noble . . . wif*] noble and verteous wife J; noble vertuous Ladie and loving wife W X.   23. *Queene*] Omitted in W.

More consulted by the King 31

themperour, vppon euery light occasion, and vppon other, to her in nobility, wisdome, vertue, favour *and* bewtye farre incomparable, to fixx his affection, meaning to make this his so light disposition an instrument to bring
5 aboute his vngodly intent, devised to allure the kinge (then alredye, contrary to his mind, nothing les lookinge for, fallinge in love w*i*th the Ladye Anne Bullen) to cast fantasy to one of the Frenche kings Sisters : wh*i*ch thing, because of the Enmity *and* warre that was at that
10 tyme betweene the French king *and* the Emperour (whom, for the cause afore remembred, he mortally maligned) he was [very] desirouse to procure; And for the better atcheving thereof, requested Langland, Bishoppe of Lincolne, *and* ghostly father to the kinge,
15 to put a scruple into [his graces] head, that itt was not lawfull for him to marry his brothers wife : wh*i*ch the kinge, not sory to heare of, opened it first to S*i*r Thomas Moore, whose councell he required therein, shewing hym c*e*rtaine places of scripture that somewhat seemed
20 to serve his appetite; wh*i*ch, when he had p*er*vsed, and

Wolsey's attempt to bring about the King's marriage with "one of the French king's sisters."

Langland reported to have suggested divorce to the King. More consulted for first time on the divorce.

Excuses himself as unmeet to meddle in such matters.

MSS. H² J H³ H¹ A M S A² D T W X B.

1. *themperour*] the foresaid Emperour Charles A² D B. 1. *light*] *Omitted in* H¹; slight M; light and slight A² D B. 2. *vertue, favour and bewtye*] favour bewty and vertue A² D B. 4. *this*] *Omitted in* J. 4. *light*] light and variable A² D B. 4. *instrument*] instrument and meane A² D B. 4. *to bring*] to compasse and bringe A² D B. 5. *his*] this his J. 5. *vngodly*] soe vngodly H³ H¹ A M T; wicked and vngodly A² D B. 5. *intent*] intent and purpose A² D B. 5. *allure*] intice and allure A² D B. 5–8. *the kinge . . . to cast*] the kinge who was then already falne into loue with the Lady Anne Bellen (which the Cardinall never dreamed of) to cast A²; D B *as* A², *but* Bullen *for* Bellen. 7. *fallinge in*] fallen into S. 7. *the*] *Omitted in* T. 8. *fantasy*] his fantasy and affection A² D B. 8. *kings*] *Omitted in* J; king W. 9. *the*] *Omitted in* J. 9. *that was*] was J. 9. *at*] *Omitted in* W. 12. *maligned*] maligned and hated A² D B. 12. *very*] *Omitted in* H² J. 12. *procure*] procure and bringe to passe A² D B. 13. *atcheving thereof*] acheiveinge and accomplishinge of this his purpose A² D B. 13. *requested*] he requested S A² D B. 14. *Bishoppe*] then Bishop A² D B. 14. *Lincolne*] Lincolnes W. 15. *his graces*] the kings H² J. 16. *his brothers*] to Brothers B. 17. *heare of*] herof H³. 17. *it first*] with the first A² D B; *in* H² it *is interlineated*. (*All* Harpsfield MSS. with the first.) 20. *his appetite*] his turne and Apetite W; *before* Appetite X *has* turne *crossed through*. 20. *pervsed*] perswaded H³ H¹ A.

thervppon, as one that * had never * professed the studye of divinity, himself excused to be vnmeete many waies to medle with suche matters, The king, not satisfied with this awneswer, so sore still pressed vppon him therefore, that in conclusion he condiscended to his graces motion. And further, forasmuche as the [case] was of such importaunce as needed [great] advisement and deliberation, he besought his grace of sufficient respite advisedly to consider of it. Wherewith the king, well contented, said vnto him that Tunstall and Clark, Byshoppes of Dirham and Bathe, with other lerned of his pryvy Councell, should also be dealers therein.

The King bids him consult with the Bishops of Durham and Bath.

So Sir Thomas Moore departing, conferred those places of scripture with *expositions [of diuers] of [the] old holy doctors; and at his cominge to the courte, in talking with his grace of thafore [sayd] | matter, he said: [p. 14]

More consults the Works of St. Jerome, St. Augustine, &c., and recommends their perusal to the King.

"To be plaine with your grace, neyther my lord of Dyrham nor my lord of Bathe, thoughe I knowe them both to be wise, vertuous, learned and honorable prelates, nor my self, with the rest of your councell, being all your graces owne seruants, for your manifold benefites

MSS. H² J H³ H¹ A M S A² D T W X B.

1. *as one that*] as that T.   1. *had never*] never had H² J A².
4. *this*] his D.   4. *sore*] fair A².   5. *that*] Omitted in J.
5. *to his*] to give such satisfacion as he could vnto his A² D B.
6–7. *further . . . was*] further forasmuche as the matter was H²; farther that the matter was J.   7. *such*] that X.   7. *great*] good H² J S.   (*All* Harpsfield MSS. good.)   7. *advisement*] advise J.   8. *deliberation*] serious deliberation A² D B.
8. *besought*] humblie besought A² D B.   9. *respite*] respect J.
9. *advisedly*] advised J.   10. *well*] beinge well A² D B.   10. *that*] Omitted in J.   11. *Byshoppes*] Bishop M.   13. *departing*] departed M.   14. *of* (1)] of the H³.   14. *scripture with*] Scripture which he had receaved of the kinge and diverse others with A² B; D *as* A² B *but* from *for* of.   14. *expositions*] thexpositions H² S; exposicione J H³ H¹ A A² D X B; exposicions M T; *omitted in* W.   (*All* Harpsfield MSS. the expositions.)
14. *of diuers*] Omitted in H²; of diuers others D.   14. *the*] Omitted in H².   15. *old*] Omitted in A².   15. *holy*] Interlineated in J; *omitted in* S.   15. *doctors*] doctors and fathers of the Church A² D B; Doctours both Greekes and Latines W.
15. *and*] Omitted in W X.   15. *at his cominge*] at the next comeing A²; at his next Comming D B.   16. *talking*] talkinge and conferringe A² D B.   16. *thafore sayd*] thafore H².   16. *matter*] matters T.   19. *vertuous*] vertuous and J H¹ A; *omitted in* W.   19. *and*] Omitted in H¹ A.   19. *honorable*] holie W X.   20. *your*] my T.   21. *your* (1)] Omitted in M.
21. *owne*] *Interlineated in* H².

dailey bestowed on vs so most bounden to you, be, in
my iudgment, meete councelors for your grace herin.
But if your grace mind to vnderstand the truth, suche
councellors may you haue devised, as neither for respecte
5 of their owne worldly comoditye, nor for feare of your
princely aucthority, will be inclined to deceave you."
To whom he named [then] St Hierome, St Awsten, and
divers other [old] holy doctors, both greekes and latines;
and moreover shewed him what aucthorities he had
10 gathered out of them; which, althoughe the kinge (as
disagreable with his * desire) did not very well like of,
yeat were they by Sir Thomas Moore, who in all his
communicacion with the king in that matter had alwaies
most discreetely behaved himself, so wisely tempered,
15 that he bothe presently tooke them in good parte, and
oftetimes had thereof conferens with him agayne.

After this were there certaine questions among his *The King appeals to the Pope to pronounce the marriage with Katherine illegal.*
councell proponed, whether the king needed in this case
to have any scruple at all; and if he had, what way
20 were best [to be taken] to deliuer him of it. The most
parté of whom were of opinion that there was good

MSS. H² J H³ H¹ A M S A² D T W X B.

2. *meete*] fit and meete A² D B.   2. *herin*] therein A².   3. *mind*] meane A² D.   4. *for respecte*] for the respecte D.   7. *named then*] named H² J H³ M; then named A² D B. (*All Harpsfield MSS.* named then.)   7. *Awsten*] Agustines T.   8. *old*] *Omitted in* H² M. (Harpsfield MSS. *vary.*)   8. *doctors*] doctors and fathers A² D B.   8. *both greekes and latines*] both greekes and latyne H³ T; both Greeke and Latine H¹ A; both of the Greeke and and [*sic*] latine Church A²; D B *as* A², *but* and *once only*.   9. *shewed*] he there also shewed A² D B.   9. *him*] them W.   9. *aucthorities*] authoritie J.   10–11. *kinge . . . like of*] kinge as disagreable with his graces desire did not very well like of H²; king did not very well like of as disagreeable to his graces desire J.   11. *disagreable*] not agreeable T, *with* not *interlineated.*   11. *with his*] to his M.   11. *like of*] like of them A² D B; like of it T.   13. *communicacion*] communicationns H³.   14. *most*] *Omitted in* T.   14. *discreetely*] wisly J.   14–15. *so . . . that he*] and soe wisely tempered his highnes that he W X.   17. *were there*] there were S; were X.   17–18. *questions . . . proponed*] Questions proposed amonge his Councell J.   17. *his*] the D B.   18. *proponed*] propounded B.   20. *were*] was D.   20. *to be taken*] *Omitted in* H² J.   21. *whom*] them H³ H¹ A D T; *omitted in* W.   20–p. 34, l. 1. *The . . . of it*] *Omitted in* W. (*Eyeslip.*)   21. *opinion*] the opinion J A A² D T B.   21. *good*] very good S.

cause [of scruple], and that for * discharginge of it, sute were [mete to be] made to the Sea of Rome, where the king hoped by liberalty to obtaine his purpose; wherein, as it * after appeared, * he was far deceaved.

<small>A Commission is appointed. [13 April, 1528.]</small>

Then was there for the triall *and* examinacion of this matrimony procured frome Rome a comission, in w*h*ich Cardinall Campegius *and* Cardinall Wolsey were ioyned Comissioners; who, for the determination thereof, sate at the Black Friers in London, where A libell was put in for the adnullinge of the said matrimony, alleaging the mariage betweene the king *and* * Queene to be vnlawfull.

<small>In support of the legality of the marriage, a dispensation and brief are produced.</small>

And for proof of the mariage to be lawfull, was there brought in a dispensation, in w*h*ich, after divers disputac*i*ons theron holden, there appeared an imperfection, w*h*ich, by an instrum*en*t or breif, vppon search found in the Tresury of Spaine, *and* sent to the Comissioners into England, was supplied. *And* so should iudgm*en*t [haue] bine geuen by the Pope accordingly, had not the king, vppon intelligens thereof, before the [same] iudgement, appealed to the next gen*er*all councell. After whos appellac*i*on the cardinall vppon that matter sate no longer.

<small>The King appeals to the next General Council.</small>

<small>More foresees the growth of heresy.</small>

It fortuned before the matter of the said matrimony

MSS. H² J H³ H¹ A M S A² D T W X B.

1. *of scruple*] *Omitted in* H² J ; of the scruple A². 1. *that*] *Omitted in* S. 1. *discharginge*] the discharginge H²; the discharge A² X; dischardge B. 1. *of it*] thereof A². 1. *sute*] that suite S. 2. *mete to be*] *Omitted in* H² S; fit to be A²; neede to be W. 2. *to the Sea*] to see M. 3. *hoped*] hopinge J. 3. *liberalty*] libertie M. 4. *as it after appeared*] as it appeared afterward H²; as after it appeared J; as after appeared A² D B. 5. *and examinacion*] *Omitted in* W X. 9. *the*] *Omitted in* W. 9. *in*] at A². 10. *the* (1)] *Omitted in* H³ H¹. 10. *alleaging*] alleadge M; affirming W X. 10–11. *the mariage*] the said marriage J. 11. *the king*] the said kinge A² D B. 11. *Queene*] the Queene H² J S T X. (Harpsfield MSS. *vary.*) 12. *lawfull*] vnlawfull H³ H¹ A. 15. *an*] a B. 15. *vppon search*] vpon the search H³. 16. *of Spaine*] in Spaine S. 17. *into*] in T W. 17. *was supplied. And*] was And T, *with* was sent *in later hand on margin.* 18. *haue*] had H². 18. *Pope*] Pope himselfe A² D B. 19. *vppon intelligens*] vppon þe inteligence H³ A. 19–20. *thereof . . . appealed*] thereof appealed H¹; thereof appealed before the same iudgment S. 20. *same*] said H². 20. *next*] *Omitted in* W X. 21. *After*] vpon A² D B. 21. *cardinall*] Cardinalls H¹ A² D W B. 21. *that*] the M S. 23. *fortuned*] fortunated that M.

More foresees the growth of heresy

brought in question, when * I, in talke with Sir Thomas
Moore, of a certaine ioy comended vnto him the happy
estate of [this] Realme, that had so chatholike a prince
that no heretike durst shewe his face, so vertuous and
[p. 15] learned a clergy, | so grave and sound a nobility, * and
6 so loving, * obedient subiectes, all in one faithe agreing
together : " Troth it is indeed, sonne Roper," quoth he,
and in comending all degrees and estates of the same
went farre beyond me, " And yeat, sonne Roper, * I pray
10 god," [said] he, * " that some of vs, as highe as we
seeme to sitt vppon the mountaynes, treading heretikes
vnder our feete like antes, live not the day that we
gladly wold wishe to be at a league and composition
with them, to let them haue their churches quietly to
15 themselfes, so that they wold be contente to let vs have
ours quietly to our selves." After that I had told him
many consideracions why he had no cause so to say :
" Well," said he, " I pray god, sonne Roper, some of vs
live not till that day," shewing me no reason why [he]
20 should put any doubte therein. To whom I said : " By
my troth, sir, it is very desperately spoken." That vyle
tearme, I cry god mercy, did I geeue him. Who, by thes

MSS. H² J H³ H¹ A M S A² D T W X B.

1. *brought*] was brought W X.   1. *when I*] when that I,
H²; when H³ H¹ A.   1–2. *with Sir Thomas Moore*] Omitted
in W X.   2. *ioy comended*] Joye I commended H³ H¹ A
(I being interlineated in A).   2. *the happy*] that happi D B.
3. *this*] the H² H³ T.   4. *face*] force M.   4–5. *so
vertuous and learned*] so learned & vertuous T.   5. *sound*] soe
sound W.   5. *a* (2)] Omitted in H¹.   5–6. *nobility, and so
loving, obedient*] nobility so loving and obedient H² J ; nobility
and so louing & obedient D.   7. *Troth*] True J.   7. *it is*]
is yt M S.   9–10. *I pray god, said he*] quothe he I pray god
H² ; I praye god, sayethe he H³ X ; I pray god A² D B.   11.
mountaynes] Mounteine W X.   11–12. *heretikes . . . antes*]
heretikes like Antes vnder our feete W.   12. *the day*] in the
day A².   13. *at a league*] at leagge J.   14–15. *to themselfes*]
by themselves H³ H¹ A.   15–16. *so . . . our selves*] Omitted
in A² D B. (*Eyeslip*.)   16. *to our selves*] by ourselves H³.
16. *had*] Omitted in T.   17. *so to say*] to say so J.   18.
Well] well well J.   18. *Roper*] Omitted in S A² D W X B. (*All
Harpsfield MSS. omit*.)   19. *me*] Omitted in H³ H¹ A.   19.
no reason] noe one Reasone H³ H¹ ; noe on A ; no more reason T.
19. *he*] I, H² J.   20. *any*] any such A² D B ; omitted in X.
21. *very*] Omitted in W X.   21. *spoken*] spoken of you A² D B.
22. *I cry god mercy*] I crye god hartelye mercye H³ H¹ A ; God
forgiue me W.   22. *thes*] those S B.

wordes perceiuinge me * in a fvme, said merily vnto me :
" Well, well, sonne Roper, It shall not be so, It shall not
be so."* Whom, in xvj yeares *and* more, being in * house
conuersant with him, I could neuer perceiue as much
as once in a fvme. 5

But nowe to retorne againe where I lefte. After the
supplieng of the Imperfections of the dispensation, sent
(as is [before rehersed]) to the Comissioners into England,
the kinge, taking the matter for ended, *and* then [mean-
inge] * no farther to proceed * in that matter, assigned 10
the Bishoppe of Durham *and* Sir Thomas Moore to goe
Embassadors to Cambray, a place neyther Emperiall
nor Frenche, to treate a peace betweene the Emperour,
the French king, *and* him. In the concluding whereof
Sir Thomas Moore so worthily handled himself, procuring 15
in our league far more benefites vnto this realme then at
that time by the kinge or his Councell was thought

Side notes: More never in a fume. More and Tunstall sent ambassadors to Cambrai. [Summer of 1529.] The great benefits More procured for England.

MSS. H² J H³ H¹ A M S A² D T W X B.

1. *me* (1)] me to be H²; *omitted in* A². 1. *in a fvme*] in some fume H¹; in a fume and chafe A² B. 2. *Well, well*] Well J. 2–3. *It* (1) . . . *so*] *Three times repeated in* H² H³ H¹ A M; *twice only in* J S A² D W X B; *once only in* T. (*All* Harpsfield MSS. *except* C *once only*; C *twice.*) 3. *and*] *Omitted in* A². 3. *being*] *Omitted in* S. 3. *house*] his house H² J; the house A² D T B. (*All* Harpsfield MSS. *except* C, his house; C, house.) 4. *conuersant*] conversant and continually A² D B. 4. *neuer*] not T. 4. *perceiue*] perceave him J H¹ A² B. 4. *as much*] soe much J S A² D. 5. *in a fvme*] to fume J; in fume A² B; in chafe D; a fume T. 6. *lefte*] left off H¹. 6–7. *After . . . Imperfections*] After suppliinge of imperfections J; After þe Suppyed [*sic*] Imperfections H¹. 7. *of the Imperfections*] *Omitted in* W. (*Eyeslip.*) 8. *before rehersed*] aforesaid H². 9. *matter for ended*] matter into consideration & beleauing it ended H¹; matter as ended W X. 9–10. *and then meaninge*] and then minded H²; and meaninge H³ H¹ A; And then minding W X. 10. *no farther to proceed*] to proceed no farther H² S W X. 10. *to proceed in that matter*] in that matter to proceede H¹. 10. *in that matter*] therein S; in that T; in the matter W X. 10. *assigned*] signed T. 11. *to goe*] *Omitted in* S. 12. *Embassadors*] Embassadour T. 12. *to*] into W X. 12. *Cambray*] Camerie J. 13. *a peace*] of a peace S D; of peace A² B. 13–14. *betweene . . . and him*] betweene the French Kinge, the Emperour and him J. 14. *him*] himselfe A² D B. 14. *concluding*] conclusion S. 15. *handled himself*] behaved himselfe and handled the matter A² D B. 16. *far*] much A². 16. *this*] his J. 17. *the*] *Omitted in* X. 17. *kinge or his Councell*] king and Councell J; king D. 17. *was*] were W. 17. *thought*] *Omitted in* J.

possible to be compassed, that for his good service in that voiage, the kinge, when he after made him Lord Chauncelo*ur*, caused the Duke of Norffolke openley to declare vnto the people (as you shall heare hereafter [more at large]) howe much all England was bound vnto him.

Nowe vppon the coming home of the Byshoppe of Dyrham *and* S*ir* Tho*mas* More from Cameray, the king was as earnest in p*er*suading S*ir* Thomas Moore to agree vnto the matter of his mariage as before, by many and divers waies p*r*ovoking him thereunto, For the w*h*ich cause, as it was thought, he the rather soone after made him Lord Chauncelor; And further declar[ing] vnto him that, thoughe at his goinge ouer * Sea to Cameray, he was in vtter dispaire thereof, yeat he had conceaved since some good hope to compasse it. For albeit his mariage, being against the positive lawes of the churche *and* the written Lawes of god, was holpen by the dispensation, yeat was there another thinge found out of Late, he said, whereby his mariage appeared to be so directly against the lawe of nature, that it could in no wise by the church be dispensable; As Doctor Stokesley

The King again consults More on the marriage, and prays him to confer with Bishop Stokesley. [1529.]

MSS. H² J H³ H¹ A M S A² D T W X B.

1. *good*] Omitted in A². 4. *you*] ye W. 4. *heare*] Omitted in M W. 4–5. *as . . . large*] as you shall heare hereafter, omitting more at large, H²; as hereafter ye shall more largly vnderstand A²; as hereafter you shall more at large vnderstand D B. 5. *all*] Omitted in W. 5. *bound*] bound and beholdinge A² B; bounden and beholding vnto him D. 7–8. *Sir Thomas More . . . to agree*] Sir Thomas More to agree W. (*Eyeslip.*) 7. *Cameray*] Camerie J. 8. *as*] Omitted in M. 9. *his*] this W X. 9. *as before*] as ever he was before A² D B. 10. *divers waies*] diuers wayes & meanes D; sundry waies W X; diuers meanes B. 10–11. *For the which cause, as it*] For which cause as it J; for which purpose as it A² D B; for as it W X. 11. *was*] is A² D T B. 12. *further*] further more A² D B. 12. *declaring*] declared H² J. 13. *his*] this H³ H¹ A. 13. *ouer Sea*] over the Sea H² J S D B. 14–15. *conceaved since*] receaued sure H¹. 15. *some*] Omitted in A² D B. 15. *albeit*] although M. 17. *and the written*] and written S W X. 17. *Lawes*] law J H¹ A S D T B. 19. *he said*] the said M; as he said A² D B. 19. *whereby*] whereof W. 19. *appeared*] most plainly appeared A² D B. 19. *to be*] Omitted in W X. 20. *lawe*] lawes J H³ H¹ A. 20. *it*] Omitted in W X. 20. *could*] would H³; shoulde T. 20. *in*] by A² B. 21. *wise . . . dispensable*] wise be by the Churche dispensable H³ H¹ A; wise by the Church be lawfully dispensed withall A² D B.

(whom he had then preferred to be Byshoppe of London,
and in that case cheifly credited) was able to instructe
him, w*i*th whom he praied him in that point to conferre.
But for all his conferens w*i*th him, he sawe nothing of
such force as coulde induce him to chaunge his opinion 5
therein : wh*i*ch notw*i*thstandinge, the | Bishoppe shewed [p. 16]
himself in his reporte of him to the kings highnes so good
and favorable that he said he found him in his graces
cause very towarde, *and* desirouse to find some good
matter wherewithe he might truly serve his grace to his 10
contentation.

Stokesley's quarrel with Wolsey.

This Bishopp Stokesley, being by the Cardinall not
long before in the Starre Chamber openley put to rebuke
and awarded to the Fleete, not brooking this contumelious vsage, *and* thincking that Forasmuch as the Cardinall, 15
for lack of such forwardnes in setting forthe the kings
divorse as his grace looked for, was out of his highnes
favour, he had nowe a good occassion offred him to
revenge his quarell against him, further to incense the
kings displeasure towards him, busily travailed to invente 20
some collorable devise for the kings furtheraunce in that

MSS. H² J H³ H¹ A M S A² D T W X B.

1. *then preferred*] then newly preferred J ; there preferred A² W.
2. *was able*] was well able D B.   2. *instructe*] instruct and
satisfy A² D B.   3. *him* (2)] him for his further satisfacion A² D B.
3. *praied*] paid M.   3–4. *point . . . sawe*] Omitted in W.
4. *his*] Omitted in W.   4. *sawe*] could finde S.   5. *force*]
force or effect A² D B.   5. *coulde*] might S.   5. *chaunge*]
Change or alter D B.   9. *towarde*] forrward D B ; towards T.
9. *find*] fynde out H³ H¹ A (oute *being interlineated in* A).
10–11. *his contentation*] his highnes good contentacion and likinge
A² D B.   12. *Bishopp Stokesley*] Bishopp of Stoksley J.
13. *openley put to rebuke*] putt to open rebuke X.   13. *to*] in
B.   14. *awarded*].   (*All* Harpsfield MSS. afterwarde sent.)   14.
this] his H³ H¹ A A² D B.   14–15. *contumelious*] contentious X.
15. *vsage*] language and vsage A² D B.   15. *thincking*] think-
inge with himselfe A² D B.   16. *forthe*] first J.   17. *looked
for*] expected and looked for A² D B.   17. *his highnes*] the
kinges S.   18. *favour*] favour and good opinion A² D B.
18. *a good*] a very good and opportune A² D B.   19.
revenge . . . him] revenge himselfe against him A².   19.
further] father J.   19. *incense*] increase H³ H¹ A S T ;
augment and increase A² D B.   (*All* Harpsfield MSS. *except*
L Y incense; L increase; Y incease.)   20. *towards*]
againe towards X.   20. *invente*] invente and finde out
A² D B.

behalfe; which (as before is mencioned) he to his grace
revealed, hoping thereby to bring the kinge to the
better liking of himself, and the more mislikinge of the
Cardinall; whom his highnes therefore soone after of
5 his office displaced, and to Sir Thomas Moore, the rather
to move him to incline to his side, the same in his steede
committed.

Fall of Wolsey. [1529.] More made Chancellor. [26 October, 1529.]

Who, betweene the Dukes of Norffolke and Suffolk,
being brought throwghe Westminster Hall to his place
10 in the Chancery, The Duke of Norffolke, in Audiens of
all the people there assembled, shewed that he was from
the kinge himself straightly charged, by speciall comission, there openly, in * presens of them all, to make
declaration howe much all England was beholdinge to
15 Sir Thomas Moore for his good service, and howe worthy
he was to haue the highest roome in the realme, and
howe dearly his grace loved and trusted him, for which,
said the duke, he had greate cause to reioyce. Wherunto Sir Thomas Moore, among many other his hvmble
20 and wise sayengs not nowe in my memory, awneswered,
That althoughe he had good cause to take comforte of
his highnes singuler Favour towards him, that he had,
farre aboue his desertes, so highly comended him,

Norfolk praises More.

His modest reply.

MSS. H² J H³ H¹ A M S A² D T W X B.

1. *is*] Omitted in A².   2. *hoping*] & hoping H¹.   2–3. *the better*] a better H³ H¹ A.   3. *the more*] to the more W X.   4. *whom*] Omitted in J.   4–5. *of his office*] from his office S; omitted in W.   6. *to move him to incline to*] to inclyne him to M; to move him to S; to move him to incline him to H¹ A A² T W X B. (*All* Harpsfield MSS. to moue him to incline to.)   6. *the same*] Omitted in S.   6. *steede*] steed and place A² D B.   8. *the*] Omitted in J.   8. *Dukes*] two dukes A² D B; Duke T.   8. *and Suffolk*] and of Suffolke D.   9. *place*] place and seate A² D B.   10. *in Audiens*] in the audience W X.   12. *charged*] charged and commanded A² D B.   13. *presens*] the presens H² A² D W X B. (*All* Harpsfield MSS. except R² H R, the presence.)   13. *of them all*] of all J; of all them T.   14. *beholdinge*] beholden J H³ H¹ A M S. (*All* Harpsfield MSS. except Y, beholding.)   16. *in the*] of the S; in all the A² D B.   17. *loved*] both loved A² D B.   19. *among many other*] amongst other(s) H³ H¹ A; amongest all other T.   19–20. *hvmble and*] Interlineated in H².   19–20. *hvmble and wise*] wise and humble X.   21. *to take comforte of*] to reioyce of J.   22. *he*] Omitted in S.   23. *farre*] Omitted in A².   23. *desertes*] meritts and desertes A² D B.   23. *so highly*] Omitted in W X.

to whom [therfore] he acknowledged himself most deeply
bounden; yeat, neuertheles, he must for his owne parte
needes confes, that in all things by his grace alleaged he
had done no more then was his duty; And further
disabled himself as vnmeete for that roome, wherein, 5
considering howe wise *and* honourable a prelate had
lately before taken so greate a fall, he had, he said,
thereof no cause to reioice. And as they had [before],
on the kings behalf, charged him vprightly to minister
indifferent iustice to the people, without corruption or 10
affection, So did he likewise charge them againe, that if
they sawe him, at any time, in | any thinge, digresse from [p. 17]
any parte of his duty in that honorable office, euen as
they wold discharge theyr owne duty *and* fidelitye to
god *and* the kinge, so should they not faile [to disclose it] 15
to his grace, who otherwise might haue iust occasion to
lay his fault wholy to their Charge.

More's doors ever open to suitors: his son-in-law's objection.

While he was Lorde Chauncelor, being * at leisure (as
seldome he was) one of his sonnes in Lawe [on a tyme]
said merily vnto him : " When Cardinall Wolsey was 20
lord Chauncelour, not only divers of his privye Chamber,
but such also as were his doorekeepers gatt greate gayne."

MSS. H² J H³ H¹ A M S A² D T W X B.

1–2. *to whom . . . bounden*] *Omitted in* J.   1. *therfore*]
Omitted in H². 1. *he*] he ever A² B. 1. *acknowledged*]
humbly acknowledged D.   2–3. *must . . . confes*] must confesse needes for his owne parte M.   3. *needes*] *Omitted in* A².
3–4. *grace . . . done*] grace hee acknowledged hee had done X.
4. *further*] furthermore W X.   5. *wherein*] therein T.   7.
before taken] taken before T ; taken W X.   7. *so greate a fall*]
suche a greate faulle H³ ; suche a great fault H¹ ; A *as* H³ *but
with* faull *as correction of* fault.   7. *he had, he said*] he said
he had W X.   8. *thereof no cause to reioice*] noe cause to
reioyce thereof M ; noe greate cause thereof to reioyce A² D B.
8. *had*] *Omitted in* J.   8. *before*] *Omitted in* H².   9. *on*]
in H³ H¹ A X.   10. *indifferent iustice*] Iustice indifferently X.
10. *or*] and X.   13. *euen as*] then as J.   15. *to disclose it*]
Omitted in H² ; to disclose T.   16. *iust occasion*] iust cause
or occasion T.   17. *their*] his D W X.   18. *While*] Afterwardes while W X.   18. *being at leisure*] being vppon a tyme
at leisure H² W ; beinge at a tyme at leisure X.   19–20. *on
a tyme said*] said H² H³ H¹ A ; at a time said A² B ; spoke W ;
spake X.   (*All* Harpsfield MSS. on a time said.)   20. *vnto
him*] vnto him sayeing W X.   22. *also*] *Omitted in* X.   22.
his] but his S A² D W B.   (*All* Harpsfield MSS. *except* R² B but
his.)

And since he had maried one of his daughters, *and* gaue
still attendaunce vppon him, he thought he mighte of
reason looke for some; where he indeed, because he
was [so] redy himself to heare euery man, * poore *and*
5 riche, *and* kepte no doores shut from them, could find
none; w*h*ich was to him a great discourage. And
wheras els, some for freindshippe, some for kinred, *and*
some for profitte, wold gladly haue [had] his furtheraunce
in bringing them to his presens, If he should nowe take
10 any thinge of them, he knewe, he said, he should do them
greate wronge, For that they might do as muche for
them selfes as he could do for them : W*h*ich condic*i*on,
althoughe he thought in S*i*r Tho*m*as Moore very comendable, yeat to him, said he, being his sonne, he found it
15 nothing profitable.

When he had told him this tale : " You saie well, More would
see justice
done even
to the Devil.
sonne," quoth he; " I do not mislike that you are of
conscience so scrupulous, but many other waies be there,

MSS. H² J H³ H¹ A M S A² D T W X B.

1. *And since*] And nowe since W X.   1. *he had*] he T ; I haue W X.   1. *his*] your W X.   1–2. *gaue still*] giue still W X.   2. *him*] you W X.   2. *he thought*] *Omitted in* A² D B. 2. *he* (1) . . . *mighte*] I thinke I might W X.   3. *some*] somwhat J.   3–4. *where* . . . *was*] But forasmuch as yourself are W X.   4. *so*] *Omitted in* H² J.   4. *himself*] yourself W; *omitted in* X.   4. *euery man*] all X.   4–5. *poore and riche*] both poore and riche H²; poore or riche H³; aswell poore as rich W; both poore as riche X, *as correction of* both poore and riche.   5. *kepte*] keepe J T W X.   5. *doores*] doore S. 5. *shut*] *Omitted in* M.   5–6. *could find none*] I can find none W X.   6. *which was to him*] was to him M; which is W X. 6. *discourage*] discouragment H³ H¹ A; whereas allso W X.   7. *for* (1)] of T.   7. *wheras els*] wheras H³ H¹ A; whereas allso W X.   7. *for* (1)] of T.   7. *some* (2)] & some H¹ A T.   7. *and*] *Omitted in* A² B.   8. *had*] *Omitted in* H² J M W X.   8. *his*] my W X.   9. *his*] your W X.   9. *If he*] if I, W X.   10. *he knewe, he said, he should*] I knowe I should W X.   10. *he said*] saide he T.   10. *them*] him A².   11. *greate*] much W X. 11. *might*] may W X.   12. *he could*] they coulde T ; I can W X.   12. *condicion*] condicions A² D B.   13. *he thought*] he thought them A² D B ; I finde W X.   13. *Sir Thomas Moore*] you W X.   14. *him*] himselfe H³ H¹; me W X. 14. *said he*] he sayed H³ H¹ A S; *omitted in* W X.   14. *his*] your W X.   14. *he found*] he thoughte A²; I find W X. 14. *it*] *Omitted in* S.   16. *had told*] told A² B.   16. *this*] his A² D T.   17. *sonne*] *Omitted in* S T.   17. *he*] Sir Thomas Moore A²; Sir Thomas D B.   17–18. *of conscience*] of a conscience X.   18. *be there*] there be A² W.

sonne, that I may both do your self good, *and* pleasure your freind also. For sometyme may I by my word stand your Frend in steede, *and* sometime may I by my letter helpe him; or if he haue a cause depending before me, at your request I may heare him before another. 5 Or if his cause be not all the best, yeat may I moue the parties to fall to some reasonable end by arbitrement. Howbeit, * this one thing, sonne, * I assure thee on my faith, that if the parties will at my handes call for iustice, then, al were it my father stood on the one side, and the 10 Divill on the tother, his cause being good, the Divill should haue right." So offred he his sonne, as he thoughte, he said, as much favour as with reason he coulde require.

<small>Decree against Heron, his own son-in-law.</small>

And that he wold for no respecte digresse from iustice, 15 well appered by a pleine example of another of his sonnes in lawe called master Heron. For when he, having a matter before him in the Chauncery, *and* presuminge to much [of] his favour, wold by him in no wise be perswaded to agre to anye indifferent 20

MSS. H² J H³ H¹ A M S A² D T W X B.

1. *both do*] doe both J; doe S.   1–2. *pleasure your freind*] pleasure friend M; pleasure your freindes A² W X B; pleasure freinds T.   2. *by my word*] doe itt by my word H¹; in words J; by my woords A².   3. *stand your Frend in steede*] standing your freind instead H¹.   3. *Frend*] freinds A².
4. *letter*] letters W X.   5. *heare*] helpe S A² D B.   5. *another*] any other T.   6. *not all the best*] not of þe best A² D; not all of the best W B; none of the best X.   7. *fall to*] Omitted in S.   8. *Howbeit . . . sonne*] Howbeit sonne this one thing H². (*Order of words in all* Harpsfield MSS. *as in* H².)   8. *sonne*] Omitted in J.   8. *thee*] you X.   8. *on*] that on A².   9. *that if the parties*] Interlineated in H²; if the partye H³; that if þe party H¹ A.   9. *handes*] hand J A² D B.   10. *then, al were it*] and albeit X.   10. *al*] Omitted in H³ H¹ A M A² B. (Harpsfield *supports* al.)   10. *the one*] one X.   11. *on the tother*] on the other syde J; on the tother side D.   12. *right*] his right A² D B.   13. *as much*] sufficient S.   13. *favour*] fauour and freindship A² D B.   14. *coulde*] woulde T.   16. *well*] As yt well H³ A B (as yt *in* A *being written out on margin, and interlineated in* B); as yt plaine H¹; as well T (*as being interlineated*).   16. *a pleine*] Interlineated in H²; a good H¹.   17. *called*] Omitted in J.   17. *he*] his said sonne W; hee said Sonne X.   19. *of his favour*] on his favour H²; of favour M.   19–20. *wold . . . wise*] would by noe meanes by him H¹.   19–20. *by him in no wise*] by no meanes by him H¹; by no wayes A²; by him no waies B.   20. *to agre*] to come to composicion and agree A² D B.

Reverence and love for his father

order, then made he in conclusion a flatt decre against him. This Lord Chauncelour vsed comonly euery after noone to sitt in his open haule, to thentent [that], if any [p. 18] persons | had any suite vnto him, they might the more
6 boldly come to his presens, and there open their complaintes before him; whose manner was also to reade euery bill himself, ere he wold award any sub pena; which bearing matter [sufficient] worthy a sub pena,
10 wold he sett his hand vnto, or els cancell it.

Care with regard to Subpœnas.

Whensoeuer he passed throughe westminster hall to his place in the Chauncery by the courte of the kinges Benche, if his father, one of the Judges there[of], had bine sate ere he came, he wold goe into the same courte,
15 and there reuerently kneeling downe in the sight of them all, duly aske his fathers blessinge. And if it fortuned that his father and he, at readings in Lincolnes Inne, mett together, as they sometime did, notwithstanding his highe office, he wold offer in argument the
20 prehemynens to his father, thoughe he, for his office sake, wold refuse to take it. And for the better declaration of his naturall affection towards his father, he not

Reverence and love for his father.

MSS. H² J H³ H¹ A M S A² D T W X B.

4. *open haule*] hall openlie M.   4. *that*] Omitted in H² J M.
5. *persons*] person T.   5. *the more*] more W.   6. *there*] then T.   6. *their*] Omitted in J.   6–7. *complaintes*] complaynt T.   7. *also*] Omitted in A².   8. *ere* . . .
award] before he would grante W X.   9. *sufficient*] Omitted in H² H³ H¹ A T X. (*All* Harpsfield MSS. sufficient.)   9. *worthy*] Interlineated in H².   9. *a*] Omitted in H¹.   10. *wold he sett*] he would sett W; would sett X.   10. *vnto*] Omitted in H³ H¹ A; vnto it W.   10. *els*] otherwise A² D B.
12–13. *by* . . . *Benche*] Omitted in X.   13. *thereof*] there H² J; *omitted in* X.   14. *sate*] there sett W; sett there X.
16. *all*] Omitted in X.   17. *that*] Omitted in W X.   17. *at readings*] in Readings H³ H¹ A; at reading T W; at a Readinge X.   17–18. *in Lincolnes Inne*] at Lincolnes Inne or any other like place A² D B.   19. *the*] of the J.   20. *prehemynens*] prehemynencye H³ H¹ A.   20–21. *thoughe*
. . . *sake*] though for his office sake, *with* his father *interlineated in different hand over* for his office S; though his father againe in regard of his said office A² D B.   21. *the*] Omitted in S A² D B.
21–22. *better declaration*] better declaracion and more stronge demonstracion A² B; D *as* A², *but* plaine *for* stronge.   22. *his naturall*] his true and naturall A² D B.

only, while he lay [on] his death bedd, [accordinge to his dutie], ofte times with comfortable wordes most kindly came to visite him, But also at his departure out of the world, with teares taking him about the necke, most lovingly kissed and imbraced him, commending him into the mercifull handes of almighty god, and so departed from him.

Defends his injunctions before the Judges.

And as fewe Iniunctions as he graunted while he was [lorde] chauncelour, yeat were they by some of the Judges of the lawe misliked, which I vnderstanding, declared the same to Sir Thomas Moore, who aunswered me that they should have litle cause to find fault with him therefore. And therevppon caused he one master Crooke, cheif of the six clerks, to make a docket contayning the whole number and causes of all such Iniunctions as either in his tyme had alredy passed, or at that present depended in any of the kings Courtes at westminster before him. Which done, he invited all the Judges to dyne with him in the councell chamber at westminster : where, after dynner, when he had broken with them what complaintes he had heard of his Iniunctions, and moreouer shewed them bothe the number and causes of euery one of them, in order, so

MSS. H² J H³ H¹ A M S A² D T W X B.

1. *while*] when J S. 1. *he lay*] his father lay W X. 1. *on*] in H² H³ A M W. (*All* Harpsfield MSS. on.) 1–2. *accordinge to his dutie*] *Omitted in* H². 3. *came*] come W. 3. *visite*] comfort X. 3. *out*] *Omitted in* H³ H¹ A. 3. *the*] this J T W X. 4. *the necke*] his necke T. 5. *kissed and imbraced him*] kissed him, embraced him T. 5. *him* (2)] *Omitted in* J. 6. *into*] to X. 8. *And*] *Omitted in* H¹. 9. *lorde*] *Omitted in* H² M. 10. *I*] I by chance A² D B. 11. *declared . . . Moore*] declared vnto him the same Sir Thomas Moore S. 12. *should*] *Omitted in* J. 13. *caused he*] he caused H¹. 16. *had*] *Omitted in* S. 17. *that*] this T. 17. *present*] present tyme J; tyme H¹; time present B. 18. *done*] when he had done A² D B. 19–20. *Judges to dyne . . . dynner, when he had*] Judges to dynner when he had T. (*Eyeslip.*) 19. *dyne*] dinner H³ H¹ A. 19. *in*] att H¹. 20. *westminster : where, after*] Westminster before him which done he inuited all the Judges where after W, *with repetition from* ll. 18–19 *above, due to recurrence of* Westminster. 20. *where*] when H¹. 21. *broken*] first broken A² D B. 21. *complaintes*] complainte S. 21. *had heard*] hard hard J. 22. *them bothe*] *Omitted in* H³; both X. 23. *causes*] cause H³. 23. *one*] *Omitted in* J. 23. *so*] *Omitted in* H³.

plainely that, vppon full debating of thos matters, they
were all inforced to confes that they, in like case, could
haue done no other wise themselfes, Then offred he this
vnto them : that if the Iustices of euery courte (vnto
5 whom the reformacion of the rigour of the lawe, by
reason of their office, most especially appertained) wold,
vppon resonable considerations, by their owne discretions (as they were, as he thought, in consciens bound)
mitigate *and* reforme the rigour of the lawe themselves,
10 there should from thenceforth by him no more Iniunctions be graunted. Wherunto when they refused to
[p. 19] condiscend, | then said he vnto them : "Forasmuch as
your selves, my lordes, drive me to that necessity for
awardinge out Iniunctions to releive the peoples iniury,
15 you canot hereafter any more iustly blame me." After
that he said secreatly vnto me : "I perceiue, sonne,
why they like not so to doe, for they see that they may
by the verdicte of the Iurye cast of all quarrells from
them selves vppon them, which they accompte their
20 cheif defens; *and* therefore am I compelled to abide
thadventure of all such reportes."

And as litle leysure as he had to be occupied in the   Refuses
study of holy scripture *and* controuersies vppon religion   reward from
                                                             the clergy
                                                             for his con-
                                                             troversial
MSS. H² J H³ H¹ A M S A² D T W X B.   writings.

1. *full*] small D.   1. *thos matters*] this matter H³; this
matters A.   2. *in like*] in the like A² D B.   2. *case*] manner
S; causes W X.   2. *could*] would H³ M A² D T B; *omitted
in* X. (*All* Harpsfield MSS. could.)   5. *of the rigour*] of
rigor J.   7–8. *discretions*] discressione H³ W X.   8. *as he
thought*] he thought H³.   8. *consciens*] Consciences H¹ A.
9. *the rigour of the lawe*] the same rigour of lawe S.   10. *by
him*] Omitted *in* D; from him T.   10. *more*] Omitted *in* T.
11. *be*] Omitted *in* M.   11. *Wherunto*] wherevpon J.   14. *to
releive*] for releiuinge W X.   14. *peoples*] people D.   14.
iniury] iniuryes T W X.   15–16. *After that*] And after that
W X.   16. *said*] had sayd J.   16. *secreatly*] Omitted *in*
S.   16. *I perceiue, sonne*] Sonne, I perceiue W X.   17–18.
see . . . cast] see that by the virdite of the Jurye they may
cast H³ H¹ A.   18. *of(2)*)] Omitted *in* A².   18. *quarrells*]
quarrell H³ H¹ A M T. (*All* Harpsfield MSS. quarells.)   20.
am 1] I am H³.   21. *thadventure*] the venture A².   22–23.
the study of] Omitted *in* A².   23. *holy*] the holy H³ H¹ A A²
D W X.   23. *scripture*] Scriptures H¹ A S.   23. *controuersies vppon*] contraversities of H³ A; Controuersyes of H¹ T
W; controversie of X.

and such other vertuous exercises, being in manner contynually busied about thaffaires of the kinge *and* the realme, yeat such watche *and* payne in setting forth of divers profitable workes, in defens of the true [Christian] religion, against hereseies secreatly sowen abrode in the Realme, assuredly sustayned he, that the Byshoppes, to whose pastorall cure [the reformacione] thereof principally app*er*tained, thinking themselfes by his travaile, wherein by their owne confession* they were not able with him to make comparison, of their duties in that behalf discharged, And considering that for all his princes favo*ur* he was no rich man, nor in yearly revenues advaunced as his worthines deserved; Therefore, at a convocatio*n* among themselfes *and* other of the clergie, they agreed together and concluded vppon a some of foure or five thowsand pound*es*, at the least, to my remembraunce, for his paynes to recompence him. To the payment whereof euery Byshop, Abbott, *and* the rest of the Clergye were, after the rate [of their abillityes], liberall contributories, hoping this porcion should be to his contentation.

MSS. H² J H³ H¹ A M S A² D T W X B.

1. *other*] other like J.　　1. *vertuous*] holy W X.　　1. *exercises*] Exercise H¹ A.　　1. *in manner*] in a manner H¹ X.　　2. *busied*] exercised X.　　2. *about*] vpon A² B.　　2–3. *and the realme*] and Realme H³ H¹ A; and of the Realme X.　　3. *setting*] sett in M.　　4. *in defens*] in the defence H³ H¹ A A² D T B. (*All* Harpsfield MSS. for the defence.)　　4. *the*] *Omitted in* S. 4. *Christian*] catholike H² J; Christian Catholick A² D B. (*All* Harpsfield MSS. Catholike.)　　5. *hereseies*] Sects and heresies A² D B.　　5. *sowen abrode in*] sowne about in diuers corners of A² D; sowen abroad in diuers Corners of the Realme B. 6–7. *to whose . . . reformacione*] to whome pastorall care and the reformacion T.　　6–7. *to whose*] to vse J.　　7. *cure*] cure and care A² D B; care T W.　　7. *the reformacione*] *Omitted in* H².　　7–8. *principally appertained*] did principally appertaine A² D B.　　8. *travaile*] traveiles S.　　9. *confession*] confessions H² S.　　9–10. *they were not able with him*] with him they were not able J.　　10. *comparison*] comparisons H¹ A.　　10–11. *duties . . . discharged*] dutie discharged J. 11. *that*] *Interlineated in* H².　　11–12. *all his princes favour*] all his paynes and princes favour J; all his princely favor X. 12. *in*] his H³.　　14. *among*] amonste H³; of W X.　　19. *of their abillityes*] *Omitted in* H².　　20. *liberall*] liberallie W X. 21. *contentation*] Contentacion and good liking A² D B.

for his controversial writings 47

Whervppon Tunstall, Bishopp of Dirham, Clark, Bishopp of Bath, *and*, as farr as I can call to mind, Vaysey, Bishop of Exeter, repayred vnto him, declaring howe thanckfully for his travailes, to their discharge, in
5 god*es* cause bestowed, they reckned themselves bounden to consider him; And that albeit they could not, according to his desert*es*, so worthily as they gladly wold, requite him therefore, but must reserve that only to the goodnes of god, yeat for a small p*a*rte of recompence, in
10 respecte of his estate so vnequall to his worthines, in the name of their whole convocac*i*on, they presented vnto him that some, w*hi*ch they desired him to take in good p*a*rte.

Who, forsaking it, said, That like as it was no small
15 comforte vnto him that so wise *and* learned men so well accepted his simple doings, for w*hi*ch he never intended to receiue reward but at thands of god onlye, to whom alone was the thanck thereof cheefly to be ascribed, So gaue he most hvmble thanckes to their honours all for
20 their [so] bountiffull [and freindly] consideration.

When they, for all their importune pressinge vppon him, that fewe wold haue went he could haue refused it, could by no meanes make him to take it, Then besought they

MSS. H² J H³ H¹ A M S A² D T W X B.

1. *Dirham, Clark*] Durham & Clarke S.   2. *can*] could W X.   3. *declaring*] declaring vnto him H³ H¹ A.   4. *his*] *Omitted in* T.   4. *travailes*] trauell W X.   7. *they*] the (? = they) M X.   7. *gladly*] *Omitted in* T.   8. *must*] *Omitted in* J.   8. *reserve*] referr D T B.   9. *god*] Allmightie God W X.   10. *worthines*] vnworthines D W.   11. *vnto*] *Omitted in* M.   14. *said*] sayed thus H³ H¹ A.   14. *was*] were J.   16. *accepted*] accepted of S A² D B; excepted T; accepte W.   16. *never intended*] intended never J.   17. *reward*] a reward X.   18. *alone*] all onelie W X.   18. *the*] *Omitted in* J.   18. *thanck*] thanks J D W X.   18. *cheefly*] *Omitted in* H³.   19. *he*] *Omitted in* A².   19. *to their*] vnto their vnto their X.   19. *all for*]. (*All* Harpsfield MSS. for all.)   20. *so*] *Omitted in* H² J M T. (Harpsfield MSS. *vary*.)   20. *and freindly*] *Omitted in* H² J.   21. *When*] & when H¹.   21. *importune*] so importune S; importunate M T; import and A².   21. *vppon him*] vpon him to take it A².   22. *that fewe . . . could*] that fewe that had want could S.   22. *went*] thought W X.   22–23. *could* (2) . . . *it*] *Omitted in* X. (*Eyeslip*.)   22. *could* (2)] yet could they S.   23. *besought they*] they besought J.

him to be content yeat that they might bestowe it vppon his wife *and* children. "Not so, my Lordes," quothe he, "I had leuer see it all cast into the Themes, then I, or any of mine, should haue thereof [the worthe of] one peny. For thoughe your offer, my lordes, be 5 indeede | very frendly *and* honorable, yet set I so much [p. 20] by my plesure *and* so litle by my profitt, that I wold not, in good faith, for so much, *and* much more to, haue losst the rest of so many night*es* sleepe as was spent vppon the same. And yeat wish wold I, for all that, vppon 10 condic*i*on that all hereseyes were suppressed, that all my bookes were burned *and* my labour vtterly lost."

Thus dep*a*rting, were they fayne to restore vnto euery man his owne agayne.

Shirt of hair and other austerities.

This Lord Chauncelo*u*r, albeit he was to god *and* the 15 world well knowen of notable vertue) thoughe not so of euery man considered) yeat, for the avoiding of singularity, wold he appeare none otherwise then other men in his apparell *and* other * behaviour. And albeit outwardly he appeared honorable like one of his callinge, 20 yeat inwardly he no such vanityes esteeming, secreatly next his body ware * a shirte of heare; w*h*ich my sister

MSS. H² J H³ H¹ A M S A² D T W X B.

1. *to be*] be J.   1. *content yeat*] yet content X.   1. *yeat that they*] that yett they D W B.   1. *that*] *Omitted in* A² X.
3. *leuer*] rather S A² D X; lether W.   3. *it all cast*] it cast it all S; it cast T W.   4. *any of*] *Omitted in* W.   4–5. *haue . . . worthe of*] haue thereof H²; haue of þe worth thereof H¹; haue the worth of X.   5. *thoughe*] *Interlineated in* H².   5. *your offer, my lordes*] my Lordes your offer W X.
6. *very frendly and honorable*] very honourable & freindly H¹.
7. *plesure . . . my*] *Omitted in* D.   (*Eyeslip.*)   8. *losst*] *Omitted in* W.   9. *many nightes*] many a nights J H¹ A M W X. (*All* Harpsfield MSS. except C, manye nightes.)   10. *wold I*] I would J.   11. *condicion*] conditions J.   12. *and my*] and all my H³ H¹ A² D B.   12. *vtterly*] *Omitted in* D T B.
14. *man*] one H¹.   14. *owne*] money A² D B.   15. *This*] The *in text of* T (p. 206), *but* This *catchword* (p. 205).   15. *was*] were S.   16. *world*] whole world X.   16. *notable*] noble H³ H¹ A T.   16–17. *not . . . considered*] not of every man so considered M.   17. *man*] one D.   17. *the*] *Omitted in* H¹.   17. *avoiding*] avoy = J (*end of line*).   18–19. *then . . . behaviour*] in his apparell & his behauiour then other men A².
19. *other behaviour*] other outward behauiour H² J; behauiour W X.   19–20. *And . . . like*] And albeit he appeared honorable outwardlie and lyke J.   21. *esteeming*] esteemed H³ T.
22. *next his*] next to his S.   22. *ware*] ware he H².

Moore, a yong gentlewoman, in the sommer, as he sate at supper, singly in his doublet *and* hose, wearing thervppo*n* a plaine shirte, w*i*thout ruffe or coller, chauncing to spye, * began to laughe at it. My wife, not ignorant
5 of his manner, p*er*ceyuinge the same, pryvily told him of it; And he, beinge sory that she sawe it, presently amended [it].

He vsed also sometymes to pvnishe his body w*i*th whippes, the cordes knotted, w*hi*ch was knowen only to
10 my wife, his eldest daughter, whom for [her] secrecy aboue all other he specially trusted, causing her, as need required, to washe the same shirte of heare.

Nowe shortly vppon his entry into the highe office of the Chauncelorshipp, the king [yeat] eftssoones agayne
15 moved him to waighe and consider his greate matter; who, falling downe vppon his knees, hvmbly besought his highnes to stand his gratious soue*r*aigne, as [he] euer since his entry into his gra[ces] service * had founde him; * sayeng there was nothing in the world had bine
20 so greiuous vnto his harte as to remember [that] he was not able, as he willingly wold, w*i*th the losse of one of

[marginal: More once again consulted on the divorce: he cannot, "with his conscience, safely serve his Grace's contentation."]

MSS. H² J H³ H¹ A M S A² D T W X B.

1. *sommer*] Sommer time W X.   1. *sate*] was sittinge S.
4. *spye*] spye it H².   6. *And*] Omitted in H³.   6. *beinge sory*] being seeing sorry W.   7. *it*] the same H².   9. *whippes, the cordes*] whips of Cords H¹; whipps X.   9. *knotted*] wherof were knotted A² D B.   10. *my wife*] his wife T.   10. *her*] Omitted in H².   11. *causing*] caused J.   11. *her*] Omitted in M.   11. *need*] cause A² D.   12. *required*] require W.   13–14. *Nowe ... Chauncelorshipp*] Now vpon entrie in the high office of the chancelorship S.   13. *vppon*] after W X.   13. *entry*] entring H¹ D.   14. *the (1)*] Omitted in H³ H¹ A M A² D B. (Harpsfield MSS. *support* the.)   14–15. *king ... moued him*] king yet oftentimes moued him againe W X.   14. *yeat*] Omitted in H² J H¹.   15. *to waighe*] very earnestly to weigh A² D B .   15. *greate*] gretest J.   16. *hvmbly*] most humblie A² D W B; *omitted* in X.   17. *soueraigne*] soueraigne Lord A² D B.   17. *he*] Omitted here in H² J T W X, *but inserted below (l.* 18) *before* had.   18. *his entry*] his first entrie S A² D W X B. (Harpsfield MSS. *vary*.)   18. *graces*] gratious H² J M T. (*All* Harpsfield MSS. graces.)   18. *had*] he had H² J T.   19. *sayeng*] In sayeng H² H³ H¹ A M T. (*All* Harpsfield MSS. saying.)   19–20. *had ... greiuous*] had so gratious A²; had bene so gratious B.   20. *that*] Omitted in H² J.   21. *he*] Omitted in A².   21. *one of*] Omitted in X.   21. *of* (2)] Omitted *in* S T.

his limbes, for that matter any thing to finde wherby
he could, [with his consciens, safely] serve his graces
contentac*ion*; As he that alwaies bare in mynde the
most godly word*es* th*at* his highnes spake vnto him at his
first coming into his noble service, the most vertuous 5
lesson that euer prince taught his servant, willing him
first to looke vnto god, *and* after god to him; as, in good
faith, he said, he did, or els might his grace well accompt
him his most vnworthy servaunt. To this the kinge
awneswered, that if he could not [therein] w*i*th his con- 10
sciens serue him, he was content taccept his service
otherwise; And vsing the aduice of other [of] his learned
councell, whose consciences could well inough agre
therew*i*th, wold neue*r*theles contynewe his gratious
favour towa*r*ds him, *and* neuer w*i*th that matter molest 15
his consciens after.

Declares to the Commons the judgment of the Universities concerning the King's marriage with Anne Boleyn.
But S*i*r Thom*a*s Moore, in processe of time, seing the
king fully | determined to p*r*oceede [forthe] in the mari- [p. 21]
age of Queene Anne, and when he, w*i*th the Bishopps
and nobles of the higher house of the parliament, were, 20
for the furtheraunce of that mariage, comaunded by the
kinge to goe downe to the comon house, to shewe vnto
them both what the vniue*r*sities, aswell of other p*a*rtes
beyond the seas as [of] Oxford *and* Cambridge, had done

MSS. H² J H³ H¹ A M S A² D T W X B.

1. *any thing to finde*] to find any thinge J. 2. *with his consciens, safely*] Omitted in H² J. 2. *his graces*] his greate T.
3. *contentacion*] contentment J. 6. *taught his*] taught to his H¹. 7. *and*] Omitted in T. 7. *god* (2)] Omitted in W. 9. *To*] Omitted in B. 10. *therein*] Omitted in H² J W. 12. *vsing*] vse J. 12. *of other of his*] of other his H² J H³ M; of others of his T; of his other X. (*All* Harpsfield MSS. of other of his.) 13. *consciences*] Omitted in M; conscience T W. 13. *could*] would H³ H¹ A D. 14. *therewith*] thereto J. 14. *wold*] he would J. 14. *gratious*] graces M. 18. *forthe*] further H² W X; for H¹. 18. *in*] Omitted in H¹. 19. *of*] Omitted in X. 19. *Queene*] the Queene, B. 19. *and*] Omitted in S A² D W X B. (*All* Harpsfield MSS. omit.) 19. *the*] Omitted in S. 20. *and*] & the D B. 20. *nobles*] Noble men H¹. 20. *the* (2)] Omitted in A² X. 21. *of . . . comaunded*] of the matter comaunded W X. 22. *to* (2)] into A². 22. *comon*] Commons H¹ X. 22. *vnto*] Omitted in A². 23. *of other*] of the other H³ W X. 23. *partes*] parties T. 24. *seas*] Sea T. 24. *of Oxford*] at Oxford H² J.

Pleads discharge from the Chancellorship 51

in that behalf, *and* their seales also testifyenge the same —All w*h*ich matters, at the kings request, not shewing of what minde himself was therein, he opened to the lower house of the p*a*rliament—Neue*r*theles, doubtinge
5 least further attemp*tes* after should followe, w*h*ich, contrary to his consciens, by reson of his office, he was likely to be putt vnto, He made sute vnto the Duke of Norfolk, his singuler deere freind, to be a meane to the kinge that he might, w*i*th his grace*s* favour, be dis-
10 charged of that chargeable roome of [the] Chauncelo*u*rshippe, wherein, for certaine infirmities of his bodye, he pretended himself vnable any longer to serve.

But is silent as to his own opinion.

Pleads for discharge from the Chancellorship, on the grounds of ill-health.

This Duke, cominge on a tyme to Chelsie to dyne w*i*th him, fortuned to find him at the Church, singing in the
15 Quier, w*i*th a surplus on his backe; To whom, after service, as they went homeward together, arme in arme, the Duke said : " God body, god body, my lord Chauncelo*u*r, a p*a*rish Clark, a p*a*rish clark ! you dishonor the king *and* his office." " Nay," quoth S*ir* Thom*a*s Moore,
20 smilinge vppon the Duke, " Yo*u*r grace may not thinck that the king, yo*u*r master *and* myne, will w*i*th me, for servinge of god, his master, be offended, or therby count his office dishonoured."

Sings in the choir at Chelsea. Norfolk censures him for acting as a parish clerk.

When the Duke, beinge therunto often sollicited, by

MSS. H² J H³ H¹ A M S A² D T W X B.

Resigns the Great Seal. [16 May, 1532.]
The King promises continuance of his favour.

1. *testifyenge*] to testefye H³; *in* H² *to is crossed through before* testifyenge.   3. *of*] *Omitted in* X.   4. *the*] *Omitted in* S X.   5. *after should followe*] should after followe J S D W X; .should followe after A² B. (Harpsfield MSS. *vary*.)   7. *likely*] like M S.   8. *deere*] *Omitted in* S; good A² B.   8. *meane*] meanes X.   9. *kinge*] kinges grace A² D B.   9. *graces favour*] gracious fauour and good leaue A² D B.   10. *chargeable*] *Omitted in* W.   10. *roome*] office A².   10. *the*] *Omitted in* H² J A² D B.   12. *himself . . . serve*] hi*m* any longer vnable to serve A²; him altogether vnable any longer to serue D B.   12. *vnable*] *Omitted in* M; not able W X.
13. *Duke*] Duke of Norffolke A² D B.   14. *at the Church*] at Church J M; in þe Church W X.   16. *homeward*] home J A² D B.   17. *the*] They H³.   17. *said*] said vnto him A² D B.   17. *God body, god body*] Gods Body for that was his vsuall oath A²; god body god body for that was his vsuall oath D; God body for that was his vsiall oath B.   17–18. *lord Chauncelour*] Lord Lord Chauncellour D.   18. *a parish clark* (2)] *Second phrase interlineated in* H²; *once only in* A² B.   19. *quoth*] said A².   22. *of*] *Omitted in* J S A² D B.   22. *be*] *Omitted in* S.   22. *therby*] *Omitted in* W.

importunate sute had at length of the king obtayned for
Sir Thomas Moore a cleere discharge of his office, Then,
at a tyme convenient, by his highnes apointment, repayred he to his grace, to yealde vpp vnto him the greate
seale. Which, as his grace, with thancks and prayse for 5
his worthy service in that office, courteously at his
handes receaved, so pleased it his highnes [further] to
say * vnto him, that for the * service that he before
had done hym, in anye sute which he should after haue
vnto him, that either should concerne his honor (for that 10
word it liked his highnes to vse vnto him) or that should
appertaine vnto his profitt, he should find his highnes
good and gratious Lord vnto him.

More discusses economies necessary to prevent the dispersion of his family.

After he had thus geuen ouer the Chauncelourshipp,
and placed all his gentlemen *and* yeomen with Byshoppes 15
and noble men, *and* his eight watermen with the Lord
Awdley, that in the same office succeded him, to whom
also he gaue his greate barge, Then, calling vs all that
were his children vnto him, *and* asking our advise howe
we mighte nowe, in this decay of his abilyty (by the 20
surrender of his office so impaired that he could not, as
he was wont, and gladly wold, beare out the whole

MSS. H² J H³ H¹ A M S A² D T W X B.

1. *importunate*] importante H³; Importunate *upon* Importante
A.   1. *at length*] at the length S A².   1. *of the king*]
Omitted in J.   1. *of the king obtayned*] obteyned of the kinge
H³ X.   2. *of his office*] for his office M.   3. *tyme convenient*] convenient tyme X.   3. *apointment*] appointed W.
3–4. *repayred he*] he repayred S.   4. *the greate*] his great S.
4–5. *to yealde . . . grace*] *Omitted in* A² B.   (*Eyeslip*.)   5.
with thancks and prayse] with praise and thankes S A² D W X B.
6–7. *at his handes receaved*] receaued att his handes X.   7.
handes] hand S.   7. *receaved*] *Omitted in* W.   7. *it*]
Omitted in T.   7–8. *further to say*] to say more H² J; to say
further W.   8. *service*] good service H² J; good and great
A² D B.   8. *that*] *Omitted in* J M.   8. *he before*] before
he A² D W X B.   9. *done hym*] done for him T.   10.
for] *Omitted in* S A² D W X B.   10–11. *that word*] that word
he said A² D B; This word W X.   11. *highnes*] grace W X.
11. *vse*] say A².   11. *should*] would J.   12–13. *his highnes
good*] his heighnes a good J H¹ D X B; his Lord a good A² B.
14. *the*] his M.   14. *Chauncelourshipp*] Lord Chauncellorshipp
T.   16. *eight*] *Omitted in* A² D B.   16. *the*] my D B.
17. *that in*] that after in J.   17. *succeded*] succeed J; next
succeded S D W X.   18. *vs all*] vs J; all vs A² D B.   20.
this decay of his] his decay of his S; this his decaye of his T; this
decay of our W.   22. *whole*] *Omitted in* S.

[p. 22] charges of them all himself) from [t]hencforth be | able to
liue *and* contynewe together, as he wished we should;
when he sawe vs * silent, *and* in that case not redy to
shewe our opinions * to him, "Then will I," said he,
5 " shewe my poore minde vnto you. I haue bine brought
vpp," quoth he, " [at] Oxforde, at [an] Inne of Chauncery, at Lyncolnes Inne, *and* also [in] the kings Courte,
and so forth from the lowest degree to the highest, *and*
yeat haue I in yearely revennewes at this present left
10 me litle aboue an hundrethe pound*es* by the yeare, So
that nowe * muste we * hereafter, if we like to live
together, be contented to become contributaries together. But, by my councell, it shall not be best for vs
to fall to the lowest fare firste : we will not therefore
15 descend to Oxforde fare, nor [to] the fare of Newe Inne,
But we will begin with Lyncolnes Inne diet, where
many right worshipp*full and* of good yeares do live full

MSS. H² J H³ H¹ A M S A² D T W X B.

1. *charges*] chardge H³ M. 1. *all*] *Omitted in* X. 1. *thencforth*] henceforth H² J. 1. *be able*] to be able W. 2. *liue and*] *Omitted in* H³ H¹ A. 2. *wished*] would wish S D; should wish A² B. (*All* Harpsfield MSS. would wishe.) 3. *vs silent*] vs all silent H² J A² D B; vs be silent X. (*All* Harpsfield MSS. except R² omit all.) 3. *and*] *Omitted in* W. 3. *redy*] ready or willing A²; ready nor willing D B. 4. *opinions to him*] opinions therein to him H². 6. *quoth he*] *Omitted in* J D B. 6. *at Oxforde*] in Oxforde H² S; at Syon at Oxforde W; at Sion at Oxon X. 6. *an*] *Omitted in* H². 6–7. *of Chauncery*] in Chauncery S. 7. *and . . . Courte*] and also at the kings Courte H² H¹; and in the kings court J; and allsoe in the kings Bench Courte M. 8. *and*] *Omitted in* J. 8. *and . . . highest*] and soe forth from the lowest to the highest degree M. 8. *forth*] *Omitted in* X. 8. *lowest*] least T. 9–10. *in yearely . . . left me*] left me in yeerely reuenewes at this presente A². 9–10. *at this present left me*] *Transposed so as to follow* yeare (l. 10) *in* J; at that tyme lefte *interlineated in* S *and* me *omitted*; left me att this present W X. 10. *an hundreths poundes by the yeare*] a hundred pound by yeare S; C¹ per annum W; C¹¹ a yeere X. 11. *nowe*] *Omitted in* J. 11. *muste we*] we muste H² J T W. (*All* Harpsfield MSS. muste we.) 11. *hereafter*] needes herafter H³ H¹ A. 12. *be contented to*] *Omitted in* A² D B. 12–13. *be . . . together*] *Omitted in* J. (*Eyeslip*.) 12. *contributaries*] contributours S; tributatories T. 13. *not*] *Omitted in* W X. 13. *not be best for vs*] be best for vs not S. 14. *the*] this X. 14. *firste*] at the first A² D B. 14. *therefore*] then A². 15. *Oxforde fare*] Oxford-shire T; oxford fare first H³. 15. *nor to the*] nor the H²; nor to T. 15. *of Newe Inne*] of the Newe Inne D. 16. *with*] at A² D B.

well; whiche, if we find not our selves the first yeare
able to maynetayne, then will we the next yeare goe one
steppe downe to New Inne Fare, wherewith many an
honest man is well contented. If that exceed our ability
to, then will we the next yeare after descend to Oxford 5
fare, where many grave, learned, and auncient fathers
be contynewally conversant; which, if our [powre]
stretch not to mayntaine neyther, then may [we] yeat,
with baggs and walletes, go a begging together, and
hoping that for pity some good folke will geeue vs their 10
charytye, at euery mans doore to singe *salue Regina*, and
so still keepe company and bee mery together."

After his resignation, he is a poor man. And whereas you haue herd before, he was by the
kinge from a very worshippfull livinge taken into his
graces service, with whom, in all the greate and waighty 15
causes that concerned his highnes or the realme, he
consvmed and spent with paynefull cares, travell[s], and
trouble[s], aswell beyond the seas as within the realme,
in effecte the whole substaunce of his life, yeat with all
the gayne he gatt thereby, being never * wastfull spender 20
thereof, was he not able, after the resignacion of his
office of [the] Lord Chauncelor,* for the maynetenaunce
of him self and such as necessaryly belonged vnto him,

MSS. H² J H³ H¹ A M S A² D T W X B.

1. *well*] merrily S. 1–2. *find . . . able*] find ourselves
the first yeare not able S. 2. *able*] not able A². 2. *yeare*]
yeere after A². 2. *one*] a H³ H¹ A. 4. *well*] *Interlineated
in* H². 4. *exceed*] exceeds X. 4. *ability*] abillities X.
6. *learned, and auncient*] anciente and learned J. 6. *and*]
Omitted in A² B. 7. *contynewally conversant*] conversaunt
continually J; continually resident S. 7. *powre*] abilyty
H² J. 8. *stretch not*] be not able W X. 8. *we*] *Omitted
in* H². 10. *good*] *Interlineated in* H². 10. *vs*] *Omitted in* J.
12. *so still keepe*] soe still so keepe W, *the first* soe *being interlineated*; soe still to keepe X. 12. *and . . . together*] merrily
together J. 12. *bee*] to be W. 13. *haue*] *Omitted in* S.
14. *into*] vnto J A². 15. *and*] *Omitted in* W X. 17–18.
cares, travells, and troubles] cares travell and trouble H² J; cares
and trauyles and troubles H³; travell and troubles M; cares
travell and troubles X. 18. *aswell*] aswell the A². 18.
the realme] this Realme D B. 19. *substaunce*] substance and
principall time A² D B. 19. *all*] *Omitted in* J. 20.
never wastfull] never no wastfull H² M. 21. *was he not*] he
was not H³ H¹ A. 21. *his*] the A². 22. *of the*] of H² S.
22. *Lord*] *Omitted in* A². 22. *Chauncelor*] Chauncelorshipp
H² S A² D B. 23. *him* (2)] himselfe W.

Prepares family for his suffering and death

sufficiently to find meate, drinck, * fuell, apparell, *and* such other necessary charges. All the land that euer he purchased, w*h*ich also he purchased before he was * lord Chauncelo*ur*, was not, I am well assured, aboue the
5 valewe of xx^(ti) markes by the yeare. And after his dett*es* paid, he had not, I knowe, his chaine excepted, in gould *and* siluer lefte him the worth of one hundreth pound*es*.

And whereas vppon the holidayes during his highe [p. 23] Chauncelo*ur*shipp, one | of his gentlemen, when service
11 at the church was done, ordinarily vsed to come to my lady his wives pue, *and* say [vnto her], " Madame, my lord is gone," the next holiday after the surrender of his office *and* depa*r*ture of his gentlemen, he came vnto
15 my lady his wifes pue himself, *and* making a lowe curtesye, * said vnto her, " Madame, my lord is gone."

In the tyme somewhat before his trouble, he wold talke w*i*th his wife *and* children of the ioyes of heuen *and* * the paynes of hell, of the lyves of holy martires, of
20 their greiuous martirdome[s], of their marvelous patiens, *and* of their passions *and* deathes that they suffred rather

His fun: " Madam, my Lord is gone."

Prepares his family for his suffering and martyrdom.

MSS. H² J H³ H¹ A M S A² D T W X B.

1. *sufficiently*] sufficient A². 1. *find*] find out W. 1. *meate, drinck*] meate and drinke T. 1. *drinck, fuell*] drinck and fuell H². 1. *apparell*] and apparell H³ H¹ A. 2. *other*] Omitted *in* A². 2. *All*] And all H³. 2. *land*] landes X. 2. *euer he*] he euer W. 3. *which also he purchased*] Omitted *in* J S A². 3. *was*] was euer H². 4. *well assured*] sure W X. 5. *the yeare*] yeare S. 7–8. *the worth . . . poundes*] aboue þe value of one hundred pounds H¹; aboue the worth of 100^(li) A²; to the worth of An hundreth poundes D B. 9. *the*] Omitted *in* H³. 9–10. *his highe Chauncelourshipp*] high Chauncellourshipp J; his highe office of Chauncellorshippe H³ H¹; A *as* H³ H¹, *but* hyght *for* highe; the highe Chauncellorshippe T. 11. *at the church*] Omitted *in* S; at his Church D. 12. *say*] would say A². 12. *vnto her*] Omitted *in* H² J. 13. *holiday*] Sunday A². 14. *and . . . gentlemen*] Interlineated *in* H². 14. *gentlemen*] gentleman T. 14. *came*] went A². 15. *wifes*] wief X. 15. *himself*] himself with his cap in his hand A². 15. *and*] Omitted *in* H³ H¹ A A². 16. *said*] he said H². 17. *In the tyme*] Omitted *in* S. 17. *trouble*] troubles W X. 18. *talke . . . children*] talke somewhat of his wife and children T. 19. *and the*] and of the H² B; & H¹ A M T W X. (*All* Harpsfield MSS. *except* B and the; and B.) 19. *of the*] or the X. 19. *of* (3)] of the D B. 19. *of* (4)] and of J. 20. *martirdomes*] martirdome H². 21. *and of*] of D B.

then they wold offend god; And what an happie *and* blessed thinge it was, for the love of god, to suffer losse of goods, imprisonem*ent*, losse of lands *and* life also. He wold * further say * vnto them that, vppon his faith, if he might p*er*ceyue his wife and children wold incourage 5 him to dye in a good cause, it should so comforte him that, for very ioy thereof, it wold make him merelye run*ne* to deathe. He shewed [vnto] them afore what trouble might [after] fall vnto him; wherewith *and* the like vertuous talke he had so longe before his [trouble] 10 incouraged them, that when he after fell into the trouble indeede, his trouble to them was a greate deale the lesse : *Quia spicula pr[e]uisa minus laedunt.*

Advice to Cromwell.
Nowe vppon this resignem*ent* of his office, came [Master] Thomas Cromewell, then in the kings highe 15 favou*r*, to Chelsey to him, [with] a message frome the kinge; Wherein when they had throughly commo*n*ed together : "M*aster* Cromewell," quoth he, "you are nowe entered into the service of a most noble, wise *and* liberall prince. If you will followe my poore advise, 20 you shall, in yo*ur* councell gevinge vnto his grace, ever

MSS. H² J H³ H¹ A M S A² D T W X B.

1. *offend god*] god offend W.   1. *an*] a D X; *omitted in* W.
1. *and*] and a J X.   2. *for*] that for T.   2. *losse*] the losse H³ H¹ A T.   3. *imprisonement*] and imprisonment W X.
4. *further say*] say further H².   4. *if*] that if W X.   5. *might*] could W X.   6. *a*] *Omitted in* B.   7. *wold*] should A².   8. *runne*] to runne J W X.   8. *vnto*] *Omitted in* H² J T.
9. *trouble*] troubles W X.   9. *after*] *Omitted in* H² J.   9. *the*] with the D B.   10. *his trouble*] his deathe H²; *omitted in* M S; his troubles indeede X.   11. *incouraged*] incourage X.   11. *he after fell*] he after that fell T; hee after hee fell X.   11. *the*] *Omitted in* H³ H¹ A T.   11. *trouble*] troubles T W X.   12. *trouble*] troubles W X.   12. *to them was*] to him was J; indeed was A²; was to them X.   12. *was*] were W.   12–13. *the lesse*] lesse A²; the les greeiuous D B.
13. *spicula*] *Space left in* A².   13. *preuisa*] prouisa H².
13. *laedunt*] ladunt A²; D B *add after this* : dangers foreseene hurt little.   14. *this*] his S; the W.   15. *Master*] Sir H² J.
15–16. *in . . . favour*] high in the kings favour S A²; highly esteemed in the kings fauour D; B *as* D *but of for* in. (*All* Harpsfield MSS. high in the kinges fauour.)   16–17. *to Chelsey . . . kinge*] with a message to Chellsey to him from þe king W; X *as* W, *but omitting* with.   16. *to him*] *Omitted in* S.   16. *with*] in H²; on J.   17. *had*] *Omitted in* W.   19. *noble*] *Omitted in* H³ H¹ A.   19–20. *wise and liberall*] and wise liberall T.   21. *your*] *Omitted in* J.

Foresees the administering of Oaths 57

tell him what he owght to doe, but never what he is
able to doe. So shall you shewe yourself a true faithfull
servant and a right worthy Councelour. For if [a] Lion
knewe his owne strength, harde were it for any man to
5 rule him."
    Shortly therevppon was there a Comission directed to *Cranmer pronounces the marriage with Katherine void. [23 May, 1533.] The King marries Anne Boleyn.*
Cranmer, then [Arch]-Bishoppe of Canterbury, to deter-
mine the matter of the matrimony betweene the king
and * Queene Katherine, at St. Albones, where, accord-
10 ing to the kings mynd, it was throughly determined :
who, pretending he had no iustice at the Popes hand[s],
frome thenceforth sequestered himself from the Sea of
Roome, and so maried the Ladye Anne Bulleyne; which *More foresees the administering of Oaths.*
Sir Thomas Moore vnderstanding, said vnto me : " God
15 geeue grace, sonne, that thes matters within a while be
not confirmed with othes." I, at that tyme seing no
likelyhoode thereof, yeat fearing least for his forespeak-
inge it wold the sooner come to pas, waxed therefore for
his so sayeing much offended with him.
20   It Fortuned not longe before the coming of Queene *Refuses to be present at Anne's coronation; but accepts the Bishops' money for a gown. [1533.]*
Anne thoroughe [the] * streetes [of] London * frome the
Tower to westminster to her Coronation, that he receaved
a letter frome the Bishopp[es] of Dyrham, Bathe and Winchester, [requestinge him] bothe to keepe them company

MSS. H² J H³ H¹ A M S A² D T W X B.

1. *him*] Omitted in T. 1. *what* (2)] tell him what J. 3. *servant*] subiecte H³; subiect *underlined in* B *and* servant *written over*. 3. *a* (1)] Omitted in W X. 3. *right*] right wise H³ A. 3. *a* (2)] the H² J. 6. *was there*] ther was H³ H¹ A. 6. *directed*] Omitted in S. 7. *then*] the A². 7. *Arch-Bishoppe*] Bishoppe H². 9. *and Queene*] and the Queene H² H³ A A²; & Queene H¹, *with* þe *interlineated and crossed through*. 10. *it*] that J. 10. *determined*] fynished J. 11. *pretending*] pretended A². 11. *he had*] that he had J. 11. *hands*] hand H² S W X. 12. *thenceforth*] thenceforth therefore S A² D W X B. 12. *sequestered*] he Sequestred D. 15. *that*] quoth he that T. 16. *no*] little S. 17. *for*] that for A; omitted in S. 18. *it*] that J. 18. *the*] Omitted in X. 18. *waxed*] wax A². 19. *so*] Omitted in J M. 19. *much*] very much D B; greatlie W X. 20. *not*] that not M. 20. *Queene*] the Queene J. 21. *thoroughe*] in tryumphe through D B. 21. *the streetes of London*] London streetes H². 22. *he*] Sir Thomas Moore S. 23. *a letter*] letteres W. 23. *Bishoppes*] Bishopp H² M A². 24. *requestinge him*] Omitted in H²; requesting them W. 24. *bothe . . . company*] to beare them company J.

frome the Tower to the Coronation, *and* also to take twenty pound*e*s that by the berer | thereof they had [p. 24] sent * him to buy him a gowne with; w*hi*ch he thanckefully receaving, *and* at home still tarienge, at their next meting said meerily vnto them : 5
"My lords, in the letters w*hi*ch you lately sent me, you required two thinges of me, The tone whereof, sith I was so well content to graunt you, The tother therefore I thought I might be the boulder to denye you. And like as the tone, [because] I took you for no beggers, *and* 10 my self I knewe to be no riche man, I thoghte I might the rather fullfill, So thother did put me in remembraunce of an Empe*r*our that had ordained a lawe that whosoeu*er* comitted a certaine offence (w*hi*ch I nowe remember not) excepte it were a virgine, should suffer the paynes 15 of death, such a reuerens had he to virginity. Nowe so it happened that the first comitter [of that offence] was indeed a virgine, whereof themp*er*our hearing was in no small p*er*plexity, as he that by some example fayne wold haue had that lawe to haue ben put in execution. 20 Wherevppon when his councell had sate long, solembly

Marginal: Parable of the offending virgin. Warns the Bishops.

MSS. H² J H³ H¹ A M S A² D T W X B.

1. *to the Coronation*] to Westminster to the Coronacion W X. 3. *him* (1)]] to him H². 3. *a gowne*] Omitted in A². 3. *with*] Omitted in S. 3. *he*] Omitted in M. 4. *receaving*] receaved J W X. 4. *tarienge*] remaininge W X. 5. *their*] the M. 6. *the*] your S. 6. *letters*] letter D B. 6. *which*] Omitted in T. 7. *required*] requested X. 7–8. *sith I*] seeing I, W X. 8. *therefore*] Omitted in H¹ S. 9. *be the boulder*] the boulder be D B. 9. *boulder*] more bolder T. 9. *And*] As B. 10. *because*] Omitted in H². 11. *I knewe*] Omitted in M; I knowe J S T W X. 11. *riche*] very ryche H³ H¹ A. 12. *rather*] better J. 12. *thother*] other J M S A² W. 13. *had*] he T. 13. *that* (2)]] Omitted in W. 14. *comitted*] had Committed D B. 14–15. *which . . . not*] Omitted in J. 15. *paynes*] payne S. 16. *had he*] he had A². 16–17. *so it happened*] so happed it S; it so hapned A² D X B; it happened W. 17. *it*] Omitted in H³ M; omitted here in A *and crossed through after* happened. 17. *of that offence*] thereof H² J; of þe offence H¹. 18. *indeed*] Omitted in H³ H¹ A S A². 18. *themperour*] this Emperour S D B. 19. *as*] and J. 19. *that by*] by T. 19. *some*] some small A². 19–20. *fayne wold*] wolde fayne H³ H¹ A S A² T W X. (Harpsfield MSS. faine would.) 20. *to haue ben*] Omitted in H³ H¹ A S A² T W; beene • X. (Harpsfield MSS. to haue bene.)

Parable of the offending virgin 59

debatinge this case, sodenly arose there vpp one of his
councell, a good playne man, among them, *and* said:
'Why make you so much adoe, my lord*es*, about so
small a matter? Let her first be deffloured, *and* then
5 after * may she * be devoured.' And so thoughe yo*ur*
lordshippes haue in the matter of the matrimony
hitherto kepte yo*ur* selves pure virgines, yeat take good
head, my lord*es*, that you keepe yo*ur* virginity still.
For some there be that by procuringe yo*ur* lord*s*hippes
10 first at the coronacion to be present, *and* next to preach
for the setting forth of it, *and* Finally to write bookes to
all the world in defens therof, are desirous to deffloure
you; *and* when they haue defloured you, then will they
not faile soone after to devoure you. Nowe my lordes," He may be devoured,
15 quoth he, " it lieth not in my power but that they maye but will not be de-
devoure me; but god being my good lord, I will provide flowered.
that they shall neuer deffloure me."
In Continewans,* when the king sawe that he could The prophecies of
by no manner of benefitt*es* winne him to his side, Then, the Nun of Canterbury
20 loe, went he aboute by terrors *and* threates to drive him are made a cause of
thereunto. The begininge of w*hich* trouble* grewe by quarrel against
MSS. H² J H³ H¹ A M S A² D T W X B. More.

1. *this*] the S. 1. *this case*] the case vpon the matter W X.
1. *there vpp*] therevpon J ; vp M T W X.   2. *man*] Interlineated in H².   3. *my lordes*] *Omitted in* J.   5. *may she*]
she may H² A² ; *omitted in* X, *which here has* lett her *crossed
through.*   5. *so*] *Omitted in* J.   6. *lordshippes*] Lordshipp
J ; lorshippes H³.   6. *the matrimony*] matrimonye J X.
8. *lordes*] Lord X.   8. *virginity*] virginities H³ H¹ A D B.
9. *there be*] be there H³ H¹ A S T.   9. *be that*] *Omitted in* X.
9. *by*] *Omitted in* A².   9–10. *your lordshippes first*] first your
Lordships A².   11. *the*] *Omitted in* H³ T.   11. *forth of it*]
of it forth J.   12. *all the world*] the whole world S.   12.
defens] the defence J H¹ M.   13. *and* . . . *you*] *Omitted
in* A² X. (*Eyeslip.*)   13. *when*] after when M ; then when W.
13. *haue*] had T.   13. *then*] *Omitted in* J.   13–14. *will they
not*] the (= *they*) will not J ; will not they M X.   15. *quoth
he*] *Omitted in* S.   15. *power*] poore H³.   16. *devoure*] deflowre B.   16. *good*] *Omitted in* T.   16. *provide*] soe
prouide W X.   17. *that they shall*] that shall J ; they shall
H³ H¹ A.   18. *Continewans*] Continewans of tyme H², *with*
of tyme *interlineated*; Continuance of tyme D.   18. *that*]
Omitted in A² X.   18–19. *could* . . . *benefittes*] could not by
any manner of benefittes X.   19. *benefittes*] benefitt M.
19. *winne*] coniure W.   20. *loe*] *Omitted in* J A².   20.
went he] he went H¹ ; went X.   20. *aboute*] *Omitted in* W X.
20. *terrors*] terror H³ H¹ A.   20. *drive*] win A².   21.
trouble] troubles H² W X.

> occasion of a certaine Nonne dwelling in canterbury, for
> her vertue *and* holines among the people not a litle
> esteemed; vnto whom, for that cause, many religious
> persons, doctors of Divynity, *and* divers others of good
> worshippe of the laity vsed to resorte; who, affirming 5
> that she had revelations from god to geeue the king
> warninge of his wicked life, and of thabuse of the sword
> *and* aucthoryty comitted vnto him by god, And vnder-
> standing my lord of Rochester, Byshopp Fisher, to be a
> man of notable vertuos livinge *and* learninge, repaired 10
> to Rochester, *and* there disclosed to him all her revela-
> cions, desiring | his advise *and* councell therein; w*hich* [p. 25]
> the Bishoppe perceyvinge might well stand with the
> Lawes of god *and* his holy Churche, advised her (as she
> before had warninge *and* intended) to goe to the kinge 15
> her self, *and* to let him vnderstand the whole circum-
> staunce thereof. Whervppon she went to the kinge,
> *and* told him all her revelations, *and* so retou*r*ned home
> againe. And in shorte space after, she, making a voiage
> to the Nonnes of Sion, by meanes of one m*aster* Raynolds, 20
> a father of the same house, there fortuned concerninge
> such secretes as had bine revealed vnto her (some p*a*rte
> wherof seemed to touche the matter of the kings supre-
> macie *and* mariage, whiche shortly therevppon folowed)
> to enter into talke with S*i*r Thomas Moore; who, not- 25

Side notes:
- The Nun discloses her revelations to Fisher, who advises her to go to the King.
- The Nun talks with More, whose conduct in this case is blameless. [1533.]

MSS. H² J H³ H¹ A M S A² D T W X B.

1. *occasion*] reason D T.   1. *dwelling*] in dwellinge W.
2. *holines*] holines of life X.   5. *worshippe*] woorth X.   5.
affirming] affirmed W X.   6. *revelations*] revelacion M A².
8–9. *vnderstanding*] vnderstandinge that M.   10. *vertuos*]
vertues M.   11. *her*] his B.   13. *might*] that it might
D B.   13. *well*] Omitted here in D, but very well inserted below
after god (*l*. 14).   14. *and his*] & like wise with his D.   14.
his] *l* interlineated in H².   14. *holy*] Omitted in J.   16. *to
let*] let H³ H¹ A T.   17. *thereof. Whervppon*] of the matter
wherevpon W X.   18. *told him*] acquainted him with D B.
18. *so*] Omitted in J.   19. *shorte*] a short H¹.   19. *a*]
Omitted in B.   19. *voiage*] Jorney H³ H¹ A T.   20.
Nonnes] nunne J; monkes T.   20. *meanes*] the meanes J A².
20. *one*] Omitted in H³ H¹ A T A².   20. *Raynolds*] Reinold D.
21. *a*] Omitted in T.   21. *the same*] that J.   22. *secretes*]
fortunes A².   22. *had bine*] shee had J.   23. *wherof* |
thereof T.   23–24. *wherof . . . supremacie*] of the matter
therof seemed to touch the kings supremacy A².   23. *seemed*]
Omitted in W X.   23. *the matter of*] Omitted in W.   24.
therevppon folowed] followed therevpon W X.   25. *with*] of S.

withstanding he might well, at that tyme, without
daunger of any lawe (thoughe after, as himself had
prognosticated before, [those] matters were stablished by
statutes *and* confirmed [by] othes) freely *and* saflye haue
5 talked with her therein; Neue*r*theles, in all the comunication betweene them (as in p*r*oces it appeared) had
alwaye so discreetely demeaned himself that he deserved
not to be blamed, but contrary wise to be comended *and*
praised.

10 And had he not bine one that in all his greate office[s] *and* doings for the kinge *and* [the] realme, so many yeares together, had from all curruption of wronge doinge or bribes taking kept him self so cleere that no man was able therew*i*th once to blemishe him, [or make
15 any iust quarrell agaynst him], Itt wold, without doubte, in this troubleous tyme of the kings indignation towardes him, haue bine deapely laid to his charge, and of the kings highnes most favorably accepted, As in the case of one Parnell it most manifestly appeared; against
20 whom, because S*ir* Thom*a*s Moore, while he was Lord Chaunceloµr, at the suite of one Vaghen, his aduersary, had made a decree, This Parnell to [his] highnes most greiuously complayned that S*ir* Thom*a*s Moore, for makinge the [same] decree, had of the [same] Vaughen

He is proved innocent of taking reward from Vaughan.

[20 Jan., 1530/31.]

MSS. H² J H³ H¹ A M S A² D T W X B.

1. *he might*] þat he might D B.   1. *at*] *Omitted in* T.   3. *those*] thes H² H¹ D.   3–4. *by statutes*] *Omitted in* S.   4. *and*] or H³.   4. *by*] with H².   5. *with her therein*] therin with her B.   5–6. *comunication*] Communications H¹.   6. *proces*] processe of tyme J B.   7. *alwaye*] he alwayes D. 10. *all*] *Omitted in* S.   10. *offices*] office H² J.   11. *the* (2)] *Omitted in* H² J H³ H¹ A.   13. *so*] *Omitted in* D B.   13. *cleere*] cleane J.   14. *therewith once*] once therewith B. 14. *once*] *Omitted in* J H¹ T.   14–15. *or . . . him*] *Omitted in* H² J. (*Eyeslip*.)   15. *any*] *Omitted in* S.   15. *doubte*] all doubt X.   16. *troubleous*] troublesome J S A² D X B. 16. *kings indignation*] Kings wroth and indignation J.   16. *towardes*] against S.   18. *most*] *Omitted in* J.   19. *it*] that J.   20. *because*] *Omitted in* J A² T.   21. *one*] *Omitted in* H³.   22. *his highnes most*] the kinges highnes most H²; the Kinges highnes had J. (*All* Harpsfield MSS. *the kinges highnes*.)   24. *makinge the*] the making of the A². 24. *same* (1)] *Omitted in* H² J; said M A² W X B.   24. *the same* (2)] the said H² H³ H¹ A; one X.

The case of Vaughan

(vnable for the gowte * to travaile abrode himself) * by thandes of his wife taken a faire greate gilte Cuppe for a bribe. Who thervppon, by the kings apointment, being called before the whole Councell, where that matter was haynously laid to his chardge, furthwith confessed that 5 forasmuch as that Cuppe was, longe after the [foresaid] decree, brought him for a newyeares gyfte, he, vppon her importunate pressinge vppon him therefore, of curtesye refused not to receaue it.

Then the Lord of Wiltshire (for hatred of his religion 10 preferrer of this sute) with muche reioycinge said vnto the Lordes, " Lo, * did I not tell you, my lordes, that you shoulde fynd this matter trewe?" Wherevppon Sir Thomas Moore desired their lordships that as they had courteously herd | him tell thone parte of his tale, so [p. 26] they wold vouchsafe of their honors indifferently to hear 16 thother. After which obtayned, he further declared vnto them That, albeit he had indeed, with much worke, receaved that cuppe, yeat immediately theruppon he caused his butler to fill it with wyne, and of that 20 cupp drancke to her; and that when [he had soe donne, and] she * pleadged him, then as freely as her husband had geuen it to him, Euen so freely gave he

MSS. H² J H³ H¹ A M S (to l. 21, when; then missing to l. 1, p. 66, that shoulde be) A² D T W X B.

1. *for the gowte to travaile abrode himself*] for the gowte abrode himself to travaile H²; to goe for the gowte or to trauell W; for the gowte himselfe to travell abroad X.   2. *greate*] *Omitted in* D.   4. *whole*] *Omitted in* J; kinges whole W X. 4. *Councell*] body of the Counsell D B.   5. *haynously laid*] layd haynously S; full heinously layd D B.   6. *foresaid*] *Omitted in* H²; same S.   7. *brought him*] brought vnto him J. 7–8. *vppon her*] at her S A² D X; at the W. (*All* Harpsfield MSS. at her.)   8. *importunate*] ymportunytie M.   8. *him*] *Omitted in* T.   8. *therefore*] *Omitted in* W; therof X.   9. *receaue*] take J W.   11. *this*] his H³ H¹ A T.   12. *did* . . . *lordes*] my lordes loe did I not tell you my lords H²; my Lordes did I not tell you J; did not I tell yow my Lordes M.   14. *lordships*] worshipps J.   14. *had*] *Omitted in* H¹.   15. *courteously herd*] heard curteously B.   15. *him*] hym selfe H³; *omitted in* D B.   18. *he* . . . *with*] indeed had with J.   19. *that*] the W X.   19. *he*] *Omitted in* A² T B.   20. *fill*] sett T.   20. *it*] that J.   21. *drancke*] drinke J T; hee drunke H¹.   21–22. *he* . . . *him*] she had pledged him H² J. 22–23. *then* . . . *him*] *Omitted in* A²; then as freely as her husband gaue it him X.   23. *it to*] *Omitted in* W; *in* H² *to is interlineated.*

The cases of Mistress Crocker and Gresham 63

the same vnto her agayne, to geeue vnto her husband
for his neweyeares gifte; which, at his instant requeste,
thoughe muche against her will, at length yeat she was
[fayne] to receave, as her self, *and* certayne other there,
5 * presently before them deposed. * Thus was the greate
mountayne turned scant to a litle molehill.

So I remember that at an other tyme, vppon a newe   *And known*
yeares day, there came to him one mistres Crocker, a *to have refused*
Rich widowe, for whom, with no small paine,* he had   *money from Mistress*
10 made a decree in the Chauncery against the Lord of *Crocker.*
Arondell, * to present him with a payre of gloves, *and*
fourty poundes in Angels in them, for a newe yeares
gifte. Of whom he thancfully receyuing the gloues, but
refucing the money, said vnto her : " Mistres, since it
15 were againste good manner[s] to forsake a gentlewomans
newe yeares gifte, I am content to take your gloues, but
as for your money I vtterley refuse." So, muche against
her mynde, inforced he her to take her gold againe.

And one master Gresham likewise, having [at] the   *He had accepted a*
20 same tyme a cause depending in the Chauncerye [before] *cup from Master*
him, sent him for a newe yeares gifte a faire gilted cuppe, *Gresham, but had*
the fashion whereof he very well likinge, caused one of *given in return one of greater value.*

MSS. H² J H³ H¹ A M A² D T W X B *only*.

1. *the same vnto her*] to her the same D B.   1. *vnto her*
(1)] *In* H² vn *is interlineated; omitted in* H³ H¹ A T W.
2. *his* (1)] *Interlineated in* H² *over* her *crossed through*.   3. *at
length yeat*] yet at length J.   4. *fayne*] *Omitted in* H².   5.
presently . . . deposed] before them deposed presently H²; presently deposed before them J; present before them deposed
H³; presentlie deposed M B.   5. *the*] this D B; theis W.
6. *litle*] *Omitted in* J A².   7. *at an other*] another H³; on
another H¹ A.   7. *a*] *Omitted in* H³.   8. *him*] me D.
8. *one*] *Omitted in* T.   8. *one mistres Crocker*] a gentlewoman
called mistress Croker D B.   9. *Rich*] *Omitted in* T.   9.
paine] paines H² J.   10–11. *of Arondell*] Arrundell H³ H¹ A.
11. *to*] and to H².   12. *in*] of A².   13. *gifte*] guifts H¹.
13–16. *Of whom . . . gifte*] *Omitted in* D. (*Eyeslip.*)   13. *receyuing*] received J T.   14. *it*] that J.   15. *againste*]
Interlineated in H².   15. *manners*] manner H² A T. (*All
Harpsfield MSS. except* R² maner.)   15. *forsake*] refuse H³.
15. *gentlewomans*] gentlewomens H³.   16. *take*] receave J.
17. *refuse*] refuse yt H³ H¹ A; the same D; refuse the same B.
19–20. *having . . . tyme*] at the same time hauing A².   19–20.
at the same tyme] the same tyme H² W; *omitted in* J.   20.
before] against H² J.   22. *caused*] and caused J.

his owne (thoughe not in his fantasie of so good a fashion, yeat better in valewe) to be browght [him] out of his chamber, which he willed the messenger, in recompens, to deliuer to his master; *and* vnder other condicion[e] wold he in no wise receave it. 5

Many * things moe of like effect, for the declaration of his innocency *and* cleerenes from all corruption or evill affection, could I heare reherse besides; which, for tedioussnes omyttynge, I refer to the readers by these fewe before remembred examples, with their owne 10 iudgme*n*tes wiselye to weighe *and* consider [the same].

<small>More and Fisher attainted of misprision of treason, the King hoping to terrify More into consent to the marriage. [1534.]</small>
Att [the] Parliame*n*t folowing, was there put into the lordes house a bill to attaint the Nonne *and* divers other religious p*er*sons of highe treson, *and* the Bishoppe of Rochester, Si*r* Thom*a*s Moore, *and* certaine others of 15 misprision of treason; The kinge presupposinge of likeli-hood that this bill would be to Si*r* Thom*a*s Moore so | [p. 27 troublous *and* terrible that it wold force him to relent and condiscend to his request—wherein his grace was

<small>More summoned [before a Committee of the Privy Council, 1534.]</small>
much deceued. To which bill Si*r* Thom*a*s Moore was a 20 suter p*er*sonally to be receaved in his owne defens to make awnswer. But the kinge, not likinge that, assigned

MSS. H² J H³ H¹ A M A² D T W X B *only*.

<small>2. him] *Omitted in* H² J.   3–4. *in recompens . . . master*] to deliver to his mistres in recompence H².   4. *to* (2)] *Interlineated in* H².   4. *condicione*] condicions H² A².   5. *wold he*] he would D B.   5. *receave*] receiue or accepte D; receiue it or accept therof B.   6. *Many things*] Many other things H².   8. *affection*] affections H¹ W X.   8. *reherse*] alleadge & rehearse D B.   10. *fewe*] *Omitted in* A² B.   10. *before*] *In* H² be *is interlineated*; fower X.   11. *weighe and*] *Omitted in* J.   11. *the same*] *Omitted in* H² J.   12. *Att*] *Omitted in* W X.   12. *the*] this H² J.   12. *folowing*] *Omitted in* J.   12–13. *was there put . . . a bill*] was there a Bill putt into the Lordes house W; there was a Bill putt into the Lordes house X.   12. *into*] in T.   13. *Nonne*] Nunne of Canterbury D B.   14–15. *and the Bishoppe . . . others*] and Sir Thomas Moore & the Bishop of Rochester and certaine other M.   15–18. *Rochester, Sir Thomas Moore . . . Sir Thomas Moore so troublous*] Rochester and Sir Thomas More so troublous W. (*Eyeslip.*)   15. *certaine*] diuers H³ X.   15–16. *of misprision*] in suspision T.   16–17. *of . . . bill*] that this Bill of likelywhood X.   17. *that*] *Omitted in* J.   18. *it*] that J.   20. *a*] an earnest D B; *omitted in* W X.   21–22. *in his . . . awnswer*] to make answer in his owne defence H¹.   21. *in his owne defens*] in the Parliament openly in his owne deffence D B.   22. *that*] of that T.</small>

the Bishoppe of Canturburye, * the lorde Chaunceloure, the Duke of Norffolke, *and* m*a*ster Cromwell, at a day *and* place appointed, to call S*i*r Thomas Moore before them. At w*hi*ch tyme I, thincking [that] I had a good 5 opportunitye, ernestly advised him to labour vnto those Lordes for the helpe of his discharge out of [that] Parliament bill. Who awneswered me he wold.

Roper begs him to labour for discharge out of the Bill.

And at his cominge before them, accordinge to theyr appointm*e*nt, they intertayned him very freindly, 10 wyllinge him to sitte downe w*i*th them, w*hi*ch in no wise he wold. Then began the Lord Chancelo*u*r to declare vnto him howe many wayes the kinge had shewed his love *and* favor towards hym; howe faine he would have had hym contynewe in his office; howe glad he would 15 haue bine to haue heaped more benefitt*es* vppon him; and finally howe he could aske no worldly hono*u*r nor p*r*ofitte at his highnes hand*es* that were likely to be denyed him; hopinge, by the declaracion of the kings kindnes *and* affection towar*des* him, to provoke him to 20 recompence his grace w*i*th the like agayne; *and* vnto those things that the parliam*e*nt, the Bishops, *and* vniu*er*sities had already passed, to adde his consente.

The Lord Chancellor enlarges upon the King's goodness to More, hoping thus to win him over in the matter of the marriage.

To this S*i*r Thomas Moore mildlye made awneswer, sayenge : " No man lyuinge is there, my lordes, that

More acknowledges the King's goodness, but remains firm.

MSS. H² J H³ H¹ A M A² D T W X B *only*.

1. *Bishoppe*] Archbuyshopp J.   1. *the lorde Chaunceloure*] and the lorde Chaunceloure *interlineated in* H².   2. *at*] to H³ H¹ A D T.   4. *thincking that I*] thincking I, H²; thincked that I, B.   4–5. *a good opportunitye*] opportunytie H³ H¹ A ; then a good opportunitie A² D W X B.   5. *to*] for to T.
5–6. *vnto . . . helpe*] with these Lordes for the helping W ; X *as* W, *but* those *for* these.   6. *discharge*] charge T.   6. *that*] the H² D B.   7. *he wold*] he would so doe D B ; would X.   10. *wyllinge*] who willing W X.   10. *him*] them X.
10. *sitte*] sett T.   11. *wold*] would doe D B.   13. *howe*] & how D.   14. *contynewe*] to continue H³ H¹ A W X ; continued A² D B.   14. *glad*] gladly J.   15. *vppon him*] vnto him M.
16. *nor*] or H³ H¹ A ; omitted in M.   17. *handes*] hand A².
18. *by*] that by W X ; at A².   19. *kindnes*] highnes B.
19. *and*] or D.   19. *affection*] favour J.   20. *agayne*] gaine D.   22. *vniuersities*] the vniuersityes A² D B.   22. *already passed*] passed already A².   22. *adde*] yeld J ; adde & yeald D B.   22. *his*] *Interlineated in* H² *over* their *crossed through*.
23. *To this*] Omitted in A².   23. *made awneswer*] answered J.
24. *No man*] None H³.   24. *lyuinge . . . lordes*] is there my Lords lyvinge T ; lyveinge is there my Lord is there X.

woulde with better will doe the thinge that shoulde be
acceptable to the kings highnes then I, which must
needes confes his manyfold * goodnes *and* bountifull
benefites * most benignely bestowed on me. Howebeit
I veryly hoped that I should neuer haue herd of this 5
matter more, consideringe that I haue, from tyme to
tyme, alwayes from the beginninge, so plainely *and* truly
declared my minde vnto his grace, which his highnes to
me euer seemed, like a most gracious prince, very well to
accepte, neuer myndinge, as he said, to molest me more 10
theerewith; Since which tyme any further thinge that
was able to move me to [any] chainge coulde I neuer
find; And if I could, there is none in all the world that
[w]ould haue bine gladder of it then I."

The King's deputies accuse More of having incited the King to write [1521] the *Assertio septem sacramentorum*, maintaining the Pope's authority.

Many things more * were there of like [sorte] vttered 15
on bothe sides. * But in the ende, when they sawe they
could by no manner of perswasions remove him from
his former determinacion, | Then began they more terri- [p. 28]
blie to touche him; tellinge him that the kinges highnes
had giuen them in Commaundment, yf they coulde by 20
noe gentellnes winne him, in his name with his greate
ingratitude to charge him; That never was there servaunte to his soveraigne so villaynous, nor subiecte to

MSS. H² J H³ H¹ A M S (*from* that shoulde be, *l.* 1, *onwards*)
A² D T W X B.

1. *thinge*] k (= " *king* ") A².   1. *be*] *Interlineated in* H².
2. *acceptable*] accepted W X.   2. *I*] *Omitted in* M.   3–4.
manyfold goodnes and bountifull benefites] manyfold benefites and
bountifull goodnes H² J; W X *as text, but* benefitt *for* benefites.
(*All* Harpsfield MSS. manifolde goodnes and bountifull benefites.)
4. *most benignely*] *Omitted in* H¹.   8. *his grace*] his highnes
A²; the kings heighnes D B.   8. *highnes*] grace A² D B.
8–9. *to me euer seemed*] ever to mee seemed M; euer seemed to
me S T; to me seemed euer A².   10. *myndinge*] meaning D B.
10. *to molest*] neuer to molest M.   12. *any*] *Omitted in* H².
12. *coulde I*] I could H³ H¹ A.   14. *would*] could H².   14.
I] my Selfe D B.   15. *were there of like sorte*] of like effecte
were there H².   15. *of like sorte vttered*] vttered of like sorte
M.   15–16. *vttered . . . sides*] on both sides vttered H² J,
on *being interlineated in* H².   17. *by*] with W X.   17.
manner of] meanes of J; *omitted in* M.   17. *perswasions*]
persuacion S A² T.   18. *determinacion*] determinations J.
19. *him* (1)] *Omitted in* T.   19. *tellinge*] *Omitted in* A².   20.
by] with A².   21. *gentellnes*] gentle meanes W X.   21.
in] on A² D.   21–22. *with . . . him*] to chardge him with his
great ingratitude W.   23. *soveraigne*] master J.

his prince so trayterous as he; For he, by his subtill
synister sleygh*tes* moste vnnaturallie procuring *and*
provokinge him to sett forth a booke of the *Assertion of
the seuen sacramen*tes and mainetayn[aunce] of the Popes
5 aucthorytie, had caused him, to his dishono*ur* througheoute all Christendome, to put a sword in to the Popes
hand*es* to fight against hime selfe.

When they had thus layd forth all the terrors they More had remonstrated with the King on this matter.
coulde ymagine againste him : " My lord*es*," quothe he,
10 " these terro*urs* [be] argumen*tes* for Children, and not
for me. But to aunswere that wherewith you doe chifly
birden me, I beleave the kinges highnes of his hono*ur*
will neuer lay that to my charge; For none is there that
can in that pointe say in my excuse more then his highnes
15 himself, who right well knoweth that I neuer was procurer nor councelo*ur* of his maiestye thereunto; But
after it was finished, by his graces apointm*ent and* consent of the makers of the same, only a sorter out *and* *
placer of the principall matters therin contayned.
20 Wherein when I founde the Popes aucthority highly
aduaunced, *and* with stronge argumen*tes* mightlye
defended, I said vnto his grace : ' I must put yo*ur*
highnes in remembraunce of one thinge, *and* that is this.

MSS. H² J H³ H¹ A M S A² D T W X B.

2–3. *procuring and provokinge*] prouokinge and procuring W X.
3. *Assertion of*] *Omitted* A². 4. *the seuen*] Seauen J. 4. *and mainetaynaunce*] and mainetayninge *interlineated in* H²; and in maintenance J; & mainteining D. 4–5. *of the Popes aucthorytie*] *Interlineated in* H². 5–6. *througheoute*] through W X B. 6. *in to*] in H³ H¹ A X. 7. *handes*] hand A² D X B. 10. *be argumentes*] are argumentes H²; be the argumentes J. 11. *me*] men B. 11. *that*] to that H³ H¹ A. 11. *doe*] *Omitted in* H¹ S. 14. *can . . . more then*] in that point cann say more in myne excuse then J; canne in that poynte say in my excuse more to me then H³; can in that point say more in mine excuse to mee then H¹; in that pointe saye in myne excuse more to me then A (*with* in myne excuse *interlineated*); in that poynte can say in myne excuse more then M; can in that point say more in my defence then A²; can in theis pointes say more in my excuse then W. 15. *neuer was*] was neuer J H³ H¹ A T. (*All* Harpsfield MSS. was neuer.) 16. *nor*] or J S A² T. (*All* Harpsfield MSS. or.) 17. *it*] that it J. 18. *only*] I was only H³ H¹ A (I was *being interlineated in* A). 18. *a sorter*] be sorter T. 18. *out*] *Omitted in* S. 19. *placer*] a placer H² T. 23. *highnes*] grace J. 23. *one*] the B. 23. *this*] *Omitted in* X B.

The Pope, as yo*ur* grace knowethe, is a prince as you are, *and* in league wit*h* all other Christian princes. It may hereafter so fall owte that yo*ur* grace *and* he may varye vppon some poin*tes* of the league, whereuppon may growe breach of amitye *and* warre betweene you bothe. I thincke it best therefore that that place be amended, *and* his aucthority more sclenderly touched.'

"'Nay,' quoth his grace, 'that shall it not. We are so muche bounden vnto the Sea of Room that we cannot doe to muche honor vnto it.'

"Then did I further put him in remembraunce of the statute of Premunire, whereby a good p*a*rte of the Popes pastoral cure here was pared away.

But the King had been obstinate.

"To that awneswered his highnes: 'Whatsoeu*er* impedim*en*t be to the contrary, we will set forthe that aucthoritye to the vttermost. For we receaued from that | Sea our crowne Imperiall'; w*hich*, till his grace with his owne mouthe tould it me, I neuer heard of before. So that I trust, when his grace shalbe [once] truly informed of this, and call to his gratious remembraunce my doinge* in that behalf, his highnes will neuer speake of it more, but cleere me thoroughly therein himself."

And thus displeasauntlye dep*a*rted they.

More rejoices at withstanding the King's deputies.

Then tooke S*ir* Thom*as* Moore his boate towar*des* his house at Chelsey, wherein by the waye he was very

MSS. H² J H³ H¹ A M S A² D T W X B.

1. *knowethe*] well knoweth W X.   2. *other*] Omitted in M.
2. *It*] that J.   5. *breach*] some breach J; a breach A² D B.
6. *that that*] that the S.   7. *more*] may A².   8. *shall it not*] it shall not J.   8–9. *We are . . . we cannot*] wee cannot W. (*Eyeslip*.)   9. *muche*] Omitted in H³ H¹ A.   11. *further put him*] put him further J; put him A².   11. *remembraunce*] mynde M.   13. *cure*] Care H¹.   13. *here*] there M; omitted in S.   13. *pared*] payed J.   14. *highnes*] grace S.
16. *receaued*] receyve H³ H¹ A T.   17. *Sea*] See of Roome (*with* Roome *interlineated*) H³; Sea, *with* of Rome *crossed through*, A.   18. *with . . . me*] told it me with his owne mouth W X.   18. *it*] Omitted in M.   18. *of*] Omitted in A².   19. *when*] when as M.   19–20. *shalbe once truly*] shalbe truly H² J; shall once truely bee H¹; shalb once truelye be A, *with* e *crossed through after* shalb.   20. *his gratious*] Interlineated in H²; his graces D W X.   21. *doinge*] doinges H² J M S X. (*Best Harpsfield MSS. doing*.)   24. *departed they*] they departed S; parted they B.

More rejoices at giving the Devil a foul fall 69

merye, *and* for that was I nothinge sorye, hopinge that he had gott himself discharged out of the parliament bill. When he was [landed and] come home, then walked we twayne alone * into his garden together; * where I,
5 desirous to knowe howe he had sped, said : " I truste, Sir, that all is well because you be so meerye."
"It is so indeede, sonne Roper, I thanck god," quothe he.
"Are you then put out of the parliament bill?"
10 said I.
"By my trothe, sonne Roper," quqthe he, " I never remembred it."
"Neuer remembred it, Sir," sayd I, "A case that toucheth your self so neere, *and* vs all for your sake. I
15 am sory to heare it; For I veryly trusted, when I sawe you so meerye, that all had bine well."
Then said he: "Wilte thow knowe, sonne Roper, why I was so meery?"
"That wold I gladly, Sir," quoth I.
20 "In good faithe, I reioyced, sonne," quothe he, "that I had geuen the divell * a fowle * fall, *and* that with those Lordes I had gone so farre, as without greate shame I could never goe back agayne."

He had never remembered the Parliament Bill.

MSS. H² J H³ H¹ A M S A² D T W X B.

1. *was I*] I was H¹ W.   2. *had*] *Omitted in* B.   2. *gott*] put T; gotten B.   2. *parliament*] *Omitted in* A² W X.   3. *landed and*] *Omitted in* H² J.   4. *twayne*] towe J.   4. *alone*] *Omitted in* D.   4. *into*] in H³ H¹ A.   4. *into . . . together*] together into his garden H².   5–6. *I truste, Sir*] Sir, I trust J.   6. *that*] *Omitted in* X.   6. *you*] that you H³ H¹ A.   6. *be*] are X.   7. *It*] That J.   9. *Are*] And are D W X B.   9. *then . . . bill*] put out of the parliament Bill then J.   13. *Neuer . . . I*] Sir sayd I never remembred it S.   13. *it*] *Interlineated in* H²; *omitted in* B.   13. *Sir*] *Omitted in* T X.   13. *sayd*] quoth H³ A² D B; sayed *as correction of* quothe A.   15. *sory*] very sorry S A² D W X B. (*All* Harpsfield MSS. very sory.)   15. *For*] *Omitted in* S.   17. *Then said he*] *Omitted in* A² X; D B *omit here but insert after* meery, l. 18.   17. *Then . . . Roper*] Wilte thou then said he knowe sonne Roper S.   18. *why*] wherfore H³ H¹ A.   18. *was*] am B.   19. *gladly, Sir*] gladlie doe sir W X.   19. *quoth*] sayd S A² D T W X B.   20. *reioyced*] reioyceth J.   20. *quothe*] said S A² W B.   21. *divell a fowle fall*] divell so fowle a fall H² J.

At which wordes waxed I very sad, for thoughe himself liked it well, yet liked it me but a litle.

The deputies persuade the King not to press the Bill against More; in the matter of the Nun he is clearly innocent.

Nowe vppon the reporte made by the Lord Chauncelour and the other Lordes to the kinge of all their whole discourse had with Sir Thomas Moore, The kinge was so [highlye] offended with him, that he plainely told them he was fully determined that thaforesaid parliament bill should vndoubtedly proceede forth against him. To whom the Lord Chauncelour and the rest of the Lords saide | that they perceaved the lordes of the vpper house [p. 30] so precisely bente to heare him, in his owne defence, make awneswere himself, that if he were not put oute of the bill, it wold without faile be vtterlye an overthrowe of all. But, for all this, needes wold the kinge haue his owne will therein; or els he said that at the passing thereof, he wold be personally present himself.

Then the Lord Awdelye and the rest, seing him so vehemently sett therevppon, on their knees most humblye besought his grace to forbeare the same, consideringe that if he should, in his owne presence, receave an overthrowe, it wold not only incourage his subiectes euer after to contemne hym, But allso throughout all christendome redound to his dishonour for ever; Addinge

MSS. H² J H³ H¹ A M S A² D T W X B.

2. *well*] very well H¹ T.   2. *yet . . . me*] it liked me W X.
3. *the* (2)] my D.   4. *Lordes*] lords of the Counsell D B.
4. *kinge*] kings Maiestie D B.   6. *highlye*] haynously H².
7. *he*] that he M S A² T X.   7. *that*] *Omitted in* J.
7. *thaforesaid*] the saide J.   8. *vndoubtedly*] *Omitted in* S.
8. *forth*] out B.   9. *the* (1)] my J.   9. *Lords*] Lord X.
11. *so*] are soe W X.   11. *him*] them M.   11. *defence*] case J.   12. *make*] made T.   12. *himself*] for himsilfe J D B.   13. *the*] þat H³; the sayd D.   13. *it*] he D B.
13–14. *vtterlye . . . all* (1)] an overthrowe to all that business D; vtterly ouerthrowne of all T; an vtter ouerthrowe of all W X; vtterly an ouerthrowe of all that busines B.   14. *needes*] *Omitted in* S.   15. *that*] *Omitted in* A² D B.   15. *passinge*] passage B.   17. *Awdelye*] Audly who was Lo : Chauncellor D; Audley who was the Lord Counsellour B.   17. *rest*] rest of the Lordes X.   18. *therevppon*] downe therevppon T.   18. *their*] his A².   18. *most*] they most T.
19. *grace*] Maiestie J.   19. *forbeare*] beare H³ H¹ A.   20. *that if*] *Interlineated in* S *over how crossed through*.   20. *if*] *Omitted in* A².   20. *should*] should there S; would A².
(*All* Harpsfield MSS. *except* H R, *insert* there.)   20. *presence*] person H¹.   22. *all*] *Omitted in* S.

More put out of the Parliament Bill

therunto that they mistrusted not in tyme [against him] to find some meeter matter to serve his * turne better. For in this case of the Nonne, he was accompted, they said, so innocent *and* cleare, that for his dealinge therein, 5 men reckned him farre worthier of prayse then reproof. Where*v*ppon at lengthe, throughe their ernest *p*ersuasion, he was content to condiscend to their petition. *[More's name struck out of the Bill.]*

And on the morowe after, m*aster* Cromewell, meeting 10 me in the p*a*rliamente house, willed me to tell my father that he was put out of the p*a*rliament bill. But because I had appointed to dine that day in London, I sente the message [by my servaunte] to my wife to Chelsey. Whereof when she informed her father, 15 "In faith, Megge," quoth he, "*quod differtur non aufertur.*" *["Quod differtur non aufertur."]*

After this, as the duke of Norfolke *and* S*i*r Thomas Moore chaunced to falle in familiar talke together, the duke said vnto him: "By the masse, m*aster* Moore, it 20 is p*er*illous stryvinge withe princes. And therefore I wold wishe you somewhat to inclyne to the kings pleasure; For by god body, master Moore, *Indignatio principis mors est.*" *[Norfolk counsels More: "Indignatio principis mors est."]*

MSS. H² J H³ H¹ A M S A² D T W X B.

1-2. *against . . . matter*] to finde some other matter against him S.   1. *against him*] Omitted *in* H² J; *for* S *see above*; *interlineated in* X.   2. *meeter*] meete J M T; other H¹; other meeter A² W X (meeter *being interlineated in* X); other meete D B.   2. *matter*] matters B.   2. *turne*] graces turne H² J.   3. *in*] Omitted *in* H³ H¹ A S.   3-4. *they said*] Omitted *in* J.   5. *reckned*] reckon W.   5. *him*] Omitted *in* A² D.   5. *farre*] Omitted *in* J; more H³; for A²; farre more W X.   5. *worthier*] worthie W X.   5. *prayse*] praise & commendacon D B.   6. *ernest*] Omitted *in* W X.   7. *persuasion*] perswasions W X.   10. *me* (1)] Interlineated *in* H² *over* him *crossed through* H².   12. *to dine that day*] that daie to dine W X.   13. *by my servaunte*] Omitted *in* H².   13. *to* (2)] at J H³ H¹ A.   14. *informed*] had informed W.   15. *differtur*] defertur H¹ A X.   17. *as*] Omitted *in* D X B.   18. *to falle*] Omitted *in* M S.   18. *in*] into M A² D W X B.   18. *in familiar*] Omitted *in* S.   18. *talke*] communicacon & talke D; *so probably* B, *but cut short*.   18-19. *the duke*] and among the rest the Duke D B.   20. *perillous*] a perilous X.   21. *wishe you*] wish you if you will followe my counsell D; *so* B, *but* wish and advise you.   22. *god*] gods J A² T W.

Summoned to appear at Lambeth

Administering of the Oath. More the only layman summoned to Lambeth. [13 April, 1534.]

"Is that all, my Lord?" quothe he. "Then in good faith is there no more differens | betweene your grace [p. 31] and me, but that I shall dye today, and yow tomorowe."

So fell it oute, within a moneth or thereaboutes after the makinge of the statute for the oathe of the supremacye and matrimonye, that all the preistes of London and Westminster, and no temporall men but he, were sente for to appeare att Lambethe before the Byshoppe of Canterbury, the lord Chauncelour, and Secretory Cromwell, Comissioners appointed there to tender the oathe vnto them.

Pious exercises before departure.

Then Sir Thomas Moore, as his accostomed manner was alwaies, ere he entered into any matter of importaunce, as when he was firste chosen of the kings privy Councell, when he was sent Embassadour, appointed speaker of the parliamente, made Lord Chauncelour, or when he tooke any like waighty matter vppon him, To goe to church and be confessed, to heare masse and * be howsled, So did he likewise in the mornynge earlye the self same day that he was summoned to appeare before the Lordes at Lambeth. And whereas he * evermore vsed * before,

Sorrow at leaving his family.

at his departure from his wife and children, whom he

MSS. H² J H³ H¹ A M S A² D T W X B.

1. *my . . . he*] quoth he my Lord A² W. 1–2. *Then . . . differens*] is there in good fayth noe more difference J. 2. *is there*] there is H³. 2. *more*] Omitted in W. 3. *that*] Omitted in W X. 3. *shall*] should S. 4. *within*] about H¹. 5. *the* (4)] Omitted in J M S D W X B. (Harpsfield *supports* the.) 7. *temporall*] more temporall S; lay or temporall D B. (*All* Harpsfield MSS. moe temporall.) 7. *men*] men *as correction of* man M; man T W X B. 7. *were*] was M X. 8. *for*] Omitted in J T. 9. *Chauncelour*] Audeley W X. 9. *Secretory*] master Secretary D B. 10. *appointed*] Omitted in J M. 10. *appointed there*] there appointed B. 13. *into*] Interlineated in H². 13. *importaunce*] consequence A². 15. *sent*] first sent A² D W X B. 15. *appointed*] when he was appointed D B. 16. *parliamente*] parliament house H³ H¹ A; *in* M howse *is crossed through.* 16. *made*] when he was made D B. 17. *like*] other like H¹ M T; other S; other like matter like X; *omitted in* B. 17. *matter*] matters M. 17. *vppon him*] in hand S. 17–18. *goe . . . be* (1)] goe to Church and to be J; goe to the Church to be H³ H¹ A B; to goe to the Church and bee X. 18. *be* (2)] to be H² H¹ S. 19. *in*] on S. 20. *the Lordes*] they Lords J. 21. *he evermore vsed*] he vsed evermore H² J. 22. *his wife*] his house J; M *has* howse *crossed through before* wife.

tenderly loved, to haue them bring him to his boate, *and* there to kisse them all, and bidd them farewell, Then wold he Suffer none of them forthe of the gate to followe him, but pulled the wickatt after him, *and* shutt them
5 all from him; *and* *with* an heauy harte, as by his counten- aunce it appeared, *with* me and our foure servan*tes* there tooke he his boate towards Lambithe. Wherein sitting still sadly a while, at the last he [sodainely] rounded me in the yeare, *and* said : "Sonne Roper, I
10 thancke our Lord the feild is wonne." What he ment thereby I then wist not, yeat loth to seeme ignorant, I awneswered : "S*ir*, I am thereof very glad." But as I coniectured afterwar*des*, it was for [that] the loue he had to god wrought in him so effectually that it conquered
15 all his carnall affections vtterlye.

[Nowe] At his cominge to Lambithe, howe wisely he behaved himself before the Comissioners, at the minis- tration of the oathe vnto him, may be found in certaine |
[p. 32] letters of his, sent to my wife, remayning in a greate booke
20 of his workes. Where, by the space of foure daies, he was betaken to the custody of the Abbott of Westminster,

MSS. H² J H³ H¹ A M S A² D T W X B.

Conscience conquers natural affection: "I thank our Lord the field is won."

Imprisoned at West- minster [13– 17 April, 1534]; the King and Council consider adminis- tering a special oath to More, but Anne exasperates the King against him.

1. *tenderly loved*] loved tenderly J.   2. *there*] Omitted in H³.   2–3. *to kisse ... followe*] kisse them all forth out of the gate and bidd them farewell Then would he suffer none of them forth out of the gate to followe W.   2. *them (2)*] them all T. 3. *the*] his A².   4. *him (1)*] Omitted in T.   4. *but pulled ... him*] Omitted in B. (*Eyeslip*.)   4. *him (2)*] them T. 4–5. *and ... him*] Omitted in D. (*Eyeslip*.)   6. *it*] is A²; omitted in W X.   6. *our*] his W X.   7. *he*] Omitted in H³ H¹ A D T.   7. *his*] Omitted in D.   7. *Wherein*] where T.   8. *still*] Omitted in B.   8. *sodainely*] Omitted in H² J.   9–10. *I ... Lord*] Omitted in A².   10. *our*] the T.   10. *he ment*] his meaning was D B.   11. *I ... not*] then I wist not J ; I could not then imagine D ; I then could not imagine B.   12. *thereof*] therefore T. 12. *thereof ... glad*] verie gladd thereof M ; thereof right hartily glad D B.   13. *that*] Omitted in H².   13. *the loue he had*] the feruour and loue which he had D B.   14. *god*] god allmighty D B.   14. *in ... effectually*] so effectually and powrefully in him D B.   14. *so*] Omitted in H³.   14. *that it conquered*] & it conquered & subdued D B.   15. *his ... vtterlye*] carnall & earthly affeccons whatsoeuer D B.   15. *carnall*] Interlineated in H² X.   15. *affections*] affectationes J. 16. *Nowe*] Omitted in H² J.   19. *my*] Interlineated over his crossed through W.   20. *workes*] accountes W.   20. *Where*] from whence D B.   21. *betaken*] committed D B. 21. *of Westminster*] att Westminster M ; of winchester D.

during w*h*ich tyme the king consulted w*i*th his councell what order were meete to be taken w*i*th him. And albeit * in the beginninge they were resolued * that w*i*th an othe not to be acknowen whether he had to the supremacye bine sworne, or what he thoughte thereof, he should be dischardged, yeat did Queene Anne, by her impou*r*tunate clamou*r*, so sore exasperate the kinge againste him, that contrary to his former resolucion, he caused the said othe of the Supremacye to be ministred vnto him. Who, albeit he made a discreete qualified awnswer, neue*r*theles was forthw*i*th comitted to the tower.

Sent to the Tower. [17 April, 1534.]

Who[m], as he was going thitherward, wearing, as he comonly did, a chayne of gould about his necke, S*i*r Richard Cromewell, that had the charge of his conveyans thither, advised him to send home his chayne to his wife, or to some of his children. "Nay, S*i*r," quoth he, "that * I will * not; for if I were taken in the feild by my enemies, I wold they shold somewhat fare the better by me."

Still wears his chain of gold.

MSS. H² J H³ H¹ A M S A² D T W X B.

1. *his*] the H³ H¹ A. 3. *in . . . resolued*] they were resolued in the beginninge H². 3. *resolued*] fully resolued D B. 4. *acknowen*] knowne M; acknowledged A² D W X B. 4. *to*] in T. 5. *sworne*] Interlineated in H². 6. *by*] through W X. 6. *her*] Omitted in H³. 7. *impourtunate clamour*] importante clamore H³; importance and clamour S; importunity and clamour D B. 7. *sore*] Omitted in S; sorely D B. 7. *kinge*] kings heighnes D B. 9. *said*] Omitted in J; same S. 9. *the* (2)] Omitted in H¹ M S. 10. *albeit*] albeit that D B. 10. *made*] had A². 10. *discreete*] deepe M; most descreete D B. 10. *qualified*] & quallified D B. 11. *neuertheles was*] was neuertheles D B. 11. *forthwith comitted*] committed forthwith W X. 13. *Whom*] Who H² J T. 14. *comonly*] most commonly D B. 15. *Cromewell*] Southwell H³; *in the text of* H¹ A Cromwell, *with* Cromwell *underlined, and* Southwell *written in margin*. 15–16. *conveyans*] conveyinge S. 16. *thither*] Omitted in D. 16. *him*] Omitted in S. (*All Harpsfield MSS. except* R² *omit him.*) 16. *home*] Omitted in H³ H¹ A. 17. *to* (2)] Omitted in J A² D X B. 17. *Nay*] No S. 18. *he*] Sir Thomas D B. 18. *I will*] will I, H² J; woulde I, H³ H¹ A. 18. *not*] not by your fauour D B. 19. *enemies*] aduersarie W X. 19. *somewhat fare*] fare somewhat A² W X. 20. *by me*] S *has* by me *as correction of* for me; for me D; *in* X *by* mee *as correction of* for mee.

At whose landing m*aster* Leiuetenant [at] the tower gate was ready to receaue him, wheare the Porter demaunded of him his vpper garment. " M*aster* Porter," quoth he, " here it is; " *and* tooke of his cappe, and
5 deliue*r*id it [him], saying, " I am very sorry it is no better for you." " No, S*ir*," quoth the Porter, " I must haue yo*ur* gowne."

And so was he by m*aster* Leiuetenaunte convayed to his lodginge, where he called vnto him one John A wood,
10 his owne servaunte, there apointed to attend vppon him [who coulde neither write nor rede]; and sware him before the Leiuetenaunte that if he should heare or see him, att any tyme, speake or write any manner of thinge against the king, the Councell, or the State of the realme,
15 he shoulde open it to the Leiuetenaunte, that [the Leiuetenaunte] mighte incontinent* reveale it to the Councell.

[p. 33] | Nowe when [he] had remayned in the Tower a litle more then a monethe, my wife, longinge to see her
20 father, by her ernest suite at length got leaue to goe to him. At whose cominge, after the seuen psalmes *and*

The Porter demands his upper garment.

Instructions to John a Wood.

Margaret's visits.

MSS. H² J H³ H¹ A M S A² D T W X B.

1. *master*] þe A²; *in* X master *as correction of* the. 1–2. *at the tower gate*] of the tower at the gate H² (at the *being interlineated*); *in* X att the Tower gate *as correction of* of the Tower gate. 3. *of him*] Omitted in T; of him as a fee belonging to his place B. 4. *quoth*] said S. 4. *quoth . . . is*] heere it is quod he A². 4. *here it is*] Omitted in B. 5. *it*] Omitted in J. 5. *him*] Omitted in H²; vnto him A². 5. *very*] Omitted in W X. 5. *it is*] its A². 7. *gowne*] gowne. O I cry you mercy good master Porter quod he. For nowe I remember that my cap is not my vpper garment only þe thatch of my poore old tenement A²; gowne which he therevpon delliuered it vnto him D; B *as* D *but omitting* it. 8. *master*] the M. 8. *to*] into J. 9. *A wood*] Wood B. 10. *attend*] tend D. 10. *vppon*] Omitted in H¹. 10. *him*] his master D B. 11. *who . . . rede*] Omitted in H². 13. *any* (2)] a M. 13. *of thinge*] of things H¹ A; *omitted in* T; or thinge *as correction of* of thinge X. 14. *the king*] Omitted in A². 14. *the* (2)] & the B. 14. *the* (3)] Omitted in H¹ A. 15–16. *the Leiuetenaunte*] he H². 16. *mighte*] againe might D B. 16. *incontinent*] incontinently H² H³ H¹ A. 18. *he*] Sir Thomas Moore H² J. 18. *a litle*] litle H³ S A² D T W. (*Most* Harpsfield MSS. litle.) 19. *longinge*] very earnestly longing D B; louinge T. 20. *length*] last X. 20. *got*] obteined D B. 20–p. 76, l. 1. *got . . . him*] A² damaged here. 20–21. *to goe to him*] to see him X.

letany* said (which, whensoeuer she came to him, ere
he fell in talke of any worldly matters, he vsed accustomably to say with her) Amonge other communicacion

More rejoices at leisure for godly meditation.

he said vnto her: "I beleeve, Megge, that they that
have putt me heare, weene they haue done me a high 5
displeasure. But I assure [thee], on my faithe, my
owne good daughter, if it had not byne for my wife *and*
you that be my children, whom I accompte the cheife
parte of my charge, I wold not haue fayled longe ere this
to haue closed my self in as straighte a roome, and * 10

Believes God will provide for his family. God "maketh him a wanton."

straighter * too. But since I am come hither without
myne owne deserte, I trust that god of his goodnes will
discharge me of my care, *and* with his graciouse helpe
supply my lack amonge you. I find no cause, I thanck
god, Megge, to reckon my self in wors case heare then 15
in my owne house. For me thinckethe god makethe me
a wanton, *and* settethe me on his lappe and dandlethe

Regards his troubles as profitable exercises of patience.

me." Thus by his gratious demeanour in tribulacion
appeared it that all the trowble[s] that euer chaunced
[vnto] him, by his patient sufferaunce thereof, were to 20
him no paynefull punishmentes, but of his paciens profitable exercises.

Foretells fall of Anne Boleyn.

And att another tyme, when he had first questioned

MSS. H² J H³ H¹ A M S A² D T W X B.

1. *letany*] letanys H² S.   1. *ere*] or H¹; before D.   2. *he* (1)] she W.   2. *fell*] *Omitted in* H³; would fall D B.   2. *of*] with T.   2-3. *accustomably*] accordingly H³; customably S. (*All* Harpsfield MSS. except B customablye.)   3. *other*] theire D.   4. *he said vnto her*] *Omitted in* X.   4. *Megge, that they*] þat they Meg A².   4. *that they that*] that they M; that they which S; they that W X.   5. *weene*] meane A²; thinke W X.   5. *high*] *Omitted in* D B; great W X.   6. *thee*] you H² J X.   7. *good*] deare J.   9. *parte*] greate D.   9. *longe*] *Omitted in* X.   10. *roome*] place S; roome as this A² D W X B.   11. *straighter*] a straighter roome H².   11. *am*] *Omitted in* J.   11. *hither*] thither A².   12. *that*] *Omitted in* W X.   13. *graciouse*] graces M.   14. *lack*] want J A².   14. *you*] *Omitted in* W.   15. *Megge*] *Omitted in* A².   15. *reckon*] find A².   15. *heare*] *Omitted in* A².   16. *me thinckethe*] me thinke S W; my thinks D; mee thinckes X.   18. *tribulacion*] tribulations J.   19. *appeared*] apperthe H³; appeareth H¹ A.   19. *trowbles*] trowble H² H³ H¹ A M T B. (*All* Harpsfield MSS. troubles.)   20. *vnto*] *Omitted in* H².   20-22. *patient . . . exercises*] patient proffitable exercises T.   20. *sufferaunce*] suffering S A².   21. *paynefull*] small D.

The Lieutenant's apology for his poor cheer 77

w*i*th my wife a while of the order of his wife, * children, *and* state of his howse in his absens, he asked her how queene Anne did. " In faith, father," quoth she, " never better." " Never better! Megge," quothe he. " Alas!
5 Megge, alas! it pitieth me to remember in[to] what misery, poore soule, she shall shortly come."

After this, m*aster* Lieutenant, cominge into his chamber to visite him, rehearced the benefittes and freindshipp* that he had many waies receaved at his hand*es, and* howe
10 much bounden he was therefore freindly to intertayne him, *and* make him good cheare; w*h*ich, since the case standing as it did, he could not do w*i*thout the kinges indignation, he trusted, he said, he wold accepte his good will, *and* suche poore cheare as he had. " Maister
15 Leivetenaunt," quothe he againe, " I veryly beleeve, as you may, so you are my good freind indeede, and wold, as you say, w*i*th your best cheere intertaine me, for the w*h*ich I most hartely thancke you; and assure yo*ur* self, [p. 34] m*aster* Leivetenant, I doe not | myslike my cheare; But
20 whensoeu*er* I soe doe, then thruste me out of yo*ur* doores."

Whereas the oath confirminge the supremacye *and*

MSS. H² J H³ H¹ A M S A² D T W X B.

Reply to the Lieutenant's apology for the poor cheer of the Tower.

The Oath as administered to More had been amplified by the Lord Chancellor and Cromwell.

1. *of* (1)] in A².   1. *wife* (2)] *Omitted in* A².   1. *children*] and children H² J.   2. *state*] estate T.   2. *asked*] at the length asked D B.   3. *faith*] *Interlineated in* J; *omitted in* M; good fayth S. 4–5. *Alas! Megge, alas!*] Alas Megg Alas Megg W; *omitted in* X. 5. *remember*] remember or thinke D B.   5. *into*] in H² J M. 6. *poore . . . come*] shee poore soule shortly shall come J; she shortly shall come A².   6. *poore soule*] *Omitted in* T.   7. *Lieutenant*] Liuetenant of the Tower D B.   8. *rehearced*] receaued X.   8. *benefittes and freindshipp*] benefittes and freindshippes H² J H³ S X; many benefitts & much friendshipp D B; freindshipp and benefittes W.   9. *that he had*] hee had that hee had X.   9. *waies*] tymes J.   9. *and*] *Omitted in* T.   9–11. *and howe . . . cheare*] *Twice over in* X.   11–12. *since . . . standing*] the case so standing W X. 12. *standing*] standeth H³ H¹ A.   12. *do*] doe it H¹; *omitted in* T.   13. *accepte*] accept of S D B.   15. *againe*] *Omitted in* H¹.   15. *veryly*] *Omitted in* W.   15. *as*] that as A² W B.   16. *so you are*] so are you H³ H¹ A M T; you are S X B. (*All* Harpsfield MSS. you are.)   16. *good*] very good H¹ A² W B.   16–18. *freind . . . hartely*] freinde I most hartily T.   17. *say*] said A² B: 17–18. *the which*] which S A² D W X B. (*All* Harpsfield MSS. which.)   19. *I doe*] quoth he I doe J.   20. *soe doe*] doe H³ H¹ A S; doe soe W B; doe I doe soe X.   20. *your*] *Omitted in* A² D W X B.

Illegality of the Oath administered to More

matrimonie was by the first statute in fewe wordes comprised, The Lord Chauncelor *and* Master Secretary did of their owne heads adde more words vnto it, to make it appeare vnto the kinges eares more pleasaunt *and* plausible. And that oath, so amplified, * caused they * to be ministred to S*ir* Thomas Moore, *and* to all other throughout the Realme. W*h*ich S*ir* Thomas Moore p*er*ceyuinge, said vnto my wife : " I may tell thee, Megg, * they that * haue committed me hither, for refusinge of [this] oath not agreable w*i*th the statute, * are not * by theyr owne lawe able * to iustifye my imprisoneme*n*t. And surely, daughter, it is greate pitye that any Christian prince should by a flexible Councell ready to followe his affections, and by a weake Cleargie lackinge grace constantly to stand to their learninge, w*i*th Flatterye * be so shamefully * abused." But at length the Lord Chauncelo*ur and* m*as*ter Secretorye, espieng their [owne] oue*r*sight in that behalf, were fayne afterward*es* to find the meanes that another statute shold be made for the confirmacion of the oath so amplified w*i*th their additions.

Later this amplification was made legal.

MSS. H² J H³ H¹ A M S A² (*damaged*) D T W X B.

1. *was . . . statute*] by the first Statute was W. 1. *by*] in B. 1–2. *in fewe wordes comprised*] comprised in few words J; in fyve woordes comprised X. 2. *Master*] Omitted in W X. 3. *vnto it*] Omitted in W. 4. *vnto . . . eares*] in the kings eares M; by the kinges eares T. 5. *plausible*] fansible H³. 5–6. *caused they*] they caused H². 7. *throughout*] throughe H³ H¹ A A² D T. 8. *Moore*] Omitted in J. 8. *may*] Omitted in B. 8. *tell*] Omitted in M. 9. *they that*] that they H²; they then X. 10. *refusinge*] the refusinge H¹ A M A² D T B. 10. *this*] the H² J. 10. *with the*] to the D B; with X. 10. *the*] this M. 11. *are not*] and they are not H², *with* and they *interlineated, evidently to make sense on account of wrong reading* that they *above*, l. 9. 11. *by . . . able*] able by theyr owne lawe H² J. 12–21. *And . . . additions*] Corresponding page of A² damaged. 13. *any*] my J. 13. *should*] should be S. 13–14. *Councell ready*] Counsell reddy in all things D B; Councell be ready T. 15. *lackinge*] wanting A². 15. *learninge*] bearing A² B. 16. *be . . . abused*] so shamefully to be abused H²; soe shamefull to be abused J; to be soe shamfully abused H³ H¹ A A² D T; bee soe shameful abused M; so shamefully abused S; be so shamefully abused D W X B. 17. *length*] the length H³ T. 17. *the*] my S W X. 18. *owne*] Omitted in H² J S. 18. *ouersight*] ouersight and errour D B.

Arranges for conveyance of his lands

After S*ir* Thomas Moore had geeuen over his office *and* all other worldly doings therewi*th*, to thentent he might from thenceforthe the more quietly set[tle] himself to the Service of god, Then made he a conveyaunce
5 for the dispositio*n* of all his lands, reseruinge to himself an estate thereof only for tearme of his owne life; *and* after his decease assuringe some p*ar*te of the same to his wife, some to his sonnes wife for a Joynture in consideracion that she was an inheretrice in possession of more
10 then an houndred pound*es* land by the yeare, *and* some to me *and* my wife in recompence of our mariage money, with divers remaynders ouer; All w*h*ich conveyaunce *and* assurance was p*ar*fitelye finished longe before that matter wheruppon he was attainted was made an offence,
15 and yeat after by statute clearely avoided. And so were all his land*es*, that he had to his wife *and* children by the said conveyaunce in such sorte assured, contrary to thorder of lawe, taken away from them, *and* brought into the kings hand*es*, saving that porcion [which] he
[p. 35] had apointed | to my wife and me; [which, although
21 he had in the foresaid conveyaunce reserued, as he did the reste, for tearme of life to him self, neuer the lesse, vpon further consideracion, two dayes after, by another conveyaunce, he gaue the same immediatlye to

Side notes: More arranges for conveyance of his lands at his death. Which conveyance was set aside, and the lands appropriated by the King after More's attainder. But lands immediately conveyed to Roper and his wife escaped the King's seizure.

MSS. H² J H³ H¹ A M S A² D T W X B.

1. *office*] office of Chauncellorship D B. 2. *all*] *Omitted in* S. 2. *other*] other his S D W X B. 2. *therewith*] therewithall D B. 3–4. *settle himself*] set himself H² J (*interlineated in* H²). 4. *to . . . god*] the service B. 5. *disposition*] disposeing W X. 5. *all*] *Omitted in* H³ T W X. 5. *to*] *Omitted in* D. 6. *owne*] *Omitted in* D B. 7. *of the same*] thereof H¹ D. 8. *some . . . wife*] *Interlineated in* H². 8. *a*] her X. 10. *land*] lands A² D B; *omitted in* W X. 10. *the yeare*] yeare S W X. 12–13. *conveyaunce and assurance*] conveyances and assurances W X. 13. *finished*] finishing B. 13. *that*] the H³ H¹ A S T W X. (Harpsfield MSS. that.) 16. *were*] *Omitted in* S. 16. *his* (1)] the W X. 17. *the said*] that A². 17. *conveyaunce*] conveyances W X. 18. *thorder*] order D. 18. *lawe*] the lawe T W. 19. *which*] that H² J A² D B; *omitted in* S. 20–p. 80, l. 1. *which . . . and me*] *Omitted in* H². (*Eyeslip at beginning of new page.*) 22. *life*] his life J. 22. *him self*] himselfe as is aforesayd D B. 22–p. 80, l. 8. *neuer the lesse . . . reserved*] A² damaged. 23. *consideracion*] considerations H³ H¹ A S. 23. *two dayes*] *Omitted in* J. 24. *the*] that J. 24. *immediatlye*] *Omitted in* M.

my wife and me] in possession. And so because the statute had vndone onely the firste conveyaunce, geeving no more to the kinge but so much as passed by that, The seconde conveyaunce, whereby it was geeven to my Wife *and* me, being dated two dayes after, was without the compasse of the statute, And so was our porcion to vs by that meanes clearely reserved.

<small>More and Margaret watch martyrs "going to their deaths as bridegrooms to their marriage." More longs to accompany them. [4 May, 1535.]</small>

As S*ir* Thom*as* Moore in the Tower chaunced on a tyme, lookinge out of his windowe, to behold one m*aste*r Reynolds, a religious, learned, *and* vertuous father of Sion, *and* three Monkes of the Charterhouse, for the Matters of the Matrimonye and Supremacye goinge out of the Tower to execution, He, as one longinge in that iourneye to haue accompanied them, said vnto my wife, then standinge there besides him : "Loe, doest thow not see, Megge, that thes blessed fathers be nowe as chearefully goinge to their deathes as bridegromes to their Mariage*? Wherefore thereby maiste thow see, myne owne good daughter, what a greate difference there is betweene such as haue in effecte spent all their dayes

MSS. H² J H³ H¹ A M S A² D T W X B.

1. *my wife and me*] me and my wife J. 1. *me*] *Omitted in* X. 1. *possession*] present possession D B. 2. *had vndone onely*] only had vndone D. 2–4. *conveyaunce . . . whereby*] A² D B *have eyeslip owing to repetition of* conveyaunce, *omitting* geeving . . . by *and* The seconde conveyaunce *and reading* that wherby, *etc.* 5. *geeven*] passed W X. 7. *was*] *Omitted in* T. 7. *porcion*] portions H³ X. 7. *to vs*] *Omitted in* S; *interlineated in* X. 7–8. *by . . . reserved*] by that meanes cleerely by that meanes reserved X. 9. *in the Tower*] while he was prisonner in the Toure D B. 9. *chaunced*] *Omitted in* S. 10. *of his*] at his H³; att þe H¹. 10. *windowe*] chamber windowe D B. 11. *and*] *Omitted in* S. 12. *Sion*] the Charterhouse of Syon S. 12. *three*] the three W X. 12. *Charterhouse*] same house S. 12. *the* (2)] *Omitted in* H³ H¹ A. 13. *Matters . . . Supremacye*] matter of the Supremicie J. 13. *Matters*] matter J H³ A W X. 13. *Matrimonye*] kings matrimony D B. 14. *to execution*] towards their execucion S A² B; to their execucion D W X. 15. *my wife*] his daughter my wife D B. 16. *thow not*] not thou D. 17. *nowe*] *Omitted in* X. 18. *deathes*] death S A² D. (*All* Harpsfield MSS. death.) 18. *to their*] be to their S A² W X. 19. *Mariage*] Mariages H² J H¹; mariage *as correction of* mariages A. 19. *Wherefore*] Whereby therefore S. 19. *thereby*] heerby A² D W B. 20. *greate*] *Omitted in* J. 21. *in effecte spente*] spente in Effecte H³ H¹ A.

in a straight, hard, penetentiall, and paynefull life religiously, and such as haue in the world, like worldly wretches, as thy poore father [hath] done, consumed all theyr tyme in pleasure *and* ease licentiouslye. For god, 5 consideringe their longe continued life in most sore *and* greavous penaunce, will no long*er* suffer them to remayne heare in this vale of Misery *and* iniquitye, but speadily hence taketh them to the fruition of his eu*er*lasting deitye; whereas thy syllye father, Megge, that like 10 a most wicked Caytiffe hath passed forth the whole course of his miserable life most sinfully, God, thinckinge him not worthy so soone to come to that eternall felicitye, leaveth him heare yet still in [the] world, further to be plonged *and* turmoyled withe 15 miserye."

Within a while after, m*aster* Secretorye, cominge to him in[to] the tower from the kinge, pretended much freindshipp toward*es* him, and for his comforte told him that the kings highnes was his good and gratious 20 Lorde, and minde[d] not [with] any matter wherein he [p. 36] should haue any cause of scruple, from henceforthe | to trouble his consciens. As soone as m*aster* Secretory was gone, to expresse what comforte he conceaved of his word*es*, he wrote wi*t*h a cole, for Incke then had he none, 25 thease verses folowinge :

<small>Cromwell's promises of the King's favour and leniency do not deceive More.</small>

MSS. H² J H³ H¹ A M S A² *(damaged)* D T W X B.

<small>1–15. *in . . . miserye*] A² *damaged*.   1. *straight, hard*] hard strict A² D B.   3. *hath*] haue H² W X.   4. *theyr*] the J.   4. *licentiouslye*] licensially H³.   5. *longe*] *Omitted in* D.   5. *life*] vnpleasant lyfe S.   6. *them*] him B.   8. *taketh*] take J.   8. *to*] into W X.   10. *most*] *Omitted in* T.   10. *wicked*] silly A².   11. *sinfully*] pittifully J.   12. *him*] *Omitted in* S. (*All* Harpsfield MSS. *except* Y *omit.*)   13. *yet still*] still yet D B.   13–14. *the world*] world H²; this world H³ H¹ A.   14. *plonged*] plagued H³ H¹ A T B. (*All* Harpsfield MSS. plunged.)   14. *turmoyled*] tormented T.   14. *withe*] in H¹.   17. *into*] in H² T.   17. *pretended*] pretending A².   20. *minded*] mindeth H² J M T W X; meaneth A² D B. (*All* Harpsfield MSS. minded.)   20. *with*] *Omitted in* H² H³ H¹ A M; in A² D W X B. (*All* Harpsfield MSS. with.)   21. *any*] *Omitted in* S.   21. *henceforthe*] thenceforth H³ S A² D B. (*All* Harpsfield MSS. thenceforth.)   23. *conceaved*] receaued T.   24. *wrote*] writt X.   24. *then*] at that tyme D B.   24. *had he*] he had H³ H¹ A X.</small>

Verses on flattering Fortune

Verses on flattering Fortune.

Ey flatteringe fortune, looke thow neuer so faire,
Nor neuer so pleasantly beginne to smyle,
As thoughe thou woldest my ruine all repaire,
Duringe my life thow shalt not me begile.
Truste I shall god, to enter in a while   5
Hys haven of heaven, sure *and* vniforme;
Ever after thy calme looke I for [a] storme.

Lady More visits her husband: she is not in sympathy with his opposition to the King's wishes.

When S*ir* Thomas Moore had continued a good while
in the Tower, my Lady, his wife, obtayned lycens to see
him; who, at her first cominge, like a simple ignorant 10
woman, *and* somewhat worldly too, w*i*th this manner
of salutacion bluntlye saluted him:
" What the good yere, m*aste*r Moore," quoth she, " I
mervaile that you, that have bine alwaies hitherto taken
for so wise a man, will nowe so play the foole to lye 15
heare in this close, filthy prison, and be content thus to
be shut vpp amongst mise *and* rattes, when you might
be abroade at yo*ur* libertye, *and* w*i*th the favour and
good will both of the kinge *and* his Councell, If yow
wold but doe as all the Byshops *and* best learned of this 20
realme [haue] done. And seinge you have at Chelsey a

MSS. H² J H³ H¹ A M S A² (*damaged*) D T W X B.

1. *Ey*] *Omitted in* T; Ay A²; Aye W; Ah X.   1. *thow*] you J W.   2. *pleasantly*] lovingly S.   3. *thoughe*] *Omitted in* H³ H¹ A M T.   (*All* Harpsfield MSS. *and* English Works, though.)   3. *woldest*] would X.   3. *ruine*] Ruynes J A² D W X B.   (*All* Harpsfield MSS. *except* R² ruine; English Works, ruine.)   4. *thow*] yow H².   5. *I shall*] shall I, S A² D B.   (*All* Harpsfield MSS. *and* English Works, shall I.)
6. *Hys*] Thy J H³ H¹ A M; The A² D W X B.   (*All* Harpsfield MSS. *and* English Works, His.)   6. *haven of heaven*] Heauen of Heauen D; heaven of heavens X; haven of heaven *as correction of* heaven of heaven B.   7. *thy*] the M A² W X; a D B.   (*All* Harpsfield MSS. this; English Works, thy.)   7. *a*] noe H² J H³ H¹ A M.   (*All* Harpsfield MSS. *and* English Works, a.)
10. *her*] the D.   10–20. *a . . . the*] A² *damaged*.   10. *ignorant*] *Omitted in* J.   12. *salutacion*] salutations J.   12. *bluntlye*] humblie T.   13. *quoth she*] *Omitted in* W X.   14. *that* (2)] who S.   16. *this close*] this close and D; a close W X.   16. *filthy*] *Omitted in* X.   16–17. *thus to be*] to be thus H¹.   18. *your*] *Omitted in* H¹.   18. *and* (1)] *Omitted in* S D W X B.   (*All* Harpsfield MSS. omit.)   18–19. *favour . . . will*] good will and fauour T.   19. *both*] *Omitted in* S.
19. *his*] *Omitted in* X.   20. *wold*] will M.   20–21. *this realme*] the Realme H³; this land H¹.   21. *haue*] hath H².

The Tower as near Heaven as is More's house 83

right faire house, yo*ur* library, yo*ur* bookes, yo*ur* gallery, your garden, yo*ur* orchard, *and* all other necessaries so handsome* aboute you, where you might in the company of me your wife, [your] children, *and* howshold be
5 meerye, I muse what a gods name you meane heare still thus fondly to tarye."

After he had a while quietly heard her, with a chearefull countenaunce he said vnto her :

"I pray thee, good m*istris* Alice, tell me one thinge."
10 "What is that ? " quoth shee.

"Is not this house," quoth he, "as nighe heauen as my owne ? "

To whom shee, after hir accustomed homely fashion, not liking such talke, awneswered, " Tylle valle, Tylle
15 valle ! "

"Howe say you, m*istris* Alice," quoth he, "is itt not so ? "

"Bone deus, bone deus, [man], will this geare neuer be lefte ? " quoth shee.

[p. 37] "Well then, m*istris* Ales, if | it be so," [quoth he], " it
21 is very well. For I see no greate cause why I should much Ioye [either] of my gay house or [of] any thinge belonginge therunto ; when, if I should but seuen yeares lye buried vnder the ground, and then arise *and* come
25 [t]hither againe, I should not faile to find some therein

More argues that the Tower is as nigh heaven as is his own house.

And his house will soon forget its master.

MSS. H² J H³ H¹ A M S A² (*damaged*) D T W X B.

1. *your gallery*] *Omitted in* H¹ W X.   2. *all*] *Interlineated in* H²; *omitted in* B.   3. *handsome*] handsomely H² J.   4. *your* (2)] and H².   5. *what a*] what the H³ ; what A².   5. *what . . . name*] a gods name what S.   7. *quietly heard her*] hearde her quietly T.   11. *quoth he*] *Omitted in* J.   11–12. *quoth . . . owne*] as nigh Heauen quoth hee as mine owne H¹.   11. *as* (1)] a H³.   11. *nighe*] neere S; neere to W X.   13–14. *shee . . . not*] after her accustomed homely fashion she not S. 13–p. 84, l. 7. *To . . . Counsaile*] A² *damaged*.   13. *homely*] *Omitted in* J.   14. *such*] his D.   14–16. *Tylle* (2) . . . *itt*] *Cut off in* B.   16–17. *quoth . . . so*] is it not soe quoth hee J.   18. *man*] *Omitted in* H².   20–21. *if . . . well*] if it be so it is very well H² J ; quothe he if it be soe it is very well H³; W *has* shee *for* he.   21. *greate*] good T.   22. *much Ioye*] Ioye much M A².   22. *either*] *Omitted in* H² J M; *interlineated in* A.   22. *of any*] any H² W X.   22. *thinge*] *Omitted in* W. 23–24. *if . . . buried*] if but seaven yeares I should lye buried S. 23. *seuen*] one vij D.   24. *lye*] be H³ H¹ A A² D B. (Harpsfield MSS. *vary*.)   24. *the*] *Interlineated in* H².   25. *thither*] hither, H².   25. *find*] *Interlineated in* H².

84 *Examinations in the Tower*

that wold bid me get [me] out of doores, and tell me it were none of mine. What cause haue I then to like such an house as wold so soone forgett his master ? "
So her perswasions moved him but a litle.

The two examinations in the Tower: More will not disclose his opinion on the Supremacy.

Not longe after came there to him the Lord Chaun- 5 celour, the dukes of Norfolke *and* Suffolk, with master Secretory *and* certaine other of the privy Counsaile, at two seuerall times, by all pollicies possible procuringe him, eyther precisely to confesse the supremacy, or precisely to denye it; wherunto, as * appeareth by his 10 examination[s] in the said great book, they could neuer bringe him.

Rich, Southwell and Palmer are sent to the Tower to confiscate More's books. Rich tries to entrap him on the question of the Supremacy.

Shortlye herevppon, master Riche, afterwardes Lord Riche, then newlye made the kings Solicitor, Sir Richard Sowthwell, and one master Palmer, servaunt to the Secre- 15 tory, were sent to Sir Thomas Moore into the Tower, to fetche away his bookes from him. And while Sir Richard Southwell and master Palmer were busye in the trussing vppe of his bookes, master Rich, pretending freindly talke with him, amonge other things, of a sett 20 cours, as it seemed, saide thus vnto him :

MSS. H² J H³ H¹ A M S A² (*damaged*) D T W X B.

1. *me* (2)] *Omitted in* H² T W.   1. *of*] of the J.   1. *it*] that J.   3. *such*] *Omitted in* M.   4. *her*] his H¹.   4. *moved*] as you see moued D.   4. *but*] not H¹.   5. *after . . . Lord*] *Bottom margin cropped so that these words cut off in* X.   5. *there*] *Omitted in* A². (*All* Harpsfield MSS. *omit.*)   6. *the dukes*] Dukes H¹; the duke X.   6. *and*] *Omitted in* J.   7. *other*] *Omitted in* A² B.   7. *privy Counsaile*] kings priuie Counsell D.   8. *pollicies possible*] possible meanes H¹; pollicy possible S A²; perswasions and pollicies possible D.   9. *supremacy*] kings Supremacy D.   10. *it*] the same D.   10. *appeareth*] it appeareth H²; plainly appeareth D.   10. *by*] *Omitted in* X.   11. *examinations*] examination H² M D B.   11–12. *in the . . . him*] set downe at large in the sayd booke of his works they could neuer by all their deuices bring him D.   13–14. *afterwardes . . . then*] afterward made Lo : Rich beeing then D.   14. *made*] *Omitted in* J.   14. *Sir*] Master T.   15–16. *the Secretory*] master Secretary D ; the said Secretary W X.   16–17. *Moore . . . his*] *Cut off in* B.   16. *into the Tower*] *Omitted in* S.   18–19. *the trussing*] trussing H³ S A² D X B; A *has the interlineated.* (*All* Harpsfield MSS. *except* L, *the trussing.*)   19. *of*] *Omitted in* S.   20. *freindly*] frendship B.   20. *talke*] talking A² D B.   21. *cours*] purpose H¹; A *has* purpose *crossed through before* course; course and pourpose D.   21. *it seemed*] by the Sequell it Seemed D.   21. *thus*] this S.

"Forasmuch as it is well knowen, master Moore, that you are a man bothe wise *and* well learned aswell in the lawes of the realme as otherwise, I pray you therefore, S*ir*, lett me be so bold as of good will to putte vnto you 5 this case. Admitt there were, S*ir*," quoth he, " an acte of p*ar*liame*nt* that all the Realme should take me for kinge. Wold not you, m*aster* Moore, take me for kinge ? "
"Yes, sir," quoth S*ir* Thomas Moore, "that * wold 10 I."*
"I put * case further," quoth m*aster* Riche, "that there were an acte of p*ar*liament that all the Realme should take me for Pope. Wold * not you * then, m*aster* Moore, take me for Pope ? "
15 "For awneswer, [Sir]," quoth S*ir* Thomas Moore, "to yo*ur* firste case : the p*ar*liame*nt* may well, m*aster* Riche, medle wi*th* the state of temporall princes. But [p. 38] to make awneswer to | yo*ur* other case, I will put you this case : Suppose the p*ar*liame*nt* wold make a lawe 20 that god shold not be god. Wold you then, m*aster* Riche, say that god were not god ? "

MSS. H² J H³ H¹ A M S A² (*damaged*) D T W X B.

1. *as . . . Moore*] master Moore as it is well knowen S. 2. *well*] *Omitted in* H¹ W. 3. *the*] our H³ H¹ A; this S A²; this our D. (*All* Harpsfield MSS. this.) 4. *lett*] of Curtesie let D. 4. *be*] *Interlineated in* H². 4. *you*] *Omitted in* H¹ A² B. 5. *there . . . acte*] sir quod he there were an act A². 6. *all*] *Omitted in* T. 6. *the*] this S D. 7. *kinge*] the King J. 7. *you*] you now S. (*All* Harpsfield MSS. *except* B *insert* nowe.) 7. *master Moore*] Sir Thomas More A². 8. *kinge*] the King J. 9. *sir*] *Omitted in* T. 9–10. *wold I*] I wold H². 11. *I put case*] I put the case H² J; Yea put case A² B; Yea but put the case D; Yea put the case W X. 12. *the Realme*] the world H¹; this Realme D. 13. *Pope*] the pope J D. 13–14. *Wold . . . Pope*] *Omitted in* A². (*Eyeslip.*) 13. *Wold . . . then*] wold you not then H² (*with* then *crossed through after* you); Would then not you J (*with* then *interlineated*); would yow not then M; A² *has omission here* (*see below*). (*All* Harpsfield MSS. *except* L B, would you not then.) 14. *take*] also take D. 14. *Pope*] the Pope J. 15. *Sir* (1)] *Omitted in* H² J; Sir Sir W. 16–p. 86, l. 3. *case . . . Riche*] A² *damaged*. 16–17. *master Riche, medle*] medle master Rich M; A *has* medle *crossed through before* master. 17. *with . . . princes*] *Omitted in* S. 18. *make*] *Omitted in* S. 18. *you*] to you A². 19. *Suppose*] Suppose that H³ H¹ A. 21. *that*] *Omitted in* J; then that A². 21–p. 86, l. 1. *god* (1) *. . . that*] *Cut off in* B. 21. *not*] *Interlineated in* H²; no X.

More indicted of treason as having spoken *maliciously* against the King's Supremacy.

"No, Sir," quoth he, "that wold I not, sith no parliament maye make any such lawe."
"No more," said Sir Thomas Moore, as master Riche reported of him, "could the parliament make the kinge Supreame head of the churche." 5

Vppon whose onlye reporte was Sir Thomas Moore indicted of treason vppon the statute [wherby] it was made treason to denye the kinge to be supreame head of the churche. Into which indictment were putt thes haynouse wordes—" Maliciously, trayterouslye, and 10 Diabolically ".

Brought to Westminster to answer his indictment. [1 July, 1535.]

When Sir Thomas Moore was brought from the tower to westminster hall to awneswer the Indictment, and at the kings bench barre before the Iudges thervppon arraigned, he openly told them that he wold vppon 15 that indictment haue abidden in lawe, but that he therby shoulde haue bine driven to confesse of himself the matter indeede, [that] was the deniall of the kings supremacye, which he protested was vntrue. Wherefore he therto pleaded not giltye; and so reserved vnto 20 himself advantage to be taken of the body of the matter, after verdicte, to avoid that Indictment; And moreouer added [that] if thos only odious tearmes, " Maliciously, traiterouslye, *and* diabolicallye," were put out of the

Pleads not guilty to having *denied* the King's Supremacy.

MSS. H² J H³ H¹ A M S A² (*damaged*) D T W X B.

1–2. *that . . . lawe*] Omitted in D.   1. *that . . . not*] Omitted in X here, but inserted below after lawe, l. 2.   1. *wold I*] I woulde A² T; probably so B, but cut off before wold.   2. *maye*] cane X.   2. *make . . . lawe*] make such a lawe W X.   7. *statute*] newe statute D.   7. *wherby . . . was*] by which it was H²; in which it was J.   9. *putt*] put by way of aggrevacon D.   10. *haynouse*] Omitted in J.   11. *Diabolically*] malitiously W.   12. *the*] this S A² D B; to the T.   13. *and*] Omitted in D.   14. *Iudges*] iudges & comissioners for that purpose appointed D.   15–p. 87, l. 12. *arraigned . . . wold not say*] A² damaged.   16. *haue*] Omitted in T.   16. *that* (2)] Omitted in J.   16–17. *he therby shoulde*] thereby he should S A² D W X B. (Harpsfield MSS. *support* thereby he should.)   17. *bine*] Omitted in W.   18. *that*] which H² J.   20. *he therto*] thereto he J; he therefore W.   20. *therto pleaded*] pleaded thereto S.   20. *so*] Omitted in W.   21. *himself*] him T.   22. *that*] the T.   23. *that*] Omitted in H² J.   23. *if thos only*] if onely those H¹ D.   23. *Maliciously*] of Maliciously H¹.   24. *put*] left X.   24. *out*] Omitted in B.   24. *the*] Omitted in H³.

Rich's false oath; More exposes his character 87

Indictment, he sawe * therein nothinge * iustlye to charge him. And for proof to the Jury that Sir Thomas Moore was guilty of this treason, master Rich was called forth to
5 giue evidence vnto them vppon his oath, as he did. Against whom [thus] sworne, Sir Thomas Moore began in this wise to say : " If I were a man, my lordes, that did not regarde an othe, I need[ed] not, as it is well knowen, in this place, at this tyme, nor in this case, to
10 stand [here] as an accused person. And if this [othe] of yours, master Riche, be true, then pray I that I neuer see god in the face; which I wold not say, were it otherwise, to winne the whole world." Then recite[d] he to the * courte the discourse of all theyr communicacion in
[p. 39] the Tower, | accordinge to the truthe, and said : " In
16 good faithe, master Riche, I am * sorye[r] for your periurye then for my owne perill. And yow shall vnderstand that neyther I, nor no man els to my knowledge, ever tooke you to be a man of such creditt as in any
20 matter of importaunce I, or any other, would at anye tyme vouchsaf to communicate with you. And I, as

Side notes: Rich's false oath. More wishes he may "never see God in the face," if Rich's testimony be true. He exposes Rich's evil character.

MSS. H² J H³ H¹ A M S A² (damaged) D T W X B.

1. *therein nothinge*] nothinge therein H² J. (Harpsfield MSS. vary.)   3. *proof*] proofe of the matter D.   4–5. *forth* . . . *evidence*] by them to give evidence J.   5. *vppon his oath*] Omitted in J.   6. *Against whom*] Vpon this against whom H¹; againe whome M T; Against when B.   6. *thus*] Omitted in H² J.   6. *sworne*] Omitted in J.   7. *in this wise*] thus T.   7. *a*] Interlineated in H².   7. *my lordes*] my Lords sayd he D.   8. *needed*] need H² J W X. (Harpsfield MSS. vary.)   8. *it is*] this H³.   9. *in this place*] to bee in this place W X.   9. *at*] and at H³ H¹ A.   9. *case*] Omitted in M.   9–10. *to stand*] stand T.   10. *here*] Omitted in H² J W.   10. *othe*] Omitted in H².   11. *yours*] your H¹.   11. *pray I*] I pray that A² D B.   11. *I neuer*] I may neuer J ; neuer H³.   12. *I wold*] wold I, H³.   13. *recited*] recites H².   13–14. *to the courte*] to the whole courte H²; vnto them J.   14. *theyr*] the A² D B; their whole W X.   14. *communicacion*] Communicacion had betweene them D.   15. *said*] further said W X.   16. *good*] Omitted in J.   16. *am soryer*] am more sorye H² (more *being interlineated*); am soryer M (*the final r being interlineated*); more Sorry D.   17. *for*] Omitted in D.   18. *no man*] euer any man A²; any man D W X B.   18–p. 89, l. 1. *man . . . Tower*] A² damaged.   19. *to be a man*] a man to be D.   19. *as*] Omitted in S.   20–21. *would . . . tyme*] at anie time wold W X.   21. *I*] Omitted in J.

you knowe, of no small while haue bine acquainted with
yow and your conuersacion, who haue knowen you from
your youth hitherto; For we longe dwelled both in one
parishe together, where, as your self can tell (I am sory
you compell me so to say) you were esteemed very light 5
of your tongue, A greate dicer, *and* of no comendable
fame. And so in your house at the temple, wheare
hath bine your cheif bringing vppe, were you likewise
accompted.

Would More disclose to Rich the opinion he had withheld from the King and his Lords?

"Can it therefore seeme likely vnto your honorable 10
Lordshipps that I wold, in so weyghty a cause, so vnadvisedlye overshootte my self as to trust master Rich, a
man of me alwaies reputed for one of so litle truth, as
your lordshipps haue heard, So farre aboue my soueraigne
Lord the kinge, or any of his noble Councellours, that I 15
wold vnto him vtter the secreates of my consciens
towchinge the kings supremacye, The speciall pointe
and only marke at my handes so longe sought for: A
thinge which I neuer did, nor neuer wold, after the
statute thereof made, reveale either to the kings highnes 20
himself, or to any of his honorable councell[ours], as it is
not vnknowne to your honors, at sundry * seuerall
times sent from his graces owne person vnto the

MSS. H² J H³ H¹ A M S A² (*damaged*) D T W X B.

1. *knowe*] well knowe H³.   1. *of no . . . acquainted*] haue
beene no small while acquaynted M A².   2. *who*] which B;
And W X.   2. *haue*] hath M.   3. *longe dwelled*] haue
dwelt A² D B.   3–4. *both . . . parishe*] in one parrish both
T W.   4. *where, as*] whereas H¹ M S X.   4. *tell*] well tell
S A² D W X B.   (*All* Harpsfield MSS. *except* Y, well tell.)   6.
and] *Omitted in* W X.   7. *in . . . temple*] in your house in
the Temple M; in your house the Temple D B; att your house
the Temple W X.   11–12. *vnadvisedlye overshootte*] farr over-
shutte J.   13. *of me alwaies*] alwayes of me S.   13. *reputed*] *Interlineated over* accompted *crossed through* H².   13.
so] *Omitted in* S T.   15. *kinge*] kings most excellent Maiestie
D.   15. *of his*] his W.   15. *noble*] most noble D.   15–16.
I . . . him] vnto him I would S.   16. *vtter the secreates*] trust
þe Secrett H¹.   18. *at*] of B.   19. *did . . . wold*] would
nor euer did H¹.   19. *neuer* (2)] euer W X.   20. *thereof*]
therefore D.   20. *the kings*] *Before* the kings H² *has* your
self *crossed through*.   21. *councellours*] councell H² W X.
21. *it*] *Omitted in* B.   22. *honors*] house J.   22–23.
sundry seuerall times] sundry and seuerall times H²; sundrie
tymes and severall J; seuerall sundry times B.   23. *from*]
for B.   23. *his*] *Omitted in* X.   23. *graces*] grace H³;
omitted in T.   23. *owne*] *Omitted in* S.

Only "*malicious*" denial is punishable

Tower vnto me for none other purpose? Can this in your iudgments, my lordes, seeme likely to be true? And [yet], if [I] had so [done] indeed, my lords, as m*aster* Rich hath sworne, seing it was spoken but in Familiar *
5 secreate talk, nothing affirminge, *and* only in puttinge of cases, without other displeasaunt circumstances, it cannot iustly be taken to be spoken maliciouslye; And where there is no malice, there can be no offence. And ouer this I can never thincke, my lord*es*, that so many
[p. 40] [worthye] Bishoppes, so many | honorable parsonages,
11 and [so] many other worshipp*full*, vertuous, wise *and* well learned men as att the makinge of that lawe were in the p*ar*liam*ent* assembled, ever ment to haue any man pvnished by death in whom there coulde be
15 found no malice, taking 'malitia' [for] 'maleuolentia'; For if 'malicia' be gener*a*lly taken for 'sinne', no man is there then that can thereof excuse himself: *Quia si dixerimus quod peccatum non habemus, nosmet ipsos seducimus, et veritas in nobis non est.*
20 And only this word 'maliciously' is in the statute

Even if he had, he cannot be charged with malicious denial. The word maliciously had been put into the Statute as a precaution against inflicting the death-penalty on insufficient grounds.

Malicious denial is the only denial punishable under the Statute.

MSS. H² J H³ H¹ A M S A² (*imperfect*) D T W X B.

1–p. 91, l. 20. *Tower . . . vnto them*] *After* Tower A² *has leaf missing: then its folios* 39–43 (*to end*) *are supplied from* MS. Add. 4474 (B. M.).   2. *lordes*] good Lords D.   2. *seeme . . . true*] as Master Riche hath sworne seeme likely to be true T.
3. *yet*] *Omitted in* H² J.   3. *I had so done*] it had bine so H²; I had done soe W.   4. *sworne*] heere sworne D.   4–5. *sworne . . . secreate*] falslie sworne sith it was spoken as he said but in familiar secrett W X.   4–5. *but . . . talk*] in familier secreat speech S.   4–5. *Familiar secreate*] Familiar frendly secreate H² (secreate *being interlineated*); secret familier H³ H¹ A T.
5. *talk*] speech S.   5. *and*] but S.   7. *iustly be taken*] be justly taken H¹.   9. *ouer*] ouer and besides D.   9. *I . . . lordes*] my Lords I can neuer thinke H¹.   9. *that so many*] as Master Rich hath sworne that so many T.
10. *worthye*] other H².   11. *and* (1)] *Omitted in* D.   11. *so*] *Omitted in* H² J M.   11. *other*] *Omitted in* S.   11. *worshippfull*] *Omitted in* W.   11. *vertuous*] *Omitted in* S.   12. *well*] *Omitted in* H³ H¹ A T W.   12. *as*] *Omitted in* H³ H¹ A T.
12. *of that lawe*] thereof D B.   13. *in the*] at the D B; in þat W.   14. *by*] with W.   15. '*malitia*'] malixi X.   15. '*malitia*' *for* '*maleuolentia*'] malitia pro maleuolentia H² J; malitiam for malevolentiam M W; malyce pro malevolentia S.
16. *if*] *Omitted in* H³.   16. '*malicia*'] maliciam M; malice S.   16. *for*] *Omitted in* X.   17. *can thereof*] thereof can S D W X B.
19. *in nobis non est*] non est in nobis W.   20. *the*] this S D W X.

materiall, as this terme 'forcible' is in the statute of forcible entries; By which statute, if a man enter peaceably, *and* put not his aduersary out forcibly, it is no offence. But if he put him out forcibly, then by that statute it is an offence, *and* so shall he be punished 5 by this tearme ' forcibly '.

The King's previous favours to More should be sufficient to convince the judges of the folly of attributing to More malice against him.

"Besides this, the manifold goodnes of the kings highnes himself, that hath bine so many waies my singuler good Lord *and* gracious soueraigne, that hath so deerely loved *and* trusted me, even att my [very] first cominge 10 into his noble service with the dignity of his honourable pryvy Councell vouchsafing to admit me, *and* to offices of greate creditt *and* worshippe most liberally advanced me, *and* finally with that waighty Roome of his graces highe Chauncelour (the like whereof he neuer did to 15 temporall man before) next to his owne roiall person the highest officer in this noble realme, so farr aboue my merittes or qualities able *and* meete therefore, of his incomparable benignity honoured *and* exalted me, by the space of XX[ti] yeares *and* more shewing his con- 20 tinewall favour towards me, And (vntill at my owne poore suite, it pleased his highnes, geving me licens, with

MSS. H[2] J H[3] H[1] A M S A[2] (*imperfect*) D T W X B.

1. *materiall . . . statute*] *Omitted in* H[3] H[1] A T. (*Eyeslip.*) 1. *this*] the D.   1. '*forcible* '] forcibly S.   1–6. *is in* . . . '*forcibly* '] *Omitted in* B.   2. *forcible*] forcibly M.   2. *entries*] entry M D W.   3. *peaceably*] patiently W.   3. *aduersary*] aduersaries H[3] T.   4–5. *But . . . punished*] and so shall he be punished T. (*Eyeslip.*)   4. *forcibly*] forceible D X.   5. *an*] a H[1].   5. *shall he*] he shal H[3].   6. *this tearme*] his terme M; this X.   6. '*forcibly* '] forceible D.   7–8. *the kings highnes*] my Soveraigne Lord the Kings Highnes J.   9. *so*] *Omitted in* H[3].   10. *and*] me and J W X.   10. *very*] *Omitted in* H[2] W X.   11. *into*] vnto W X.   11. *noble*] honorable H[3] H[1] A T.   11. *with*] *Omitted in* X.   12. *and*] *Omitted in* J W X.   12. *offices*] office S.   13. *creditt*] *Interlineated in* H[2].   14. *that*] the S.   14. *waighty*] worthy H[3] H[1] A T.   14. *graces*] Maiesties W.   15. *Chauncelour*] Chauncellorshipp J; S *has* shyp *erased.*   15. *to*] to any W (any *being interlineated*).   16. *man*] Men H[1].   16. *owne*] *Omitted in* W.   17. *officer*] office H[1] W X.   17. *this*] his S D B.   17. *noble*] whole H[3] H[1] A.   18. *merittes*] merryt X.   18. *or*] *Interlineated in* H[2] *over* and *crossed through.*   18. *and*] or H[1] S.   18. *his*] his owne H[3]; his owne and H[1] A T.   19. *benignity*] *Space left in* X.   21. *And*] *Omitted in* S.   22. *poore*] poore humble S D W B. (*All* Harpsfield MSS. *except* B, poore humble.)

his ma*ies*ties favour, to bestowe the residue of my life
for the p*ro*vision of my soule in the service of god, of
his especiall goodnes thereof to discharg *and* vnburthen
me) most beningly heaped honours continually more
5 *and* more vppon me : All this his highnes goodnes, I say,
[p. 41] [so long] thus | bountifully extended towards me, were
in my minde, my Lordes, matter sufficient to convince
this sclaunderous surmise by this man so wrongfully
imagined against me."
10 Master Rich, seing himself so disproved, *and* his credit   Southwell
so fowlye defaced, cawsed S*ir* Rich*ard* Southwell *and*   and Palmer
                                                             are sworn;
m*aster* Palmer, that at [the] time of their com*m*unicacion they had
                                                             paid no
were in the chamber, to be sworne what word*es* had   heed to
                                                      the con-
passed betweene them. Wheruppon m*aster* Palmer,   versation.
15 vppon his deposition, said that he was so buysye about
the trussinge vppe of S*ir* Thomas Moores bookes in a
sack, that he tooke no head to their talke. S*ir* Rich*ard*
Southwell likewise, vppon his deposition, said that because he was apointed only to looke vnto the convey-
20 aunce of his bookes, he gaue no eare vnto them.
After this were there many other Reasons, not nowe   In spite
                                                      of More's
                                                      proven
MSS. H² J H³ H¹ A M S A² (*imperfect*) D T W X B.   innocence,
                                                      the Jury
                                                      find him
2. *provision*] providinge S; preservacion W X.   2. *in*]   guilty.
into W.   3. *vnburthen*] disburthen H³ B.   4. *heaped*]
heapinge S D W X B. (*All* Harpsfield MSS. heaping.)   4.
continually] Omitted in J.   4–5. *more and more vppon me*]
vppon me more and more T.   5. *goodnes*] Omitted in W.
6. *so long*] Omitted in H².   6. *thus*] this X.   6.
thus . . . me] continued towards me J.   7. *minde*] mynd
& Simple iudgement D.   7. *Lordes*] good Lords D; *space
left in* X.   7. *matter*] matters H³.   8. *this* (1)] the S.
8. *sclaunderous*] scandalous W X.   8. *wrongfully*] falsely
& wrongfully D.   9. *imagined*] imagined & deuised D.   10.
seing] beinge T.   10. *so disproved*] so disgracefully disproued
D; thus disproved T.   12. *that*] Omitted in S.   12–13.
that . . . sworne] at that tyme of their Comunicacion present
in the chamber with them to be sworne S.   12. *at*] in H¹.
12. *the*] that H² J S X (*that being interlineated in* H²).   12.
communicacion] examynacion M.   13. *were . . . chamber*]
were present in theire Chamber with them D; were in the
Chamber with them W X B.   14. *betweene*] betwixt J S W X B.
15. *so*] Omitted in D B.   15–16. *about the trussinge*] aboute
trussinge H³ H¹ A; in the trussing X.   16. *of*] Omitted in J.
17. *to*] of D B.   17. *talke*] wordes H³; tale W.   19. *vnto*]
vppon X.   20. *his*] Sir Thomas Moore his H³ A; Sir Thomas
Mores H¹.   20. *eare*] great eare W X.   21 *to end*.]   *For* A²
see collations to 89/1–91/20.   21. *not nowe*] that nowe T.

in my remembraunce, by Sir Thomas Moore in his owne
defens alleaged, to the discredit of master Riches aforesaid evidence, and proof of the cleerenes of his owne
consciens. All whiche notwithstandinge, the Jury found
him guilty. And incontinent vppon the[ir] verdicte, 5
the Lord Chauncelour, for that matter cheif Comissioner,
begininge [to proceede] in iudgment against him, Sir
Thomas Moore said to him : "My Lord, when I was
toward the Lawe, the manner in such case was to aske
the prisoner before Iudgment why Iudgment should not 10
be geuen agaynste him." Wherevppon the lord Chauncelour, stayeng his Iudgment, wherein he had partely
proceeded, demaunded of him what he was able to say
to the contrary. Who then in this sorte moste humbly
made awneswer : 15

"Forasmuch as, my Lorde*," quoth he, "this Indictment is grounded vppon an acte of parliamente directly
repugnant to the lawes of god and his holy churche, the
supreeme gouer[n]ment of which, or of any parte whereof,
may no temporall prince presume by any lawe to take 20
vppon him, as rightfully belonging to the Sea of Roome,
a spirituall preheminence by the mouth of our Sauiour
hymself, personally present vppon the earth, [only] to
St Peeter and his successors, Byshopps of the same Sea,

MSS. H² J H³ H¹ A M S A² (damaged) D T W X B.

1. *Moore*] *Omitted in* X.   2–3. *Riches aforesaid*] Riche his
foresaid J W X.   2–3. *aforesaid*] sayd S.   3. *proof*] pra
X.   3. *owne*] *Omitted in* A² D B.   4. *All*] At T.   5.
incontinent] *In* H² *ly is added on the margin in fainter ink*; incontinently H³ H¹ A.   5. *their*] the H² J M; that A².   6.
cheif] chefelie M.   7. *to proceede*] *Omitted in* H² J.   7–8. *Sir
. . . said*] Sir Thomas More interrupting the same sayd D.
9. *toward the*] a Student in the S.   9. *case*] a case J ;
cases S D W X. (Harpsfield MSS. *vary between* case *and* cases.)
10. *why*] what he could say for himselfe why D.   11–p. 93,
l. 7. *agaynste . . . with*] A² damaged.   12. *had*] *Omitted in* H³.
14. *then*] *Omitted in* W.   14. *moste*] *Omitted in* J H³ H¹.
14. *humbly*] mildlie J.   16–17. *Forasmuch . . . Indictment*]
Forasmuch my Lord quoth he that this Indytement S.   16.
Lorde] Lordes H² T.   16–17. *Indictment*] Judgement M X.
17. *vppon*] with W.   17. *directly*] direct D.   18. *repugnant*]
oppugnaunt J.   19. *gouernment*] gouerment H²; gouernour B.
19. *whereof*] thereof H³ A² W X.   20. *no*] not M.   20.
presume] *Omitted in* M.   20. *any*] *Omitted in* M.   21. *as*]
Omitted in S.   23. *the*] *Omitted in* S.   23. *only*] *Omitted in* H².

He denounces rejection of the Pope's Supremacy

by speciall prerogative graunted; It is therefore in lawe amongest Christen men insufficient to charge any Christen man." And for proofe thereof, like as, amonge [diuers] other reasons and aucthorities, he declared that
5 this Realme, being but one member and [smale] parte
[p. 42] of the Church, might not make a particuler lawe | disagreable with the generall lawe of Christes vniuersall Catholike Churche, No more then the city of London, beinge but one poore member in respecte of the whole
10 realme, might make a lawe against an acte of parliament to bind the whole realme; So farther shewed he that it was contrary both to the lawes and statutes of our owne Land yeat vnrepealed, As they might evidently perceaue in *Magna charta: Quod ecclesia Anglicana*
15 *libera sit, et habeat omnia * iura sua * integra et libertates suas illæsas*; And also contrarye to that sacred oath which the kinges highnes himself and euery other christian prince alwaies with greate solemnitye receaved at their Coronations; Alleaginge moreover that no more
20 might this realme of England refuse obediens to the Sea of Roome then might the child refuse obediens to his

MSS. H² J H³ H¹ A M S A² (*damaged*) D T W X B.

1. *speciall*] spirituall S.   1. *therefore*] thereof M.   3–5. *like . . . being*] like as amonge many . . . being H²; amongst diuers other Reasons and auctorityes he declared that like as this Realme beinge H³; like as amongst diuers other Reasons & Authorityes hee declared that as this Realme being H¹; lyke as amongest divers other reasons and aucthorytyes he declared that like as this Realme beinge A T; A² *damaged*.   5. *smale*] Omitted in H²; a small S X.   6. *Church*] Christian Church D. 6–7. *disagreable*] disagreeinge H³ H¹ A D X B. (*All* Harpsfield MSS. disagreable.)   7. *with*] to T W X.   7–8. *vniuersall . . . Churche*] holye Catholique Church J.   9. *poore*] Omitted in X. 9. *member*] *After* member H² *has, crossed through, and* parte of the churche mighte not make a particular lawe.   10. *might*] may A².   11. *So*] vnto So J.   12. *both*] Omitted in A². 13. *our owne*] this J.   14. *perceaue*] apeare A².   14. *Quod*] where it is sayd Quod D.   15. *libera*] *Interlineated in* H². 15. *habeat*] *Interlineated in* H²; habet H³ H¹ A.   15. *iura sua*] sua iura H² W X.   16. *also*] Omitted in J.   17. *other*] Omitted in S.   18–19. *with . . . Coronations*] at theire Coronations receaved J.   18. *receaved*] Receyvethe H³.   19. *Coronations*] Coronation H¹.   19–p. 94, l. 16. *Coronations . . . there against*] A² *damaged*.   20. *this*] the A² B.   20. *the Sea*] *Interlineated in* H² *over* this realme *crossed through*.   21. *to*] of A².

[owne] naturall father. For, as St Pawle said of the Corinthians : " I haue regenerated you, my children in Christ," So might St Gregorye, Pope of Roome, of whom, by St Austyne, his messenger, we first receaved the Christian faithe, of vs Englishmen truly saye : 5 " Yow are my children, because I haue geuen to you euerlasting salvacion, a farr [higher and] better inheritaunce then any carnall father can leaue to his child, and by [re]generation made you my spirituall children in Christe." 10

More is accused of "stiffly sticking," contrary to the Bishops and learned men of the Realm.

Then was it by the Lorde Chauncelour therunto awneswered, that seinge all the Byshoppes, Vniuersities *and* best learned of [this] Realme had to this acte agreed, It was muche mervayled that he alone against them all would so stiffly stick [therat], *and* so vehemently argue 15 there against.

He claims the support of the Clergy and learned men of the past.

To that Sir Thomas Moore replied, sayenge : " If the number of Bishoppes *and* vniuersytyes be so materiall as your lordeshippe seemethe to take it, Then se I litle cause, my lorde, why that thing in my consciens should 20 make any chainge. For I nothinge doubte but that, thoughe not in this realme, yeat in Christendome aboute, of thes well lerned | Bishoppes and vertuous men that [p. 43]

MSS. H² J H³ H¹ A M S A² (*damaged*) D T W X B.

1. *owne*] Omitted in H² J.   1. *said of the*] sayed to the H³ H¹ A; saith to the W X.   3. *Pope*] bp A².   3. *of*] Interlineated in H² over by *crossed through*.   4. *of whom*] Omitted in T.   6. *geuen*] give J.   6. *to*] Omitted in D. 7. *higher and*] Omitted in H² J.   8. *leaue to his*] leaue his H³ H¹ A; giue to his W.   8. *child*] children W X.   9. *regeneration*] generation H² H³ H¹ A M; spirituall generation J. 9. *spirituall*] Omitted in W.   11–12. *by . . . awneswered*] therevnto by the Lord Chauncellour answeared J.   12. *that . . . Vniuersities*] Cropped in B.   12. *the*] Omitted in H³. 13. *learned*] learned men S.   (*All* Harpsfield MSS. learned men.) 13. *this*] the H².   (*All* Harpsfield MSS. the.)   13. *acte*] Omitted in B.   13. *agreed*] Omitted in M.   14. *mervayled*] marveyll H³ H¹ A W X.   (*All* Harpsfield MSS. except C, meruaile.) 15. *therat*] Omitted in H² J.   15. *so* (2)] Omitted in J.   18. *number of*] Omitted in J.   18. *and*] Crossed through in B. 19. *lordeshippe*] lordshippes J.   20. *lorde*] Lords J.   21. *For*] Omitted in W.   21. *but that*] Omitted in S.   22. *not*] Omitted in W.   22. *aboute*] Omitted in W X.   23–p. 95, l. 1. *of thes . . . alive*] Omitted in J.   23. *thes*] those S D A² B; all those W X.   (Harpsfield MSS. vary between these *and* those.) 23. *vertuous*] learned H³ H¹ A.

are yeat alive, they be not the fewer parte that be of my mind therein. But if I should speake of those whiche already be dead, of whom many be nowe holy sainctes in heaven, I am very sure it is the farre * greater parte of
5 them that, all the while [they] lived, thoughte in this case that waye that I thinck nowe. And therefore am I not bounde, my lord, to conforme my consciens to the Councell of one Realme against the generall Councell of Christendome."

10 Nowe when Sir Thomas Moore, for thavoydinge of the Indictment, had taken as many exceptions as he thought meete, and [many] moe reasons then I can nowe remember alleaged, The Lord Chauncelour, loth to haue the burthen of that Iudgmente wholye to depend vppon
15 himself, there openlye asked thadvise of the Lord Fitz James, then Lord Cheif Justice of the kings Bench, and ioyned in Comission with him, whether this indictment were sufficient or not. Who, like a wise man, awneswered: "My lords all, By St Julian" (that was euer his
20 oath), "I must needes confes that if thacte of parliament be not vnlawfull, then is not the Indictment in my conscience insufficient."

Wherevppon the Lord Chauncelour said to the rest of the Lordes: "Loe, my Lordes, loe, you heare what

The Lord Chief Justice admits that "if the Act of Parliament be lawful, then the Indictment is good enough."

Sentence is passed against More.

MSS. H² J H³ H¹ A M S A² (damaged) D T W X B.

1. *fewer*] least J; fourthe H³ H¹ A S A² D T B. (*All* Harpsfield MSS. fewer.)   1. *be* (2)] are S A² D W X B.   1. *my*] *Omitted in* M.   2–3. *whiche . . . dead*] that be allreadie dead J D B; that are alreadie dead S X. (*All* Harpsfield MSS. that are already dead.)   3. *be nowe*] be D; nowe be W X.   3. *holy*] *Omitted in* J.   4. *very*] *Omitted in* A² D W B.   4–5. *it . . . lived*] that þe farre greater part of them all þe while they liued H¹; the farre greater parte of them there lived J; the farr greater part of them while they liued B.   4. *it is*] *Omitted in* W X B.   4. *farre*] farre farre H² M.   4. *parte*] *Omitted in* M.   5. *that, all the*] *Omitted in* A² W X.   5. *they*] *Omitted in* H².   5. *this*] *Omitted in* T.   6. *that I*] which I, B.   6–7. *am I*] I ame H³.   7. *lord*] *A correction of* lords H²; Lords J.   7–p. 96, l. 2. *lord . . . him*] A² *damaged*.   8. *one*] our S.   8. *of* (2)] of all H³ H¹ A D.   12. *meete*] meete & convenient D.   12. *many*] *Omitted in* H² J M.   12. *nowe*] *Omitted in* S A² W X B.   13. *alleaged*] had alleaged A² D W X B.   14. *that*] the H³ H¹ A T.   14. *Iudgmente*] Inditement T. (*All* Harpsfield MSS. Indictment.)   16. *Lord*] the Lord J M.   18. *not*] noe D.   18. *wise man*] man wise W.   19. *lords all*] Lords all, sayd hee D; Lord all T.

He prays for his judges.

my lord cheif Iustice saith," and so ymmediately gave he Iudgemente against him.

After whiche ended, the Comissioners yeat further curteouslye offred him, if he had any thinge els to alleage for his defence, to graunt him favorable audience. Who 5 awneswered : " More haue I not to say, my Lordes, but that like as the blessed Apostle St Pawle, as we read in thactes of the Apostles, was present, *and* consented to the death of St Stephen, and kepte their clothes that stoned him to deathe, and yeat be they [nowe] both 10 twayne holy Sainctes in heaven, and shall continue there frendes for euer, So I verily [truste], *and* shall therefore right hartelye pray, that thoughe yo*ur* lordshippes haue nowe [here] in earthe bine Judges to my condemnacion, we may yeat hereafter in heaven meerily all meete 15 together, to our euerlasting saluac*ion*."

Roper not present at More's trial, but had received the report from those present.

Thus much towching S*ir* Thomas Moores arrainem*en*t, being not thereat present my self, haue I by the credyble reporte, [partely] of the right worshipp*full* S*ir* Anthony Seintleger, knight, *and* partely of Ri*chard* Heywood *and* 20 John Webbe, gentlemen, | withe others of good creditt, [p. 44]

MSS. H² J H³ H¹ A M S A² (*damaged*) D T W X B.

1. *so*] *Omitted in* H³.   1. *ymmediately*] imediatly without more adoe D.   1-2. *gave he*] gaue the J T; gaue H³; A² *imperfect*.   2. *against him*] against him according to the vsuall manner in such cases D.   3. *further*] *Omitted in* J.   4-5. *if . . . defence*] *Omitted in* B.   6. *haue I*] I haue A² D T W X B.   7. *that*] *Omitted in* J S A² D B.   7. *like*] *Omitted in* D.   8. *consented*] contented M.   9-10. *and . . . deathe*] *Omitted in* D.   10. *nowe*] *Omitted in* H².   11. *twayne*] *Omitted in* A² B.   11. *there*] therof X.   12. *frendes for euer*] *Space left in* X.   12. *for euer*] together for ever A S D T W; for euer and euer A².   12. *verily truste*] verily hope H²; trust verely T.   12. *therefore*] *Omitted in* M.   13. *right*] most H³ H¹ A.   13. *your*] in your J.   13-14. *your . . . here*] now you Lordships haue here B.   14. *here*] *Omitted in* H² J M.   14. *in*] one D; on B.   15. *in heaven . . . meete together*] meete in heauen together W; meete in heauen merrely altogether X.   15. *all meete*] meete A²; meet all D B.   16. *our*] *Omitted in* H³ H¹ A T.   17. *arrainement*] Arrainment & Condemnacon D.   18-p. 97, l. 15, *being . . . your*] A² damaged.   18. *thereat present*] present thereat M; thereat personally present D; there present T.   18. *the*] *Omitted in* S.   19. *partely*] *Omitted in* H² W.   19. *of the*] by the T.   19. *the right worshippfull*] *Omitted in* J.   19. *Sir*] *Omitted in* X.   21. *gentlemen*] gentleman J; gent X.   21. *withe others*] and others W X.

at the hearing thereof present themselves, as farre as my poore witt *and* memory wold serue me, here truly rehersed vnto you.

Nowe, after this arraignem*e*nt, dep*a*rted he from the 5 barre to the Tower againe, ledde by S*ir* Willi*a*m Kingston, a talle, stronge, *and* comely knighte, Constable of the Tower, *and* his very deare freind. Who, when he had brought him from westminster to the old Swanne towards the Tower, there w*i*th an heavy harte, the 10 teares runinge downe by his cheekes, bade him farewell. *More returns to the Tower. Kingston's farewell.*

S*ir* Thom*a*s Moore, seinge him so sorowefull, comforted him w*i*th as good words as he could, sayenge : " Good m*a*ster Kingston, trouble not yo*u*r self, but be of good cheare ; for I will pray for you, *and* my good Lady, 15 yo*u*r wife, that we may meete in heuen together, where we shalbe meery for ever *and* ever." *More will pray for Kingston and his wife.*

Soone after, S*ir* willi*a*m Kingston, talking w*i*th me of S*ir* Thomas Moore, said*e* : " In good faith, m*a*ster Roper, I was ashamed of my self, that, at my dep*a*rting 20 from yo*u*r father, I found my harte so feeble, *and* his so stronge, that he was fayne to comfort*e* me, wh*i*ch should rather have comforted him." *Kingston praises More's stout heart.*

When S*ir* Thomas Moore came from westminster to the Towerward againe, his daughter, my wife, desirous *Margaret's farewell to her father.*

MSS. H² J H³ H¹ A M S A² (*damaged*) D T W X (*to l.* 21, *he*) B.

1. *as* (2)] fourth as J.   2. *here*] *Omitted in* W.   2. *truly*] truly and faithfully D.   3. *rehersed*] rehearsed and related D.   4. *this*] his H³ S D T W.   5. *barre*] Tower barre X.   6. *Constable*] then Constable W.   7. *deare*] good S; great W.   9. *the Tower*] to Tower W.   9. *an*] a J S.   9. *the* (2)] his H¹.   10. *downe*] *Omitted in* W. 10. *by*] *Omitted in* J T.   12. *as* (1)] *Omitted in* W.   15. *meete*] one day meet meete D.   16. *ever and ever*] euer and euer and so they parted D.   17–22. *Soone . . . him*] *Omitted here in* S, *but inserted below, after* weape, p. 99, l. 8.   17. *after*] after this W X.   18. *saide*] sayd vnto me D.   18. *good*] *Omitted in* J.   19. *departing*] departure J A² D B.   20. *your*] my A².   20–21. *so stronge*] stronge M.   21–p. 100, l. 10. *was fayne . . . death*] *Omitted in* X.   21. *which*] that H³ H¹A T; who A² D.   22. *him*] him when Sir Tho : More came from his arraignement D.   23. *When*] As D.   23. *came*] was come S.   23–24. *came . . . his*] was of comming vnto the Towre againe from his Arraignement his D.   23. *from westminster*] *Omitted in* S.   24. *Towerward*] Toward M. 24. *desirous*] beeing desirous D.

to see her father, whom she thought she should neuer see in this world after, *and* also to haue his Finall blessinge, gaue attendaunce aboute the Tower wharf, where she knewe he should passe by, before he could enter into the Tower, There tarienge for his coming home. Assone as she sawe him, after his blessing on her knees reue*r*ently receaued, Shee hastinge towards him, *and*, w*i*thout consideracion or care of her self, pressinge [in] amonge [the middest of] the thronge and company of the garde that w*i*th halberd*es and* bills wente round aboute him, hastely ranne to him, *and* there openly, in the sight of them all, imbraced him, toke him about the neck, *and* kissed him. Who, well liking her moste naturall *and* deere daughterlye affection towarde*s* him, gaue her his fatherly blessinge *and* many [godly] word*es* of | comforte [p. 45] besides. From whom after she was dep*a*rted, she, not satisfied w*i*th the former sighte of [him, and like one that had forgotten herselfe, being all ravished with the entyre loue of] her deere father, having respecte neyther to her self, nor to the presse of [the] people *and* multitude

He blesses and comforts her.

MSS. H² J H³ H¹ A M S A² (*damaged*) D T W X (*imperfect*) B.

1–p. 99, l. 2. *see* . . . *as*] A² *damaged*. 2. *after*] againe after D. 2–3. *and* . . . *blessinge*] *Interlineated in* H². 2. *Finall*] last and finall D. 3. *attendaunce*] dilligent attendaunce D. 4. *should*] would A²; must of necessity D. 4. *before*] ere J. 5. *tarienge*] tarriyng and abiding D. 5–6. *his* . . . *after*] the comming home of her Father and as soone as shee saw him after D. 5. *coming home*] coming. Whom S. (*All* Harpsfield MSS. comming. Whom.) 6. *him*] *Omitted in* S. (*All* Harpsfield MSS. *omit*.) 6. *his*] her H³. 6. *blessing*] blessinges J; fatherly blessing D. 6–7. *on* . . . *receaued*] revently [*sic*] vpon her knees receaved M. 7. *him, and*] *Omitted in* J. 8. *or*] of J. 8. *in*] *Omitted in* H² T. 9. *the middest of*] *Omitted in* H². 9. *company*] the Companie J. 10. *with*] *Omitted in* M. 10. *wente*] weare J; as in such cases the manner is went D. 12. *them all*] all them J H³ A. 12. *imbraced him, toke him*] embraced and tooke him J; ymbraced him M. 13. *moste*] *Omitted in* W. 13–14. *naturall* . . . *affection*] daughterlye loue and affection J. 14. *deere*] *Omitted in* M. 14. *daughterlye*] daughterlike S. 15. *godly*] goodly H². 17. *the*] her H³. 17–19. *him* . . . *loue of*] *Omitted in* H² J. (*Eyeslip*.) 18. *the*] *Omitted in* M S D B. (*All* Harpsfield MSS. *omit*.) 19. *deere*] *Interlineated in* M; *omitted in* T. 19. *respecte neyther*] neither respect W. 20. *presse*] greate preasse D. 20. *the* (2)] *Omitted in* H² M S A² W. (Harpsfield MSS. *vary*.)

Letter to Margaret 99

that were [there] aboute him, sodainely *torned back Margaret's second farewell.
againe, ranne to him as before, tooke him about the
neck, *and* divers tymes together most lovingly kissed
him; and at last, with a full heavy harte, was fayne to
5 dep*ar*te from him : The beholding whereof was to many
of them that were present thereat so lamentable that it
made them for very sorowe [therof] to mourne and
weape.

So remayned S*ir* Thomas Moore in the tower more More sends his hair-shirt and a letter to Margaret.
10 then a seuennight after his iudgme*nt*; From whence, the
day before he suffred, he sent his shirte of heare (not
willinge to haue it seene) to my wife, his deerely beloved
daughter, *and* a letter written wi*th* a coale, contayned
in the foresaid booke of his workes, plainely expressing
15 the fervent desire he had to suffer [on] the morowe, in
these words folowinge :

" I comber you, good Margaret, much, but I wold be He longs to die on the Eve of St. Thomas.
sory if it should be any longer then to morowe; For to
morowe is St Thomas even, *and* the vtas of St Peeter;
20 And therefore too morowe longe I to goe to god; it
were a daye very meete *and* convenient for me, etc. I
neuer liked your manner* [towardes me] better then
when you kissed me last. For I like when daughterly

MSS. H² J H³ H¹ A M S A² (*damaged*) D T W X (*imperfect*) B.

1. *were there aboute*] were aboute H² H³; there were aboute W.
1. *torned*] retorned H².   2. *ranne*] and rann J; *omitted in* M.
2. *to him*] *Omitted in* M.   2. *tooke*] & tooke H¹.   3. *together*] *Omitted in* A².   3. *most*] *Omitted in* T.   3. *lovingly*] entirelie W.   4. *at*] at the W.   6. *them*] the Spectators D.
6. *present*] there present M.   6. *thereat*] *Interlineated in* H²; thereat & wittnesses thereof as some of them haue since themselues related vnto me D.   6. *lamentable*] lamentably T.
7. *therof*] *Omitted in* H² J M.   7–8. *mourne and weape*] weepe and mourne T.   8–9. *weape. So*] Between weape *and* So, S *inserts paragraph* Soone . . . him *which was missing above, p.* 97, *ll.* 17–22.   9. *Moore*] *Omitted in* W.   10. *iudgment*] sayd iudgement & condemnacon D.   12. *to* (1) . . . *seene*] to bee seene M; that the same should be seene D.   14. *booke*] bookes A².   14–p. 100, l. 10. *expressing . . . death*] A² *damaged*.   15. *on*] in H² T.   15. *morowe*] morrowe after D.   16. *folowinge*] *Omitted in* J.   19. *vtas*] *Space left in* W.   20. *too morowe longe I*] longe I tomorrowe T.   20–21. *it were*] that weare J.   21. *me, etc. I*] mee And I, J; me I, T.   22. *your*] *Omitted in* I, T.   22. *manner*] manners H² J M.   22. *towardes me better*] better H² J H³ H¹ A; better toward me W.

loue *and* deere charitye hath no leysure to looke to
worldly curtesye."

Pope brings him word that he is to die that day. [6 July, 1535.]

And so vppon the next morowe, beinge Tuesdaye, St
Thomas even, *and* the vtas of Saincte Peeter, in the
yeare of our lord, * one thowsand five hundreth thirtye 5
and five (according as he in his letter [the daye] before
had wished) earlye in the morninge came to him S*ir*
Thomas Pope, his singuler freind, on message from the
kinge *and* his Councell, That he should before nyne of
the clock * the same morning suffer death; and that 10
therefore furthwi*th* he should prepare him self therunto :

Gratitude to the King for giving him leisure to prepare for death.

"M*aste*r Pope," quoth he, "for yo*ur* good tydings I
most hartelye thancke you. I haue bine alwaies much
bounden to the Kings highnes for the benefit*es and*
honoures that he hath still from tyme to tyme most 15
bountyfully heaped vppon me; and yeat more bound
am I to his grace for puttinge me into this place, where
I haue had convenient time *and* space to haue remem-

He is ready and glad to die, and thanks, and will pray for, the King.

braunce of my end. And so helpe me, god, most of all,
m*aster* Pope, am I bound to his | highnes that it pleaseath [p. 46]
him so shortly to ridde me out of the miseries of this 21
wretched woorld. And therefore will I not faile ernestly

MSS. H² J H³ H¹ A M S A² (*damaged*) D T W X (*imperfect to l.* 10, *death*) B.

2. *curtesye*] curtesie &c. S.   3. *so*] *Omitted in* W.   3. *next*] *Omitted in* S.   3. *morowe*] morninge J.   3. *Tuesdaye*] Thursday A².   3–4. *St Thomas even*] *Omitted in* A².   4. *vtas*] *Space left in* W.   5. *lord*] lord god H² J S.   5–6. *one . . . five*] 1537 J; 1635 (*underlined for correction, but not corrected*) H¹; 1538 M (*Baker's transcript of* M *in MS.* Harleian 7030, *has* 1535).   6. *letter*] letteres W.   6. *the daye*] *Omitted in* H².   8. *singuler*] singular good D W.   9. *his*] the M.   10. *the same*] of the same H²; in the same J.   11. *therefore*] therto A².   11. *therunto*] *Omitted in* H³ H¹ A.   12. *quoth he*] sayth he J; *omitted in* T.   13. *most*] *Omitted in* T.   13–14. *alwaies . . . highnes*] all waies to the kings highnesse much bounden W X.   13–14. *much bounden*] bounden much J.   14. *Kings*] kinge H³ A.   15. *that*] which J; *omitted in* M W.   16. *heaped*] bestowed H³.   16. *bound*] so bounden W.   17. *am I*] I ame J.   17. *into*] in W.   17. *this*] *Omitted in* B.   18. *had*] *Omitted in* T.   19. *helpe me, god*] god helpe me A² D B.   19–20. *most . . . Pope*] Master Pope most of all W.   20. *master Pope*] *Omitted in* X.   20. *am I*] I am B.   20. *pleaseath*] pleased J W X.   21. *so*] *Omitted in* H³ H¹ A A².   21. *me*] him D.   21. *out*] of J.   22. *wretched*] wicked H³.   22–p. 101, l. 2. *And . . . world*] *Omitted in* A². (*Eyeslip.*)   22. *ernestly*] most earnestlye J.

to pray for his grace, bothe heare *and* also in another world."

"The kings pleasure is further," quoth m*aster* Pope, "that at yo*ur* execution you shall not vse many words." *He is commanded to use few words at his execution.*

5 "M*aster* Pope," quothe he, "you do well to geeue me warninge of his graces pleasure, for other wise I had purposed at that tyme somewhat to have spoken, but of no matter wherew*ith* his grace, or any other, should haue had cause to be offended. Neue*r*theles, whatsoeuer
10 I intended, I am ready obediently to conforme my self to his graces commandem*entes*. And I beseeke you, good m*aster* Pope, to be a meene vnto his highnes that my daughter Margaret may be * at my buriall." *He pleads that Margaret may be present at his burial.*

"The kinge is * content already," quoth m*aster* Pope,
15 "that yo*ur* wife, children *and* other [your] freinds shall haue libertie to be present thereat."

"O howe much beholden then," said S*ir* Thomas Moore, "am I to his grace, that vnto my poore buriall vouchsafeth to haue so graciouse consideracion."

20 Wherewithall m*aster* Pope, takinge his leaue of hym, could not refrayne from wepinge. Which S*ir* Thomas Moore perceiuinge, comforted him in this wise : "Quiet yo*ur* self, good m*aster* Pope, *and* be not discomforted; For I trust that we shall, once in heaven, *Comforts Pope.*

MSS. H² J H³ H¹ A M S A² (*damaged*) D T W X B.

1–2. *also . . . world*] in another world also S.   4–20. *at . . . takinge*] A² *damaged.*   5. *to geeue*] that you giue J.
6. *of . . . pleasure*] *Omitted in* S.   6. *pleasure*] pleasure heerein D.   6. *I had*] had I, J.   8. *other*] *Omitted in* T.
10. *intended*] Intend, J.   10. *ready*] *Omitted in* D B.   10. *obediently*] obedient D.   11. *commandementes*] commaundement S A² X B; good pleasure and comaundment D. (*All* Harpsfield MSS. commaundement.)   11. *you*] *Omitted in* B.
12. *to be*] be H³ H¹ A T.   12. *meene*] meanes X.   13. *be*] be present H² J.   14. *kinge*] kings Maiestie D.   14. *content already*] well content already H² J; allready content D.   15. *that*] *Omitted in* W.   15. *wife*] wife and H³ H¹ A A².   (*All* Harpsfield MSS. wife.)   15. *children*] your children D.   15. *your* (2)] *Omitted in* H² J; your good H³; of your W X.   (Harpsfield MSS. vary.)   16. *libertie*] free libertie J D.   17. *beholden*] beholding M A² W X; bounden & beholding D.   17. *said*] quoth W.   18. *grace*] noble grace D.   19. *vouchsafeth*] he vouchsafeth T.   19. *consideracion*] consideracions X.
20. *his*] *Omitted in* B.   20. *of*] with H³ H¹ A T.   24–p. 102, l. 1. *we . . . see*] in heauen we shall once see A² D B.

see eche other full merily, where we shalbe sure to live *and* loue together, in ioyful blisse eternally."

The Lieutenant prevents him from wearing his best apparel at his execution.

Vppon whose dep*ar*ture, S*ir* Thom*as* Moore, as one that had bine invited to [some] solempne feaste, chaunged himself into his best apparell; w*hi*ch m*aste*r Leiueten- 5 aunt espienge, advised him to put it of, sayenge that he that should haue it was but a Javill.

"What, m*aste*r Leiuetenaunt," quoth he, "shall I accompte him a Javill that shall doe me this day so singuler a benefitt? Nay, I assure you, were it clothe 10 of gold, I wolde accompt it well bestowed on him, as St Ciprian did, who gaue his executioner thirtie peeces

But More sends gold to his executioner.

of gould." And albeit at length, throughe m*aste*r Leiuetenaun*tes* importunate p*er*suasion, he altered his apparell, yeat after thexample of | that holy martir St [p. 47] Ciprian, did he, of that litle money that was lefte him, 16 send one Angell of gold to his executioner.

Jests on the weakness of the scaffold.

And so was he by m*aste*r Leiuetenaunte brought out of the Tower, *and* from thence led to[wardes] the place of execution. Where, goinge vppe the scaffold, w*hi*ch 20

MSS. H² J H³ H¹ A M S A² (*damaged*) D T W X B.

1. *see . . . merily*] full merrily see each other W X.   1. *eche other*] one another B.   1. *sure*] sure full merrely D.   1–2. *live and loue*] loue and liue B.   3. *Sir Thomas Moore*] Omitted in X.   4. *some*] a H² J; omitted in H³.   5–6. *Leiuetenaunt*] Leiuetenant of the Towre D.   6. *advised*] aduising H¹ A A².   7. *that*] which S.   8. *quoth he*] Omitted here in A², but inserted below after Javill (*l.* 9).   8. *shall*] should S.   9. *a*] for a A².   9. *shall*] Omitted in J; should W X.   10. *you*] Omitted in D.   10. *were it*] if it were M.   10–p. 103, l. 4. *clothe . . . my self*] A² damaged.   11. *accompt*] accompted J.   12. *did*] Omitted in S.   12. *his*] to his S A² D W X B.   (*All Harpsfield MSS. to his.*)   13. *at length*] Omitted in X.   13. *throughe*] he through T.   13–14. *master Leiuetenauntes*] the Leiftennantes W X.   14. *importunate*] earnest and importunate D; important W.   14. *persuasion*] perswasions J W.   14. *he*] Crossed through in T.   14. *altered*] was contented to alter D.   15. *that*] Omitted in A².   15. *holy*] blessed and holy D.   16–17. *of . . . to his*] giue that money which was left him which was one Angell of gould to his W; giue that litle money that was left him which was one Angell of gold to this X.   16. *that* (2)] Omitted in S.   18. *by . . . brought*] brought by master Lieuetenaunt J.   19. *led*] Omitted in T; was led was led W; was ledd, X.   19. *towardes*] to H².   19–20. *place of execution*] place of execucon being one the Towre Hill D.   20. *Where*] here X.   20. *vppe the*] vpp to the M.   20. *which*] that it H¹; that A².

was so weake that it was ready to fall, he saide merilye
to m*aster* Leiuetenaunte : " I pray you, m*aster* Lieue-
tenaunte, see me salf vppe, *and* for my cominge downe
let me shifte for my self."
5 Then desired he all the people thereaboute to pray *Speech at the scaffold, and the manner of his death. [6 July, 1535.]*
for him, *and* to beare witnes w*i*th him that he should
[nowe there] suffer death in *and* for the faith of the holy
chatholik churche. Whiche done, he kneled downe,
and after his prayers said, * turned to thexecutioner,
10 *and* w*i*th a cheerefull countenaunce spake [thus] to him :
" Plucke vpp thy spirites, man, *and* be not afrayde to
do thine office; my necke is very shorte; take heede
therefore thow strike not awrye, for savinge of thine
honestye."
15 So passed Sir Thomas Moore out of this world to god,
vppon the very same daye in w*hi*ch himself had * most
desired.*
Soone after whose deathe came intelligence thereof to *How Charles the Emperour talked with Elyot of More's death, and paid tribute to his wisdom.*
the Emp*er*our Chareles. Whervppon he sent for S*ir*
20 Thomas Elliott, our english Embassado*ur*, *and* said vnto
him : " My Lord Embassador, we vnderstand that the
Kinge, yo*ur* m*aster*, hath put his faithfull seruaunt *and*
grave, wise Councelo*ur*, S*ir* Thom*as* Moore, to deathe."
Wherunto S*ir* Thom*as* Elliott awneswered that he

MSS. H² J H³ H¹ A M S A² (*damaged*) D T W X B.

1. *weake*] weakly built D.   1. *that*] Omitted in H¹.   1. *merilye*] Omitted in J.   2. *I . . . you*] Omitted in D.   2–3. *master Leiuetenaunte*] Omitted in D W; good Master Leivtenaunt X.   3. *see*] doe you see D.   5. *Then*] Thus T.   6. *to beare*] bare H³.   7. *nowe there suffer*] then suffer H² J; there nowe suffer A². (Harpsfield MSS. *vary*.)   8. *chatholik*] Omitted in W X.   8. *downe*] downe and prayed very devoutly D.   9. *said*] ended D.   9. *turned*] he turned H² J D.   10. *a*] Omitted in S.   10. *countenaunce*] voyce D.   10. *thus*] Omitted in H² J.   11. *man*] Omitted in H³ H¹ A.   12. *my*] for my H³; A *has* for *crossed through before* my.   13. *of*] Omitted in J.   15. *out . . . god*] to god out of this world S.   16–17. *most desired*] desired most H².   17–p. 104, l. 10. *desired . . . accordingly*] A² damaged.   18. *whose*] his H¹ T.   18. *came intelligence*] intelligence came H³.   18. *thereof*] Omitted in M.   19. *the*] *I*nterlineated in H²; omitted in J H³ H¹ A T.   19. *Chareles*] Charles the Fift D.   19. *for*] to H¹.   20. *Embassadour*] Embassadour in his courte D.   21. *that*] Omitted in H³.   24. *Wherunto*] Whervpon H³ T.   24. *that he*] he H³ H¹ A.

vnderstood nothing thereof. "Well," said the Emperour, "it is too true. And this will we say, that if we had bine maister of such a servante, of whose doings our selfe haue had these many yeares no small experience, we wold rather haue lost the best city of our dominions 5 then haue lost such a worthy councello*ur*." Which matter was by the same S*ir* Thomas Eliott to my self, to my wife, to maister Clement *and* his wife, to m*as*ter John Haywood *and* his wife, and [vnto] diuers other his Freinds accordingly reported. 10

<small>Roper had learnt this from Elyot himself.</small>

Finis. Deo gratias.

MSS. H² J H³ H¹ A M S A² (*damaged*) D T W X B.

1. *vnderstood*] heard S W X. 2. *too*] verye J. 2. *will we*] we will A². 2. *say*] say of him D. 2. *that*] *Omitted in* S X. 4. *haue . . . yeares*] A² *damaged* : . . . ny yeeres haue had. 5. *we*] *Omitted in* S. 5. *of our*] of all our D; in our W X. 6. *councellour*] councell W. 7. *the same*] *Omitted in* J. 7–8. *to . . . wife* (1)] to my wife to my selfe D. 8. *to* (1)] and H³ H¹ A. 8–9. *to maister Clement . . . wife*] *Omitted in* S. (*Eyeslip.*) 8. *maister*] my T. 8–9. *to master John . . . wife*] *Omitted in* B. (*Eyeslip.*) 9. *vnto*] *Omitted in* H² M; *interlineated in* J. 9–10. *other his*] others of his J. 10. *his Freinds*] *Omitted in* W X. 11. *Finis. Deo gratias*] Finis 26 Maij 1598 H¹ A; Deo gratias S; *omitted in* B.

HISTORICAL NOTES

NOTE.—For the matters treated by Roper, and incorporated by Harpsfield, Prof. Chambers' Notes to Harpsfield should usually be consulted for more detailed discussion. These are indicated below by **H** and page and line (*e.g.* **H, 10**/18–19). The corresponding Notes in Roper usually contain only the minimum of essential information, and are mostly summarised from the Notes to Harpsfield.

Exceptions, however, occur where the corresponding Note in Harpsfield indicates that the matter will be more fully treated in the edition of Roper—the Colts (6/11–22, below), the children of More and their marriages (7/4–5, 40/19, 42/16–17, below), and Dame Alice More (82/8–9, below). The Clements are more fully treated in the Roper Notes (104/8–9, below). Much of the material for these Notes was kindly put at my disposal by Prof. Chambers.

Where further information, later than the edition of Harpsfield, has come to hand, this is included in the Roper Notes; as, for example, in the case of the dates of More's appointments, 11/1–3, 12/8–10, below.

3/3–6. *as witnessethe Erasmus, more pure and white,* etc. (**See H, 208**/21–4.)

3/11–12. *William Roper . . . his sonne in lawe,* etc. See above, Introd., pp. xxix–xlvii.

3/15–16. *resident in his house . . . xvj yeares and more.* See above, Introd., p. xxxii.

5/1. *This Sir Thomas Moore.* For date and place of More's birth (probably 6 Feb. 1478, in the parish of St. Giles, Cripplegate Without) see **H, 9**/6.

Prof. Chambers there argued that the ages marked on the Basle sketch pointed to 1477 as the more probable year of More's birth. He adheres to this, but he now points out to me that such probability is outweighed by another consideration. In the Trinity College manuscript John More entered the birth of his son Thomas as "the Friday next after the Feast of the Purification in the seventeenth year of Edward IV," *i.e.* 6 February, 1478. The entry "to wit the 7th of February" was added later, probably by John More, and cannot carry the same authority as the original entry. The arguments drawn from the Basle sketch are only surmises, and cannot count against the fact that documentary evidence favours 6 February, 1478.

5/2. *St. Anthonies in London.* A free school attached to the Hospital of St. Anthony in Threadneedle Street. (**See H, 10**/18–19.)

5/3. *his father.* Judge John More, born probably in 1451; died 1530. (**See H, 10**/6–7.) On 24 April, 1574, he married Agnes Graunger, by whom he had six children, Thomas (the second) being born probably on 6 February, 1478. (**See H, 9**/6, and Note to 5/1 above.)

Judge John had three later wives. (**See H, 10**/16.) For authorities on his life, see **H, 9**/9.

5/6–7. *wold . . . steppe in among the players.* (**See H, 11/2–3.**)

5/16. *at Oxford.* Apparently at Canterbury College, now Christchurch. (**See H, 12/13.**)

5/16–17. *in the greake and latine tongue.* (**See H, 12/15–16.**)

5/19. *Newe Inne.* When an Inn of Chancery, this was connected with the Middle Temple. (**See H, 12/26.**)

5/21. *admitted to Lincolnes Inne.* 12 February, 1496. (**See H, 13/2–12.**)

6/3–4. *St. Lawrens . . . Doctor Grosin.* Grocyn was Vicar of St. Lawrence, Jewry, and it is probable that More's "lectures" were given at his invitation. (**See H, 13/23–25**, etc.)

Prof. Reed points out to me the account of the Church in Newcourt's *Repertorium Ecclesiasticum Parochiale Londinense* (1708–10), Vol. I, pp. 384–6; *Novum Repertorium*, etc., compiled by G. Hennessy (1898), pp. 264–7. The ancient church was a Rectory, given to Balliol College, Oxford, May 30, 1294. Since then the Church has had a Vicar—Balliol (Master and Scholars) presenting, except for occasional "lapses," calculated in respect of tithes. Grocyn was appointed Vicar by the Bishop of London, Thomas Savage, on 26 December, 1496, "by lapse," the nine preceding presentations being by Balliol, as also the five following. He resigned in 1517.

6/7. *Fvrnivals Inne.* An Inn of Chancery attached to Lincoln's Inn. (**See H, 14/17.**)

6/10–11. *in the Charter house of London . . . without vowe, about iiij^{er} yeares.* More apparently tested his call to the religious life. (**See H, 17/11–15.**)

6/11–22. *Vntill he resorted to the house of one Master Colte, a gentleman of Essex . . . having three daughters . . . he . . . framed his fancy towardes her* [the eldest] *and . . . maryed her.* For general information concerning the Colts and their estates, see Morant's *Essex* (1768), Vol. II; G. R. F. Colt's *History and Genealogy of the Colts*, Edinburgh, 1887; Page's *Supplement to the Suffolk Traveller*, 1844, pp. 929–30. As noted below, the statements of these authorities must be accepted with caution.

The tombs and brasses of John Colt and some of his forbears are in Roydon Parish Church, Essex, about a mile from Netherhall. I am much indebted to the present Rector (the Rev. C. Copland) for kindly checking and supplementing information to be derived from them. The tomb and brass of Jane's brother Thomas and his wife, Magdalen, are in Waltham Abbey.

The pedigree of the Colts appears to be as on p. 107.

The maiden name of Johanna, wife of Thomas Colt the first, is not recorded. In the *Cal. Inquis. post mortem*, Vol. IV, 13 Edward IV, No. 28, p. 361, the entry concerning her runs:

Johanna quæ fuit uxor Willielmi Parre militis prius nupta Thomæ Colt.

But on p. 371, there is an entry under 15 Edward IV, No. 34:

Johanna quæ fuit uxor Willielmi Parre militis postea nupta Thome Colt.

It is generally assumed that Thomas Colt was her first husband. The first entry speaks of his estates in Cumberland; the second of many estates, including Netherhall in Essex, and Grays, Peches, Peytones, Chelworth in Suffolk.

Historical Notes

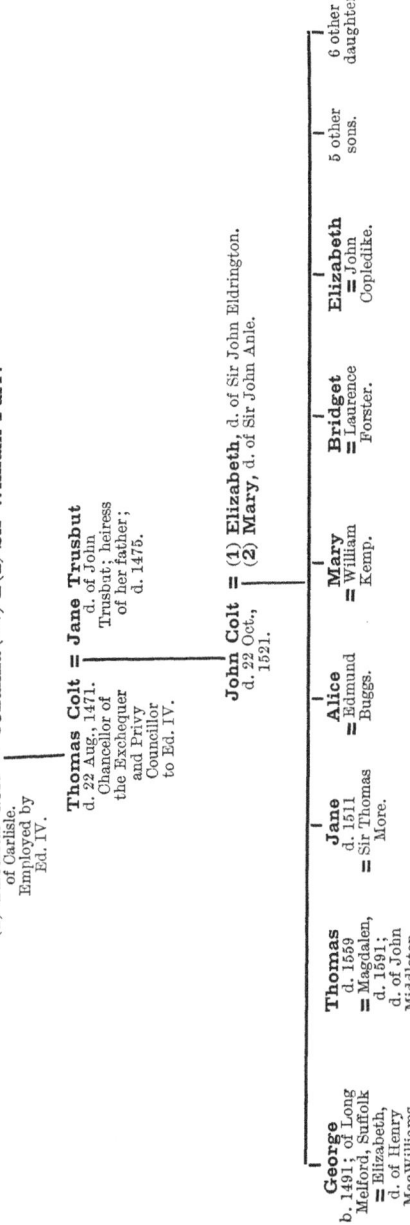

Authorities differ somewhat as to the list of the Colts' estates, but rather in fullness of detail than in actual fact. It seems clear that Thomas of Carlisle owned estates in Cumberland, and that the Essex and Suffolk family properties are later, some through the various wives. Whatever their source, considerable lands and several Manors came to belong to John Colt, Jane's father—the Manors of Netherhall and Downehall, and lands known as Burleys, Daylands, Wardlands, Pylgrims, Harvies, Heyward, Hobards, etc., in Essex; also Titless Hall, Shouldham Priory, Colt Hall, etc. His father, Thomas Colt, owned Grays (*i.e.* Grays Hall, later Colt Hall) in Cavendish, Suffolk; Chelworth, Boxstead, Aketon, etc., in Suffolk; and Netherhall and "another manor" (? Downehall) in Essex.

Morant and Colt err in stating that the death of Thomas Colt the second took place in 1476. P. S. Allen (*T.L.S.*, 26 Dec. 1918) correctly calculated it as 22 August, 1471. The brass makes this clear: "MC quater semel LX v bis et I   Augusti mensis x bis   et I bis."

The "Master Colte" referred to by Roper is John Colt of Netherhall. He married twice. On the brass the name of Elizabeth Eldrington precedes that of Mary Anle (Morant and Colt spell "Alne"), which would seem to indicate that Elizabeth was the first wife (Morant and Colt reverse this order). On John Colt's brass eighteen children are depicted—on his right four sons and eight daughters, on his left three sons and three daughters, apparently the issue by each wife. (Allen, *op. cit.*, gives twelve children; Colt states that there was no issue by the first wife—according to him Mary Alne—and by the second the two sons and five daughters noted in the pedigree above.) The name of Jane's mother cannot be definitely decided from the information at present available, but seems more likely to have been Elizabeth Eldrington.

For proof that the home of the Colts in Essex, where More met his young bride, was Netherhall (not "Newhall," as stated by Cresacre More, and some later authorities) see P. S. Allen, *op. cit.* Allen gives an account of the ruins still standing.

More's marriage to Jane Colt was not later than January, 1505. Their eldest child, Margaret, was born not later than 1 October, 1505. These approximate dates may be deduced from the evidence of the Basle sketch for Holbein's picture of the More family group, and from Richard Hyrde's note of Margaret's age on 1 October, 1524.

According to his father's first statement in the Trinity College, Cambridge, manuscript (**see H, 9/6**) Thomas More was born on Friday, 6 February, 1478 (N.S.). The Basle sketch notes that More was in his fiftieth year, and that note must therefore have been written in between 6 February, 1527, and 5 February, 1528.

Anne Cresacre is stated on the Burford Priory picture to have been born in the third year of Henry VIII, *i.e.* between 22 April, 1511, and 21 April, 1512. According to the records preserved in the Eyston family, she was born on 3 May, 1511, and was therefore in her fifteenth year between 3 May, 1525, and 2 May, 1526. But Holbein had not arrived in England by 2 May, 1526, so the statement that she was born on 3 May, 1511, must be erroneous. The brass-

Historical Notes 109

plate which covered Anne Cresacre's tomb in the church at Barnborough recorded that she died on 2 December, 1577, in her sixty-sixth year. She was therefore born not earlier than 2 December, 1511, and, as we have seen, not later than 21 April, 1512. The Basle sketch states that she was in her fifteenth year, which can then only have been between 2 December, 1525, and 21 April, 1527.

If the birthdays of Thomas More and Anne Cresacre are correct, the names must have been written into the Basle sketch not earlier than 6 February, 1527, to suit Thomas More, and not later than 21 April, 1527, to suit Anne Cresacre.

In the Basle sketch Margaret Roper and Margaret Gigs are in their twenty-second year. They were therefore born between 6 February, 1505, and 21 April, 1506. And from this evidence the marriage of More and Jane Colt cannot be *later* than the middle of 1505.

Richard Hyrde, in his Preface to Margaret Roper's translation of Erasmus's *Precatio Dominica*, says that Margaret was " XIX yere of age. 1524." He dates his Preface to the first edition " at Chelcheth, the year of our Lord God a thousand five hundred xxiiij. The first day of October." Margaret Roper was therefore born not later than 1 October, 1505. And from this evidence the marriage of More and Jane Colt cannot have been *later* than January, 1505, but may have been earlier.

For More's other children, see below, Note to 7/4–5.

Jane Colt died in 1511, and within a month More married a second time. Jane Colt was still living on 19 May, 1511, when Ammonius obviously refers to her in a letter to Erasmus:

. . . Morus noster mellitissimus cum sua facillima coniuge, quæ nunquam tui meminit quin tibi bene precetur, et liberis ac vniuersa familia pulcherrime valet. (*Opus Epist. Des. Erasmi*, ed. Allen, No. 221, Tom. I, p. 458.)

More had married Dame Alice before 27 October, 1511, when Ammonius, in writing to Erasmus, implies that he has fled from More's house to avoid "the crooked-beaked harpy"—Dr. P. S. Allen's brilliant emendation of the passage which had puzzled all previous scholars :

. . . Ego in Collegium diui Thomæ tandem immigraui, vbi sum nihilo magis ex sententia mea quam apud Morum. Non video τῆς ἁρπυίας τὸ ἀγκύλον ῥάμφος (*ibid.*, No. 236, p. 476).

For Dame Alice, see below, Note to 82/8–9.

6/23–5. *Lyncolnes Inne . . . called to the bench . . . and had read there twice.* (See **H, 13/2-12.**)

7/4. *Bucklersbury.* This led from the east end of Cheapside to Charlotte Row, the west side of the Mansion House. (See **H, 19/12.**) More's famous house there, "The old Barge," passed into John Clement's possession in 1524, when More moved to Chelsea. On Low Sunday, 12th April, 1534, More was dining with Clement at "The Barge," when he was served with the warrant to appear before the Commissioners at Lambeth. (See Stapleton, *Tres Thomae*, cap. 15 (end); Hallett's translation, p. 160.)

7/4–5. *three daughters and one Sonne.* Margaret, b. not later than 1 October, 1505, d. 1544; Elizabeth, b. 1506; Cecily, b. 1507; John, b. about 1509, d. 1547. In 1521 Margaret married William Roper: see Introduction, p. xxxii, above. In 1525 Elizabeth was married to William Daunce, and Cecily to Giles Heron : see below, Notes to 40/19, and 42/16–17.

In 1529 John married Anne Cresacre, only child and heir of Edward Cresacre of Barnborough Hall, Yorkshire. Anne Cresacre was a ward of More's, and a member of his household. (For the marriage of John and Anne Cresacre and their ages, **see H, 9/6, 66/2–3,** and Note to 6/11–22, above.) Their eldest child, Thomas, was born in his grandfather's house at Chelsea, 8 August, 1531. For Thomas's later history, and some account of other children of John More and Anne Cresacre, see Harpsfield, pp. 294–6, and footnotes.

For John More's share in the Plot of the Prebendaries against Cranmer, and pardon, see below, Note to 40/19.

The Eystons of Hendred House, East Hendred, are the lineal descendants of John More, through Bridget More, and thus the representatives of Sir Thomas More's family, Bridget's brothers Thomas and Christopher having become priests. The pedigree on pp. 112 and 113 illustrates their descent.

7/16–17. *the kings demaundes thereby were cleane ouerthrowne.* It is estimated that a "Fifteenth" at this date was approximately £29,000. Instead of getting three Fifteenths as the Aid consequent upon the marriage of his daughter, Henry VII had to be satisfied with a grant of £40,000 in lieu of two Aids, the one for the making knight of Arthur, late Prince of Wales, the other for the marriage of Margaret. **(See H, 15/15–16.)**

7/18. *master Tyler.* Presumably Sir William Tyler, knight of the King's body, controller of the King's works, and master of the King's jewels. **(See H, 15/16.)**

8/4–5. *Doctor Fox, Bishoppe of Winchester,* born *c.* 1448, died 1528. Founder of Corpus Christi College, Oxford.

8/14–16. *master Whitford . . . after a Father of Syon. I.e.* Richard Whitford, translator of *The Imitation of Christ,* and of the *Martyrology* used at the Bridgettine monastery of Syon at Isleworth, Middlesex. He was a great friend of More and of Erasmus. **(See H, 16/19–21.)**

9/2. *foure hundreth poundes.* In pre-war (1914) value this was considered equivalent to £4,000. In present currency one would multiply by 15 to 20.

9/9–12. *at the suite and instaunce of the Englishe merchauntes . . . twise Embassador . . . betweene them and the merchauntes of the Stilliarde.* The Steelyard was the colony of the Hanseatic League in London : it stood on the site of Cannon Street Station. Roper, and Harpsfield following Roper, are not correct in making both embassies relate to matters between the English merchants and those of the Steelyard : the second embassy was to Calais, and for the purpose of negotiating, not with the Hanseatic, but with French merchants. **(See H, 20/23–21/3.)**

11/1–3. *mayster of the requests . . . and within a moneth after knighte, and one of his privy Councell.* Roper's arrangement here confuses the sequence of

Historical Notes 111

events, and Harpsfield takes over Roper verbatim. Miss E. M. G. Routh, *Sir Thomas More and his Friends*, p. 92, and footnote 3, gives the dates of appointment:
> When More returned from Calais in October 1517, he was appointed one of the King's councillors, and a Judge in the Court of Requests, or, as it was then called, the "Poor Men's Court," or "Court of Poor Men's Causes." The title "Master of Requests" did not come into use until some time after More held the office. He does not appear to have taken up regular duties at Court before the spring of 1518.
>
> ... The title "Master of Requests" would be familiar to Roper when he wrote his biography; More was not knighted, however, before 1521. Mr. I. S. Leadam says, "I first find the name 'Court of Requests' in 1529" (*Select Cases in the Court of Requests,* introd., p. xiv). For "Masters of Requests," *ibid.*, pp. xvi, xix, and xxxi. ... The date of More's admission to the King's Council (which was not yet known as the Privy Council) was for some time in doubt. Erasmus wrote on 17 Apr. 1518, *Morus totus est aulicus, regi semper assistens* (Allen, iii, no. 816). In July 1518 he alluded to More as "one of the council" (*ibid.*, no. 855), and in September, Giustiniani spoke of his being "newly-made councillor" (*Letters and Papers*, ii, no. 4438). An annuity of £100 was granted to More by the King himself, 21 June, 1518, to date from Michaelmas 1517. This latter date apparently gives the approximate time of More's appointment to the Council (Public Record Office, C 66, no. 637, m. 12 (patent roll); E 405, no. 202).

12/8-10. *Then died one master Weston, thresurer of thexchequer, whose office ... the kinge ... gaue vnto Sir Thomas Moore.* Roper's memory here is much at fault:

(1) The office in question was that of Under-Treasurer. The Treasurer was the Duke of Norfolk, who resigned in December 1522, and was succeeded by his son Thomas, Earl of Surrey.

(2) More's predecessor as Under-Treasurer was, not Weston, but Sir John Cutte. **(See H, 24/9-10.)** The exact date of More's appointment has been established by the researches of Miss C. Jamison at the Record Office. See Miss E. M. G. Routh's *Sir Thomas More and his Friends*, p. 107, and footnote 3:

> On the 2nd of May 1521, without any request of his own, he [More] was given the post of Under-Treasurer, with the usual large salary of £173 6s. 8d. per annum [multiply by 15 to 20 for present value], in succession to Sir John Cutte, who died on the 4th of April 1521. The Under-Treasurer was customarily a knight, and the date of More's knighthood, which has been the subject of some discussion, may no doubt be assigned to this time.
>
> ... More followed Sir John Cutte in this office a month after Cutte's death. [Miss Jamison] has discovered in the records of the Treasury of Receipt a rough entry book of daily receipts by the Tellers (E 405, no. 480), with ... note against an entry of the payment, on 26 October, 13 Hen. VIII (1521) ... of £71 14s. 6d.: "For Sir Thomas More, Knight, Sub-Treasurer of England ... owed from 2nd May, 13th year, until the feast of Michælmas next following for 151 days." ...

TABLE OF THE EYSTON BRANCH OF MORE'S DESCENDANTS

(See Note to 7/4–5, above)

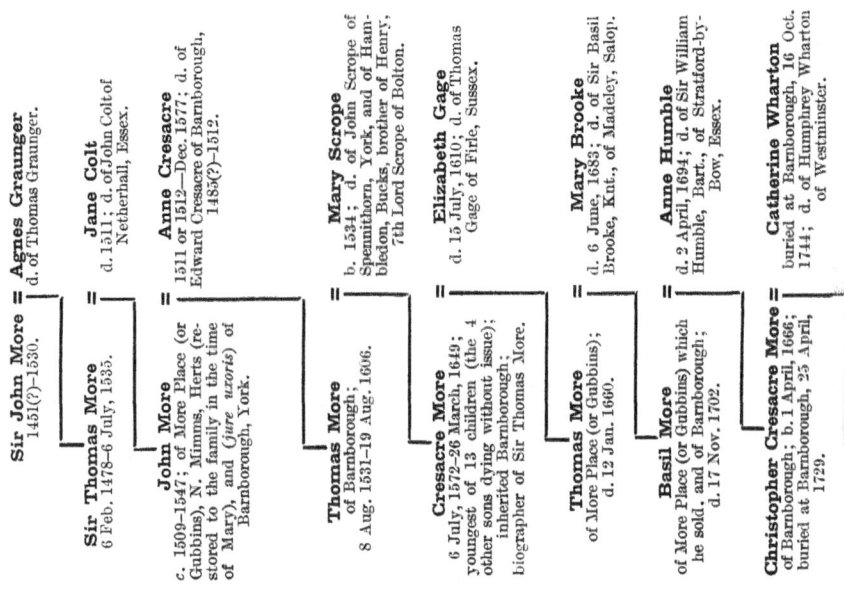

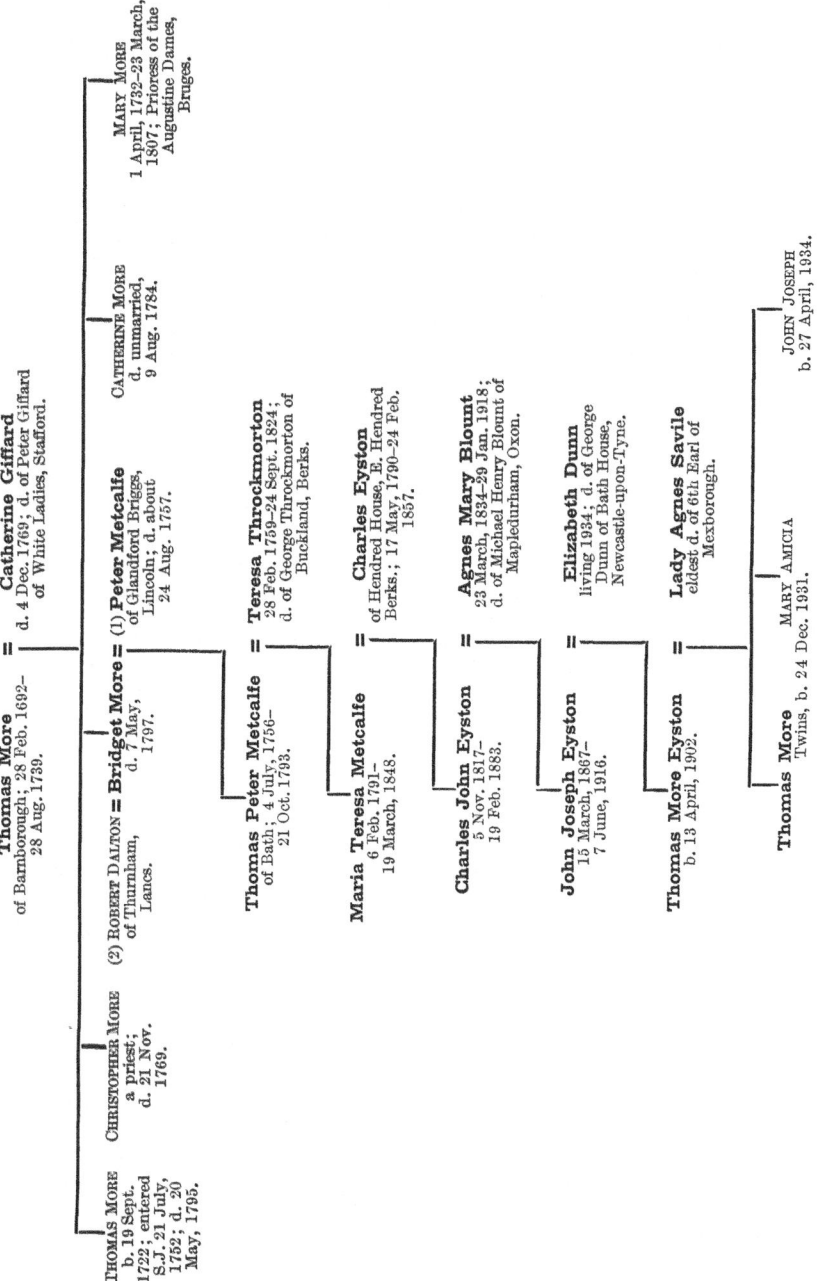

The last payment of his [More's] fee as Sub-Treasurer was made up to 24 Jan. 1525/6, when Sir William Compton assumed office. Sir Richard Weston succeeded Compton in 1528.

(3) Weston lived for some twenty years after the date when he is alleged by Roper to have died.

12/14. *not nowe extant.* A summary, however, is given in Hall's *Chronicle* and in Harpsfield. **(See H, 26/19 ff.)**

12/16–17. *he spake vnto his grace in forme folowinge.* **(See H, 27/13–14 ff.)**

17/1–3. *It fortuned at that parliament A very greate subsedy to be demaunded,* etc. Though More disliked Wolsey's arrogance, he loyally co-operated in persuading the Commons to grant this unpopular subsidy, and the letters of More and Wolsey at this period show that any friction between them was of short duration. **(See H, 31/12 ff.)**

18/9–10. *master Marney (after lord Marney). I.e.* Sir John Marney. His father, Sir Henry Marney, Lord Privy Seal, had been raised to the peerage on 12 April, 1523, a few days before the meeting of this Parliament, and died a few weeks later, 24 May, 1523. **(See H, 32/14.)**

19/12–13. *gallery att whitehall. I.e.* York House.

19/21–24. *the cardinall . . . councelled the king to send him Embassodor into Spayne.* Though there is no ground for attributing to Wolsey any murderous intent, it was a well-known trick of his to send abroad rivals whose power he feared. And More also seems to have known that for him the Spanish climate would be dangerous. Richard Sampson had been sent in the autumn of 1522, and on 18 April, 1525, Tunstall and Sir Richard Wingfield were sent to join him. Wingfield fell ill almost immediately, and died at Toledo on 22 July, 1525, whilst Tunstall and Sampson were both seriously ill. So More's fears of the climate were not unfounded. **(See H, 33/19–22.)**

20/20. *vppon the death of Sir Richard Wingfeild.* See above, Note to 19/21–24.

20/23–4. *his house att Chelsey.* Truce was made with France on 14 Aug. 1525, so Henry's visit was probably in 1524–5. **(See H, 24/27–26/3.)**

23/1–3. *Who, beinge Chauncelour of the duchie, was made Embassador twice.* An error in chronology, as regards the first embassy of 1521. More became Chancellor of the Duchy in 1525. See above, p. 20, ll. 19–20, and Introduction, p. xlvi.

23/5. *the water baily of London.* One of the four gentlemen attendant upon the Lord Mayor, the others being the Sword Bearer, the Common Crier, and the Common Hunt. Prof. Sisson has pointed out that the Water Bailiff referred to here must be Sebastian Hilary, who died at Shrove-tide, 1545. See above, Introd., p. xlii.

28/5–7. *at such tyme as my wife . . . was sick of the sweating sicknes.* There were, according to Hall, two great attacks of this "sweating sickness," one in 1517, and one in 1528. Margaret most probably was attacked in 1528. **(See H, 81/18–19.)**

Historical Notes 115

29/19–30/8. *Nowe while Sir Thomas Moore was Chauncellour of the Duchy, the sea of Roome chaunced to be void . . . Cardinall Adrian . . . was . . . chosen Pope.* An error in chronology, Sir Thomas More being Chancellor of the Duchy of Lancaster from 1525 to 1529. See Introd., p. xlvi.

30/14–17. *Cardinall Wolsey . . . studied to invent all waies of reuengment of his grief against the Emperour: which, as it was the begininge of a lamentable tragedye.* For discussion of the origin of the divorce, see Harpsfield, pp. 40–42, and **H**, **41**/2–4.

31/8. *one of the Frenche kings Sisters.* An error of Roper and other writers. See above, Introd., p. xlvi, and **H**, **43**/8–9.

31/13–15. *requested Langland, Bishoppe of Lincolne, . . . to put a scruple into his graces head.* Harpsfield notes Langland's repentance, and Chapuys writes of it to Charles V on 3 Jan. 1534. (**See H**, **41**/21.)

Prof. Reed points out to me Tyndale's allegation in the *Practice of Prelates* of Wolsey's influence over Langland:

He promoted the Byshop of Lyncolne [Langland] that now is, his most faythfull frend and old companion and made him confessour: to whom of what soeuer the kynges grace shroue him selfe, thinke ye not that hee spake so loude that the Cardinall heard it ? (*Workes of Tyndall, Frith and Barnes*, 1573, pp. 368–9; cf. *William Tyndale*, by R. Demaus, new ed., revised by R. Lovett, 1886, p. 243.)

31/16–18. *the kinge . . . opened it first to Sir Thomas Moore.* Roper distinguishes only three consultations, Harpsfield four:

1. Roper, pp. 31–33; Harpsfield, pp. 44–6.
2. Not in Roper; Harpsfield, pp. 47–8; More's Letter to Cromwell, *English Works*, p. 1425.
3. Roper, pp. 37–38; Harpsfield, pp. 48–9.
4. Roper, pp. 49–50; Harpsfield, pp. 56–7.

34/15–17. *breif . . . found in the Tresury of Spaine, and sent to the Comissioners into England.* Erroneous statements: see above, Introd., pp. xlvi–vii, and **H**, **46**/20–23.

36/3–4. *in xvj yeares and more, being in house conuersant with him.* See above, Introd., p. xxxii.

38/12–14. *Bishopp Stokesley, being by the Cardinall . . . put to rebuke and awarded to the Fleete.* There is no historical confirmation of this episode, and Dr. A. F. Pollard thinks that Roper may be confusing Stokesley's troubles in 1538; but there is no doubt there was some quarrel between Wolsey and Stokesley. **See H**, **49**/16–18, and the passage there cited from Tyndale's *Practice of Prelates*: "or some quarel was picked agaynst him, and so was thrust out of the Court, as Stokesley was " (*Workes of Tyndall, Frith and Barnes*, 1573, p. 368; cf. *William Tyndale*, by R. Demaus, new ed., revised by R. Lovett, 1886, p. 242).

40/19. *one of his sonnes in Lawe.* Obviously William Daunce, as Roper would not so refer to himself, and " another of his sonnes in lawe called master Heron " is referred to below, 42/16–17.

More's second daughter, Elizabeth, married Daunce on 29 Sept. 1525; at the same time Giles Heron married the youngest daughter Cecily. In the summarised and translated form of the *Allegations for Marriage Licences issued by the Bishop of London, 1520–1610, Harleian Soc. Pub.*, Vol. XXV, p. 4, their marriage licence runs thus :

    29 September : W. Dansey and Elizabeth More.⎫
    29 September : Giles Hern and Cecilia More. ⎭
        to marry in Oratorio of Mr. Giles Alynton, par. Willesden, dioc. of London.

Prof. A. W. Reed in *T. L. S.*, April 3, 1930, gives the full licence from the Vicar-General's books at Somerset House, first volume (Foxford's), f. 100 r., under the year 1525. He notes the interesting features of the licence : that the marriage was not taking place in a parish church; that it was so unusual to include four people in one licence that the Vicar-General states that it was issued under the seal of the Bishop, More's friend Tunstall; and the provisions that the two rites should not be merged, and the pairs not crossed.

Giles Alington—later Sir Giles—was the second husband of Alice, daughter of More's second wife Alice by her first husband, John Middleton. Alice junior had been previously married to Thomas Elrington.

William Daunce was the son of Sir John Daunce, Knight of the Body and Privy Councillor, etc. to Henry VIII. For indenture between Sir Thomas More and Sir John Daunce, dated 17 Hen. VIII, making certain arrangements in connection with the marriage, see *Notes and Queries*, 7th Series, I, June 19, 1886, p. 488.

In the *T. L. S.*, March 27, 1930, Dr. A. F. Pollard writes :

The two bridegrooms of 1525 were politically united four years later by being both returned for Thetford to the Reformation Parliament elected in October, 1529; and this leads on to the notable fact that all the male members of More's family (except his son John, who was a minor . . .) found seats in the Parliament which More himself opened as Lord Chancellor. His eldest daughter, Margaret, had married William Roper, who was returned for Bramber; Giles Alington sat for Cambridgeshire; John Rastell, who had married More's sister Elizabeth, found a seat at Dunheved (Cornwall); while young Daunce's father, Sir John, sat for Oxfordshire. More himself sat, of course, in the House of Lords, to which his father, Sir John, must also have been summoned by the " writs of assistance " regularly sent to Judges of the King's Bench and Common Pleas. Alington and Sir John Daunce no doubt owed their election to their own territorial influence, but the return of W. Daunce and Giles Heron for Thetford and of William Roper for Bramber was almost certainly due to the Duke of Norfolk, who had promoted More's own appointment as Chancellor. Norfolk may also have assisted in Rastell's return for Dunheved, where both members were non-resident nominees.

William Daunce was implicated with John More, John Heywood and other notable Catholics, in the Plot of the Prebendaries against Cranmer, 1543. Daunce and John More recanted and had their pardon together. John Heywood remained firm longer, but finally made a humiliating submission. German Gardiner and John Larke, More's Parish priest of Chelsea, were executed.

See *L. & P.* 1544, Pt. i. 444(5) :

Wm. Daunce, of Cayshobere, Herts, *alias* late of Cannons, Midd., *alias* of London. Pardon of all treasonable words against the King's supremacy,

Historical Notes   117

concealments of treason, and treasonable conversations with John More or others concerning the King, the kingdom, and certain prophecies; with restoration of goods. Greenwich, 24 April, 36 Hen. VIII. *Del.* Westm. 26 April.

Also *L. & P.* 1544, Pt. i. 444(6):

John More of Chelsith, Midd. *alias* of Bamburgh, Yorks., *alias* of London. Pardon of all treasonable words with the detestable traitors, John Eldryngton, Germain Gardyner, John Bekynsale, John Heywood, Wm. Daunce, John Larke, clk., John Irelande, clk., Roger Irelande, clk., and any others, in wishing ill to the King and arguing against the King's supremacy, and all concealments of treasons, of which he has been accused; with restoration of goods. Greenwich, 24 April, 36 Hen. VIII. *Del.* Westm. 26 April.

And see for *John Heywood*:

L. & P. 1544, Pt. i. 812(109):

John Heywode, late of London, *alias* of Northmymmes, Herts. General pardon. Westm., 26 June, 36 Hen. VIII.

Del. Westm. 30 June.

L. & P. 1544, Pt. i. 853:

6 July. Recantation of John Heywood. Willingly declares the great clemency of the King, whose supremacy had often been opened to him both by word and writing, etc.

Somewhat earlier William Roper had been thrown into the Tower, but his fault seems rather to have been in aiding distressed Catholics, notably Beckinshaw, and he was released on payment of £100 fine. (See above, Introd., p. xxxiv.)

In spite of the fortitude of Margaret Roper described by Harpsfield (pp. 78-9) these anxious years must have told on her health. She died at Christmas, 1544 (see above, Introd., p. xlii).

42/16–17. *another of his sonnes in lawe called master Heron.* Giles Heron married More's youngest daughter, Cecily, at the same time (29 Sep. 1525) that her elder sister, Elizabeth, married William Daunce. See above, Note to 40/19.

Giles Heron was son and heir of Sir John Heron, Treasurer of the Chamber to Henry VIII. A brief account of Sir John Heron's career as a Civil-servant is given by Newton in *Eng. Hist. Rev.*, xxxii, pp. 355-8. Newton points out that the last entries in Sir John's hand in the accounts occur in Feb. 1521, and that he died on 10 June, 1522. (Morant, *Essex*, Vol. II, p. 620, had given the date of his death as 8 July, 1521.) Newton terms Sir John " the greatest of all Treasurers of the Chamber."

Sir John Heron's Will is in *Prerogative Court of Canterbury, Inquisitions post mortem, Chancery Series*, Vol. XL, nos. 72 & 113. At the time of his father's death, Giles was a minor. His wardship was granted to Sir Thomas More, 18 March, 1523. See *L. & P.*, Henry VIII, Vol. III. 2, no. 2900 (*Patent Rolls*, 14 Hen. VIII, p. 2, m. 26.):

Wardship of Giles, son and heir of Sir John Heron, with the profits of his lands from Michælmas last. Greenwich, 7 March, 14 Henry VIII. *Del.* Westm. 18 March.

Some details as to the genealogy of the Herons are given in Mundy's *Col-*

lection of Arms and Descents of the Gentry in Middlesex, MS. Harl. 1551, fo. 84:

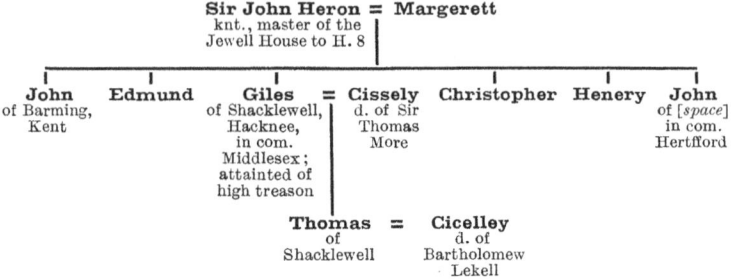

The Petition of Heron's sons (see below) gives us information of another son of Giles, viz. John.

For Giles Heron and William Daunce as members for Thetford in the 1529 Parliament, see above, Note to 40/19.

Giles Heron was attainted of high treason on 12 April, 1540. See *Parl. Roll*, 32 Henry VIII, c. 56:

 That where Gyles Heron, late of Hackney in your Countie of Midd., Esquier, by the instigation of the devill, putting aparte the dreade of god and the excellent benefites receyued of your highnes, hath not only moste traiterously refused his duetie and allegeaunce whiche he ought to beare vnto your highnes, but also hath comitted and perpetrated diuers and sondrye detestable and habomynable treasons, to the moste fearefull and extreme perrill and daungier of the destruction of your moste roiall persone, and to thutter losse, disherison and desolation of this your Realme, if god of his goodnes had not in due tyme brought his said treasons to knowlege. For the whiche, being plainely and manyfestly proued, that it may be enacted by auctoritie of this present parlament that thesaid Gyles Heron, for his abhominable and detestable treasons by him mooste abhomynably committed and doon againste your maiestie and this Realme, shalbe by auctoritie of this present parlament conuicted and attainted of high treason.

The forfeiture of his lands is to date back to include those in possession on 28 January, 1539:

 in possession the xxviijth day of Januarye in the thyrtie yere of your moste noble Reigne, or at any tyme after.

 As far as the evidence has been collected at present, the "abominable and detestable treasons" of poor Giles Heron, so dangerous to King and State, and so plainly and manifestly proved, seem to reduce themselves to "mumblings" and plottings between Sir Thomas More and Heron (*L. & P.*, 1534; no. 290) and the putting of one Lyons out of his farm (see below); and to depend upon this same Lyons as single witness.

 The progress of events can be traced from *L. & P.*:

 24 Feb., 1539: no. 358. Recognisance given by Giles Heron . . . for his

appearance before the Council when called to answer articles laid to his charge within 2 years hereafter.
6 July, 1539 : no. 1219. Giles Heron then was sent to the Tower, it is said for treason.
2 Oct., 1539 : no. 359. [*Wrongly dated* 20 Oct.] Deposition of Thos. Reygate, smith, and Ric. Forest, husbandman.
Prof. Reed supplies me with the full transcript of this deposition, showing Lyons' efforts to incriminate Heron :

At maye last past att crafford in the 9tie of Kent in the house of one Rychard Fayremā : thomas Reygate smythe : and Rychard forest husbondmā. Wyttnessythe that one lyons enquyryd for M^r heron wether he were there cens and they sayd yes he was there : then sayd lyons I have no cause to praye for hym for he putt me owt off my ferme where I had a prattye lyvȳg therefor and I lyve I shall displease hym : then sayd theye he semythe to us an honest gentylmā : Well sayd he I woll be quytte w^t hym. Whye ⱷ Forest and yff you knowe any thynge by hym that is nott good you doo nott well to kepe it long in close and yor mattre shall rather be agaynst you than w^t you : well ⱷ he and sayd no more but deptyd.

Also the sayd lyons w^t importune entyces wold have hyryd one thomas torner at ij sondrye tymys for VIs VIIId to haue assystyd hym agaynst gylys heron before my lord p've seale in suche causys as he wold devyse by byllys sayiğ to the [s^d] Torner Mr Heron hath putt the owt off thy house and me also. Wherefore I woll dysplease hym in that I maye for he hathe now undone me : and I shall also get John Hayle to put up a byll to my lord P've Seale agaynst the sayd Gylys heron for now that he is in the fleate in troble a lytle complaynt shall take effect and yff thou wolt come to suche a place as I shall appoȳt the I shall so ordre the mattre : that I shall warrant the a large amends and I woll dwell styll in my howse etc nay ⱷ he I woll nott for yff he haue done me wrong I truste he woll make me amendes hereafter.

Wytnessythe thys confessyon off the sayd thomas tornor sayiğ he had no mynd to accompanye wt hym bycause he was a busye felowe

Wyllym Upchyrche   constable
thoīnas seetle   smythe   ⎫
Wyllym lansforde   ⎬ off Shortdyche
thomas boowden   ⎭

w^{t}owt bysshoppesgate ij daye off october in the xxxj yere of the reyn of or lord kyng Henry VIII.

Apparently no other case could be made out against Heron. The entries in *L. & P.* are of the vaguest and scantiest :

1539. *Cromwell's Remembrances* (nos. 424, 494) :
To proceed against . . . Heron.
Touching Giles Heron and what is to be done with him for as much as there is but one witness.

20 Nov., 1539. *Prisoners in the tower* (no. 554) :
The lady Salisbury, the lady Marquis, Mr. Edw. Cowrtney, Mr. Henry Poolle . . . Giles Heryne, etc.

1540. *Cromwell's Remembrances* (nos. 438, 439) :
Touching Gyles Heron, etc.
Gyles Herons offence.

It was not till 4 August, four months after his attainder, that Heron laid down his life at Tyburn. And Cromwell, my lord Privy Seal, had met his fate first: from March, 1540, he had himself been numbered among the Prisoners in the Tower, and on 28 July he was executed.

The Tudor biographers of More never hint at Heron's martyrdom. Roper's *Life* is a slight sketch, with admittedly important omissions: he does not even tell us of Fisher's end. But Harpsfield goes out of his way (p. 212) to remind his readers of the execution of Germain Gardiner (7 March, 1544). If denial of the King's supremacy had been attributed to Heron, one would have thought that Harpsfield and Stapleton would have stressed his courage in following More's example.

The following accounts of the death of Giles Heron and of his fellow-sufferers are substantially the same:

Wriothesley's Chronicle, ed. Hamilton, Camden Soc., 1875, p. 121.

A.D. 1540. This yeare the fowerth daie of Awgust were drawen from the Tower of London to Tiburne, Giles Heron, gentleman, Clement Philpott, gentleman, late of Callis, and servant to the Lord Lile, Darbie Gynning, Edmonde Bryndholme, priest, William Horn, late a lay brother of the Charter Howse of London, and another, with six persons more, were there hanged, drawen and quartered . . . all which persons were attaynted by the whole Parliament for treason.

Two London Chronicles, ed. Kingsford, p. 16, *Camden Miscellany*, Vol. XII, 1910.

The iiij day of August wer drawne from ye Towre to Tyborne vj persons, & one led between ij sargantis, & ther hangyd & quarteryd; one of them was ye prior of Dancastor, a monke of ye Chartarhouse of London, Gyles Herne, a monke of Westmystar, one Fylpot, & one Carrow, & a fryar: all were put to death for treason.

Stow's Chronicle, 1580, says the same: giving Lawrence Cooke . . . William Horne . . . Giles Horne, Clement Philpot, Edmond Bromham, Darby Kenham, Robert Birde, Jaruis Carrow—all put to death for treason (pp. 1019, 1020).

Holinshead, 1586, says simply: "had beene atteinted of treason by parlement" (p. 952).

The Annales, or Generall Chronicle of England, by Iohn Stow . . . continued . . . by Edmond Howes, 1615, p. 581, gives the list with slight variations, and adds:

and had been attainted by parliament for deniall of the kings supremacie.

The *Proceedings of the Privy Council*, Vol. VII, 1540–1542, show the informer Lyons plotting against Giles Heron's brothers, Christopher, Henry, John, "John the Bastard" (described as "of Chisilherst in Kent, gent.") and "two other brethren." All were apprehended and imprisoned:

[*25 Aug. 1540*] p. 11. A lettre sent from Mr Sadler to Mr Wriothesley, touching the apprehension of Christopher Heron and Henry Heron, brethern unto the late Giles Heron, upon the accusacion of Lyones, was red before the Counsaill and delivred again to Mr Wriothesley.

[*25 Aug. 1540*] p. 11. Christopher Heron, that of late had bene Mr Sadlers servant, being sent for upon thaccusacion of Lyons, appered before the Counsaill, and being charged generally for his trueth towardes the Kinges highnes, defended himself so vehemently to be true to the King, that he refused the Kinges generall pardon, and yet nevertheles was committed to the porters ward untill the cumming of the said Lyons; and Henry Heron, who was also sent upp at the same tyme, was before his examinacion delivred to the Knight marshalls keping.

[*26 Aug. 1540*] pp. 12, 13. John Heron, the bastard brother of Giles Heron [was apprehended] . . . touching conjuracions, and . . . was examyned touching his knoweledge, suspicion and consent, aswell of the treasons whereof his brother Giles was atteynted as of any other, and it could by no meanes be gathered by any woord or otherwise that he was fawty of the same.

[*26 Aug. 1540*] p. 13. Henry Heron, . . . examyned of the same pointes that his brethern wer, made the same aunswer that Christopher did in effect, and yet he was pressed vehemently bothe by hope and dispaire to have confessed.

[*28 Aug. 1540*] p. 14. [Directions as to the custody of Christopher, Henry, John the Bastard and Lyons] untill the cummyng of twoo other brethern which wer sent for into the north.

[*2 Sep. 1540*] p. 27. All the brethern of Giles Heron except the bastard brother shuld be dispeched with honest reward for their chardges cummyng and going, and that alsoo lettres shuld be written to Mr Sadler, his Highnes Secretarye, in the favour of Christopher and John Heron his servauntes, and that the bastard shuld be still reteined in warde and further to be examyned vpon the practise of necromancye.

[*2 Sep. 1540*] p. 28. A lettre was sent to the Warden of the Flete for the delyverye of Christopher and Henry Herons, prisoners ther, without taking any fees of theim.

[*2 Sep. 1540*] p. 28. A lettre was sent to Mr Sadler, the Kinges secretarye, by the Kinges speciall commandment, in the favor of Christopher and John Heron his servantes, to kepe the same still in service notwithstanding this their examinacion, which was to be noted rather a tryall of theire trueth and a purgacion of theim from all suspicion thenne any ignomynie or shame.

[*4 Sep. 1540*] p. 30. John Heron, the bastard brother of Giles Heron . . . examyned of his practise of astronomye and necromancie . . . and aunswering indirectly was remitted to warde again . . .

[*16 Sep. 1540*] p. 38. John Heron, the bastard brother of Gyles Heron, was . . . browght before the Counsail, and . . . knowledging his foly in using of fantastical practises in astronomye, was set at libertie, and was bownd in a recognisaunce of one hundred markes.

With regard then to all the Heron brothers except John the Bastard, the informer Lyons had evidently failed in his accusations and proofs. They seem to have been falsely and maliciously slandered, and charged with treason and sedition, but nothing could be construed even into disaffection. It is good to learn they had some redress for the expense and inconvenience to which they had been put. The divinations of John the Bastard must have been suspected as of a treasonable tendency, and before being set at liberty, he was forced to promise to abandon all inquiries and experiments.

In *L. & P.* no. 450, 3 April, 1540, there is reference to a "letter from J. and T. Heron to Mr Sadler." This is the appeal of the two sons of Giles Heron, John and Thomas, to Ralph Sadler, Secretary to Henry VIII, for some help towards their maintenance and education. It is in Latin, French, and English, the English version describing the petitioners "as chylldren havying a father not able to helpe hym selfe nor hys desolat chyldren." (See Royal MS. 7. C. xvi, 152.)

It was fourteen years before the Herons came back to their own. Queen Mary restored the estates in Essex to Thomas Heron, the eldest son, 23 July, 1554. See *Letters Patent*, 2 Mary, 23 July, 1554; *Patent Rolls* 879, Sheet 5:

Regina om*n*ibus ad quos etc. salutem. SCIATIS quod nos pro diu*er*sis bonis iustis & rac*i*onabilib*us* causis et consideracionibus nos specialiter mouentib*us* et instigantib*us* ac pro exoneracione consciencie nostre de gracia nostra speciali ac ex certa sciencia et mero motu nostris dedimus & concessimus ac restituimus. . . . Thome Heron generoso filio seniori Egidii heron de alta prodicione nuper convicti et attincti . . . totum illud manerium nos*t*rum, etc.

For information concerning the Heron estates, see Stowe's *Survey*, ed. Strype, 1720, II, 122 (Wansted House, "Naked Hall Hawe" [*i.e.* Court] and lands in Wansted and Ilford in Essex); Morant's *History of Essex*, 1768, I (Aldersbroke, Little Ilford; Higham Bemsted Manor, Walthamstow); William Robinson's *History of Hackney*, 1842, I, 115 (Shacklewell House); Lysons' *Environs of London*, 1795, II, 459 (Shacklewell House).

The *matter before* More *in the Chauncery* (42/18) and the *flatt decre* against Heron (43/1–2) seem to be the Case of *Giles Heron v. Nicholas Millisante* (Land in Withern wrongfully entered on by defendant during complainant's nonage), *Early Chancery Proceedings*, Bundle 643, No. 32.

44/13–14. *master Crooke, cheif of the six clerks.* *I.e.* John Croke, son of Richard and Alicia Croke, afterwards (1549) a Master in Chancery. Sir Thomas Pope was his pupil. (See below, Note to 100/78.) Croke died on 2 Sep. 1554. The Six Clerks of the Court of Chancery were among its principal officers, and received very high salaries. They were abolished in 1842. **(See H, 55/6.)** For "Master Crooke," see "John Croke, alias Le Blount" in *A Genealogical History of the Croke Family*, by Sir A. Croke (1823, 2 vols.), Bk. IV, pp. 393–407.

48/22. *a shirte of heare.* This was sent by More to Margaret Roper the day before his execution (see above, p. 99, ll. 11–12). From her it passed to her adopted sister and namesake, Margaret Gigs, later the wife of Dr. John Clement. Through their daughter, Mother Margaret Clement, it passed to the Community of St. Monica's, Louvain, and thence to its present guardians, the Canonesses of Newton Abbott, who were founded from the Louvain Community. **(See H, 65/22–3.)** More's shirt of hair was a source of vexation to his second wife: see below, Note to 82/8–9.

48/22–49/1. *my sister Moore.* *I.e.* Anne Cresacre, wife of John More. See above, Note to 7/4–5.

Historical Notes

51/11. *for certaine infirmities of his bodye.* Harpsfield adds: "Truth it is that this was no bare and naked pretence . . . for he was troubled with a disease in his breast." **(See H, 59/7-9.)**

57/9-13. *at St. Albones . . . and so maried the Ladye Anne Bulleyne.* The court was actually held at Dunstable Priory, and sentence given on 23 May, 1533. The King had been secretly married to Anne since about 25 January, and five days after giving sentence at Dunstable, Cranmer declared the marriage lawful. Harpsfield copies these errors from Roper, though he has "Dunstable" correctly in the *Pretended Divorce.* **(See H, 148/5-6.)**

60/1. *a certaine Nonne.* *I.e.* Elizabeth Barton, "the Holy Maid of Kent."

60/20. *the Nonnes of Sion.* *I.e.* the Bridgettine monastery of Sion, near Isleworth, between Kew and Richmond. **(See H, 156/4-5.)**

60/20. *master Raynolds.* *I.e.* Dr. Richard Reynolds, executed 4 May, 1535. See above, 80/10-11. **(See H, 179/1-2.)**

61/18-21, ff. *in the case of one Parnell . . . at the suite of one Vaghen.* Geoffrey Vaughan and Richard his son, citizens and mercers of London, had business dealings with John Parnell, citizen and draper, also of London, and brought an action against him for not fulfilling his part of the bargain. After various unsuccessful suits, the Vaughans finally won the case when More was Chancellor, 20 Jan. 1530(31). **(See H, 153/7-8.)**

64/13. *a bill to attaint the Nonne.* **(See H, 156/26.)**

67/3-4. *the Assertion of the seuen sacramentes.* Henry published the *Assertio* in 1521. Luther replied in 1522. More replied for the King under the pseudonym "Gulielmus Rosseus," 1523. **(See H, 105/21-3 ff.)**

71/11. *he was put out of the parliament bill.* **(See H, 165/12-13.)**

72/5-6. *the statute for the oathe of the supremacye and matrimonye.* *I.e.* the Oath of the Succession. The Act of Succession, 25° Hen. VIII, cap. xxii, declared the marriage with Catherine void, that with Anne valid, limited the succession to Anne's children, and ordained that all subjects should swear to keep the Act. But the Oath administered included an undertaking *to beare faith, truth and obedyence alonely to the Kynges Majestye . . . and not to any . . . foreyn Auctorite or Potentate.* These added words are referred to by Roper, p. 78, ll. 2-12; he also notes the later Statute (26° Hen. VIII, cap. ii) made to confirm the addition, p. 78, ll. 16-21. Harpsfield omits the references to these additions, but see Note to reference in the *Rastell Fragments*, **H, 228/24-27.**

73/19-20. *in a great booke of his workes.* See above, Introd., p. xlv, note 4.

73/21. *the Abbott of Westminster.* *I.e.* William Benson, a native of Boston, hence taking the surname "Boston." He died in 1549. **(See H, 169/17.)**

74/14-15. *Sir Richard Cromewell.* The son of Thomas Cromwell's sister Katherine and her husband, Morgan Williams. He entered his uncle's service, and took his name. He was the great-grandfather of the Protector. **(See H, 170/1-2.)**

75/1. *master Leiuetenant. I.e.* Sir Edmund Walsingham, 1490?-1550; lieutenant of the Tower, 1525-1547. (See *D.N.B.*)

75/9. *John A wood.* (See **H, 170**/16.)

77/2-3. *he asked her how queene Anne did.* (See **H, 72**/13-18.)

77/22-78/21. *Whereas the oath . . . amplified with their additions.* See above, Note to 72/5-6.

79/4. *Then made he a conveyaunce,* etc. (See **H, 146**/11-12.)

80/10-11. *one master Reynolds.* See above, Note to 60/20.

80/12. *three Monkes of the Charterhouse. I.e.* John Houghton, Prior of the Charterhouse of London, Robert Laurence, Prior of Beauvale, and Augustine Webster, Prior of Axholme. This is the first band of Carthusians to be executed. (See **H, 229**/29-**230**/14, for note on Rastell's account in the *Rastell Fragments*.)

82/8-9. *When Sir Thomas Moore had continued a good while in the Tower, my Lady, his wife . . .* Roper has never acquainted his reader with More's first wife's death and his second marriage. Jane died in 1511, and within a month More married Alice, widow of John Middleton, Citizen and Merchant of London, and Merchant of the Staple at Calais, who had died in 1509, possessed of considerable property. His Will is dated 4 Oct., 1509, and was proved 13th November, 1509 (*Prerogative Court of Canterbury,* fol. 22, Bennett). He leaves many pious benefactions—to Estrington Church, Yorkshire; to St. Kateryn Colman, London (where he wishes to be buried); and to the parish church of Hitchin; also to houses of friars in London and Hitchin. He arranges for obits, trentalls, etc. for the good of his soul and the souls of his kin. He leaves his property at Hitchin, Herts—lands, tenements, rents, meadows, etc.—to his wife Alice for her life, and after her death to their children. Bequests are arranged for his sisters Agnes and Isabel and their children; for his daughters Alice and Helen; and for other possible issue after his death. The daughter Alice became a member of More's household, and was as one of his own children. She married twice, first Thomas Elrington, and secondly Sir Giles Alington. She was Lady Alington at the time of More's attainder, and pleaded with Audley on his behalf. (See letter to Margaret, *Works,* 1557, pp. 1433-4.)

Dame Alice's maiden name has not yet been established, but her arms in Chelsea Church are those of the Arden family. It is suggested by Mrs. Carwardine Probert, of Bevills, Bures, Suffolk, who has been endeavouring to trace the connections of John Middleton and his wife Alice, that John Middleton belonged to the Stockeld Middletons, as his daughter Alice (Lady Alington) carries the Stockeld Middletons' arms on her tomb in Horseheath Church, Cambridgeshire.

For a copy of John Middleton's Will, I am much indebted to Mr. Reginald L. Hine of Hitchin. He informs me that he has found the Arden family "as natives of Yaxley and Kelshall and Coddington, near Hitchin, but not of this parish itself." Also that Thomas More and his father had property in Hitchin —"in 1504 a third part of the Manor of Charlton, Hitchin, was granted to John More, Serjeant-at-Law, and in 1523, in the Lay Subsidy Rolls, John More is assessed 'in goods' at £4, and his son Thomas is assessed 'in stipend' at 20s."

Historical Notes

In the *English Hist. Review*, Vol. VII, 1892, Oct., pp. 712–15, James Gairdner prints a letter in the Public Record Office, sent to Dame Katheryn Manne by Dan John Bouge (?Bonge), 1535. The writer was at the time a Carthusian of Axholme, but he had been Sir Thomas More's confessor during his early married years. Bouge notes the month's interval that elapsed between the death of More's first wife and his marriage with the second :

> Item, as ffor Sir Tomas More, he was my paryschener at London. I crystynyd hym ij goodly chyldern. I berryd hys ffirst wyff, and wᵗin a monythe after he cam to me on a Sonday at nyte late and ther he browt me a dyspensacyon to be marryd þᵉ next Monday wᵗowt any banys axyng; and as I understond sche is ȝett a lyff.

He goes on to praise More's virtues, and tells how Dame Alice begged him to use his influence to prevent More's use of the hair-shirt :

> kepe yow thys prevyly to your selff, he ware a gret heyer next hys skynne, in so myche þᵗ my mastres marvelyd wher hys schyrtes was weschyd. Item, þⁱˢ mastres hys wyff desyryd me to counsell to put þᵗ hard and row schyrte off hayer, and ȝet is very longe, almost a twelmonythe, or sche knew thys haburyon off heyyr; yt tamyd hys fflesche tyll þᵉ blod was sene in hys clothys, etc.

84/10–11. *as appeareth by his examinations in the said great book.* See above, Introd., p. xlv, footnote 4 ; also 73/19–20, 99/13–14.

84/13–14. *master Riche, afterwardes Lord Riche. I.e.* Sir Richard Rich (1496–1567) knighted 1533; created first Baron Rich, 1547; lord-chancellor, 1548. In addition to his perjury against More, he is probably the "mischievous messenger" who entrapped Fisher. (See *Rastell Fragments*, pp. 232–5, in Appendix I to edition of Harpsfield's *Life of More*, and **H, 240/**5–6.)

84/14–15. *Sir Richard Sowthwell*, 1504–64. (See **H, 181/**27–**182/**1, and *D.N.B.*)

84/15. *one master Palmer.* In the Historical Note to **H, 181/**27–**182/**1, Prof. Chambers suggested that this might be Sir John Palmer. He now points out that Cromwell's servant was Thomas Palmer. See R. B. Merriman's *Life and Letters of Thomas Cromwell*, Vol. II, no. 313.

86/7–9. *indicted of treason vppon the statute,* etc. There were two distinct Acts : (1) 26 Henry VIII, cap. 1 : *An Acte concernynge the Kynges Highnes to be supreme heed of the Churche of Englande*, etc. (2) 26 Henry VIII, cap. 13 : *An Acte wherby divers offences be made high treason.* (**See H, 174/**20–25.)

86/12–13. *Moore . . . brought . . . to westminster hall to awneswer the Indictment.* The Paris News Letter (see Harpsfield, Appendix II, pp. 253–66) must be combined with Roper's account (as in Harpsfield) to get the whole story of the trial.

88/7. *the temple. I.e.* the Middle Temple.

89/7–90/1. *maliciouslye ; And where there is no malice, there can be no offence. . . . And only this word 'maliciously' is in the statute materiall.* The inclusion of this word in the Statute was specially stressed. Rastell notes that it is twice inserted in the Act. (See Note to *Rastell Fragments*, **H, 229/**2–8.)

90/15–16. *he neuer did to temporall man before.* This has often been wrongly interpreted. Roper does not say that More was the first layman to be made Chancellor, but that *he*, Henry VIII, never gave the Chancellorship to *temporal man before.* (See **H, 191**/17–19.)

92/4–5. *the Jury found him guilty.* For names of the Jury, see **H, 192**/24–5.

95/15–16. *the Lord Fitz James, then Lord Cheif Justice of the kings Bench.* I.e. Sir John Fitz James, 1470?–1542? Chief Justice, 1526. One of the Commissioners also at Fisher's trial.

96/19–20. *Sir Anthony Seintleger, knight* (1496–1559). A member of Gray's Inn, and probably present, like Richard Heywood, in a legal capacity at More's trial. He was not knighted till 1539. His later career was distinguished— "gentleman of Henry VIII's privy chamber, 1538; . . . escorted Anne of Cleves to England, 1539; lord-deputy of Ireland, 1540 . . . confirmed as deputy by Edward VI, 1547 . . . recalled for alleged papistical practices, 1551; . . . reappointed 1553," etc. (See *D.N.B.*)

96/20. *Richard Heywood* (1509–1570). Brother of John Heywood, the dramatist, and son of William Heywood. He entered Lincoln's Inn in 1534, and was present in a legal capacity at More's trial. He shared with William Roper the office of Prothonotary of the King's Bench. (See above, Introd., p. xxxv, and A. W. Reed, *Tudor Drama*, pp. 30, 32–3, 82.)

97/5. *Sir William Kingston* (d. 1540) . . . "fought at Flodden, 1513; knighted, 1513; took part in the Field of the Cloth of Gold; captain of the guard, 1523; constable of the Tower, 1524; brought Wolsey to London, 1530; received Anne Boleyn in the Tower, 1536," etc. (See *D.N.B.*)

99/9–10; 100/3–4. *more then a seuennight after his iudgment; Tuesdaye, St. Thomas even, and the vtas of Saincte Peeter.* An error, in which Harpsfield follows Roper. More was executed on the fifth day (July 6) after his trial (July 1). (See above, Introd., p. xlvii, and **H, 200**/18–19; **201**/9–10.)

100/7–8. *Sir Thomas Pope* (?1507–1559) had been articled to Master John Croke (see above, Note to 44/13–14) and, as a young official in the Court of Chancery, must have been well known to More. He was the founder of Trinity College, Oxford, 1555, and the guardian from 1555 to 1558 of the Princess Elizabeth. (See **H, 201**/13.)

103/19–23. *the Emperour Chareles . . . sent for Sir Thomas Elliott . . . and said . . . the Kinge, your master, hath put . . . Sir Thomas Moore to deathe.* An error of Roper, taken over by Harpsfield. Elyot's only known embassy to Charles V, 1531–2, had ceased long before More's death. But Roper's story must have some foundation in fact. The list of witnesses (see below, p. 104, ll. 8–10) proves that there was some definite scene in his mind—probably after More's resignation in 1532, the Emperor's words to Elyot referring to Henry's loss of his wise councillor by that act.

There is no authority for the statement in *D.N.B.* that Elyot was ambassador again to the Emperor in 1535. (See **H, 205**/16–**206**/8.)

103/19–20. *Sir Thomas Elliott* (? 1490–1546), well known to students of literature as author of the "Boke called the Governour," 1531. See *D.N.B.* for his public and diplomatic career, and Note to 103/19–23, above.

Historical Notes

104/8–9. *maister Clement and his wife . . . master John Haywood and his wife.* The Mores, Heywoods, Clements and Rastells were connected by marriage, as may be shown most clearly by the following table of the persons concerned here :

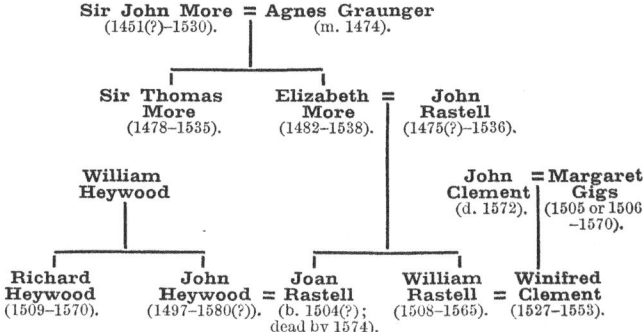

"Maister Clement," *i.e.* John Clement, M.D., was educated at St. Paul's School, and then taken into More's household. He was with More at Antwerp in 1515, and present at Peter Giles's house when *Utopia* was planned: see Prefatory Letter to Peter Giles :

For John Clement, my boye, who as yow knowe was there present with vs, etc.

Clement became proficient in Latin and Greek, and in 1519 was appointed Cardinal Wolsey's Lecturer in Rhetoric at Oxford, and later Reader in Greek. In 1526 he married Margaret Gigs, who was also an inmate of More's household (see below), and had by her eleven children, Winifred being presumably the eldest.

Clement turned his attention to medicine, in which his wife was also skilled (see **H, 90/21–91/19**). He qualified, and became Court Physician, 1528–40. In 1528 he was elected Fellow of the College of Physicians, and in 1544 their President. In 1529 he attended Wolsey in his illness.

On 21 December, 1549, to escape the religious difficulties under Edward VI, he and his wife and family fled to Louvain. They were accompanied by their married daughter Winifred and her husband, William Rastell. On 17 July, 1553, Winifred died of fever in Louvain, just before Mary's accession, and was buried at St. Peter's. The Clements and William Rastell then returned to England, and Clement took up again his medical career.

Under the Elizabethan rigours, the Clements and William Rastell, on 3rd January, 1562(3), again fled to Louvain, and this time none returned. William Rastell died in 1565 at Louvain, and was buried with Winifred, his wife. In 1570 Margaret Clement died at Mechlin, and in 1572 John Clement died there also; both were buried at St. Rumbold's.

The most famous of the Clement children was Margaret, born 1540, died 1612, Prioress of St. Ursula's, Louvain. There is record also of a son Thomas and three other daughters, Dorothy, Bridget and Helen. Bridget was Mary Bassett's god-daughter (see Mary Bassett's Will, *Notes & Queries*, 11th Series, Vol. VI, Aug. 3, 1912).

Margaret Gigs was brought up with More's children, and "numbered," as he says, "amongst his own." Her parentage is not clear. In the Basle sketch by Holbein for his picture of the More family group (see frontispiece to Harpsfield) she is described as :
Margareta giga clementis uxor thome mori filiabus condiscipula et cognata anno 22.
Margaret Roper is there described as :
Margareta Ropera thome mori filia anno 22.
Bridgett (*Life of More*, p. 125, n.) takes *cognata* as indicating that Margaret Gigs was a relative of the Mores. Prof. Reed has another suggestion, and writes in a letter :
> In this word *cognata* I see the explanation of the coincidence of the ages. Mother Giggs was foster-mother or wet-nurse to Meg. The two infants were brought up together, and More played the game, and not only gave them both the same name but the same breeding. There is *Utopia* in the making. . . . When John Clement recovered *The Old Barge* in his suit at law, he described his property as being "a great messuage with the appurtenances wherein yor said orator nowe dwellethe, *and of one mese or tenement with thappurtenances therunto adjoyning sett* and being in the barge at Bucklersbury." Later on he gives the value of the adjoining tenement as £6 a year, and later again this tenement is described as "late in the tenure of Thomas Gyggs." It may be that this Gyggs came in after Clement's flight, but I think it more likely that he indicates (as the occupant of the smaller tenement adjoining the big house) the relation of the Giggs' household to the Mores'.

As noted above (Note to 6/11–22), Margaret Gigs was a contemporary of Margaret Roper, and born between 6 February, 1505, and 21 April, 1506. Her birth has been usually placed in 1508, and her marriage in 1530, but both dates are impossible. Her marriage date has been based upon the fact that in the pictures of the More family group, she is sometimes called "Gigs," sometimes "Clement," sometimes both : it has therefore been assumed that she was married whilst the picture was being painted, and so the date 1530 was reached—the date wrongly attributed to the picture. The Basle sketch was probably made early in 1527 ; the two Margarets are there noted as in their 22nd year, so their birth-date 1505 or 1506 is arrived at. (**See H, 9/6.**) And from Richard Hyrde's statement as to Margaret Roper's age, her birth at any rate cannot have been later than October, 1505 (see above, Note to 6/11–22).

Early in 1526 is the latest possible date for the Clements' marriage. Margaret Clement died on 6 July, 1570, and her husband writes on her tomb : *Hæc mihi plus quam quadraginta et quatuor annos iuncta fuit* (Pits. p. 768, Æt. 16, 1018). Also her daughter Winifred died on 17 July, 1553, aged 26½ (Pits. p. 765, Æt. 16, 1014).

For authorities on the Clements, **see H, 90/6–7.**

John Heywood, the well-known dramatist, married Joan Rastell about 1522. For his part in the Plot of the Prebendaries against Cranmer, see above, Note to 40/19. He and his wife and sons, Jasper and Ellis, remained in England under Edward VI, when the Clements and William Rastell fled. But in the second flight they shared, the parents fleeing on 20th July, 1564, and Jasper and Ellis being already in Rome. The sons became Jesuits, and all died in exile.

For further details, see Reed's *Early Tudor Drama.*

GLOSSARY

Note.—The Glossary is not a complete concordance, but aims at including all words of which the meaning is of interest or of difficulty.
Infinitives which do not occur in the text, if used as headwords, are placed within square brackets.

[**Abide,** *s. v.*] await submissively; *p. p.* **abidden,** 86/16.
Accompt, *w. v.* obsolete form of "account," 50/8 ; 1 *sg. pr. ind.* **accompte,** 76/8; 3 *pl. pr. ind.* **accompte,** 45/19; *p. p.* **accompted,** 3/10, 18/13, etc.
Acknowen, *p. p.* acknowledged, confessed. To be **acknowen,** to avow, confess, 74/4.
Affection, *sb.* partiality, 40/11.
Among, *adv.* from time to time, now and then, 15/7.
Angell, *sb.* gold coin of the value of 6*s.* 8*d.* to 10*s.*, 102/17; *pl.* **angels,** 63/12.
Avoid, *w. v.* make void, 86/22; *p. p.* **avoided,** 79/15 ; *vbl. sb.* **avoydinge,** 95/10.
[**Awarde,** *w. v.*] sentence, consign to custody; *p. p.* **awarded,** 38/14.

Barrister, Vtter, *sb.* one who pleads "without" (outside) the Bar, as distinguished from Benchers, who are sometimes admitted to plead "within" the Bar, 5/23. (See *N.E.D.—Bar, Barrister.*)
Beholdinge, *pr. p. adj.* beholden, indebted, 39/14.
[**Betake,** *s. v.*] deliver, entrust; *p. p.* **betaken,** 73/21.
Boystyous, *adj., older and obsolete form of* "boisterous," *which is an obscure variant of it,* rough, unpolished, 15/1.
[**Breake with,** *s. v.*] broach a matter; *p. p.* **broken,** 20/4, 44/21.
Breif, *sb.* papal letter less formal and more compendious than a Bull, 34/15.

Chargeable, *adj.* burdensome, of great responsibility, 51/10.

Civillian, *sb.* one learned in civil law, 10/5.
Coler, *sb.* pretence, appearance of right, 8/11.
Collorable, *adj.* specious, plausible, 38/21.
[**Common,** *w. v.*] commune, have intercourse with; *p. p.* **commoned,** 56/17.
Complexion, *sb.* constitution (physical), 20/6.
Condiscend, *w. v.* agree, concur, assent, 45/12, 64/19 ; 3 *sg. pret. ind.* **condiscended,** 32/5.
Conf(f)erre, *w. v.* (1) compare ; 3 *sg. pret. ind.* **conferred,** 32/13. (2) discuss, 11/11, 13/18-19, etc.
Conuersation, *sb.* behaviour, 6/14.
Convince, *w. v.* confute, prove wrong, 91/7.
Courte, *sb.* Inn of Court, 7/9.
Cunninge, *adj.* learned, skilful, 6/5.

Deare, Deere, *adj.* (1) high-priced, costly, 9/19. (2) precious in estimation, 51/8.
Desperately, *adv.* hopelessly, in extremity of despair, 35/21.
[**Disable,** *w. v.*] discredit, belittle; 3 *sg. pret. ind.* **disabled,** 40/5.
Disagreable, *adj.* not agreeing, discordant, 33/11, 93/6-7.
Discharge, *w. v.* unburden, relieve from obligation or duty, 16/13, 76/13, 91/3 ; *p. p.* **discharged,** 15/19, 46/11, etc.
Discharge, *sb.* relief from duty or obligation, 12/15, 47/14, etc.
Disposition, *sb.* nature, condition of body, 20/6.
Doubte, *sb.* fear, dread, 15/20, 16/8, 16/12.

THOMAS MORE   129   K

Glossary

Eftssoones, *adv.* soon afterwards, 49/14.
Enhable, *w. v.*, obsolete form of " enable," declare fit, regard as competent, 12/24.

Fayne, *adj.* constrained, forced of necessity, 48/13, 63/4, 78/18.
Forbeare, *s. v.* deny oneself, be without, dispense with, 10/22.
Forsake, *s. v.* decline, refuse, 63/15; *pr. p.* **forsaking,** 47/14.
Forth(e), *adv.* forwards, onwards, without deviation, continuously, 50/18, 70/8.
Fowle, *adj.* shameful, ignominious, 27/23.

Ge(e)ue, *s. v.*, obsolete form of " give "—*passim*.
Generally, *adv.* in the wide or general sense, 89/16.
Glister, *sb.* clyster, enema, 29/3.
Gods markes, *sb.* 29/11. See *N.E.D.*—*God*, IV, 16. c : " the markes of the plague, commonly called Goddes markes " (Warde, 1558). (Cf. similar reference to the Great Sickness in More's *Four Last Things*, 80. B. 6.)
Good yere : What the good yere! *a phrase expressing impatience, imprecation, etc.*, 82/13.
Greif, Grief, *sb.* (1) difficulty, trouble, 9/1. (2) grudge, displeasure, anger, 30/16 ; *pl.* 19/14.
Grudge, *sb.* uneasiness, 14/1. (Cf. More's *Rich. III*, 38. C. 2 : " grudge and heart-brennyng.")
Guise, *sb.* habit, custom, 25/19.

Honest, *adj.* virtuous, seemly, 6/14.
[Howsel, *w. v.*] (1) *tr.* to administer the Eucharist to. (2) *pass.* to receive the Eucharist; *p. p.* **howsled,** 72/18.

Impertinent, *adj.* irrelevant, 30/18.
Incense, *w. v.* kindle, enflame, 38/19.
Incontynent(ly), *adv.* immediately, 29/2, 75/16.
Indifferent, *adj.* impartial, 40/10, 42/20.
Indifferently, *adv.* impartially, 62/16.
Iniunctions, *sb. pl.* orders to stop proceedings till the Court of Chancery was satisfied as to their equity, 44/8, etc.

Instant, *adj.* urgent, insistent, 63/2.
Instrument, *sb.* formal legal document, 34/15.
[Intreate, *w. v.*], obsolete form of " entreat," handle a matter or subject; *p. p.* **intreated,** 15/14.

Javill, *sb.* worthless scoundrel, rogue, 102/7, 9.

Leades, *sb. pl.* lead roof, 11/13.
Leese, *s. v.* lose, 9/21.
Let, *w. v.* hinder, 15/16.
Lewd, *adj.* wrong, villainous, 23/15.
Lewdly, *adv.* maliciously, wrongly, 23/19.
Libell, *sb.* document of plaintiff, plea, 34/9. (*Not with modern bad sense.*)
[List, *w. v.*] desire; 3 *pl. pr. ind.* **they list,** 23/20.

Maistry, *sb.* achievement, 26/11.
[Malign, *w. v.*] hate; 3 *sg. pret. ind.* **maligned,** 31/12.
Markes, *sb. pl.*, 55/5. (*The " mark " was worth* 13*s.* 4*d.*)
Meate, *sb.* food in general, 7/7.
Misprision of treason, *sb.* 64/16. See *N.E.D.* : " originally an offence . . . akin to treason . . . but involving a lesser degree of guilt, and not liable to the capital penalty. As various statutes enacted that concealment of a person's knowledge of treasonable actions or designs should be regarded as *misprision of treason*, this term came to be used as the ordinary designation for such concealment." See important reference in *N.E.D.* to Act 25 Hen. VIII, C. 22 (a° 1533–4) : " Yf any person . . . being commaunded . . . to take the seid othe . . . obstynatly refuse that to doo . . . that every such refusall shalbe . . . adjudged mesprysion of high treason."

Parte, *sb.*, *obsolete form of* " party," 9/5, 10/12; *pl.* **partes,** 25/5.
Pillars, *sb. pl.* pillars of silver carried before the Cardinal as an emblem of his being a Pillar of the Church, 17/13.
[Plonge, *w. v.*] overwhelm, overpower; *p. p.* **plonged,** 81/14.

Glossary 131

Pollaxes, *sb. pl.* long-handled weapons carried by escort of a great personage, 17/14.
Precisely, *adv.* (1) particularly, specifically, 70/11. (2) definitely, expressly, in precise terms, 84/9.
Presently, *adv.* promptly, immediately, 5/8.
[Propone, *w. v.*] propound, propose; *p. p.* **proponed**, 33/18.
Provoke, *w. v.* incite, urge, stimulate to action, 26/8.

Reforme, *w. v.* alter, revoke, 12/19.
Roome, *sb.* place, position, 11/2, 39/16, 40/5.
[Round, *w. v.*] whisper; 3 *sg. pret. ind.* **rounded**, 73/9.
Rude, *adj.* uneducated, inexperienced, 15/1.

Salf, *adj.* safe, 103/3.
Scant, *adv.* barely, hardly, 63/6.
Serve, *w. v. in usual sense, passim* ; gratify, furnish means for satisfying, 31/20; 3 *sg. pret. ind.* **served**, prompted, inclined, 6/16.
Seuerall, *adj.* separate, 19/7, 84/8, 88/22.
Seuerally, *adv.* separately, 18/12.
Showes, *sb. pl.* shoes, 30/11.
Shrewd, *adj.* injurious, harmful, 27/11.
Singly, *adv.* simply, without more, 49/2.
Singuler, *adj.* special, particular, above the ordinary, 3/2, 10/5, 11/5, 51/8, 90/8, 102/10.

Singulerly, *adv.* particularly, specially, 21/9.
Subpœna, *sb.* summons to give evidence, 43/8, 9.
Suffrages, *sb. pl.* prayers, intercessions, 25/18.
Sythe, *conj.* since, 12/18.

[Tender, *w. v.*] love; 3 *sg. pret. ind.* **tendred**, 28/14.
Towarde, *adj.* inclined, 38/9.
Towardnes, *sb.* (1) forwardness in learning, 5/10. (2) readiness, willingness, 18/3.
Travers, *sb.* apartment screened off, 11/8.
Trustie, *adj.* involving trust, responsible, 11/6.
[Turmoil, *w. v.*] torment, harass; *p. p.* **turmoyled**, 81/14.
Tylle valle, *exclamation of impatience*, 83/14.

Vnconingly, *adv.* unskilfully, 16/18.
Vtas, *sb.* octave, 100/4.
Vtter, *adj.* complete, fully qualified, 5/23.

Wanton, *sb.* pet, pampered darling, 76/17.
[Wene, *w. v.*] think ; 3 *pl. pr. subj.* **weene**, 76/5 ; *p. p.* **went**, 47/22.
[Wit, *pret. pr. v.*] know; 2 *pl. pr. ind.* **wote**, 17/10; 3 *sg. pret. ind.* **wist**, 19/22.
Wood, *adj.* mad, angry, 30/14.

GENERAL INDEX

Note.—The Historical Notes to Harpsfield's *Life of More* (E.E.T.S.) should be consulted for further information concerning matters treated by Roper and taken over by Harpsfield. The references below are to pages of the Roper text, and to the Historical Notes to Roper (= R) and to Harpsfield (= H).

Adrian, Cardinal: is made Pope [1522] to the disappointment of Wolsey, 30; description of his first entrance into Rome, 30 (**see Note to H, 42/8-15**).

Alice, Mistress, [second] wife of Sir Thomas More (**see Note to R, 82/8-9**): is teased by More—"Madam, my Lord is gone," 55; visits More in the Tower, and is not in sympathy with his opposition to the King's wishes, 82-4.

Anne, Queen. See *Boleyn, Anne.*

Anthony, St., School of: More educated at, 5 (**see Note to H, 10/18-19**).

[Arthur, Prince of Wales], brother of Henry, later Henry VIII of England: first husband of Katherine of Aragon, 31.

Arundel, [William Fitz Alan], Earl of: loses his case against Mistress Crocker, 63.

Assertion of the seuen sacramentes: Henry VIII's book, More accused of responsibility for, 67-8 (**see Note to H, 105/21-3 ff.**).

Audeley, [Sir Thomas], Lord Chancellor of England [1532-44]: succeeds More as Chancellor, 52; is given More's eight watermen, 52; one of the King's deputies before whom More is summoned in the case of the Nun of Canterbury, 65; one of those who persuade the King to put More out of the Parliament Bill, 70-71; one of the Commissioners appointed to tender the Oath of the Succession, 72; gets legalised the amplification of the oath as administered to More, 78; attempts to discover More's opinion on the Supremacy, 84; stays his judgement, 92; accuses More of "stiffly sticking," 94; appeals for advice to the Lord Chief Justice, 95.

Augustine, St. [of Canterbury, died *c.* 607]: sent by Gregory to convert the English, 94.

Augustine, St. [of Hippo; Aurelius Augustinus, b. 354, d. 430]: More "reads" in the Church of St. Lawrence the *De Civitate Dei* of, 6 (**see Note to H, 13/23-5**); More advises the King to consult the works of, 33.

[Barton, Elizabeth], the Nun of Canterbury. See *Nun of Canterbury* [i.e. *Elizabeth Barton*].

Bath, [John] Clarke, Bishop of [1523-41]: one of the learned men consulted on the divorce, 32; one of the Clergy who request More to accept reward for his controversial writings, 47; one of the Bishops who request More to accompany them to Anne's coronation, 57.

Blackfriars: commission for the trial of the King's marriage at, 34.

Boleyn, Anne, Queen of Henry VIII of England: Henry VIII falls in love with, 31; marries Henry VIII, 57; More refuses to attend the coronation of, 57-8; Henry VIII is exasperated against More by, 74; More foretells the fall of, 77 (**see Note to H, 72/13-18**).

Bucklersbury: More's house at, 7 (**see Note to H, 19/12**).

Bullen, Anne. See *Boleyn, Anne.*

Cambrai: More and Tunstall ambassadors at, 36 (**see Note to H, 48/18-19**).

Cambridge : More's disputations with learned men of, 21 ; More attends the King on his progresses to, 22 ; More declares to the Commons the judgement of the University of, on the divorce, 50–51.
Campegius, [Laurentius], Cardinal : one of the Commissioners appointed to judge the divorce, 34.
Canterbury, Thomas Cranmer, Archbishop of [1533–56] : determines the matter of the marriage, 57 ; one of the King's Deputies before whom More is summoned in the case of the Nun of Canterbury, 65 ; one of the Commissioners appointed to tender the Oath of the Succession, 72.
See also *Morton, [John], Cardinal*.
Canterbury, Nun of. See *Nun of Canterbury*.
Carthusians : martyrdom of the [first band of], 80–81 **(see Notes to H, 178/26–179/1, 229/29–230/14)**.
Catherine, Queen. See *Katherine, Queen*.
Chain of Gold : More's, 74.
Chancellor of the Duchy of Lancaster : More made, 20.
Chancellor, Lord, of England. See *Morton, [John], Cardinal ; Wolsey, [Thomas], Cardinal ; More, Sir Thomas ; Audeley, [Sir Thomas] ; Rich, [Sir Richard]*.
Chancery : 42, 43.
Charles V, Emperor : procures the election to the papacy of Cardinal Adrian [1522], and so incurs the anger of Wolsey, 30 ; nephew to Queen Katherine, 30–31 ; peace concluded between the Kings of England and France and, 36 ; pays tribute to More's wisdom, 103–4 **(see Note to H, 205/16–206/8)**.
Charterhouse, of London : More spends four years with the monks of the, 6 **(see Note to H, 17/11–15)**.
See also *Carthusians* (one of the three " Monkes of the Charterhouse," 80, being John Houghton, Prior of the Charterhouse of London).
Chelsea : Henry VIII visits More at his house at, 20 **(see Note to H, 24/27–26/3)** ; More sings in the Parish Church at, 51.
Clarke, John. See *Bath, [John] Clarke, Bishop of*.
Clement, [John], Doctor : hears Elyot's report of the Emperor's tribute to More's wisdom, 104.
Clement, [Margaret], Mistress [*i.e.* Margaret Gigs] : hears Elyot's report of the Emperor's tribute to More's wisdom, 104.
Clergy : More refuses reward from the, 45–8.
Colte, [Jane] : [first] wife of Sir Thomas More, 6 **(see Note to R, 6/11–22)** ; her children, 7 **(see Note to R, 7/4–5)**.
Colte, Master [John] : gentleman of Essex, and father-in-law of More, 6 **(see Note to R, 6/11–22)**.
Commons. See *Parliament*.
Conveyance of More's lands : 79–80 **(see Note to H, 146/11–12)**.
Corinthians : St. Paul's children in Christ, 94.
Cranmer, Thomas. See *Canterbury, Thomas Cranmer, Archbishop of*.
[Cresacre, Anne]. See *More, [Anne]*.
Cromwell, Sir Richard : conveys More to the Tower, 74 **(see Note to H, 170/1–2)**.
Cromwell, Thomas, Master Secretary : More's advice to, 56–7 ; one of the King's Deputies before whom More is summoned in the case of the Nun of Canterbury, 65 ; tells Roper that More is put out of the Bill, 71 ; one of the Commissioners appointed to tender the Oath of the Succession, 72 ; gets legalised the amplification of the Oath as administered to More, 78 ; promises More the King's favour, 81 ; attempts to discover More's opinion on the Supremacy, 84.
Crooke, Master : prepares docket of More's injunctions, 44 **(see Note to H, 55/6)**.

De Civitate Dei, St. Augustine's : " read " by More in the Church of St. Lawrence, 6.
Devil : likened by More to an Ape, 27 ; More would see justice done even to the, 42.

General Index

Divorce, between Henry VIII and Queen Katherine : events preceding the, 29–31, 33–4, 57 **(see Notes to H, 41/2–4, 46/12–13, 46/20–23, 46/26–47/1)**; Wolsey considered by Roper the originator of the, 30–31 **(see Notes to H, 41/2–4, 41/4–42/1)**; More consulted on the, 31–3, 37–8, 49–50 **(see Note to H, 44/17–18).**

Durham, [Cuthbert] Tunstall, Bishop of [1530–52 and 1553–9] : one of the learned men consulted on the divorce, 32 ; on embassy with More at Cambrai, 36 ; one of those who request More to receive reward for his controversial writings, 47 ; one of those who request More to accompany them to Queen Anne's coronation, 57.
See also (1) *London*, [*Cuthbert*] *Tunstall, Bishop of*.

Elyot, Sir Thomas : told of More's martyrdom by Charles the Emperor, 103–4 **(see Note to H, 205/16–206/8).**

Embassies, More's : for the English merchants, 9 **(see Note to H, 20/23–21/3)** ; with Wolsey in Flanders and France, 23 ; with Tunstall at Cambrai, 36–7.

Emperor, the. See *Charles V, Emperor.*

Erasmus : 3.

Exeter, [John] Veysey (Vaysey, Vesey, Voysey), Bishop of [1519–51 and 1553–4] : one of those who request More to accept reward for his controversial writings, 47.

Fisher, John. See *Rochester, John Fisher, Bishop of*.

Fitz-James, [Sir John], Lord Chief Justice : appealed to by the Lord Chancellor at More's trial, 95.

Flanders : More and Wolsey ambassadors in, 23.

Fleet : Bishop Stokesley sent by Wolsey to the, 38 **(see Note to H, 49/16–18).**

Fortune : More's verses on flattering, 82.

Fox, Dr. [Richard]. See (1) *Winchester, Dr. [Richard] Fox, Bishop of*.

France : More and Wolsey ambassadors in, 23.

French King, the [*i.e.* Francis I] : Wolsey tries to arrange a marriage between Henry VIII and the " sister " (error) of, 31 **(see Note to H, 43/8–9)** ; concludes a peace with Henry VIII and Charles the Emperor at Cambrai, 36.

Friday : devoted by More to spiritual exercises, 26.

Furnival's Inn : More Reader at, 6 **(see Note to H, 14/17).**

Gardiner, [Stephen]. See (2) *Winchester, [Stephen] Gardiner, Bishop of.*

Gregory [I], St., Pope : sends Augustine to convert the English, 94.

Gresham, Master : More's exchange of cups with, 63–4.

Grocyn, [William], Dr. : one of More's audience, 6.

Hampton Court : Wolsey's gallery at, 19.

Health, More's : reason advanced for discharge from the Chancellorship, 51 **(see Note to H, 59/7–9).**

Henry VII, King of England : More incurs the hostility of, 7–8 **(see Notes to H, 15/15–16, 15/21 ff.)** ; death of, 8.

Henry VIII, King of England : takes More into his service, 10 ; his love of More, 11 ; excuses More from the proposed embassy to Spain, 20 **(see Note to H, 33/19–22)** ; visits More at Chelsea, 20–21 **(see Note to H, 24/27–26/3)** ; employs More to answer orations, 22 ; consults More on the divorce, 31–3, 37–8, 49–50 **(see Note to H, 44/17–18)** ; the Peace of Cambrai concluded between the Emperor, the French King and, 36 **(see Note to H, 48/18–19)** ; displaces Wolsey from the Chancellorship and appoints More, 39 ; promises More the continuance of his favour, 52 ; Fisher advises the Nun of Canterbury to go to, 60 ; hopes to use More's attainder in the case of the Nun to win his consent to the Marriage, 64 ; his undue stressing of the Pope's authority in his *Assertio septem sacramentorum* blamed on More, 66–7; highly offended with More, 70; exasperated by Anne against More, 74; More's lands seized by, 79 (**see Note to H, 146/11–12**); sends Master Pope to warn More that he is to die that day, and commands him not to use many words at his execution, 100–101; More will pray for, 101.

See also *Divorce; More, Sir Thomas; Wolsey.*

Heron, [Giles], son-in-law of Sir Thomas More: More issues a decree against, 42–3 (**see Notes to H, 53/24–8, and R, 42/16–17**).

Heywood, [Joan], Mistress, [*i.e.* Joan Rastell, wife of John Heywood]: hears Elyot's report of the Emperor's tribute to More's wisdom, 104.

Heywood, John: hears Elyot's report of the Emperor's tribute to More's wisdom, 104.

Heywood, Richard: present at More's trial, 96.

[Holy Maid of Kent]. See *Nun of Canterbury* [i.e. *Elizabeth Barton*].

Indictment: Sir Thomas More's, 86.

See also *Harpsfield, Appendix III.*

Injunctions: More defends his, 44–5.

Jerome, St.: More advises the King to consult the works of, 33.

Jury, at More's trial, 92 (**see Note to H, 192/24–5**).

Katherine, Queen [daughter of Ferdinand of Spain]: her delight in More's company, 11; aunt to the Emperor, 30–31; wife, first to Prince Arthur, and after to Prince Henry, sons of Henry VII of England, 31.

See also *Divorce; Henry VIII; Wolsey.*

[Kent, Holy Maid of]. See *Nun of Canterbury* [i.e. *Elizabeth Barton*].

King's Bench, Court of the: More's father a Judge of, 43.

Kingston, Sir William, Constable of the Tower: conveys More back to the Tower after his trial, sorrows for him, and praises his fortitude, 97.

Lambeth: More summoned to take the Oath at, 72.

Langland, [John]. See *Lincoln, [John] Langland, Bishop of.*

Lawrence, St., Church of: More "reads" the *De Civitate Dei* in the, 6 (**see Note to H, 13/23–5**).

Letter, More's, to Margaret: 99.

Lincoln, [John] Langland, Bishop of [1520–47]: urged by Wolsey to question the lawfulness of Henry VIII's marriage to Katherine, 31 (**see Note to H, 41/21**).

Lincoln's Inn: More admitted to, 5 (**see Note to H, 13/2–12**); after his marriage, More continues his studies at, and is made Bencher, 6 (**see Note to H, 19/8–9**); More and his father meet at readings at, 43; the fare of, 53.

London: More educated at St. Anthony's School in, 5 (**see Note to H, 10/18–19**); More lectures at the Church of St. Lawrence in, 6; More spends four years with the monks of the Charterhouse of, 6 (**see Note to H, 17/11–15**); More's home at Bucklersbury in, 7 (**see Note to H, 19/12**); More's popularity and office of Under-sheriff in, 8–9 (**see Notes to H, 19/2–20/2, 20/1**); the Water-bailiff of, 23–4 (**see Note to R, 23/5**); the Commissioners sit to judge the divorce at Blackfriars in, 34; Stokesley appointed to the Bishopric of, 38.

(1) London, [Cuthbert] Tunstall, Bishop of [1522–30]: ambassador with More at Cambrai, 36–7 (**see Note to H, 48/18–19**).

See also *Durham, [Cuthbert] Tunstall, Bishop of.*

(2) London, [John Stokesley, Bishop of [1530–39]: his conference on the marriage with More, and his report of More to the King, 38; his revenge against Wolsey, 38–9 (**see Note to H, 49/16–18**).

Lord Chancellor of England. See under *Morton, [John], Cardinal; Wolsey, [Thomas], Cardinal; More, Sir Thomas;*

General Index 137

Audeley, [Sir Thomas]; Rich, [Sir Richard].

Margaret More, later Roper. See *Roper, Margaret*.

[Margaret Tudor], eldest daughter of Henry VII of England : marries [James IV], King of Scotland, 7.

Marney, Master, after Lord [John] : 18 (see Note to H, 32/14).

Master of Requests : More made, 11 (see Note to R, 11/1-3).

Merchants : More's embassies in the interests of, 9 (see Note to H, 20/23-21/3); of the Stillyard, 9 (see Note as above); the Water-bailiff angered by hearing the railing against Sir Thomas More of certain, 23.

[Middleton], Alice, later More. See *Alice, Mistress, [second] wife of Sir Thomas More*.

More, [Anne], [i.e. Anne Cresacre, wife of More's son John] : laughs at More's shirt of hair, 48-9 (see Note to H, 66/2-3).

More, [Cecily], [later wife of Giles Heron] : youngest of the three daughters of Sir Thomas More, 7 (see Note to R, 7/4-5).

More, [Elizabeth], [later wife of William Daunce] : second of the three daughters of Sir Thomas More, 7 (see Notes to H, 19/15-17, and R, 7/4-5).

More, Jane. See *Colte, [Jane]*.

More, [Sir John], father of Sir Thomas More : Judge, 43 (see Notes to H, 9/9, 10/6-7); More's courtesy to, and love for, 43-4.

More, [John] : son of Sir Thomas More, 7 (see Note to R, 7/4-5).

More, Margaret. See *Roper, Margaret*.

More, Sir Thomas, Lord Chancellor of England [1529-32]: at St. Anthony's School, 5 (see Note to H, 10/18-19); in household of Archbishop Morton, 5 ; impromptu acting, 5 (see Note to H, 11/2-3); sent to Oxford, 5 (see Notes to H, 12/13, 15-16); studies for the Bar, 5, 6-7 (see Notes to H, 12/26, 13/2-12); made an utter barrister, 5 ; lectures on *De Civitate Dei* of St. Augustine, 6 (see Note to H, 13/23-25); Reader at Furnival's Inn, 6 (see Note to H, 14/17); four years without vow with the monks of the Charterhouse of London, 6 (see Note to H, 17/11-15); marries Mistress [Jane] Colte, 6 (see Note to R, 6/11-22); their children, 7 (see Notes to H, 19/13-15, 15-17, and to R, 7/4-5); continues his study of the law, called to the Bench, 6-7 (see Note to H, 19/8-9); made Burgess of the Parliament, 7 ; incurs hostility of Henry VII by opposing subsidy, 7-8 (see Notes to H, 15/15-16, 15/21 ff.) ; an Under-sheriff of London, 8 (see Notes to H, 19/22-20/2, 20/1); his income therefrom, 9 ; embassies in the interests of the English merchants, 9 (see Note to H, 20/23-21/3); ability in case of the Pope's ship, 9-10 ; enters the Royal service, Master of Requests, knight and Privy Councillor, 10-11 (see Notes to R, 11/1-3, 12/8-10); wins the royal affection, 11 ; [Under]-Treasurer, 12 (see Note to R, 12/8-10); chosen Speaker, 12 (see Note to H, 26/17); pleads for freedom of speech for the Commons, 12-16 (see Note to H, 27/13-14 ff.); Wolsey's visit to the Commons, More defends the liberties of the House, incurs Wolsey's displeasure, 16-20 (see Note to H, 31/12 ff.); defeats Wolsey's plot to send him to Spain, 19-20 (see Note to H, 33/19-22); Chancellor of the Duchy of Lancaster, 20 (see Note to H, 24/11); the King visits More at Chelsea—" If my head could win him a castle in France," 20-21 ; modesty in argument, 21-22 ; *ex tempore* orations, 22 ; embassies with Wolsey to Flanders and France, 23 ; the Waterbailiff jealous for More's reputation, 23-4 (see Note to R, 23/5); three things in Christendom that More wished to see, 24-5 ; not ambitious of worldly honour or reward, 25 ; family prayer, 25 ; his New Building—devotes Fridays there to spiritual exercises, 25-6 ; pious counsels to his family, 26-8 ; at his prayer Margaret recovers from the sweating sickness, 28–9; More consulted for the first time on the divorce, 31–3 (**see Note to H, 44/17–18**); More foresees the growth of heresy, 34–6; never in a fume, 36; again consulted on the divorce, 37–8 (**see Note to H, 44/17–18**); on the fall of Wolsey, More made Chancellor, 39 (**see Notes to H, 50/25–6, 50/26–51/1**); Norfolk's praise of More and his modest reply, 39–40; doors ever open to suitors, 40–42; decree against Heron, 42–3 (**see Note to H, 53/24–8**); care concerning subpœnas, 43; reverence and love for his father, 43–4; defends his injunctions, 44–5; refuses reward from the clergy, 45–8; shirt of hair and other austerities, 48–9 (**see Note to H, 65/22–3**); once again consulted on the divorce, 49–50 (**see Note to H, 44/17–18**); declares to the Commons the judgment of the Universities concerning the marriage, 50–51; pleads for discharge from the Chancellorship, 51; " a parish clerk," 51; resigns the Great Seal—the King promises continuance of his favour, 51–2; discusses economies with his family, 52–4; poverty after his resignation, 54–5; " Madam, my Lord is gone," 55; prepares his family for his suffering and martyrdom, 55–6; advice to Cromwell—" If a Lion knew his own strength," 56–7; foresees the administering of oaths, 57; refuses to be present at Anne's coronation, but accepts the Bishops' money for a gown—parable of the offending virgin, 57–9; the Nun of Canterbury talks with More, 60–61; incorruptibility—the Vaughan (**see Note to H, 153/7–8**) Crocker and Gresham cases, 61–4; attainted of misprision of treason in the case of the Nun, and accused of inciting the King to write the *Assertio septem sacramentorum*—his name struck out of the Bill, 64–71 (**see Note to H, 165/12–13**); " *Quod differtur non aufertur*," 71; foretells Norfolk's disgrace, 72; summoned to Lambeth to take the Oath, 72 (**see Notes to H, 166/1–3, 228/24–7**); pious exercises before departure, 72; conscience conquers natural affection, 72–3; imprisoned at Westminster, 73; sent to the Tower, 74; retains his chain of gold, 74; the Porter demands his upper garment, 75; instructions to John a Wood, 75; Margaret's visits, 75–6; rejoices at leisure for godly meditation, 76; trusts his family to God, God " maketh him a wanton," 76; foretells fall of Anne Boleyn, 76–7 (**see Note to H, 72/13–18**); reply to the Lieutenant's apology for the poor cheer of the Tower, 77; illegality of the Oath administered to More, its subsequent confirmation, 77–8; arranges conveyance of his lands, 79–80; envies martyrs going gladly to execution, 80–81; not deceived by Cromwell's promises, 81; verses on flattering Fortune, 82; Mistress Alice visits More in the Tower, and is not in sympathy with his opposition to the King's wishes, 82–4; examinations in the Tower, 84; his books are taken from him, 84; Rich tries to entrap him on the question of the Supremacy, 84–6; indicted of treason, 86 (**see H, Appendix III**); trial and condemnation, 86–97 (**see H, pp. 183–197 and Notes; H, Appendix II**); farewell to Kingston, 97; farewell to Margaret, 97–9; sends his hair-shirt and a letter to Margaret, 99–100; Pope brings word that More is to die that day, 100 (**see Note to H, 200/18–19, 201/9–10**); More is beholden to the King's " gracious consideration," 101; comforts Pope, 101–2; is prevented from wearing his best apparel for his execution, 102; sends gold to his executioner, 102; jests on the weakness of the scaffold, 102–3; the manner of his death, 103; Charles V pays tribute to his wisdom, 103–4 (**see Note to H, 205/16–206/8**).

Morton, [John], Cardinal, [1493], [**Lord Chancellor of England,** 1487–1500], [**Archbishop of Canterbury,** 1486–1500] : More in the household of, 5; More's great future predicted by, 5; More sent to Oxford by, 5.

General Index

New Building, More's: used for pious exercises, 26; petition for the recovery of Margaret at, 28.
New Inn: More studies at, 5 (see Note to H, 12/26); fare of, 53, 54.
Norfolk, [Thomas Howard, 2nd Earl of Surrey], [3rd] Duke of: praises More when made Chancellor, 39; More makes suit to the Duke for discharge from the Chancellorship, 51; censures More for acting as a parish clerk, 51; one of the King's Deputies before whom More is summoned for the matter of the Nun of Canterbury, 65; warns More that *Indignatio principis mors est*, 71-2; More foretells his disgrace, 72; attempts to discover More's opinion on the Supremacy, 84.
Nun of Canterbury [i.e. *Elizabeth Barton*]: the matter of the, 59-61; attainted of treason, and Fisher and More attainted of misprision of treason, 64 (see Note to H, 156/26).

Oath of the Succession, the: More summoned to Lambeth to take, 72-4 (see Note to H, 228/24-7).
Old Swan: 97.
Oxford: More sent to, 5 (see Note to H, 12/13); More declares to the Commons the judgement of the University of, concerning the divorce, 50; fare of, 53, 54 (see Note to H, 144/13).

Palmer, Master [Thomas]: 'servant to Cromwell, sent to take away More's books, 84 (see Note to R, 84/15); professes he paid no heed to the conversation between More and Rich, 91.
Parliament and **Lower House of the Parliament (Commons)**: More burgess of, 7 (see Note to H, 14/20-21); More opposes subsidy demanded by Henry VII from, 7 (see Note to H, 15/15-16); More chosen Speaker, 12 (see Note to H, 26/17); More pleads toleration for himself and freedom of speech for, 12-16 (see Note to H, 27/13-14 ff.); Wolsey's visit to, and More's defence of the liberties of, 16-19 (see Note to H, 31/12 ff.);

More declares the judgement of the Universities concerning the divorce to, 50-51.
Parnell, Master [John]: More's decree against, 61-3 (see Note to H, 153/7-8).
Paul, St.: the Corinthians the children in Christ of, 94; More refers at his trial to the presence at the death of St. Stephen of, 96.
Peter, St.: the spiritual pre-eminence of, 92.
Peter, St., Utas of: day of More's execution, 100.
(1) **Pope [Leo X, 1513-21]**: case of the ship of, 9-10; Henry VIII in his *Assertio septem sacramentorum* unduly stressed the authority of, 67.
(2) **Pope [Adrian VI, 1522-3]**: elected (to the disappointment of Wolsey), 30 (see Note to H, 42/8-15).
(3) **Pope [Clement VII, 1523-34]**. See *Divorce*.
Pope, Sir Thomas: sent by the King to prepare More for death, and his sorrow, 100-102 (see Note to H, 201/13).
Porter of the Tower. See *Tower of London, Porter of the*.
Privy Councillor: More made, 11.
Psalms, the Seven. See *Seven Psalms, the*.

Reynolds, [Richard, Dr.], father of [the Bridgettine Monastery of] Sion: visited by the Nun of Canterbury, 60; executed, 80 (see Note to H, 179/1-2).
Rich, [Sir Richard, Solicitor-general: afterwards Lord Chancellor, 1547-51]: attempts to entrap More on the question of the Supremacy, 84-6; perjury of, 87; More discloses the character of, 87-8.
Rochester, [John] Fisher, Bishop of [1504-35]: his interview with the Nun of Canterbury, 60; indicted of misprision of treason in the case of the Nun of Canterbury, 64.
Rome: Pope Adrian's first entrance into, 30 (see Note to H, 42/8-15); Commission to judge the divorce procured from, 34 (see Note to H, 46/12-13); spiritual pre-eminence of the See of, 92.

140 General Index

Roper, Margaret, eldest daughter of Sir Thomas More: wife of William Roper, 3 (**see Note to R, 3/11-12**); her miraculous recovery from the sweating sickness, 28-9 (**see Note to H, 81/18-19**); is trusted with the secret of More's shirt of hair, 49; More is informed by, that he is put out of the Parliament Bill, 71; visits her father in the Tower, 75-7; More predicts the fall of Anne Boleyn to, 77 (**see Note to H, 72/13-18**); More conveys a portion of his lands to Roper and, 79-80; watches, with her father, the Carthusians and Master Reynolds going to execution, 80 (**see Note to H, 229/29-230/14**); bids her father farewell, 97-9; More sends his shirt of hair and a letter to, 99-100 (**see Note to H, 65/22-3**).

Roper, William: why qualified to write More's life, 3-4; marries Margaret More, 3 (**see Note to R, 3/11-12**); congratulates More on possession of King's favour, 21; More describes to, the three things desirable in Christendom, 24-5; commends the happy state of the Realm to More, 34-5; has never observed More "in a fume," 36; offended at More's prediction of the administering of oaths, 57; urges More to labour for his discharge out of the Parliament Bill, 65; is grieved that More has neglected to do so, 69-70; sends message to his wife that More is put out of the Parliament Bill, 71; accompanies More in the boat to Lambeth, 73; More's conveyance of certain lands to, 79-80; not himself present at More's trial, 96; Kingston praises More's fortitude to, 97; had learnt from Sir Thomas Elyot of the Emperor's praise of More's wisdom, 104.

St. Albans: 57 (**see Note to H, 148/5-6**).
St. Anthony's School. See *Anthony, St., School of.*
St. Lawrence, Church of. See *Lawrence, St., Church of.*
St. Leger, Sir Anthony: present at More's trial, 96.

Secretary, Master. See *Cromwell, Thomas.*
Seven Psalms, the [*i.e.* 6th, 31st, 37th, 50th, 101st, 129th, and 141st]: said daily by More and his family, 25; and by Margaret and More on Margaret's visits to the Tower, 75.
Ship, the Pope's: the case of, 9-10.
Shirt of Hair, More's: laughed at [by Anne Cresacre], 48-9; sent to Margaret, 99 (**see Note to H, 65/22-3**).
Sion [the Bridgettine Monastery of]: [Richard] Whitford one of the fathers of, 8 (**see Note to H, 16/19-21**); the Nun of Canterbury visits the nuns of, 60 (**see Note to H, 156/4-5**); [Richard] Reynolds a father of, 60, 80 (**see Note to H, 179/1-2**).
Southampton: 9.
Southwell, Sir Richard: sent to the Tower to take away More's books, 84 (**see Note to H, 181/27-182/1**); professes he paid no heed to the conversation between More and Rich, 91.
Spain: Wolsey's plot to send More to, 19 (**see Note to H, 33/19-22**); Pope Adrian coming from, 30; brief concerning the marriage of Henry and Katherine found in the Treasury of, 34 (**see Note to H, 46/20-23**).
Speaker: More made, 12 (**see Note to H, 26/17**).
Star Chamber: case of the Pope's ship heard in the, 10; Stokesley rebuked by Wolsey in the, 38 (**see Note to H, 49/16-18**).
Stephen, St.: his martyrdom referred to by More, 96.
Stillyard, merchants of the: 9 (**see Note to H, 20/23-21/3**).
Stokesley, [John]. See (2) *London, [John] Stokesley, Bishop of.*
Subpœnas: More's care with regard to, 43.
Suffolk, [Charles Brandon], Duke of: attends Sir Thomas More to the Chancery on his being made Lord Chancellor, 39; attempts to discover More's opinion on the Supremacy, 84.
Supremacy, the King's: More accused of denying, 86.
Sweating sickness: Margaret's miraculous recovery from the, 28-9 (**see Note to H, 81/18-19**).

General Index

Thames, River: 24, 48.
Thomas, St., of Canterbury, Eve of: More executed on, 100.
Tower of London, the: More committed to, 74; Margaret's visits to More in, 75–77; More not grieved by his imprisonment in, 76; the Lieutenant's apology for the poor cheer of, 77; More watches the martyrs going to execution from his window in, 80; Cromwell's visit to More in, 81; More's wife visits him in, 82–4; as near Heaven as is More's own house, 83; More's examinations in, 84; after his sentence, More returns to, 97; More brought from, to execution, 102.
Tower of London, Constable of the. See *Kingston, Sir William.*
Tower of London, Lieutenant of the [*i.e.* Sir Edmund Walsingham]: receives More, 75; apologises for the poor cheer of, 77; prevents More from wearing his best apparel at his execution, 102; More jokes on the weakness of the scaffold with, 102–3.
Tower of London, Porter of the: demands More's upper garment, 75.
Trial, More's: 86–97.
Tunstall, [Cuthbert], Dr. See (1) *London, [Cuthbert] Tunstall, Bishop of*; and *Durham, [Cuthbert] Tunstall, Bishop of.*
Tyler, Master [William]: reports to Henry VII More's opposition to the subsidy, 7 (see Note to H, 15/16).

Under-Sheriff of London: More made an, 8 (see Notes to H, 19/22–20/2, 20/1).
[Under]-Treasurer of the Exchequer: More made, 12 (see Note to R, 12/8–10).
Utas of St. Peter. See *Peter, St., Utas of.*

Vaughan, Master [Geoffrey or Richard]: More accused of taking reward from, 61–3 (see Note to H, 153/7–8).
Vaysey, John. See *Exeter, [John] Veysey, Bishop of.*

Water-bailiff of London: jealous for More's reputation, 23–4 (see Note to R, 23/5).
Webbe, John: present at More's trial, 96.
Westminster, [William Benson or Boston], Abbot of: More in the custody of, 73 (see Note to H, 169/17).
Westminster, city of: 19, 57, 97.
Westminster Hall: 43, 86.
Weston, [William], [Under]-Treasurer: death of, 12 (see Notes to H,24/9–10, R, 12/8–10).
Whitehall: 19.
Whitford, Richard: chaplain to Richard Fox, Bishop of Winchester, and later a Father of Sion, his warning to More, 8 (see Note to H, 16/19–21).
Wiltshire, [Sir Thomas Boleyn], Earl of: charges More with bribery and extortion, 62.
(1) Winchester, Dr. [Richard] Fox, Bishop of [1501–28]: tries to entrap More, 8 (see Note to H, 16/8).
(2) Winchester, [Stephen] Gardiner, Bishop of [1531-50 and 1553-5]: one of those requesting More to accompany them to Anne's coronation, 57.
Wingfield, Sir Richard: Chancellor of the Duchy of Lancaster before More, death of, 20 (see Note to H, 24/11).
Wolsey, [Thomas], Cardinal, Lord Chancellor of England [1515–29], Archbishop of York [1514–30]: labours to procure More for the Royal service, 9; case of the Pope's ship tried before, 10; visit to the Commons, 16–19 (see Note to H, 31/12 ff.); anger against More, and unsuccessful plot to send More to Spain, 19 (see Note to H, 33/19–22); Roper had seen the King walk arm in arm with, 21; twice joined in embassy with More, 23; his failure to obtain the Papacy, and his consequent revenge against the Emperor and Queen Katherine, considered by Roper the origin of the divorce, 30–31 (see Notes to H, 41/2–4, 41/4–42/1); desire to bring about for the King a French marriage, 31 (see Note to H, 43/8–9); one of the Com-

ERRATUM.

Page 141. *For* Weston [William] *read* Weston [Sir Richard].

missioners appointed to decide the divorce, 34 ; his quarrel with Bishop Stokesley, 38–9 (**see Note to H, 49/16–18**) ; his fall, 39 ; his fall referred to by More when More made Lord Chancellor, 40.

Wood, John a : More's servant, instructions to, 75 (**see Note to H, 170/16**).

York, Archbishop of. See *Wolsey, [Thomas], Archbishop of York.*

Early English Text Society.

OFFICERS AND COMMITTEE:

Honorary Director:
Dr. A. W. POLLARD, C.B., F.B.A., 40, MURRAY ROAD, WIMBLEDON, S.W. 19.

Assistant Director and Secretary:
Miss MABEL DAY, D.Lit., 15, ELGIN COURT, ELGIN AVENUE, LONDON, W. 9.

Committee:

Prof. R. W. CHAMBERS, D.Lit., F.B.A.
Sir W. A. CRAIGIE, D.Litt., F.B.A.
Dr. ROBIN FLOWER.
Dr. W. W. GREG, F.B.A.
Mr. HENRY LITTLEHALES.

Dr. ALLEN MAWER, F.B.A.
Dr. R. B. McKERROW, F.B.A.
Miss A. C. PAUES, Ph.D.
Mr. ROBERT STEELE.
Sir G. F. WARNER, D.Lit., F.B.A.

American Committee
Chairman: Professor G. L. KITTREDGE, Harvard Coll., Cambr., Mass., U.S.A.
Hon Sec.: Professor CARLETON BROWN, New York University N.Y., U.S.A.

Bankers:
THE NATIONAL PROVINCIAL BANK LIMITED,
2, PRINCES STREET, LONDON, E.C. 2.

The Subscription to the Society, which constitutes full membership, is £2 2s. a year for the annual publications, from 1921 onwards, due in advance on the 1st of January, and should be paid by Cheque, Postal Order, or Money Order, crost 'National Provincial Bank Limited,' to the Secretary, Dr. Mabel Day, 15, Elgin Court, Elgin Avenue, London, W. 9. The Society's Texts can also be purchased separately from Mr. Humphrey Milford (Oxford University Press), through a bookseller at the prices put after them in the Lists, or through the Secretary, by members only, for their own use, at a discount of 2d. in the shilling.

Any Member could save time and trouble by sending the Secretary an order on the Member's Banker to pay the subscription each January, until countermanded. A printed form for this purpose would be sent on application to the Secretary.

THE EARLY ENGLISH TEXT SOCIETY was founded in 1864 by Frederick James Furnivall, with the help of Richard Morris, Walter Skeat and others, to bring the mass of unprinted Early English literature within the reach of students and provide sound texts from which the New English Dictionary could quote. In 1867 an Extra Series was started of texts already printed, but not in satisfactory or readily obtainable editions. At a cost of nearly £35,000, 160 volumes were issued in the Original Series and 125 in the Extra Series prior to 1921. The two series were then amalgamated in order to give greater freedom in bringing out in any given year the volumes ready for publication. Since then some 30 more volumes have been issued.

As originally envisaged, the task of the Society may be completed in another twenty years. Some of the texts now being issued are naturally less interesting than those which claimed the first attention of the founders of the Society. It is well to print them, as otherwise students would continually be wasting time in investigating their uncertain merits; but individual members of the Society have for some time been allowed, after consultation with the Secretary, to select earlier volumes from the rich store of the Society's publication instead of those of the current year. All they are asked is to contribute annually to the Society, so that it may go on with its work.

The Society exists not only to print early texts, but to foster the study of them. It has survived its financial difficulties mainly by the support of Universities and libraries. It now asks for a largely increased number of individual students, and from these, to meet the needs of those who cannot afford more, Annual Subscriptions of One Guinea, entitling the subscriber to books within that value from the Society's list, will in future be welcomed. For Universities and other Institutions the minimum subscription will remain, as at present, Two Guineas, and it is hoped that as many individual students as can will also pay the full amount.

ORIGINAL SERIES. *(One guinea each year up to 1920.)*

1. **Early English Alliterative Poems**, ab. 1360 A.D., ed. Rev. Dr. R. Morris. 16s. — 1864
2. **Arthur**, ab. 1440, ed. F. J. Furnivall, M.A. 4s. — ,,
3. **Lauder on the Dewtie of Kyngis**, &c., 1556, ed. F. Hall, D.C.L. 4s. — ,,
4. **Sir Gawayne and the Green Knight**, ab. 1360, ed. Rev. Dr. R. Morris. 3s. 6d. — ,,
5. **Hume's Orthographie and Congruitie of the Britan Tongue**, ab. 1617, ed. H. B. Wheatley. 4s. — 1865
6. **Lancelot of the Laik**, ab. 1500, ed. Rev. W. W. Skeat. 8s. — ,,
7. **Genesis & Exodus**, ab. 1250, ed. Rev. Dr. R. Morris. 8s. — ,,
8. **Morte Arthure**, ab. 1440, ed. E. Brock. 7s. — ,,
9. **Thynne on Speght's ed. of Chaucer**, A.D. 1599, ed. Dr. G. Kingsley and Dr. F. J. Furnivall. 10s. — ,,
10. **Merlin**, ab. 1440, Part I., ed. H. B. Wheatley. 2s. 6d. — ,,
11. **Lyndesay's Monarche**, &c., 1552, Part I., ed. J. Small, M.A. 3s. — ,,
12. **Wright's Chaste Wife**, ab. 1462, ed. F. J. Furnivall, M.A. 1s. — ,,
13. **Seinte Marherete**, 1200-1330, ed. Rev. O. Cockayne. — 1866
14. **Kyng Horn, Floris and Blancheflour**, &c., ed. Rev. J. R. Lumby, D.D., re-ed. Dr. G. H. McKnight. 5s. ,,
15. **Political, Religious, and Love Poems**, ed. F. J. Furnivall. 7s. 6d. — ,,
16. **The Book of Quinte Essence**, ab. 1460-70, ed. F. J. Furnivall. 1s. — ,,
17. **Parallel Extracts from 45 MSS. of Piers the Plowman**, ed. Rev. W. W. Skeat. 1s. — ,,
18. **Hali Meidenhad**, ab. 1200, ed. Rev. O. Cockayne, re-edited by Dr. F. J. Furnivall. (*v.* under 1920.) ,,
19. **Lyndesay's Monarche**, &c., Part II., ed. J. Small, M.A. 3s. 6d. — ,,
20. **Richard Rolle de Hampole, English Prose Treatises of**, ed. Rev. G. G. Perry. (*v.* under 1920.) ,,
21. **Merlin**, Part II., ed. H. B. Wheatley. 4s. — ,,
22. **Partenay or Lusignen**, ed. Rev. W. W. Skeat. 6s. — ,,
23. **Dan Michel's Ayenbite of Inwyt**, 1340, ed. Rev. Dr. R. Morris. 10s. 6d. — ,,
24. **Hymns to the Virgin and Christ; the Parliament of Devils**, &c., ab. 1430, ed. F. J. Furnivall. 3s. — 1867
25. **The Stacions of Rome, the Pilgrims' Sea-voyage, with Clene Maydenhod**, ed. F. J. Furnivall. 1s. ,,
26. **Religious Pieces in Prose and Verse**, from R. Thornton's MS., ed. Rev. G. G. Perry. 5s. [1913.] ,,
27. **Levins's Manipulus Vocabulorum, a ryming Dictionary**, 1570, ed. H. B. Wheatley. 12s. — ,,
28. **William's Vision of Piers the Plowman**, 1362 A.D.; Text A, Part I., ed. Rev. W. W. Skeat. 6s. ,,
29. **Old English Homilies** (ab. 1220-30 A.D.). Series I, Part I. Edited by Rev. Dr. R. Morris. 7s. ,,
30. **Pierce the Ploughmans Crede**, ed. Rev. W. W. Skeat. 2s. — ,,
31. **Myrc's Duties of a Parish Priest**, in Verse, ab. 1420 A.D., ed. E. Peacock. 4s. — 1868
32. **Early English Meals and Manners**: the Boke of Norture of John Russell, the Bokes of Keruynge, Curtasye, and Demeanor, the Babees Book, Urbanitatis, &c., ed. F. J. Furnivall. 12s. — ,,
33. **The Knight de la Tour Landry**, ab. 1440 A.D. A Book for Daughters, ed. T. Wright, M.A. 8s. ,,
34. **Old English Homilies** (before 1300 A.D.). Series I, Part II., ed. R. Morris, LL.D. 8s. — ,,
35. **Lyndesay's Works, Part III.**: The Historie and Testament of Squyer Meldrum, ed. F. Hall. 2s. ,,
36. **Merlin**, Part III. Ed. H. B. Wheatley. On Arthurian Localities, by J. S. Stuart Glennie. 12s. — 1869
37. **Sir David Lyndesay's Works**, Part IV., Ane Satyre of the Three Estaits. Ed. F. Hall, D.C.L. 4s. ,,
38. **William's Vision of Piers the Plowman**, Part II. Text B. Ed. Rev. W. W. Skeat, M.A. 10s. 6d ,,
39. **Alliterative Romance of the Destruction of Troy.** Ed. D. Donaldson & G. A. Panton. Pt. I. 10s. 6d. ,,
40. **English Gilds, their Statutes and Customs**, 1389 A.D. Edit. Toulmin Smith and Lucy T. Smith, with an Essay on Gilds and Trades-Unions, by Dr. L. Brentano (reprinted 1924). 30s. — 1870
41. **William Lauder's Minor Poems.** Ed. F. J. Furnivall. 3s. — ,,
42. **Bernardus De Cura Rei Famuliaris, Early Scottish Prophecies**, &c. Ed. J. R. Lumby, M.A. 2s. ,,
43. **Ratis Raving, and other Moral and Religious Pieces.** Ed. J. R. Lumby, M.A. 3s. — ,,
44. **The Alliterative Romance of Joseph of Arimathie, or The Holy Grail**: from the Vernon MS.; with W. de Worde's and Pynson's Lives of Joseph : ed. Rev. W. W. Skeat, M.A. 5s. — 1871
45. **King Alfred's West-Saxon Version of Gregory's Pastoral Care**, edited from 2 MSS., with an English translation; by Henry Sweet, Esq., B.A., Balliol College, Oxford. Part I. 10s. ,,
46. **Legends of the Holy Rood, Symbols of the Passion and Cross Poems**, ed. Rev. Dr. R. Morris. 10s. ,,
47. **Sir David Lyndesay's Works**, Part V., ed. Dr. J. A. H. Murray. 3s. — ,,
48. **The Times' Whistle, and other Poems**, by R. C., 1616 ; ed. by J. M. Cowper, Esq. 6s. — ,,
49. **An Old English Miscellany**, containing a Bestiary, Kentish Sermons, Proverbs of Alfred, and Religious Poems of the 13th cent., ed. from the MSS. by the Rev. R. Morris, LL.D. 10s. — 1872
50. **King Alfred's West-Saxon Version of Gregory's Pastoral Care**, ed. H. Sweet, M.A. Part II. 10s. ,,
51. **The Life of St Juliana**, 2 versions, A.D. 1230, with translations; ed. T. O. Cockayne & E. Brock. 2s. ,,
52. **Palladius on Husbondrie**, englisht (ab. 1420 A.D.), ed. Rev. Barton Lodge, M.A. Part I. 10s. ,,
53. **Old-English Homilies**, Series II., and three Hymns to the Virgin and God, 13th-century, with the music to two of them, in old and modern notation ; ed. Rev. R. Morris, LL.D. 8s. — 1873
54. **The Vision of Piers Plowman, Text C: Richard the Redeles** (by William, the author of the *Vision*) and The Crowned King; Part III., ed. Rev. W. W. Skeat, M.A. 18s. — ,,
55. **Generydes, a Romance**, ab. 1440 A.D. ed. W. Aldis Wright, M.A. Part I. 3s. — ,,
56. **The Gest Hystoriale of the Destruction of Troy**, in alliterative verse ; ed. by D. Donaldson, Esq., and the late Rev. G. A. Panton. Part II. 10s. 6d. — 1874
57. **The Early English Version of the "Cursor Mundi"**; in four Texts, edited by the Rev. R. Morris, M.A., LL.D. Part I, with 2 photolithographic facsimiles. 10s. 6d. — ,,
58. **The Blickling Homilies**, 971 A.D., ed. Rev. R. Morris, LL.D. Part I. 8s. — ,,
59. **The "Cursor Mundi" in four Texts**, ed. Rev. Dr. R. Morris. Part II. 15s. — 1875

4   The Original Series of the "Early English Text Society."

60. **Meditacyuns on the Soper of our Lorde** (by Robert of Brunne), edited by J. M. Cowper. 2s. 6d.   1875
61. **The Romance and Prophecies of Thomas of Erceldoune**, from 5 MSS.; ed. Dr. J. A. H. Murray. 10s. 6d.   ,,
62. **The "Cursor Mundi,"** in four Texts, ed. Rev. Dr. R. Morris. Part III. 15s.   1876
63. **The Blickling Homilies**, 971 A.D., ed. Rev. Dr. R. Morris. Part II. 7s.   ,,
64. **Francis Thynne's Embleames and Epigrams**, A.D. 1600, ed. F. J. Furnivall. 7s.   ,,
65. **Be Domes Dæge** (Bede's *De Die Judicii*), &c., ed. J. R. Lumby, B.D. 2s.   ,,
66. **The "Cursor Mundi,"** in four Texts, ed. Rev. Dr. R. Morris. Part IV., with 2 autotypes. 10s.   1877
67. **Notes on Piers Plowman**, by the Rev. W. W. Skeat, M.A. Part I. 21s.   ,,
68. **The "Cursor Mundi,"** in 4 Texts, ed. Rev. Dr. R. Morris. Part V. 25s.   1878
69. **Adam Davie's 5 Dreams about Edward II.**, &c., ed. F. J. Furnivall, M.A. 5s.   ,,
70. **Generydes**, a Romance, ed. W. Aldis Wright, M.A. Part II. 4s.   ,,
71. **The Lay Folks Mass-Book**, four texts, ed. Rev. Canon Simmons. 25s.   1879
72. **Palladius on Husbondrie**, englisht (ab. 1420 A.D.). Part II. Ed. S. J. Herrtage, B.A. 15s.   ,,
73. **The Blickling Homilies**, 971 A.D., ed. Rev. Dr. R. Morris. Part III. 10s.   1880
74. **English Works of Wyclif**, hitherto unprinted, ed. F. D. Matthew, Esq. 20s.   ,,
75. **Catholicon Anglicum**, an early English Dictionary, from Lord Monson's MS. A.D. 1483, ed., with Introduction & Notes, by S. J. Herrtage, B.A. ; and with a Preface by H. B. Wheatley. 20s.   1881
76. **Aelfric's Metrical Lives of Saints**, in MS. Cott. Jul. E 7., ed. Rev. Prof. Skeat, M.A. Part I. 10s.   ,,
77. **Beowulf**, the unique MS. autotyped and transliterated, edited by Prof. Zupitza, Ph.D. 25s.   1882
78. **The Fifty Earliest English Wills**, in the Court of Probate, 1387-1439, ed. by F. J. Furnivall, M.A. 7s.   ,,
79. **King Alfred's Orosius**, from Lord Tollemache's 9th century MS., Part I. ed. H. Sweet, M.A. 13s.   1883
79 *b*. *Extra Volume.* **Facsimile of the Epinal Glossary**, ed. H. Sweet, M.A. 15s.   ,,
80. **The Early-English Life of St. Katherine** and its Latin Original, ed. Dr. Einenkel. 12s.   1884
81. **Piers Plowman** : Notes, Glossary, &c. Part IV, completing the work, ed. Rev. Prof. Skeat, M.A. 18s.   ,,
82. **Aelfric's Metrical Lives of Saints**, MS. Cott. Jul. E 7., ed. Rev. Prof. Skeat, M.A., LL.D. Part II. 12s.   1885
83. **The Oldest English Texts, Charters**, &c., ed. H. Sweet, M.A. 20s.   ,,
84. **Additional Analogs to 'The Wright's Chaste Wife,'** No. 12, by W. A. Clouston. 1s.   1886
85. **The Three Kings of Cologne**. 2 English Texts, and 1 Latin, ed. Dr. C. Horstmann. 17s.   ,,
86. **Prose Lives of Women Saints**, ab. 1610 A.D., ed. from the unique MS. by Dr. C. Horstmann. 12s.   ,,
87. **The Early South-English Legendary** (earliest version), Laud MS. 108, ed. Dr. C. Horstmann. 20s.   1887
88. **Hy. Bradshaw's Life of St. Werburghe** (Pynson, 1521), ed. Dr. C. Horstmann. 10s.   ,,
89. **Vices and Virtues**, from the unique MS., ab. 1200 A.D., ed. Dr. F. Holthausen. Part I. 8s.   1888
90. **Anglo-Saxon and Latin Rule of St. Benet**, interlinear Glosses, ed. Dr. H. Logeman. 12s.   ,,
91. **Two Fifteenth-Century Cookery-Books**, ab. 1430-1450, edited by Mr. T. Austin. 10s.   ,,
92. **Eadwine's Canterbury Psalter**, from the Trin. Cambr. MS., ab. 1150 A.D., ed. F. Harsley, B.A. Pt. 1. 12s.   1889
93. **Defensor's Liber Scintillarum**, edited from the MSS. by Ernest Rhodes, B.A. 12s.   ,,
94. **Aelfric's Metrical Lives of Saints**, MS. Cott. Jul. E 7, Part III., ed. Prof. Skeat, Litt.D., LL.D. 15s.   1890
95. **The Old-English version of Bede's Ecclesiastical History**, re-ed. by Dr. Thomas Miller. Part I, § 1. 18s.   ,,
96. **The Old-English version of Bede's Ecclesiastical History**, re-ed. by Dr. Thomas Miller. Pt. I, § 2. 15s.   1891
97. **The Earliest English Prose Psalter**, edited from its 2 MSS. by Dr. K. D. Buelbring. Part I. 15s.   ,,
98. **Minor Poems of the Vernon MS.**, Part I., ed. Dr. C. Horstmann. 20s.   1892
99. **Cursor Mundi.** Part VI. Preface, Notes, and Glossary, ed. Rev. Dr. R. Morris. 10s.   ,,
100. **Capgrave's Life of St. Katharine**, ed. Dr. C. Horstmann, with Forewords by Dr. Furnivall. 20s.   1893
101. **Cursor Mundi.** Part VII. Essay on the MSS., their Dialects, &c., by Dr. H. Hupe. 10s.   ,,
102. **Lanfranc's Cirurgie**, ab. 1400 A.D., ed. Dr. R. von Fleischhacker. Part I. 20s.   1894
103. **The Legend of the Cross**, from a 12th century MS., &c., ed. Prof. A. S. Napier, M.A., Ph.D. 7s. 6d.   ,,
104. **The Exeter Book** (Anglo-Saxon Poems), re-edited from the unique MS. by I. Gollancz, M.A. Part I. 20s.   1895
105. **The Prymer or Lay-Folks' Prayer-Book**, Camb. Univ. MS., ab. 1420, ed. Henry Littlehales. Part I. 10s.   ,,
106. **R. Misyn's Fire of Love and Mending of Life** (Hampole), 1434, 1435, ed. Rev. R. Harvey, M.A. 15s.   1896
107. **The English Conquest of Ireland**, A.D. 1166-1185, 2 Texts, 1425, 1440, Pt. I, ed. Dr. Furnivall. 15s.   ,,
108. **Child-Marriages and -Divorces, Trothplights, &c.** Chester Depositions, 1561-6, ed. Dr. Furnivall. 15s.   1897
109. **The Prymer or Lay-Folks Prayer-Book**, ab. 1420, ed. Henry Littlehales. Part II. 10s.   ,,
110. **The Old-English Version of Bede's Ecclesiastical History**, ed. Dr. T. Miller. Part II, § 1. 15s.   1898
111. **The Old-English Version of Bede's Ecclesiastical History**, ed. Dr. T. Miller. Part II, § 2. 15s.   ,,
112. **Merlin**, Part IV : Outlines of the Legend of Merlin, by Prof. W. E. Mead, Ph.D. 15s   1899
113. **Queen Elizabeth's Englishings of Boethius, Plutarch &c. &c.**, ed. Miss C. Pemberton. 15s.   ,,
114. **Aelfric's Metrical Lives of Saints**, Part IV and last, ed. Prof. Skeat, Litt.D., LL.D. 10s.   1900
115. **Jacob's Well**, edited from the unique Salisbury Cathedral MS. by Dr. A. Brandeis. Part I. 10s.   ,,
116. **An Old-English Martyrology**, re-edited by Dr. G. Herzfeld. 10s.   ,,
117. **Minor Poems of the Vernon MS.**, edited by Dr. F. J. Furnivall. Part II. 15s.   1901
118. **The Lay Folks' Catechism**, ed. by Canon Simmons and Rev. H. E. Nolloth, M.A. 5s.   ,,
119. **Robert of Brunne's Handlyng Synne** (1303), and its French original, re-ed. by Dr. Furnivall. Pt. I. 10s.   ,,
120. **The Rule of St. Benet in Northern Prose and Verse**, & Caxton's Summary, ed. by E. A. Kock. 15s.   1902
121. **The Laud MS. Troy-Book**, ed. from the unique Laud MS. 595, by Dr. J. E. Wülfing. Part I. 10s.   ,,
122. **The Laud MS. Troy-Book**, ed. from the unique Laud MS. 595, by Dr. J. E. Wülfing. Part II. 20s.   1903
123. **Robert of Brunne's Handlyng Synne** (1303), and its French original, re-ed. by Dr. Furnivall. Pt. II. 10s.   ,,
124. **Twenty-six Political and other Poems** from Digby MS. 102 &c., ed. by Dr. J. Kail. Part I. 10s.   1904
125. **Medieval Records of a London City Church**, ed. Henry Littlehales. Part I. 10s.   ,,
126. **An Alphabet of Tales**, in Northern English, from the Latin, ed. Mrs. M. M. Banks. Part I. 10s.   ,,
127. **An Alphabet of Tales**, in Northern English, from the Latin, ed. Mrs. M. M. Banks. Part II. 10s.   1905

The Original Series of the "Early English Text Society." 5

128. **Medieval Records of a London City Church**, ed. Henry Littlehales. Part II. 10s. — 1905
129. **The English Register of Godstow Nunnery**, ed. from the MSS. by the Rev. Dr. Andrew Clark. Pt. I. 10s. ,,
130. **The English Register of Godstow Nunnery**, ed. from the MSS. by the Rev. Dr. A. Clark. Pt. II. 15s. 1906
131. **The Brut, or The Chronicle of England**, edited from the best MSS. by Dr. F. Brie. Part I. 10s. ,,
132. **John Metham's Works**, edited from the unique MS. by Dr. Hardin Craig. 15s. ,,
133. **The English Register of Oseney Abbey, by Oxford**, ed. by the Rev. Dr. A. Clark. Part I. 15s. 1907
134. **The Coventry Leet Book**, edited from the unique MS. by Miss M. Dormer Harris. Part I. 15s. ,,
135. **The Coventry Leet Book**, edited from the unique MS. by Miss M. Dormer Harris. Part II. 15s. 1908
135 b. *Extra Issue.* Prof. Manly's **Piers Plowman & its Sequence**, urging the fivefold authorship of the *Vision*. 5s. [*On sale to Members only.*]
136. **The Brut, or The Chronicle of England**, edited from the best MSS. by Dr. F. Brie. Part II. 15s. ,,
137. **Twelfth-Century Homilies in MS.** Bodley 343, ed. by A. O. Belfour, M.A. Part I, the Text. 15s. 1909
138. **The Coventry Leet Book**, edited from the unique MS. by Miss M. Dormer Harris. Part III. 15s. ,,
139. **John Arderne's Treatises on Fistula in Ano, &c.**, ed. by D'Arcy Power, M.D. 15s. 1910
139 b, c, d, e, f, *Extra Issue.* **The Piers Plowman Controversy**: b. Dr. Jusserand's 1st Reply to Prof. Manly; c. Prof. Manly's Answer to Dr. Jusserand; d. Dr. Jusserand's 2nd Reply to Prof. Manly; e. Mr. R. W. Chambers's Article; f. Dr. Henry Bradley's Rejoinder to Mr. R. W. Chambers (issued separately). 10s. [*On sale to Members only.*] ,,
140. **Capgrave's Lives of St. Augustine and St. Gilbert of Sempringham**, A.D. 1451, ed. by John Munro. 10s. ,,
141. **Earth upon Earth**, all the known texts, ed., with an Introduction, by Miss Hilda Murray, M.A. 10s. 1911
142. **The English Register of Godstow Nunnery**, edited by the Rev. Dr. Andrew Clark. Part III. 10s. ,,
143. **The Wars of Alexander the Great**, Thornton MS., ed. J. S. Westlake, M.A. 10s. ,,
144. **The English Register of Oseney Abbey, by Oxford**, edited by the Rev. Dr. Andrew Clark. Part II. 10s. 1912
145. **The Northern Passion**, ed. by Miss F. A. Foster, Ph.D. Part I, the four parallel texts. 15s. ,,
146. **The Coventry Leet Book**, ed. Miss M. Dormer Harris. Introduction, Indexes, etc. Part IV. 10s. 1913
147. **The Northern Passion**, ed. Miss F. A. Foster, Ph.D., Introduction, French Text, Variants and Fragments, Glossary. Part II. 15s. ,,
[An enlarged re-print of No. 26, **Religious Pieces in Prose and Verse**, from the Thornton MS., edited by Rev. G. G. Perry. 5s.]
148. **A Fifteenth-Century Courtesy Book and Two Franciscan Rules**, edited by R. W. Chambers, M.A., Litt.D., and W. W. Seton, M.A. 7s. 6d. 1914
149. **Sixty-three Lincoln Diocese Documents**, ed. by the Rev. Dr. Andrew Clark. 15s. ,,
150. **The Old-English Rule of Bp. Chrodegang, and the Capitula of Bp. Theodulf**, ed. Prof. Napier. 7s. 6d. ,,
151. **The Lanterne of Light**, ed. by Miss Lilian M. Swinburn, M.A. 15s. 1915
152. **Early English Homilies**, from Vesp. D. XIV., ed. by Miss Rubie D.-N. Warner. Part I, Text. 15s. ,,
153. **Mandeville's Travels**, ed. by Professor Paul Hamelius. Part I, Text. 15s. 1916
154. **Mandeville's Travels** (Notes and Introduction). 15s. ,,
155. **The Wheatley MS.**, ed. by Miss Mabel Day, M.A. 30s. 1917
156. **Reginald Pecock's Donet**, from Bodl. MS. 916; ed. by Miss E. Vaughan Hitchcock. 35s. 1918
157. **Harmony of the Life of Christ**, from MS. Pepys 2498, ed. by Miss Margery Goates. 15s. 1919
158. **Meditations on the Life and Passion of Christ**, from MS. Add., 11307, ed. by Miss C. D'Evelyn. 20s. ,,
159. **Vices and Virtues**, Part II., ed. Prof. F. Holthausen. 12s. 1920
[A re-print of No. 20, **English Prose Treatises of Richard Rolle de Hampole**, ed. Rev. G. G. Perry. 5s.] ,,
[A re-edition of No. 18, **Hali Meidenhad**, ed. O. Cockayne, with a variant MS., Bodl. 34, hitherto unprinted, ed. Dr. Furnivall. 12s.]
160. **The Old English Heptateuch**, MS. Cott. Claud. B. IV., ed. S. J. Crawford, M.A. 42s. 1921
161. **Three O.E. Prose Texts**, MS. Cott. Vit. A. XV., ed. Dr. S. Rypins. 25s. ,,
162. **Facsimile of MS. Cotton Nero A. x (Pearl, Cleanness, Patience and Sir Gawain)**, Introduction by Sir I. Gollancz. 63s. 1922
163. **Book of the Foundation of St. Bartholomew's, Smithfield**, ed. the late Sir Norman Moore. 10s. 1923
164. **Pecock's Folewer to the Donet**, ed. by Miss E. Vaughan Hitchcock. 30s. ,,
165. **Middleton's Chinon of England**, with Leland's Assertio Arturii and Robinson's translation, ed. Prof. W. E. Mead, Ph.D. 25s. ,,
166. **Stanzaic Life of Christ**, ed. Dr. Frances A. Foster. 35s. 1924
167. **Trevisa's Dialogus inter Militem et Clericum, Sermon by FitzRalph, and Bygynnyng of the World**, ed. A. J. Perry, M.A. 25s. ,,
168. **Caxton's Ordre of Chyualry**, ed. A. T. P. Byles, M.A. 15s. 1925
169. **The Southern Passion**, ed. Dr. Beatrice Brown. 15s. ,,
170. **Walton's Boethius**, ed. Dr. M. Science. 30s. ,,
171. **Pecock's Reule of Cristen Religioun**, ed. Dr. W. C. Greet. 35s. 1926
172. **The Seege or Bataylе of Troy**, ed. Miss M. E. Barnicle. 25s. ,,
173. **Hawes' Pastime of Pleasure**, ed. Prof. W. E. Mead. 15s. 1927
174. **The Life of St. Anne**, ed. R. E. Parker. 10s. ,,
175. **Barclay's Eclogues**, ed. Miss Beatrice White, M.A. 25s. ,,
176. **Caxton's Prologues and Epilogues**, ed. W. J. B. Crotch, M.A. 15s. ,,
177. **Byrhtferth's Manual**, ed. Dr. S. J. Crawford. 42s. 1928
178. **The Revelations of St. Birgitta**, ed. Dr. W. P. Cumming. 10s ,,
179. **The Castell of Pleasure**, ed. Miss R. Cornelius. 12s. 6d. ,,
180. **The Apologye of Syr Thomas More**, ed. Dr. A. I. Taft. 30s. 1929
181. **The Dance of Death**, ed. Miss F. Warren. 10s. ,,
182. **Speculum Christiani**, ed. G. Holmstedt. 25s. ,,
183. **The Northern Passion (Supplement)**, ed. Dr. W. Heuser and Dr. Frances Foster. 7s. 6d. 1930
184. **The Poems of John Audelay**, ed. Dr. Ella K. Whiting. 28s. ,,

6 The Extra Series of the "Early English Text Society."

185. Lovelich's Merlin, Pt. III, ed. Dr. E. A. Kock. 25s.		1930
186. Harpsfield's Life of More, ed. Dr. Elsie V. Hitchcock and Prof. R. W. Chambers. 36s.		1931
[The section of the introduction to this by Prof. Chambers on The Continuity of English Prose is published separately by the Oxford University Press. Price 6s.]		
187. Whittinton and Stanbridge's Vulgaria, ed. Miss B. White. 12s.		,,
188. The Siege of Jerusalem, ed. Prof. E. Kölbing and Dr. Mabel Day. 15s.		,,
189. Caxton's Fayttes of Armes and of Chyualrye, ed. A. T. Byles. 21s.		1932
190. English Mediæval Lapidaries, ed. Dr. Joan Evans and Dr. Mary Serjeantson. 16s.		,,
191. The Seven Sages, ed. Prof. K. Brunner. 24s.		,,
192. Lydgate's Minor Poems, ed. Dr. H. N. MacCracken. Part II, Secular Poems. 30s.		1933
193. Seinte Marherete, re-ed. Dr. Frances Mack. 15s.		,,
194. The Exeter Book, Pt. II, ed. Prof. W. S. Mackie. 18s.		,,
195. The Quatrefoil of Love, ed. Sir I. Gollancz and Miss M. Weale. 5s.		1934

EXTRA SERIES. (One guinea each year up to 1920.)

The Publications for 1867-1920 (one guinea each year) are:—

I. William of Palerne; or, William and the Werwulf. Re-edited by Rev. W. W. Skeat, M.A. 13s.		1867
II. Early English Pronunciation, by A. J. Ellis, F.R.S. Part I. 10s.		,,
III. Caxton's Book of Curtesye, in Three Versions. Ed. F. J. Furnivall. 5s.		1868
IV. Havelok the Dane. Re-edited by the Rev. W. W. Skeat, M.A. 10s.		,,
V. Chaucer's Boethius. Edited from the two best MSS. by Rev. Dr. R. Morris. 12s.		,,
VI. Chevelere Assigne. Re-edited from the unique MS. by Lord Aldenham, M.A. 3s.		,,
VII. Early English Pronunciation, by A. J. Ellis, F.R.S. Part II. 10s.		1869
VIII. Queene Elizabethes Achademy, &c. Ed. F. J. Furnivall. Essays on early Italian and German Books of Courtesy, by W. M. Rossetti and Dr. E. Oswald. 13s.		,,
IX. Awdeley's Fraternitye of Vacabondes, Harman's Caveat, &c. Ed. F. J. Viles & F. J. Furnivall. 7s. 6d.		,,
X. Andrew Boorde's Introduction of Knowledge, 1547, Dyetary of Helth, 1542, Barnes in Defence of the Berde, 1542-3. Ed. F. J. Furnivall. 18s.		1870
XI. Barbour's Bruce, Part I. Ed. from MSS. and editions, by Rev. W. W. Skeat, M.A. 12s.		,,
XII. England in Henry VIII.'s Time: a Dialogue between Cardinal Pole & Lupset, by Thom. Starkey, Chaplain to Henry VIII. Ed. J. M. Cowper. Part II. 12s. (Part I. is No. XXXII, 1878, 8s.)		1871
XIII. A Supplicacyon of the Beggers, by Simon Fish, 1528-9 A.D., ed. F. J. Furnivall; with A Supplication to our Moste Soueraigne Lorde; A Supplication of the Poore Commons; and The Decaye of England by the Great Multitude of Sheep, ed. by J. M. Cowper, Esq. 6s.		,,
XIV. Early English Pronunciation, by A. J. Ellis, Esq., F.R.S. Part III. 10s.		,,
XV. Robert Crowley's Thirty-One Epigrams, Voyce of the Last Trumpet, Way to Wealth, &c., A.D. 1550-1, edited by J. M. Cowper, Esq. 12s.		1872
XVI. Chaucer's Treatise on the Astrolabe. Ed. Rev. W. W. Skeat, M.A. 6s.		,,
XVII. The Complaynt of Scotlande, 1549 A.D., with 4 Tracts (1542-48), ed. Dr. Murray. Part I. 10s.		,,
XVIII. The Complaynt of Scotlande, 1549 A.D., ed. Dr. Murray. Part II. 8s.		1873
XIX. Oure Ladyes Myroure, A.D. 1530, ed. Rev. J. H. Blunt, M.A. 24s.		,,
XX. Lovelich's History of the Holy Grail (ab. 1450 A.D.), ed. F. J. Furnivall, M.A., Ph.D. Part I. 8s.		1874
XXI. Barbour's Bruce, Part II., ed. Rev. W. W. Skeat, M.A. 4s.		,,
XXII. Henry Brinklow's Complaynt of Roderyck Mors (ab. 1542): and The Lamentacion of a Christian against the Citie of London, made by Roderigo Mors, A.D. 1545. Ed. J. M. Cowper. 9s.		,,
XXIII. Early English Pronunciation, by A. J. Ellis, F.R.S. Part IV. 10s.		,,
XXIV. Lovelich's History of the Holy Grail, ed. F. J. Furnivall, M.A., Ph.D. Part II. 10s.		1875
XXV. Guy of Warwick, 15th-century Version, ed. Prof. Zupitza. Part I. 20s.		,,
XXVI. Guy of Warwick, 15th-century Version, ed. Prof. Zupitza. Part II. 14s.		1876
XXVII. Bp. Fisher's English Works (died 1535), ed. by Prof. J. E. B. Mayor. Part I, the Text. 16s.		,,
XXVIII. Lovelich's Holy Grail, ed. F. J. Furnivall, M.A., Ph.D. Part III. 10s.		1877
XXIX. Barbour's Bruce. Part III., ed. Rev. W. W. Skeat, M.A. 21s.		,,
XXX. Lovelich's Holy Grail, ed. F. J. Furnivall, M.A., Ph.D. Part IV. 15s.		1878
XXXI. The Alliterative Romance of Alexander and Dindimus, ed. Rev. W. W. Skeat. 6s.		,,
XXXII. Starkey's "England in Henry VIII's time." Pt. I. Starkey's Life and Letters, ed. S. J. Herrtage. 8s.		,,
XXXIII. Gesta Romanorum (englisht ab. 1440), ed. S. J. Herrtage, B.A. 15s.		1879
XXXIV. The Charlemagne Romances:—1. Sir Ferumbras, from Ashm. MS. 33, ed. S. J. Herrtage. 15s.		,,
XXXV. Charlemagne Romances:—2. The Sege off Melayne, Sir Otuell, &c., ed. S. J. Herrtage. 12s.		1880
XXXVI. Charlemagne Romances:—3. Lyf of Charles the Grete, Pt. I., ed. S. J. Herrtage. 16s.		,,
XXXVII. Charlemagne Romances:—4. Lyf of Charles the Grete, Pt. II., ed. S. J. Herrtage. 15s.		1881
XXXVIII. Charlemagne Romances:—5. The Sowdone of Babylone, ed. Dr. Hausknecht. 15s.		,,
XXXIX. Charlemagne Romances:—6. Rauf Colyear, Roland, Otuel, &c., ed. S. J. Herrtage, B.A. 15s.		1882
XL. Charlemagne Romances:—7. Huon of Burdeux, by Lord Berners, ed. S. L. Lee, B.A. Part I. 15s.		,,
XLI. Charlemagne Romances:—8. Huon of Burdeux, by Lord Berners, ed. S. L. Lee, B.A. Pt. II. 15s.		1883
XLII. Guy of Warwick: 2 texts (Auchinleck MS. and Caius MS.), ed. Prof. Zupitza. Part I. 15s.		,,
XLIII. Charlemagne Romances:—9. Huon of Burdeux, by Lord Berners, ed. S. L. Lee, B.A. Pt. III. 15s.		1884
XLIV. Charlemagne Romances:—10. The Four Sons of Aymon, ed. Miss Octavia Richardson. Pt. I. 15s.		,,
XLV. Charlemagne Romances:—11. The Four Sons of Aymon, ed. Miss O. Richardson. Pt. II. 20s.		1885
XLVI. Sir Bevis of Hamton, from the Auchinleck and other MSS., ed. Prof. E. Kölbing, Ph.D. Part I. 10s.		,,
XLVII. The Wars of Alexander, ed. Rev. Prof. Skeat, Litt.D., LL.D. 20s.		1886
XLVIII. Sir Bevis of Hamton, ed. Prof. E. Kölbing, Ph.D. Part II. 10s.		,,

The Extra Series of the "Early English Text Society." 7

XLIX. **Guy of Warwick**, 2 texts (Auchinleck and Caius MSS.), Pt. II., ed. Prof. J. Zupitza, Ph.D. 15s. 1887
L. **Charlemagne Romances** :—12. **Huon of Burdeux**, by Lord Berners, ed. S. L. Lee, B.A. Part IV. 5s. ,,
LI. **Torrent of Portyngale**, from the unique MS. in the Chetham Library, ed. E. Adam, Ph.D. 10s. ,,
LII. **Bullein's Dialogue against the Feuer Pestilence**, 1578 (ed. 1, 1564). Ed. M. & A. H. Bullen. 10s. 1888
LIII. **Vicary's Anatomie of the Body of Man**, 1548, ed. 1577, ed. F. J. & Percy Furnivall. Part I. 15s. ,,
LIV. **Caxton's Englishing of Alain Chartier's Curial**, ed. Dr. F. J. Furnivall & Prof. P. Meyer. 5s. ,,
LV. **Barbour's Bruce**, ed. Rev. Prof. Skeat, Litt.D., LL.D. Part IV. 5s. 1889
LVI. **Early English Pronunciation**, by A. J. Ellis, Esq., F.R.S. Pt. V., the present English Dialects. 25s. ,,
LVII. **Caxton's Eneydos**, A.D. 1490, coll. with its French, ed. M. T. Culley, M.A. & Dr. F. J. Furnivall. 13s. 1890
LVIII. **Caxton's Blanchardyn & Eglantine**, c. 1489, extracts from ed. 1595, & French, ed. Dr.L. Kellner. 17s. ,,
LIX. **Guy of Warwick**, 2 texts (Auchinleck and Caius MSS.), Part III., ed. Prof. J. Zupitza, Ph.D. 15s. 1891
LX. **Lydgate's Temple of Glass**, re-edited from the MSS. by Dr. J. Schick. 15s. ,,
LXI. **Hoccleve's Minor Poems**, I., from the Phillipps and Durham MSS., ed. F. J. Furnivall, Ph.D. 15s. 1892
LXII. **The Chester Plays**, re-edited from the MSS. by the late Dr. Hermann Deimling. Part I. 15s. ,,
LXIII. **Thomas a Kempis's De Imitatione Christi**, englisht ab. 1440, & 1502, ed. Prof. J. K. Ingram. 15s. 1893
LXIV. **Caxton's Godfrey of Boloyne, or Last Siege of Jerusalem**, 1481, ed. Dr. Mary N. Colvin. 15s. ,,
LXV. **Sir Bevis of Hamton**, ed. Prof. E. Kölbing, Ph.D. Part III. 15s. 1894
LXVI. **Lydgate's and Burgh's Secrees of Philisoffres** ('Governance of Kings and Princes'), ab. 1445—50, ed. R. Steele. 15s. ,,
LXVII. **The Three Kings' Sons**, a Romance, ab. 1500, Part I., the Text, ed. Dr. Furnivall. 10s. 1895
LXVIII. **Melusine**, the prose Romance, ab. 1500, Part I, the Text, ed. A. K. Donald. 20s. ,,
LXIX. **Lydgate's Assembly of the Gods**, ed. Prof. Oscar L. Triggs, M.A., Ph.D. 15s. 1896
LXX. **The Digby Plays**, edited by Dr. F. J. Furnivall. 15s. ,,
LXXI. **The Towneley Plays**, ed. Geo. England and A. W. Pollard, M.A. 15s. 1897
LXXII. **Hoccleve's Regement of Princes**, 1411-12, and 14 Poems, edited by Dr. F. J. Furnivall. 15s. ,,
LXXIII. **Hoccleve's Minor Poems**, II., from the Ashburnham MS., ed. I. Gollancz, M.A. 5s. ,,
LXXIV. **Secreta Secretorum**, 3 prose Englishings, one by Jas Yonge, 1428, ed. R. Steele. Part I. 20s. 1898
LXXV. **Speculum Guidonis de Warwyk**, edited by Miss G. L. Morrill, M.A., Ph,D. 10s. ,,
LXXVI. **George Ashby's Poems**, &c., ed. Miss Mary Bateson. 15s. 1899
LXXVII. **Lydgate's DeGuilleville's Pilgrimage of the Life of Man**, 1426, ed. Dr. F. J. Furnivall. Part I. 10s. ,,
LXXVIII. **The Life and Death of Mary Magdalene**, by T. Robinson, c. 1620, ed. Dr. H. O. Sommer. 5s. ,,
LXXIX. **Caxton's Dialogues, English and French**, c. 1483, ed. Henry Bradley, M.A. 10s. 1900
LXXX. **Lydgate's Two Nightingale Poems**, ed. Dr. Otto Glauning. 5s. ,,
LXXXI. **Gower's Confessio Amantis**, edited by G. C. Macaulay, M.A. Vol. I. 15s. ,,
LXXXII. **Gower's Confessio Amantis**, edited by G. C. Macaulay, M.A. Vol. II. 15s. 1901
LXXXIII. **Lydgate's DeGuilleville's Pilgrimage of the Life of Man**, 1426, ed. Dr. F. J. Furnivall. Pt. II. 10s. ,,
LXXXIV. **Lydgate's Reason and Sensuality**, edited by Dr. E. Sieper. Part I. 5s. ,,
LXXXV. **Alexander Scott's Poems**, 1568, from the unique Edinburgh MS., ed. A. K. Donald, B.A. 10s. 1902
LXXXVI. **William of Shoreham's Poems**, re-ed. from the unique MS. by Dr. M. Konrath. Part I. 10s. ,,
LXXXVII. **Two Coventry Corpus-Christi Plays**, re-edited by Hardin Craig, M.A. 10s. ,,
LXXXVIII. **Le Morte Arthur**, re-edited from the Harleian MS. 2252 by Prof. Bruce, Ph.D. 10s. 1903
LXXXIX. **Lydgate's Reason and Sensuality**, edited by Dr. E. Sieper. Part II. 15s. ,,
XC. **English Fragments from Latin Medieval Service-Books**, ed. by Hy. Littlehales. 5s. ,,
XCI. **The Macro Plays**, ed. Dr. Furnivall and A. W. Pollard, M.A (reprinted 1924). 15s. 1904
XCII. **Lydgate's DeGuileville's Pilgrimage of the Life of Man**, Part III., ed. Miss Locock. 10s. ,,
XCIII. **Lovelich's Romance of Merlin**, from the unique MS., ed. Dr. E. A. Kock. Part I. 10s. ,,
XCIV. **Respublica**, a Play on Social England, A.D. 1553, ed. L. A. Magnus, LL.B. 12s. 1905
XCV. **Lovelich's History of the Holy Grail**, Pt. V. : The Legend of the Holy Grail, by Dorothy Kempe. 6s. ,,
XCVI. **Mirk's Festial**, edited from the MSS. by Dr. Erbe. Part I. 12s. ,,
XCVII. **Lydgate's Troy Book**, edited from the best MSS. by Dr. Hy. Bergen. Part I, Books I and II. 15s. 1906
XCVIII. **Skelton's Magnyfycence**, edited by Dr. R. L. Ramsay, with an Introduction. 7s. 6d. ,,
XCIX. **The Romance of Emaré**, re-edited from the MS. by Miss Edith Rickert, Ph.D. 7s. 6d. ,,
C. **The Harrowing of Hell, and The Gospel of Nicodemus**, re-ed. by Prof. Hulme, M.A., Ph.D. 15s. 1907
CI. **Songs, Carols**, &c., from Richard Hill's Balliol MS., edited by Dr. Roman Dyboski. 15s. ,,
CII. **Promptorium Parvulorum**, the 1st English-Latin Dictionary, ed. Rev. A. L. Mayhew, M.A. 21s. 1908
CIII. **Lydgate's Troy Book**, edited from the best MSS. by Dr. Hy. Bergen. Part II, Book III. 10s. ,,
CIV. **The Non-Cycle Mystery Plays**, re-edited by O. Waterhouse, M.A. 15s. 1909
CV. **The Tale of Beryn, with the Pardoner and Tapster**, ed. Dr. F. J. Furnivall and W. G. Stone. 15s. ,,
CVI. **Lydgate's Troy Book**, edited from the best MSS. by Dr. Hy. Bergen. Part III. 15s. 1910
CVII. **Lydgate's Minor Poems**, edited by Dr. H. N. MacCracken. Part I, Religious Poems. 15s. ,,
CVIII. **Lydgate's Siege of Thebes**, re-edited from the MSS. by Prof. Dr. A. Erdmann. Pt. I, The Text. 15s. 1911
CIX. **Partonope**, re-edited from its 3 MSS. by Dr. A. T. Bödtker. The Texts. 15s. ,,
CX. **Caxton's Mirrour of the World**, with all the woodcuts, ed. by O. H. Prior, M.A., Litt.D. 15s. 1912
CXI. **Caxton's History of Jason**, the Text, Part I, ed. by John Munro. 15s. ,,
CXII. **Lovelich's Romance of Merlin**, ed. from the unique MS. by Prof. E. A. Kock, Ph.D. Pt. II. 15s. 1913
CXIII. **Poems by Sir John Salusbury, Robert Chester, and others**, from Christ Church MS. 184, &c., ed. by Prof. Carleton Brown, Ph.D. 15s. ,,
CXIV. **The Gild of St. Mary, Lichfield**, ed. by the late Dr. F. J. Furnivall. 15s. 1914
CXV. **The Chester Plays**. Part II, e-edited by Dr. Matthews. 15s. ,,
CXVI. **The Pauline Epistles**, ed. Miss M. J. Powell. 15s. 1915
CXVII. **Bp. Fisher's English Works**, Pt. II, ed. by the Rev. Ronald Bayne. 15s. ,,

CXVIII.	The Craft of Nombrynge, ed. by R. Steele. 15s.	1916
CXIX.	The Owl and Nightingale, 2 Texts parallel, ed. by the late G. F. H. Sykes and J. H. G. Grattan. 15s. [*At Press.*	,,
CXX.	Ludus Coventriae, ed. by Miss K. S. Block, M.A. 30s.	1917
CXXI.	Lydgate's Fall of Princes, Pt. I, ed. Dr. H. Bergen. 15s.	1918
CXXII.	Lydgate's Fall of Princes, Pt. II, ed. Dr. H. Bergen. 15s.	,,
CXXIII.	Lydgate's Fall of Princes, Pt. III, ed. Dr. H. Bergen. 15s.	1919
CXXIV.	Lydgate's Fall of Princes, Pt. IV, ed. Dr. H. Bergen. 15s.	,,
CXXV.	Lydgate's Siege of Thebes, Part II, ed. Prof. Erdmann and Prof. Ekwall. 20s.	1920

Forthcoming issues will be chosen from the following, and will be issued as completed:—

Sir Firumbras, ed. Miss M. I. O'Sullivan. [*At Press.*
Bokenham's Lives of Holy Women (Lives of the Saints), ed. Dr. Mary Serjeantson. [*At Press.*
Short English Metrical Chronicle, ed. Dr. E. Zettl. [*At Press.*
Byrhtferth's Manual, Pt. II, ed. Dr. S. J. Crawford.
English Poems of Charles of Orleans, ed. R. Steele. [*At Press.*
Mum and the Sothsegger, ed. R. Steele and Dr. Mabel Day. [*At Press.*
Valentyne and Orson, ed. Dr. Arthur Dickson. [*At Press.*
The Minor Poems of Hawes, ed. G. S. Humphreys.
The Earliest English Apocalypse with a Commentary, ed. Dr. Anna C. Paues. [*At Press.*
Piers Plowman, the A Text, ed. Prof. R. W. Chambers and J. H. G. Grattan. [*At Press.*
Lydgate's Troy Book, ed. Dr. Hy. Bergen. Part IV, Introduction, Notes, &c. [*At Press.*
Harleian MS. 2253 (English Poems), ed. Miss Hilda Murray.
Thomas Castleford's Chronicle, ed. Dr. Blach and Dr. E. Zettl.
The Life of St. Norbert, ed. W. H. Clawson.
The Mirror of Simple Souls, ed. Dr. B. Radtke.
Jacob's Well, Pt. II, ed. Dr. G. R. Owst.
Lives of More by William Roper and Ro. Ba., ed. Dr. Elsie V. Hitchcock and Prof. R. W. Chambers. [*At Press.*
Barlaam and Josaphat, ed. Dr. M. Science.
Speculum Sacerdotale, ed. Dr. E. H. Weatherly. [*At Press.*
Vegetius on the Art of War, ed. Miss K. Garvin.
Homilies of Ælfric, ed. Dr. J. Pope.
Non-Ælfrician Homilies, ed. Dr. R. Willard.
Palsgrave's Acolastus, ed. P. L. Carver. [*At Press.*

Other texts are under consideration.

November 1934.

The manufacturer's authorised representative in the EU for product safety is Oxford University Press España S.A. of El Parque Empresarial San Fernando de Henares, Avenida de Castilla, 2 - 28830 Madrid (www.oup.es/en or product.safety@oup.com). OUP España S.A. also acts as importer into Spain of products made by the manufacturer.
Printed and bound by CPI Group (UK) Ltd, Croydon, CR0 4YY

22/04/2026

02094916-0001